THE GIRLS' GUIDE TO LOVE AND SUPPER CLUBS

THE
girls' guide
TO
love
AND
supper clubs

Dana Bate

HYPERION

NEW YORK

Page 373: "Old-Fashioned Braised Brisket" by Kelly Alexander. First published as
"Lil Pachter's Jewish-Style Brisket" in *Saveur* magazine and reprinted
by permission of the author.

Page 378: "Braised Green Beans with Fire-Roasted Tomatoes." Originally
published in the *Washington Post*. Copyright © 2004 by Ed Bruske, aka the
Slow Cook. Reprinted by permission of Ed Bruske.

Page 381: "Turkey Leg Confit" by Grace Parisi. First published
in *Food & Wine* magazine and reprinted by permission. Copyright
American Express Publishing Corporation.

Library of Congress Cataloging-in-Publication Data

Bate, Dana.
   The girls' guide to love and supper clubs / Dana Bate. — 1st ed.
     p. cm.
   ISBN 978-1-4013-1100-1
   1. Single women—Fiction. 2. Dinners and dining—
Fiction. 3. Cooking—Fiction. 4. Self-realization—Fiction.
5. Washington (D.C.)—Fiction. I. Title.
   PS3602.A8534G57 2013
   813'.6—dc22   2012026961

Hyperion books are available for special promotions and premiums. For details
contact the HarperCollins Special Markets Department in the New York office
at 212-207-7528, fax 212-207-7222, or email spsales@harpercollins.com.

Book design by Jennifer Daddio/Bookmark Design & Media Inc.

FIRST EDITION

10 9 8 7 6 5 4 3 2 1

to my parents

CHAPTER

one

a s soon as Adam pulls into his parents' driveway, I panic: maybe the carrot cake was a mistake. Two days ago, it seemed like a great idea. Everyone loves my carrot cake. Everyone. Even my boss, Mark—a man who subsists on cheese sandwiches and hot dogs—even *he* loves my carrot cake. But the Prescotts aren't like everyone else. They drive Lexuses and summer in Tuscany and keep a personal wine cellar at The Capital Grille. Adam's mother will probably take one look at the cake and call it quaint. That's what she called me once: quaint. A polite way of saying unsophisticated.

I should have made something fancier, like chocolate mousse. Or a Sacher torte. Why didn't I listen to Adam when he said bringing dessert was a silly idea? Probably because "silly" has become his favorite word to describe my obsessive interest in food, followed immediately by "crazy." His criticism functions as muddled background music, like when my parents talk about my "future" and "direction." The words barely register anymore.

Adam parks the car along the cobblestone circular driveway in front of his parents' Georgetown home, a pale yellow mansion that takes up the better part of a city block. Among the Federalist brick and clapboard town houses, all sandwiched together along the tree-lined streets, the Prescotts' stand-alone home towers above the rest, with its creamy facade, jet-black shutters, and series of rectangular columns covered by tumbling sprays of wisteria and knotted ivy. It is one of the most beautiful homes I have ever seen. It is also one of the most intimidating.

Adam smoothes his gelled, chestnut hair with his hands and shoots me a sideways glance as he unbuckles his seat belt. "You okay?"

"Fine," I say. But of course I'm not okay. Everything about this evening lies outside my comfort zone, and I wish Adam would turn the car around and drive the two miles back to our apartment in Logan Circle, a neighborhood whose character is more vintage thrift shop than Vineyard Vines. But we're here, and I have a carrot cake in my lap. Turning around is not an option.

I throw off my seat belt and steal a glance in the car's side mirror. Disaster. I spent an hour and a half grooming myself, but thanks to the July heat and humidity, my forehead glistens with sweat, and my wavy locks have swollen into a fluffy orange mass. One more thing for the Prescotts to love: their son is dating Carrot Top. Carrot Top with the carrot cake. Perfect.

Adam fumbles for the door handle as I shudder at my reflection. "Relax," he says. "There's nothing to be nervous about."

"I know." But that isn't true. There's plenty to be nervous about, and we both know it. It's no accident that, in the fifteen months we've been dating, this is the first time his parents have invited me to their home, despite the fact that we live in the same city. I would say "better late than never," but at the moment, the idea of "never" seems just fine.

"Oh, but could you not mention the apartment?" Adam asks. "I still haven't told them."

"We've been living together for three months."

Adam scratches his square jawline and looks through the front windshield. "I'm waiting for the right time."

Whatever that means. We dated for six months before he finally introduced me to his parents. Then, too, he was waiting for the "right time." At this rate, it will probably be November before he tells them we moved in together. If we're still together then. The way Adam has been acting lately, I don't know what to think.

I hop out of the car and follow Adam as he makes his way to the front door, scrambling to keep up as I balance the carrot cake on my arms. "You know I'm the worst at keeping secrets," I say.

"It's just for tonight. Please? For me?"

I sigh. "Yeah, okay, whatever."

"Thank you. We don't need a repeat of The Capital Grille."

That's where his parents took us for lunch the first time they met me, and suffice it to say, the lunch did not go as planned. They immediately sniffed out my lack of good breeding, which came to a head when I accidentally spilled a glass of Martin Prescott's 1996 Château Lafite in his lap and proceeded to wipe the area around his crotch with my napkin, while uttering a few words and thoughts I probably should have kept to myself. By the time lunch was over, the Prescotts had made up their minds: I lacked the poise and refinement required of a future First Lady, which meant I was an unsuitable match for their son. I can't say I blame them.

Balancing the carrot cake on one hand, I smooth my navy sundress with the other, checking to make sure everything is in its right place. The dress's bulk adequately disguises my curvy figure without looking like a nun's habit—a strategic move on my part, because although Adam may enjoy staring at my ample bosom, I guarantee his mother will not. Adam is dressed in his typical uniform: navy polo shirt, khaki pants, and penny loafers. A generous squirt of gel holds his dark brown hair in place, and his skin is a toasty butterscotch, thanks to a few summer weekends on the tennis court.

I follow Adam up the broad front steps, past the potted boxwoods and hydrangea bushes, and as we reach the top, the front door swings open.

"Adam!"

Sandy Prescott bursts onto the front steps like a little

hurricane of pastels and pearls and frosted hair. She wraps her arms around Adam and kisses him on the cheek, squeezing his shoulders with her bony hands. Martin stands with one hand tucked into the pocket of his salmon-colored chinos and extends the other toward me. Between his boat shoes and Sandy's pastels, I feel like I interrupted a photo shoot for the Brooks Brothers summer catalog.

"Hannah," Martin says, grabbing my right hand. He squeezes until I lose feeling in my fingers, the sort of crippling grip one might expect from a high-profile Washington lobbyist. "Good to see you again."

"Likewise."

Sandy nods and flashes a quick smile as she glances at my chest, which, apparently, I haven't disguised well enough. "Hello, Hannah."

She drags her eyes up and down the length of my figure and makes a light, almost imperceptible clucking sound with her tongue when she spies my faux-leather sandals. Strike one. Two, actually, if you count my unfortunate anatomy.

Sandy tears her eyes from my feet and motions toward the doorway. "Shall we?"

Adam pulls me through the front door into the foyer, a room roughly the size of Alaska with about as much warmth. The ceiling rises fifteen feet, with a crystal chandelier that descends from the top and sparkles like a mini-solar system in the summer sun. A curved staircase sweeps up to the second floor and envelops a round, Louis Quinze table, which sits atop the sleek white marble floor. The entire house reeks of money, even more money than I realized Adam's family had, and I see now why his parents bristle at my blatant disinterest in Washington society.

"What do we have here?" Sandy asks, pointing to the crinkly mound of aluminum foil perched on my arms. I tried to cover the cake without letting the foil touch the cream cheese frosting—a goal easier in theory than in practice—which means the cake now resembles a fifth-grade science project.

"Dessert," I say, pausing before mentioning the inevitable. "A carrot cake."

Sandy smiles tightly. "Carrot cake," she says, taking the cake from my hands. "How fun."

Adam sighs. "It's one of Hannah's specialties. Making it is at least a two-day project. Quite the ordeal."

Sandy stares at the mountain of foil and knits her brows together as she shakes her head. "That sounds like an *awful* lot of trouble for something like a carrot cake. I guess I've always figured that's what bakeries are for."

She lets out a bemused sigh and carries the cake into the kitchen.

See? The carrot cake was a mistake. I knew it.

What follows is a carefully choreographed dance involving me on one side and the Prescotts on the other. I don't want to step on the Prescotts' toes, and they don't want to step on mine, but really, all of us would be a lot happier if we didn't have to dance at all. I, for one, would much rather sit along the sidelines and watch everyone else dance while I stuffed my face with candy.

But round and round we go, and the longer we dance, the more the smile tattooed on my face begins to ache and tingle and develop its own pulse. And yet I keep smiling, mostly because I am Adam's girlfriend and they are his parents and, well, it's pretty clear whose position is the least secure. I don't expect the Prescotts to love me by the end of this dinner, but I would like, at the very least, for them to stop calling Adam every weekend to voice their concerns about our relationship while he hides in the bathroom and pretends I'm not sleeping ten feet away in our shared bed. In the scheme of things, I do not think this is an unreasonable goal.

We blow through a bottle of Veuve Clicquot as we nibble canapés on the Prescotts' brick patio, and the champagne both calms my nerves and impairs my ability to focus on what, exactly,

Adam and his parents are talking about. As our discussion progresses around the dinner table, I find myself drifting in and out of the conversation, as if the Prescotts are a TBS Sunday afternoon movie playing in the background while I fold my laundry and send e-mails. I hear what they are saying, and I am saying things in response, but significant periods of time pass where I'm not sure what is going on.

As I float away on my champagne wave, I lose myself in the thorny world of my own thoughts: how lately Adam seems mortified by everything I do, how moving in together has only magnified our differences and obscured our similarities, and how consequently I now feel as if I am in the wrong everything—the wrong job, the wrong relationship, possibly even the wrong city.

I snap out of my trance when someone mentions my name, though I'll be damned if I can figure out who it was. But everyone is staring at me, so I think it's safe to assume a question was involved.

"Sorry?"

"Your parents," Martin says. "How are they?"

"They're good. On sabbatical in London until October."

"Wonderful," Sandy says. She hands her empty soup bowl to Juanita, the Prescotts' housekeeper. "Your parents do such interesting work."

My parents are the only part of my pedigree of which the Prescotts approve. When Sandy heard my parents were Alan and Judy Sugarman, both esteemed economics professors at the University of Pennsylvania, she saw a glimmer of hope. I didn't come from a wealthy or powerful family, but at least my parents carried the sort of academic heft that would look good in a *New York Times* wedding announcement.

"They aren't the only ones doing interesting work," Martin says. "Adam showed us the paper you coauthored on quantitative easing. Very impressive."

"Thanks—although my boss was the one who wrote it. I only helped with the research."

"She's being modest," Adam says, rubbing my shoulder. "You put a lot of work into that paper. And it showed. It was excellent."

Martin smiles. "Looks like we have another Professor Sugarman in our midst, hmm?"

It is the question I dread most—and, I should add, the one I get asked all the time. Everyone assumes I aspire to be my parents someday, my every professional choice driven by a deep-seated desire to carry on their legacy. The way everyone poses the question suggests I *should* want that for myself—that I'd be crazy not to. And so what am I supposed to say when someone like Martin Prescott puts me on the spot? That I'd rather stab myself with a rusty knife than become a professor? That what I'd really like to do is start an offbeat catering company someday, but that my parents would go ballistic if I ever did? No, I can't say those things, not when it's clear that the one thing the Prescotts rate me for is a career I no longer care about and a scholarly legacy I want nothing to do with.

So instead I smile and simply say, "We'll see."

I grab for my wineglass and take a long sip and then, against my better judgment, I add, "But who knows. Maybe I'll do something wild someday like start my own catering company."

Sandy blanches. An obvious disappointment.

"Catering?" Martin chuckles, swirling his wineglass by its base. "Surely you can aim a little higher than *that*."

Juanita returns to the dinner table, carrying three dinner plates on one arm and holding the forth in her opposite hand. She hands me the last of the plates, a gilded disk of porcelain filled with roasted potatoes, green beans, and some sort of meat.

"It's slow-roasted leg of lamb," Sandy says as I study my plate. She smiles. "I was planning to serve a pork roast, but I wasn't sure if you would eat that."

Ah, yes. The Jew ruins the party once again. The truth is, I love pork. I eat it all the time. But I can't expect her to know that, and by her tone, it is clear that Jews are as foreign to her as aliens or cavemen.

I tuck into my portion of lamb, and the meat melts on my tongue, buttery and rich with red wine and the faintest hint of rosemary. "Wow, Sandy, what did you put in this? It's fabulous."

"Oh, I didn't *make* this," she says as she cuts her lamb into bite-size pieces and pushes most of it to the far corners of her plate, burying the meat under wedges of roasted potatoes.

Adam clears his throat. "Mom has a personal chef."

"Oh," I say. Of course she does.

"I'd love to cook," she says, "but who has the time? I can't afford to spend two days baking a cake."

The implication, of course, is that only unimportant people have that kind of time. Unimportant people like me. I wait for Adam to jump in and save me, but instead he shoves a forkful of lamb into his mouth and feigns deep interest in the contents of his dinner plate. For someone with Adam's political ambitions and penchant for friendly debate, I'm always amazed at the lengths he goes to avoid confrontation with his parents.

"I have a full-time job," I say, offering Sandy a labored smile, "and somehow I manage."

Sandy delicately places her fork on the table and interlaces her fingers. "I beg your pardon?"

My cheeks flush, and all the champagne and wine rush to my head at once. "All I'm saying is . . . we make time for the things we actually want to do. That's all."

Sandy purses her lips and sweeps her hair away from her face with the back of her hand. "Hannah, dear, I am very busy. I am on the board of three charities and am hosting two galas this year. It's not a matter of *wanting* to cook. I simply have more important things to do."

For a woman so different from my own mother—the frosted, well-groomed socialite to my mother's mousy, rumpled academic— she and my mother share a remarkably similar view of the role of cooking in a modern woman's life. For them, cooking is an irrelevant hobby, an amusement for women who lack the brains for more high-powered pursuits or the money to pay someone to perform such a humdrum chore. Sandy Prescott and my mother would agree on very little, but as women who have been liberated from the perfunctory task of cooking a nightly dinner, they would see eye to eye on my intense interest in the culinary arts.

Were I a stronger person, someone more in control of her faculties who has not drunk multiple glasses of champagne, I would probably let Sandy's remark go without commenting any further. But I cannot be that person. At least not tonight. Not when Sandy is suggesting, as it seems everyone does, that cooking isn't a priority worthy of a serious person's time.

"You would make the time if you wanted to," I say. "But obviously you don't."

Martin stabs a piece of lamb with his fork and shoves his glasses up the bridge of his nose. "Is this really *appropriate*, ladies?"

The correct answer, obviously, is no. Picking a fight with my boyfriend's mother, a woman who already dislikes me, is not appropriate. It also is not wise. But by this point in the evening, I don't care. I just want this dinner to end, and the sooner that happens the better.

Unfortunately dinner stretches on for an interminable two hours, giving me ample opportunity to take a minor misstep and turn it into a totally radioactive fuckup. And, knowing me, that's exactly what I'll do. Whether it's muttering expletives while wiping Martin's lap at The Capital Grille or railing against those who order chicken at a steakhouse—which Sandy ultimately did—I always manage to say exactly the wrong thing when the Prescotts are around.

Adam tries to play referee, jumping in with a story about his latest coup, an assignment to a Supreme Court case. He embellishes wildly, crediting himself with far more responsibility and power than he actually has, but Sandy and Martin eat up every word. They love it.

This is Adam at his best: the future politician, captivating the table with his charm and panache. From the moment I met Adam, I was, like any woman with a pulse, attracted to his chiseled features, his intelligence, and his ambition, but his charisma—that's what sucked me in. That's what hooked me. When Adam is "on," being around him is electrifying, a total thrill of a ride you never want to end. He made me feel interesting. He made me feel *alive*. He took me to parties filled with political movers and shakers— White House Correspondents' Dinner afterparties and charity galas and Harvard alumni events. He treated me like someone important—like someone who mattered. How could I not fall for someone like that? The man is magnetic, enchanting everyone he meets with his smiles and jokes and shiny white teeth.

All of which seems great until I realize tonight he is acting this way to shut me up.

Every time I attempt to join the conversation, Adam raises his voice and plows over me like a bulldozer, crushing me with his anecdotes and convivial banter. He kicks, squeezes, and prods me beneath the table, like I am an out-of-control five-year-old at a dinner party. I can't get a word out, which, it becomes clear, is the point.

And that, I decide, is total bullshit. Adam used to love my spunk. That's what he told me, anyway. I was nothing like the girls Sandy tried to fix him up with, girls who'd had debutante balls and regularly appeared in *Capitol File* magazine. Sure, I went to an Ivy League school, but in his Harvard-educated eyes, I "only" went to Cornell, which he considered a lesser Ivy. I grew up in a house the size of his parents' foyer, wrote about financial regulation for a living, whipped up puff pastry from scratch. I was *different*, damn it. And that made me special. But tonight I do not feel special. Tonight I feel as I have on so many occasions recently: like part of a social experiment gone awry.

During a lull in Adam's act, Juanita appears with my carrot cake, an eight-inch tower of spiced cake, caramelized pecan filling, cream cheese frosting, and toasted coconut. Miraculously, none of the frosting stuck to the foil—a small triumph. Juanita starts cutting into the cake, but I shoo her away and volunteer to serve the cake myself. If Adam wants to cut me out of the conversation, fine, but no one will cut me out of my culinary accolades.

I hand a fat slice to Sandy, whose eyes widen at the thick swirls of frosting and gobs of buttery pecan goo. I cannot tell whether she is ecstatic or terrified. Something tells me it's the latter.

"My goodness," she says. She lays the plate in front of her, takes a whiff, and then pushes it forward by four inches. I gather this is how she consumes dessert. "By the way, Hannah," she says as I serve up the last piece of cake, "I read some very scary news last week about your neighborhood. Something about a rash of muggings?"

"Really? I hadn't heard that."

"You should be careful. Apparently Columbia Heights is still very much . . . shall we say, on the *edge*."

"Oh, I don't live in Columbia Heights anymore. Adam and I found a place together in Logan Circle about three months ago. We—"

I catch myself. Adam's eyes widen in horror and fix on mine.

"I'm sorry, what?" Sandy says, her eyelids fluttering rapidly. "Did I hear you correctly? You two have been living together?"

Neither of us says anything.

Sandy's voice grows tense. "Adam? Is this true? You've been living together—for *three months*?"

Adam clears his throat. "No. Yes. Let me explain . . ."

But before he can say anything more, Sandy clenches her jaw and shakes her head and leaps up from the table. Adam chases after her, and then Martin throws his napkin on the table and stomps out of the room after both of them, leaving me in the dining room, alone.

I stare at the mess of plates and napkins, scattered around the table amid the overturned forks and the slices of uneaten cake. The Prescotts haven't touched my dessert, and given the hushed tones coming from the next room, they probably never will. I pull my plate closer, saw off a corner of carrot cake, and shovel a forkful into my mouth. The cake is delicious, the best I've made in months, bursting with the sweet flavor of cinnamon and carrots and the crunch of caramelized pecans and toasted coconut. It's a masterpiece, and no one will ever know. I'm sure there are worse ways this evening could have gone, but at the moment, I'll be damned if I can think of any of them.

CHAPTER
two

Let's be honest: the Prescotts were going to find out at some point. All I did was speed up the process.

And, really, with all of the champagne and red wine, combined with the prospect of sugary frosting and pecan goo, it almost wasn't my fault. I was distracted. Who *hasn't* made a few bad decisions under the spell of sugar and alcohol? Besides, Adam acted like a jerk for most of the evening. I'm hardly the only one at fault.

But something tells me none of these excuses will fly with my boyfriend, who has ignored me for the remainder of the evening. As he speeds toward the Q Street Bridge, I'm struck by how little he has said since we left his parents. The air-conditioning blasts through the vents in Adam's Lexus, chilling the interior of the car as we move like a cool, hermetically sealed bubble through the thick, sticky summer air. Even at nine-thirty, the summer sky still holds a faint purple glow, draping the night in a dreamlike veil. Old-fashioned streetlamps dot the sidewalk, surrounded by leafy trees of varying sizes and blooming impatiens. The spires belonging to a series of Dupont Circle town houses loom on the horizon.

As we approach the bridge, Adam grips the wheel of his Lexus with two tense fists and presses down on the gas pedal. He races up behind a white Prius, a car moving at the speed limit, and rides its tail all the way across. When the opposing lane clears, he jerks the car over the double yellow line, speeds up, passes the Prius, and cuts back in front of it.

"Asshole," he says as he gives the driver the finger.

I have no idea how driving the speed limit makes someone an asshole, and I am inclined to ask, but given Adam's scarily aggressive tone, I decide not to bother.

Adam speeds up again as we cross Connecticut Avenue, flying through the very heart of Dupont Circle with its crowded streets and bustling sidewalks, and I clutch my seat and close my eyes, not at all comfortable with these hostile maneuvers, even though I recognize my earlier behavior is likely behind them. Regardless, I'd rather not die tonight.

But I will concede tonight was a disaster. An indisputable, excruciating disaster. Why do interactions with Adam's parents always end this way? Because I'm me, that's why. And Adam is Adam. I am chatty and unpredictable, and Adam is uptight and cautious, and when you throw us into a room with his parents, we somehow become exaggerated versions of ourselves, which is to say, polar opposites. I am the loose cannon, and Adam is the guy with a stick up his ass, and it is clear which kind of person the Prescotts prefer.

What Adam's parents think of me shouldn't matter, but it does—to both of us. Adam may have grown up surrounded by luxury and privilege, but we were both raised by parents who invested a significant proportion of their time and money into our upbringing and whose opinions always mattered—on the right schools, the right majors, the right careers and lifestyles. Why should their opinions about our significant others carry any less weight? I've always respected people who could flout their parents' wishes on a regular basis and blaze their own trails in the face of their parents' disapproval. But Adam and I aren't like that. It's one thing we've always had in common.

Adam turns onto the wider and less crowded thoroughfare of

Fourteenth Street, and I decide to break the silence. "The carrot cake came out well."

Carrot cake. That's all I've got.

"Like it matters," he mumbles under his breath.

"I'm sure they'll get used to it. Us living together."

Adam huffs as he races through a yellow light. "Don't count on it."

We don't speak again until we reach the apartment.

Adam unlocks the door to our fifth-floor, loft-style apartment, which is located in the heart of Logan Circle. When I interned in Washington as a college student, Logan Circle was still considered "up-and-coming," and I heard stories about the prostitutes who would loiter up and down Fourteenth Street. But over the past few years, dozens of shops and restaurants and galleries have moved into the area—everything from Whole Foods to the hip Cork Wine Bar and low-key Logan Tavern—and now the Fourteenth Street corridor bustles with young professionals, who have moved into the area in droves. Our building sits on a lot where a run-down auto repair shop once stood, but now the decaying warehouse of beat-up cars has been replaced by eighty-four luxury rental apartments—none of which I could afford without Adam's monthly financial contribution.

I follow Adam into the apartment, leaving a few feet between us as he storms into the living room. He throws his keys on the steel console, setting off a clang that echoes off the brushed cement floors.

"I can't believe you told them," he says as he throws himself onto our leather couch—*his* leather couch, actually, since I sold all my furniture before we moved in together, an idea that seemed to make sense at the time but now makes my stake in this apartment, this *relationship*, rather tenuous.

"I didn't mean to," I say. "It just sort of . . . slipped out."

"Right. It slipped out. After I specifically asked you not to say anything."

"I told you, I've never been good at keeping secrets." Adam stares at me, unmoved. "At least they know the truth."

Adam lets out a huff. "Yeah. Great."

"They were going to find out eventually . . ."

Adam presses his palms against his temples and lets out a grunt. "You know what? I can't deal with this right now. We'll talk tomorrow." He pushes himself off the couch and marches into the bathroom.

Okay, so he's pissed. Or, more accurately, given the banging I hear going on in the bathroom, he's flat-out angry. But if we have any shot at making this relationship work, his parents will have to accept and respect our decision to live together. We can't live a lie forever. At least I can't.

What worries me is I'm beginning to think Adam could. When I said Adam has never defied his parents, that's not entirely true. He's dating me, after all. That has been his one rebellion against them, his small act of resistance. But tonight, instead of charging forward in the face of their disapproval, he waved a little white flag and left me open to attack. And lately all the characteristics that drew him to my side—the way I was talkative and offbeat and sometimes a little weird—are pushing him away, as if I am a constant source of embarrassment.

He didn't used to see me that way. When we first started dating, he introduced me to all his friends and colleagues as his little firecracker. That's what he started calling me after our third date, when he brought me to a Redskins party at his friend Eric's place. Eric had decided to make buffalo chili, but, in what became clear to both me and everyone else at the party, he had no idea what he was doing. Two hours into the party, after all of us had blown through the bags of tortilla chips and pretzels, Eric was still chopping red peppers. Determined not to let a room of fifteen people go hungry, I rolled up my sleeves, marched into the kitchen, and grabbed a knife. "Okay, Bobby Flay," I said as I wielded my knife.

"Time to get this show on the road." I chopped and minced and crushed at rapid-fire speed, and in no time, dinner was served. "Get a load of this firecracker," Eric said as he watched me work my magic. After that, the name sort of stuck.

For a while, the nickname seemed like a good thing. Every time I would rail against fad diets or champion the importance of sustainable agriculture or lament the lack of food options in inner cities, Adam would laugh and say, "That's my little firecracker." He made me feel special, as if I were a vital part of his life. His parents were the only people from whom he seemed to hide me, and though it bothered me a little, I understood. I was the anti-Sandy. That's what made me attractive. But he hasn't called me his little firecracker in what feels like months now, and lately I feel as if he's hiding me from everyone. When did this little fire-cracker become a grenade?

I follow Adam into the bathroom and stare at his reflection as he brushes his teeth. "I'm sorry dating me is such a huge embar-rassment."

Adam spits a foamy, white lump of toothpaste into the sink and rinses out his mouth, swishing the water back and forth be-tween his cheeks. He spits the water into the sink and meets my eyes in the mirror. "I never said that."

"It's what you're thinking."

Adam shoves his toothbrush into the toothbrush holder. "No, it's not. But come on, did you need to mention the apartment?"

"I told you, that was an *accident*."

"What about arguing with my mom about cooking? Was that an accident, too?"

I play with the fringe on one of our hand towels. "I wasn't ar-guing with her."

Adam huffs. "Sure sounded that way."

"Well, I'm sorry. I guess I can't do anything right."

"That's not what I'm saying." He massages the bridge of his nose and sighs. "But, okay, just as an example, why did you have to bring up the whole catering fantasy? What made you think that would go over well? I'm surprised you didn't start telling them about food carts or your obsession with underground supper clubs."

Ever since I introduced Adam to the idea surrounding underground supper clubs—secret, unlicensed restaurants run by off-duty chefs or enthusiastic novice cooks out of their homes—he has considered it an obsession. Sure, I have lobbied him repeatedly to let me host one out of our apartment, and sure, I have researched the crap out of what it would take to run one, but that hardly makes it an *obsession*. It's more of an interest. An intense, unshakeable interest.

Adam reaches for the mouthwash, but I grab the bottle before he can lay his hands on it. "Starting a catering company isn't a crazy fantasy, Adam. Your mom employs a personal chef. Cooking is a legitimate career."

"Yeah, for people who don't have the brains to do something else. Which you do."

"God, you sound like my parents."

"I sound like someone who's right."

"No, you sound like an asshole."

Adam rolls his eyes. "For my parents' sake, couldn't you have made up something else?"

Typical Adam: when reality doesn't suit your audience, create an alternate reality that suits them better. Adam Prescott for president!

But I know Adam wishes my intense interest in food weren't a reality at all. When we first started dating, my talent in the kitchen was a turn-on. The prospect of me in the kitchen, wearing a skimpy apron and holding a whisk in my hand—he thought that was *sexy*. And, as someone with little insight into how to work her own sex appeal, I pounced on the opportunity to make him want and need me.

I spent four days preparing my first home-cooked meal for him, a dinner of wilted escarole salad with hot bacon dressing, osso bucco with risotto Milanese and gremolata, and a white-chocolate toasted-almond semifreddo for dessert. At the time, I lived with three other people in a Columbia Heights town house, so I told all of my housemates to make themselves scarce that Saturday night. When Adam showed up at my door, as the rich smell of braised veal shanks wafted through the house, I greeted him holding a platter of prosciutto-wrapped figs, wearing nothing but a slinky red apron. He grabbed me by the waist and pushed me into the kitchen, slowly untying the apron strings resting on my rounded hips, and moments later we were making love on the tiled kitchen floor. Admittedly, I worried the whole time about when I should start the risotto and whether he'd even want osso bucco once we were finished, but it was the first time I'd seduced someone like that, and it was lovely.

Adam raved about that meal—the rich osso bucco, the zesty gremolata, the sweet-and-salty semifreddo—and that's when I knew cooking was my love language, my way of expressing passion and desire and overcoming all of my insecurities. I learned that I may not be comfortable strutting through a room in a tight-fitting dress, but I can cook one hell of a brisket, and I can do it in the comfort of my own home, wearing an apron and nothing else.

Adam loved my food, and he loved watching me work in the kitchen even more, the way my cheeks would flush from the heat of the stove and my hair would twist into delicate red curls along my hairline. As the weeks went by, I continued to seduce him with pork ragu and roasted chicken, creamed spinach and carrot sformato, cannolis and brownies and chocolate-hazelnut cake.

But once the honeymoon period was over, about six months into our relationship (which, incidentally, coincided with the first time I met his parents), he tired of the fricassees and pound cakes and soufflés. It was a distraction, he said. I'd gone beyond what one might consider a future wifely duty and had entered the realm of obsession—constantly talking about what I planned to make for dinner and rhapsodizing over every new recipe I found, spending three days preparing a brisket and wreaking havoc in the kitchen. He was fine with cooking as a hobby, but once he realized it was more than that, he'd had enough. You cook so you can eat, and you eat so you can live, and that's that. Serious and intelligent people don't make a *career* of cooking.

"So, what, I should have lied to your parents?" I ask, flicking my finger against the plastic Listerine bottle. Adam doesn't reply. I hand him the mouthwash and grab my toothbrush off the counter. "Yeah, great idea. Then maybe they'll never get to know me."

"Maybe that would be better . . . ," Adam mumbles.

I freeze, the toothbrush half hanging out of my mouth. "Excuse me?"

"Never mind," he says.

"No, what was that supposed to mean?"

"It means you're right: I'm sick of dating a total misfit. It's not cute anymore. I can't be in a relationship with someone who's always making me apologize for her behavior."

I pluck the toothbrush from my between my lips. "Is that so?"

"Listen, all I'm saying is I should be able to take you places without worrying about what you might say or do."

"Come on, Adam. You don't have to worry about me."

"Oh, I don't? What about almost lighting Eric's Christmas tree on fire last year when you insisted on lighting a menorah right next to it? Or the infamous dinner with my boss last month?"

Ugh. I knew he'd bring that up. "I was just trying to explain the correct way to make spaghetti carbonara."

"And by doing so implied that he had done it *incorrectly*."

"Well . . . I mean . . . he had."

Adam sighs. "Do you see what I'm saying? You're a loose cannon."

"No I'm not. I'm just . . . a stickler when it comes to certain things. But you don't have to worry about me. Promise."

"Yeah, well, I'll believe that when I see it."

"Oh, you'll see it, all right," I say, shoving my toothbrush back in my mouth. "Trust me."

I'm not entirely sure what I mean by this last statement, but I suppose what I'm trying to say is I can be the genteel, taciturn woman he describes—even if, deep down, I think the whole idea of proving myself to him is absurd. Because it is. That wasn't the deal we struck. He chose to date me *because* I was sassy and opinionated. But lately Adam seems to have buyer's remorse, as if I am some wild shirt he bought on a whim, a bright orange button-down that now doesn't go with his lifestyle or anything else in his closet.

And that scares the crap out of me. Adam is the first person I let myself fall in love with in a slobbery, all-consuming way. What will happen if everything falls apart? I have no experience to draw from, no playbook to reference. This is an embarrassing admission to make at twenty-six years of age, but it is also true. I sacrificed opportunities and friendships to make our relationship work—ruling out a better-paying job in Boston so that I could stay in DC with him, deciding against a weekend cheese-making class because it would mean less "together time" for the two of us. Adam became the center of my world, and I let my other friends drift away, and now I barely have any friends left who aren't connected to Adam. If I lose him, I'll lose my entire social life, on top of this apartment and the entire life we've built together—the movie nights, the Sunday brunches, the trips to Harris Teeter to buy groceries, and the walks along the Tidal Basin to see the cherry blossoms and the memorials. I'll be alone. All that sacrifice will have been for nothing.

I can't let that happen. I have to make this relationship work again, to re-create the spark that attracted us to each other in the first place: his magnetic energy, my seductive wit, his fascination with me, my admiration for him. I owe that to both of us. All I need is a little Sugarman magic to prove to Adam that he has nothing to worry about, and neither do I.

three

apparently I have plenty to worry about because, despite my best efforts, I cannot sleep. I toss and turn, throwing the covers off and pulling them back on. The evening's events replay in my head on a continuous loop, and I dissect each gaffe over and over again until my head feels like it might explode. Which, in the end, makes sleeping rather difficult.

At five-thirty, I stop trying. I pull myself out of bed and drag myself into the living room, each movement a struggle, as if I am walking through a large container of Marshmallow Fluff. I plop down in front of my laptop and stare at the screen, letting the *Washington Post* headlines wash over me: "All Eyes Turn to Meeting of Fed Committee" . . . "Trade-Ins Catch On in a Down Economy" . . . "Preparing for Swine Flu's Return" . . . It all blends together, mostly because at the moment I cannot process anything above a third-grade reading level.

Instead of reading through today's news, I log on to Facebook, where the stable and successful lives of my four hundred friends—many of them fellow Cornell alumni—stare me in the face, mocking me. Isaiah's *New York Times* article was the third most e-mailed article on the *Times*'s Web site yesterday—hooray! Kate's nonprofit was mentioned in President Obama's speech yesterday, and she and a few of her coworkers have been invited to the White House—so exciting! Meredith passed the bar, and Jonathan won his case, and Katherine's wedding was the most beautiful and fun and important wedding of the century. Isn't it wonderful, all this happy news? Isn't it just *marvelous*? No, not really.

It's not that I begrudge my friends their successes, although maybe I do, just a little. But at a time when I feel so lost—about my career, about my relationship, about everything—every status update and photo set and link reminds me how stuck I am and how, while everyone else soars upward with aplomb, I continue to sputter in circles, like a wind-up toy running out of juice. I want to post about my amazing career or the achievement of my dreams or my life-changing trip to Abruzzo, but the best I can do is post a photo of the strawberry tart I baked or the salted caramel ice cream I made. It's my way of saying, "I'm here—I'm charging ahead like the rest of you," even if the opposite is true.

I glance at the upper corner of my screen and click on my profile picture, a photo of me and Adam taken almost a year ago at my friend Rachel's housewarming party. Adam is handing me an enormous chocolate cupcake with white buttercream frosting, and I am sitting beside him with a lovesick smile planted on my face, an expression directed at Adam and the cupcake in equal proportion. The cupcake was the last one, and Adam grabbed it because he knew I'd been too busy plowing my way through the guacamole and salsa to check out the dessert table. In those first few months of dating, Adam thrived on random acts of kindness, always looking out for me, always trying to make me happy.

That was then. What strikes me, as I stare at the photo, is how much the image resembles someone else's present life and not my own. The picture tells the story of a girl in love, whose days brighten because she knows someone out there is thinking about her as much as she is thinking about him. When did that girl stop being me? I cannot remember the last time I felt the way I did in that photo. Not since we moved in together, that's for sure.

The impetus behind our move wasn't so much romantic as it was practical: both our leases were about to run out, and I was sick of living in a group house. As a lawyer whose parents still provide him with a monthly stipend, Adam could afford a nicer apartment than I could, but combined, we realized we could get an even better place together. We pooled our resources and scored a luxury apartment in Logan Circle with exposed ductwork, polished cement floors, floor-to-ceiling windows, and granite countertops—the kind of place that would have been completely out of my reach without Adam.

Everyone told me it was too soon to move in together: my friends, my parents, even my boss, Mark, cautioned against it. And that's because everyone thinks I am incapable of managing my own life.

"So, what, after a year of dating, now you're thinking about marrying this guy?" my mom asked when I told her.

Adam and I hadn't discussed marriage—ever—but I assured my mom we'd talked through the move, and it made financial and practical sense. End of story. Why did moving in together have to lead to *marriage*?

But now I see her point, and everyone else's. The move was . . . well, it was a little hasty. There's no way I could afford this apartment without Adam, and so if we were to break up . . .

I slam my laptop shut and jump up from my seat. No. I can't think about that now. I can't think about how my relationship is on the brink, how all those people who told me moving in together was a mistake might have been right. Because thinking about those things will lead me into darker territory, like what would happen if Adam and I broke up, where I would live, how I would afford a new apartment and new furniture. I would be forced to examine my backup plan, which does not, in fact, exist.

So I do what I always do when my life seems out of control: I bake.

Baking and cooking bring me inner peace, like a tasty version of yoga, without all the awkward stretching and sweating. When my life spins out of control, when I can't make sense of what's going on in the world, I head straight to the kitchen and turn on my oven, and with the press of a button, I switch one part of my brain off and another on. The rules of the kitchen are straightforward, and when I'm there I don't have to think about my problems. I don't need to think about anything but cups and ounces, temperatures and cooking times.

When I was a freshman at Cornell, I heard a plane had flown into the World Trade Center while sitting in my Introduction to American History lecture. My friends and I ran back to our dorm rooms and spent the next few hours glued to the television. I kept my TV on all day, but after talking to my parents and watching three hours of the coverage, I headed straight to the communal kitchen and baked a triple batch of brownies, which I then distributed to everyone on my floor. Some of my friends thought I was crazy ("Who bakes brownies when the country is under attack?"), but it was the only thing I could do to keep from having a panic attack or bursting into tears. I couldn't control what was happening to our country, but I could control what was happening in that kitchen. Baking was my way of restoring order in a world driven by chaos, and it still is.

I preheat the oven and pull the flour, sugar, and baking soda from the cupboard, but before I can grab my recipe for sour cream coffee cake, Adam trudges out of the bedroom.

"What are you doing?" he groans, holding his hand above his eyes to block out the kitchen light.

I rub my hands along the counter and bite the inside of my lip. I can't tell if he is still angry about last night, but I suspect he is. "Baking a coffee cake," I say.

"Isn't there half a carrot cake in the fridge?"

"This is for the office."

"Well could you keep it down? I don't have to get up for another hour."

"Sure." I start to move toward him, about to tell him he doesn't have to be such a jerk about everything, but before I can say anything more, he turns around and heads into the bedroom and shuts the door behind him.

The coffee cake takes thirty minutes longer to bake than expected, which makes no sense at all. I made it exactly the way I always make it—handfuls of cinnamon streusel, a hefty dose of vanilla, the perfect ratio of butter, eggs, and flour—but the toothpick kept coming out with goo all over it. Maybe our oven is broken. Wouldn't that be fitting? Broken, like most other things in my life at the moment.

But, broken or not, the broader consequence of all of this is that, despite having been up since five-thirty, I am late for work. Again.

I race out of the apartment and hobble along the seven hot-and-sticky blocks to my office at the Institute for Research and Discourse—IRD, or as my friends and I call it, "NIRD," which describes pretty much everyone who works there.

NIRD is a prominent Washington think tank whose scholars think and talk and write about public policy, and then think and talk and write about it some more. It's run by a brilliant but completely insane seventy-year-old named Charles Shenkenfrauder, a one-time head of the Congressional Budget Office who fancies himself an expert on the presidencies of Jimmy Carter and Ronald Reagan, the two presidents under whom he served. For fun, he travels to Chesapeake, Virginia, each December to participate in a Revolutionary War reenactment of the Battle of Great Bridge—or at least he used to. Apparently last year he was involved in an unfortunate incident involving a dove and a musket, and, well, according to Charles things are a little up in the air this year.

I push my way through the revolving door and bolt toward the elevator, balancing a coffee cake and half a carrot cake in my arms. Adam informed me he would be working late every night this week and wouldn't have time to eat the carrot cake, so I decided to foist the leftovers on my coworkers instead. Personally, I don't see how working late has any impact on one's ability to consume a carrot cake, but since the cake reminds me of dinner at the Prescotts', I'm happy to get rid of it.

my desk from her perch in the health policy department, carrying a sliver of my coffee cake. She slides up to my desk for one of our daily heart-to-hearts, looking characteristically chic in a sleeveless cream blouse and chocolate pencil skirt, the kind of outfit I could never wear because I actually have hips. Rachel, on the other hand, is built like a willowy nymph. Everything about her is lean and trim, from her narrow face and delicate nose to her boyish hips and long, sleek brown hair. If she were a few inches taller, I bet she could have been a model. I would say she's the Jackie O. to my Marilyn, but I'm pretty sure Marilyn Monroe never wore fleece.

"Awesome coffee cake," she says in her faint Chicago accent, the *a* in *ah-some* drawn out like a song. She licks the crumbs off her slender fingers. "Melts in your mouth. What's in the streusel? Cinnamon?"

I nod. "And a little cocoa powder."

"Nice. So how was dinner last night?"

"I don't want to talk about it."

"That bad?"

"That bad."

She comes around to my side of the desk and sits on the edge. "Care to give me the CliffsNotes version?"

"Let's see. Should I begin with the part where I picked a fight with Adam's mother, or the part where I told his parents Adam and I are living together?"

"They didn't know?"

"No. As you can imagine, the news went over really well."

"I'm sure." Rachel scrunches up her lips and studies the tip of her brown, snakeskin shoe, admiring its pointy toe. "Hey—in the end, you did everyone a big favor. It's Adam's fault for not telling them months ago."

Rachel Cohen has never been one for mincing words, particularly when it comes to Adam. Her candor is one of the things I love about her. A graduate of George Washington University, she started at NIRD a few months before I did, and one of the first

I burst through the elevator doors and walk face-first into a mass of curls, the sort of coarse, fruity-smelling ringlets that can belong to only one woman: Millie Roberts.

Millie, like me, works as a NIRD research assistant, though to hear her tell it, you would think she ran the place at the age of twenty-six. She frequently begins sentences with, "When I was in the Peace Corps," or "As I told Wolf Blitzer," or "When I cowrote an op-ed published in the *Wall Street Journal*." Her status updates on Facebook are always saturated in self-importance ("*Need to finish writing this congressional testimony, then heading to the Hilton to meet the Veep—wish there were more hours in the day!!*"), as if it is her work, and her work alone, that keeps this institution from falling apart. She generally causes annoyance and discomfort wherever she goes—ergo the reason I have christened her The Hemorrhoid.

"Watch it," Millie says as she spins around. She purses her lips when she realizes I am the offender in question. "Oh, hi, Hannah." She looks at her watch. "Just getting here?"

"Household emergency," I say, only partly lying.

"Is everything okay?" she asks, moving in close. I nod, ignoring her mock concern. Millie and Adam dated in high school, when he was a senior and she was a sophomore at Georgetown Day School, and they are now "best friends," the sort of warm-and-fuzzy friendship that makes my stomach churn. As far as I can tell, Millie harbors hope the two of them will reunite in a scene straight out of *When Harry Met Sally*. I foresee something more along the lines of *Fatal Attraction*.

Millie deserves a little credit, I guess. She introduced me to Adam. We met at one of her parties, and much to her surprise, Adam and I hit it off. Even then—when I was at my fittest—my petite, curvy frame couldn't hold a candle to Millie's five-foot-seven-inch frame of pure marathon-runner muscle. She never thought Adam would show interest in someone as clumsy and out of shape as me. I would be lying if I said I took no pleasure in proving her wrong.

Millie draws closer, lowering her voice to a whisper as she widens her eyes. "I heard about last night. *Yikes.*"

I can't see my watch through the stack of cakes, but I know it's no later than nine-thirty. I cannot fathom how she already knows about last night's dinner. I'm sure it has something to do with the nature of her friendship with Adam, where they talk every day and tell each other everything. Which, of course, pleases me to no end.

"That's not why I'm late," I say, glazing over her reference to last night's events. "My . . . dad called from London."

"Oh, right, they're in England. London School of Economics, right?" I nod. She stares at the foil tower nestled in my arms, eyeing it suspiciously. "What's that?"

"Coffee cake and leftover carrot cake."

"*Two* cakes? Are you trying to make us all obese?"

"Yes, Millie. That's why I bake for the office. To make you all obese."

Millie raises an eyebrow. "I don't see why you couldn't bring in something healthy every once in a while."

Adam once told me that when Millie was thirteen, her mom sent her to fat camp, and from what I can tell, she has lived in mortal fear of eggs and butter ever since. I am about to remind Millie that the carrot cake does contain vegetables, and therefore possesses a modicum of nutrition one could rationalize into healthfulness, but before I can speak I hear a voice calling my name at the end of the hallway.

"Hannah? Hannah, where are you?"

Mark Henderson. My boss. Crap.

"Gotta run." I dash past Millie and dump my cakes in the kitchen before scurrying to my desk.

"Where have you been?" Mark asks, knitting together his apricot-colored eyebrows, which jut a full inch beyond the rim of his round, tortoiseshell glasses. He speaks, as always, with the faintest hint of an English accent, a mystery to all of us, seeing as Mark was born and raised in Indiana. From what I can tell, the

accent is an affectation, much like his extensive collection of ties and handkerchiefs. Mark used to be a member of the Federal Reserve Board of Governors, where for a whopping fourteen he was in charge of setting interest rates and overseeing the banking system. These days, he churns out papers and op-ed fiscal and monetary policy and occasionally makes the round the cable news networks. As a prolific DC commentator, he is of the economic equivalent of Terry Bradshaw or John McEn albeit without the charisma and with a much larger collection tweed.

"Sorry," I say. "Family emergency."

He crosses his arms and sighs. He's heard it all before. "W now that you're finally here, I need you to get going on the prep rations for the conference."

"The conference?" This is the first I've heard of any confe ence.

"Yes, the conference. On the economic recovery? And finan cial risk? In December?"

Again, this is the first I've heard of any of this. "Right," I say "The . . . conference."

"I need you to get the ball rolling—contacting the speakers, reserving a room, coordinating with marketing. You know the drill."

I pull out a pen and paper, awaiting further instructions on what speakers I am supposed to get in touch with and when, exactly, he wants to hold this conference, but when I look up, Mark has disappeared into his office. This might be more concerning if it didn't happen at least three times a day.

Hoping to find guidance in the form of an e-mail or announcement, I log on to my computer and scrub my in-box where I find . . . nothing. I search through the piles of papers on my desk, mostly old research papers and printouts from Mark, but again I cannot find a single mention of the December conference. I give up.

I let out a loud groan and look up to see Rachel gliding toward

things she said to me, as I reached for a chicken salad sandwich in the NIRD lunchroom, was, "I wouldn't do that unless you have a bottle of Pepto in your desk." I didn't have many friends in Washington before I met Rachel, but with her by my side, I never had to worry about eating alone at lunch or enduring an afternoon of gastrointestinal distress.

Over the past three years, in what is as much a surprise to me as anyone else, she has become, in addition to my best friend at work, my best friend in all of DC. Had we met at a different stage of life, I'm not sure that would be true. My college friends and I were kindred spirits, homebodies who preferred sweatpants to high fashion, a night watching old movies to a night on the town. But those friends are spread across the country, in Boston and Seattle and New York, and now Rachel is the one who knows the intimate details of my daily life—Rachel, the woman everyone notices when she walks into a room, who can make sweatpants look like high fashion, in a way I never could. In addition to writing about domestic health care policy for her boss at NIRD, she runs a wildly successful fashion and design blog called Milk Glass—further proof she is beauty and brains personified. None of my other friends are like her, and yet some days I feel closer to her than I do to them, for the simple reason that she's here and they're not.

"Don't worry," Rachel says. "The Prescotts will get over it."

"I hope so."

"You hope what?" Millie's voice pierces through the low hum of the fluorescent lights and computers peppering the eighth floor. She stalks up to my desk and inserts herself into the discussion, as is her wont.

"Nothing," I say.

Millie lets out a frustrated sigh. "Whatever. Why haven't you hoes responded to my birthday Evite? The party is this weekend."

"I'm still trying to move a few things around," Rachel says.

Millie places a hand on her hip and turns to face me. "You'll be there, Hannah. I know you don't have plans."

I choose to assume she has already spoken to Adam about this, rather than interpret her remark as a commentary on my lack of a social life. "Wouldn't miss it for the world," I say.

"Good," Millie says. "And keep your weekend open. I'm trying to put together a brunch on Sunday followed by an afternoon at the movies."

Millie stalks back to her desk, and Rachel sighs, twirling one of her long, chestnut locks around her finger. "A weekend of Millie," she says. "Good luck with that."

"You're not coming?"

"I have a date."

"Shocker," I say. Rachel always has a date. How she manages to find so many datable men in DC is a mystery to me.

"I don't want to traumatize this guy by introducing him to Millie on our first date."

"True, but come on. You can't send me out there alone."

"You'll have Adam," she says. This provides surprisingly little consolation. "I'm sure it'll be fun."

But as she says the words, she can't help but snicker, because although Millie's party may be many things—loud, smelly, unbearable—the one thing it won't be, for me at least, is fun.

four

i look forward to Millie's party as much as I look forward to a
Pap smear or a tooth extraction. Which is to say, not at all.

But before I know it, Saturday is already here, and my anxiety
gives way to resigned acceptance. Adam and I are going to this
party together, and that's the end of it. Adam and I haven't talked
about the party—we haven't talked about much of anything all
week—but I know that as painful as tonight may be, it is also an
opportunity for me to remind Adam why he fell in love with me
in the first place—how he used to love my quirks and how they
don't always spell disaster. There was a moment two nights ago,
after I made a crack about Mark's mammoth eyebrows and how it
is only a matter of time before I grab a pair of scissors and trim
them myself, when I saw, out of the corner of my eye, a smirk cross
Adam's lips. In that moment, I knew there was still hope for us. I
can still make him laugh. I can still make him smile. All I need to
do is sail through this party with grace and dignity, and then I can
finally stop having anxiety dreams about being single, lonely, and
homeless.

As I stand in front of the bathroom mirror, tugging at my
unruly hair, Adam shouts from the living room, filling the apartment with the sound of his voice. "Jesus, Hannah, you're going to
make us late—again!"

"Coming!"

What I leave out is the "will be"—as in she *will be* coming round the mountain when she comes. And I *will be* coming out of the bathroom . . . as soon as I throw my hair into a ponytail and give my eyelashes one more coat of mascara. And try on another color of lipstick. Before checking my ass in the mirror. Twice.

"One sec!" I tear into the bedroom and shove my wallet, phone, and keys inside my purse, grab a bottle of Vouvray for Millie, and hurry into the living room. "Okay," I say. "Let's go."

A few months ago, Adam would have said something about my new white maxidress or given me a kiss or at least done something to validate the effort I put into pulling myself together. That's part of what I fell in love with, I think—how good he made me feel about myself. I was curves, brains, and snark all in one, a loveable mishmash of Christina Hendricks and Maureen Dowd and Kathy Griffin. Or at least that's what he led me to believe. He always found something to compliment: my eyes, a paper I'd written, the softness of the skin along my doughy belly. The night we met at Millie's party, he told me I had an infectious laugh. It was one of the first things he said to me. I turned to goo and made a terrible joke about infections and swine flu—with, as I recall, some bizarre reference to Batman and the Joker—but Adam chuckled anyway, saying he'd be happy to catch anything I'd give him. And, for the first time, I didn't worry I'd made a total fool of myself in front of an attractive member of the opposite sex. He put me at ease. He always knew the right thing to say.

But tonight he says nothing. He hasn't commented on anything I've said or done for the past week, ever since our argument last Sunday. I bet I could go out wearing nothing but a bra and pajama bottoms, and he wouldn't even notice.

We walk side by side from our apartment in Logan Circle to Millie's place in Kalorama, a hilly neighborhood just north of Dupont Circle, peppered with grand Victorian and Art Deco buildings, elegant prewar condos, and tree-lined streets. Millie frequently reminds us that the neighborhood has been home to everyone from Woodrow Wilson to Betty Friedan and, in more recent history, people like Ted Kennedy and Christopher Hitchens. So, by Millie's way of thinking, she fits right in. That I dislike this woman should come as a surprise to no one.

As Adam and I make our way up Eighteenth Street in the thick, sticky heat, charged silence swirls around us like electricity. Our shoulders are only three inches apart, but we might as well be walking on opposite sides of the street.

One of Millie's college friends buzzes us into her Beaux Arts lobby, a grand foyer lined by grand plaster columns, richly upholstered furniture, and wrought iron banisters. We walk through the cavernous marble hallway toward her first-floor apartment, located at the end of a long hallway. When we reach her apartment, we bang on her door, which shakes and rattles to the rhythm of Lady Gaga.

"Hey!" Millie shouts above the music as she opens the door. She smoothes her hands down the sides of her skintight strapless black dress and welcomes us into her darkened apartment, a large one-bedroom with an open floor plan and exposed brickwork along the back wall. I make as much money as Millie and could never afford this place, but unlike me, Millie gets a cushy stipend each month from her parents, both of whom are successful K Street lawyers.

My eyes take a minute to adjust to the dimmed lighting, but I can already see the place is packed. People are drinking and eating, and a few guests have started dancing in the middle of the living room, bumping and grinding to the deafening music. The apartment smells, as it does at all of Millie's parties, like sweat and desperation.

Millie wraps her arms around Adam's neck and gives him a peck on the cheek, letting her taught, dark curls brush against his face. I clench my jaw and hand Millie the bottle of wine. She releases Adam from her grip and studies the bottle. "It's too warm," she says, scrunching up her nose. "I can't put this out. I'll have to refrigerate it."

She marches into the kitchen with the wine, and Adam grabs my shoulder. "Listen—I know she can be difficult, but please. Behave yourself. She's my friend."

"And I'm your girlfriend and barely know anyone here."

"So?"

"So don't leave me to fend for myself."

"Why don't you worry a little less about my behavior and worry a little more about your own?"

Why don't you stop being such a prick? I think. But I can't say that—not when I've made some bullshit promise to be on my best behavior. So instead, I say, "Then help me. Stick by me tonight. Don't ditch me for a bunch of people I've never met."

Adam rolls his eyes, and for a moment I almost forget he is my boyfriend. He is acting like my boss. Or my father. Or a teacher, even. But definitely not a person with whom I share an apartment and a bed and supposedly a life. Something in our relationship has permanently shifted, like a doorway that has warped from the cold, preventing the door from closing flush with the frame, and I am beginning to think there's nothing I can do to smooth us back into place.

It takes me all of ten minutes to discover there is no one I want to talk to at this party, which consists of a bunch of think tank wonks, uptight lawyers, and Millie's running buddies, who only want to talk about their next race and latest training regimen. One guy named Tim (or Tom, or Bill) pounced on me as soon as I put down my purse and launched into a lengthy and detailed description of his work on ERISA law, which was almost as interesting as it sounds, but not quite. I now know far more than I ever wanted to know about the Pension Benefit Guaranty Corporation.

But I'm playing the role of Adam's gracious partner, and so far I'm doing a pretty good job—though it is becoming increasingly clear this is not a role I enjoy playing. If I have to listen to one more person erupt in a frenzy over "regulatory arbitrage" or "inverted yield curves," I might actually try to take my own life.

Adam has been working the room since we arrived, abandoning me in precisely the way I asked him not to, and by the time I extricate myself from a series of dull conversations, I've lost track of him. I am now standing in the corner of the living room by myself, the only sober person among the throng of gyrating wonks, a distinction I feel compelled to eliminate. At this point, alcohol is a means for survival.

I push my way to the bar, elbowing my way through a crowd that has now started dancing aggressively to Justin Bieber. The bar is in total disarray, littered with half-empty bottles and dirty cups. I grab a half-decent bottle of Cabernet and fill a clear plastic cup to the rim. As I sip my wine, I spot Adam across the room, whispering into Millie's ear as he cups her shoulder. I empty my glass in a single gulp and fill it up with another varietal, followed by another, and another. Pretty soon I've lost track of Adam and Millie, and I'm not sure how many glasses of wine I've drunk, but what I do know is that if I don't get something solid in my stomach soon, very bad things will happen.

Stumbling through the crowd, I make my way to the dining room table, whose offerings have been pillaged by a crowd almost as inebriated as I am. Millie always makes all the food at her parties, and it's never any good. A few months ago she made a bowl of vegan chocolate mousse that tasted like burnt chalk, and Adam went on and on about how delicious it was, which made me want to throttle him—mostly because the mousse was inedible, but also because it had been months since he'd spoken of anything I'd made with such effusive praise.

At this point, though, I'm willing to eat anything, so I scan the table for a decent snack and grab a skewer from what appears to be a large platter of beef satay.

It is not beef satay.

I'm sure it's *supposed* to be beef satay, but what I put in my mouth tastes like armpits and sweaty feet, and as I chew, I feel as if I am eating a pair of wet socks. I search around for a receptacle in which I can spit this culinary atrocity, but all I can find is the empty cup I'm holding in my hand. So, without a better alternative, I cough up the beef into my cup.

Tim/Tom/Bill shuffles over to my position along the table, disgust painted all over his pasty, pock-marked face. "What was *that*?" he shouts, his nasal voice piercing through the music.

"What?" I shout back.

He points to my cup. "What the hell is that?"

I look down at the mangled piece of meat and back up at Tim/Tom/Bill, of whom there now appears to be two. "It tastes like rancid possum," I say, as if that will make what I'm holding in my hand any less disgusting.

He cups his hand to his ear. "Sorry, it tastes like what?"

"RANCID POSSUM. It tastes like something crawled in my mouth and *died*!"

It is at this moment that Millie's friend Sarah decides to change songs on Millie's iPod. And it is at this exact moment, in the brief five seconds of silence between "Rock Your Body" and "Poker Face," that the room is filled with the slurred, strained sounds of my drunken voice.

The crowd momentarily stops dancing and turns in my direction, wondering, most likely, what the hell is going on and why someone is shrieking like a lunatic about rancid possums. Sarah clutches her chest, embarrassed at being partially responsible for bringing the party to a crashing halt, though she and I might disagree about the extent of her role here.

Not knowing what to do in the face of my screeching, Sarah adjusts the volume on Millie's iPod and waves her arms at the group, encouraging everyone to *go on, go on, keep dancing*, which some of them do and some of them don't. Millie pushes her way through the crowd until she is standing in front of me with her hands on her hips, looking as if she might rip out my eyeballs.

"I beg your pardon?" she asks, her voice competing with Lady

Gaga's *p-p-poker face* for the crowd's attention. "What, my food isn't good enough for you?"

I stand in silence and bite my lip. What am I supposed to say? That her beef satay tastes like a jockstrap?

"No answer? That's a first," she says. She surveys the crowd, half of whom have started dancing again. The rest are either talking or swaying drunkenly from side to side. "Way to ruin everyone's good time, Hannah."

"I—I didn't ruin anything. Everyone is having a great time." Under the spell of far too many glasses of wine, my lips feel fat and numb, providing a substantial challenge to my attempts at proper diction, and so what I say sounds more like "Ereewon issaaaving a graytime."

But everyone *is* having a great time, aren't they? Everyone except me. I scan the room and spot Sarah a few feet away, rocking back and forth to the music as she grabs a snack off the table. "Look at Sarah getting her groove on," I shout in Sarah's direction. "You're still having a good time, aren't you, Sarah?"

Sarah looks up from the table and frowns. "My name is Danielle," she says.

"Oh. Sorry."

Fantastic.

I look for Adam's face in the crowd, but I cannot find him anywhere, and so my only option is to retreat gracefully into the bathroom.

Or not so gracefully. Millie's floor tilts from side to side like the deck of a ship, a circumstance under which grace eludes me. I stagger drunkenly toward the bathroom and slam the door shut behind me, but when I try to fasten the lock, my hands won't let me. They're slippery with sweat and tremble uncontrollably. What have I done? Reassuring Adam was my only goal for the evening, and I've already blown it.

I reach for Millie's medicine cabinet, in search of Tums or Maalox to quell the fire burning in my stomach, and catch a glimpse of myself in her mirror. My hair is wet and dark along my hairline, with tiny wisps stuck to my forehead. Red blotches cover my face, and my mascara and eyeliner have leached from my lids and settled along my lower eye sockets, resembling small patches of bicycle grease. I look—and feel—as if I've been punched in the face.

Millie's cabinet is organized alphabetically and by function, and in the antacids section, I have my choice of Gas-X (G), Maalox (M), Rolaids (R), or Tums (T), in various strengths and flavors. I pop four lemon cream Extra Strength Maalox in my mouth, wipe the makeup from under my eyes, and splash some cold water on my face. I close my eyes, take two deep breaths, and put my hand on the door handle, hoping that when I open it I will be transported like Dorothy in *The Wizard of Oz* to a magical, happy place. Everyone will smile when I return, welcoming me like the Lollipop Guild with smiles and treats.

But we are not in Oz, and so instead I am forced to push my way through the crowd, withstanding the occasional raised eyebrow, while everyone bumps and grinds to the music blasting through Millie's speakers. When I get to the other side of the room, I find Millie and Adam talking in the corner, next to the cup of masticated beef.

As I approach, Millie narrows her dark brown eyes into tiny slits, anger oozing from every pore. Even her hair looks angry, as if a steamy inner rage is unraveling each coil into a frizzled mass.

"What do you want?" she asks.

What I want is for her to disappear—to evaporate into thin air—but since that isn't going to happen, and since I'm stuck at this damn party, I might as well smooth things over until Adam and I can leave.

"I . . ." I take a deep breath and force the words to come out. "I'm . . . sorry."

My gaze shifts between Millie and Adam, but Adam stares into the distance, his almond-shaped eyes focused on the dancing crowd. He tucks his hands into his pockets, the sleeves of his blue-and-white-striped button-down rolled up around his elbows. No matter what I do to grab his attention, he won't look at me.

Millie crosses her arms over her chest. "Apology denied," she says. "We can talk about this Monday. Until then, please leave before you ruin the rest of my party."

I wait for her to say something more, but she doesn't and glares at me with her flinty eyes. Normally I would balk at Millie's histrionics. I would mirror her haughty stance, slowly and dramatically crossing my arms over my chest, and stare at her in silence until she turned fuchsia and stomped off like a three-year-old. Tonight, however, I will gladly accept her invitation to get the hell out of here.

I grab my purse off one of the dining room chairs, but when I turn to walk toward the door, Adam doesn't move. He remains by Millie's side, hands tucked into his khakis, staring at the floor.

"Adam?" I lay my hand on his shoulder.

"I'm not leaving yet," he says, shrugging my hand off his shoulder without looking at me.

For a moment I think he's sticking up for me—Ha! Take that! We're not leaving!—but then I realize he said "I" not "we," and when he moves closer to Millie, I understand. The key, however, is pretending that I don't.

I scrunch my eyebrows together and play dumb. "So . . . we're staying, then."

"No, I'm staying," he says.

"Well, if you're staying, I'm staying."

"Except Millie asked you to leave."

"So, what, Millie is the boss of you now?"

The two of them exchange a glance, and then Adam looks back at me. "Don't make this uglier than it already is."

I've never seen him like this—his voice and demeanor like ice—and even in my drunken state, I know he is angrier with me now than he has ever been. And as much as I want to fight him on this, to make him choose me over Millie, I know there's no point. He has made up his mind. He wants me to leave.

"Fine," I say, trying to keep my lip from quivering. "I'll see you at home."

I clutch my purse in my hand and walk with purpose toward Millie's entryway, holding myself together until I'm out of their sight. But when I look over my shoulder, I see it doesn't matter. Adam isn't watching. He is staring at the ground, his hands tucked into his pockets, and he doesn't look up as I walk out the door.

five

the light from the TV bounces off the cement walls of our living room, and I look at the clock for what feels like the hundredth time: 2:01 A.M. I left Millie's apartment more than two hours ago, and still no sign of Adam.

I get out my phone and start to call him but hang up before his phone starts ringing. I shouldn't call. He'll be home any minute.

I shiver in the chilled apartment air, which feels colder than usual, probably because I am sitting alone in the dark watching reruns of *Will & Grace* while I wait for my boyfriend to come home and yell at me. Adam likes to keep the temperature somewhere between that of a meat locker and the grocery freezer aisle, but I waved the white flag in our thermostat war months ago. When we first moved in together, the battle was silent but constant. I'd raise the temperature three degrees when he was out; he'd lower it four degrees when he returned and I wasn't looking. Back and forth, back and forth. But one day, I didn't have the energy for it anymore. My resignation came as a surprise, but the battle felt more like an eternal stalemate, and for what? I told myself love is all about compromise, though I wondered if love is also supposed to feel like defeat.

"The chicken's great," says Grace on the TV screen as she gnaws on a chicken bone, much to Will's disgust. I've always felt a kinship with Grace Adler's character. Maybe it's the red hair, or the fact that she's Jewish, or the way in one episode she pretended to be an alcoholic so that she could get free Krispy Kreme doughnuts and hot cocoa at AA meetings. I can relate to all of those things. There's very little I wouldn't do for a free Krispy Kreme doughnut.

But I can also empathize with her incompetence when it comes to relationships. Before Adam, my longest relationship lasted two months. His name was Edwin Michaels, and we met junior year of college at the annual Apple Harvest Festival in Ithaca. He asked if I wanted to share a pumpkin funnel cake, a query that, to me, seemed like a trick question. Of course I *wanted* a pumpkin funnel cake; who wouldn't want a pumpkin funnel cake? A crazy person, that's who. But did I want to share? Not really. I wanted my own. But he was adorable—all limbs and freckles, topped off with a froth of brown curls that seemed to defy the laws of gravity—and I couldn't turn him down. We shared one funnel cake, and then another, and by the end of the day we were sharing a bed in his off-campus apartment. All told, the day was a raging success.

I quickly discovered Edwin loved to cook and eat, and we proceeded to go on a series of dates that consisted of trips to Wegmans followed by a home-cooked meal at his apartment, followed by some quality schtupping. Looking back on it, I see that he was almost perfect: smart, funny, interested in food, attentive in the bedroom. But I didn't want to rush into anything serious, and I didn't want to seem too eager. My male friends hated the constant texts and calls from their girlfriends, so I tried to seem mysterious and aloof. I ignored some of Edwin's calls, pretended to have other plans when I didn't, acted as if I had a very busy and productive life that had nothing to do with him. I played it cool—a little *too* cool, as it turns out, because after two months of me canceling dates and acting busy all the time, Edwin broke up with me.

That was pretty much the pinnacle of my dating career until I met Adam. Along the way, I told myself my repeated failures with men weren't my fault; it was all these losers I kept meeting. I was too much woman for them to handle, clearly. But in moments of complete honesty, I worried I was defective in some way— undateable, even. And then I met Adam, who shockingly didn't tire of me after two weeks, or even two months. He actually seemed to like me—and not simply because I had big boobs and curvy hips. He liked my attitude. He found me refreshing.

In the beginning, dating Adam felt like a dream. He was sexy and intelligent and wanted by half the young women in Washington, and yet he had chosen me—me!—over everyone else. After we had been dating for a month or so, Adam invited me to a Harvard young alumni event he was cohosting, which featured speeches by two former solicitors general. Adam gave the opening remarks, and from the moment he started speaking, it was as if Cupid had shot me through the heart. His gift for oratory, his palpable brilliance, his ability to captivate an entire room with his sheer charisma—I was smitten. I'd never met someone as intellectually gifted as Adam, and I haven't since. I was in awe of him.

The first three months of our relationship flew by, and on our three-month anniversary, as we walked along the Tidal Basin, he told me he loved me. I turned and kissed him and collapsed in his arms and told him I felt the same. I'd never said that to anyone before, but it felt true. Isn't that what love is? That feeling of being swept away? It's not that I'd never loved anyone before, but I'd always been too afraid to give myself over to someone who might reciprocate the feeling. That felt too dangerous, like walking through a bad neighborhood with your wallet wide open. But being with Adam, that felt safe.

Or at least it used to . . .

I hear footsteps in the hall. I sit up straight as the steps get louder and closer, but they soon pass and enter the apartment next to ours. I look at the clock: 2:40.

Where *is* he?

I look down at the blanket, a gift from my parents from one of their many trips to Asia, and notice I've been pulling at the fringe around the edge, fraying it. I can't shake the feeling from earlier, when Adam wouldn't even look at me—when he asked me to leave.

I hear a sound at our door, followed by the jingle of keys. Someone fumbles with the lock, and the door opens with a snap. Adam stumbles in, slamming the door behind him, and flicks on the light.

"Why are you sitting in the dark?" he asks as he throws his keys on the counter.

"I was waiting up for you. Are you . . . okay?"

"Fucking great." He pours a glass of water and sips it slowly. He hasn't looked at me since entering the apartment.

"It's pretty late," I say. Silence. My fingers continue to pick at the blanket fringe. "Listen, about earlier—"

"Stop," Adam snaps, looking me in the eye. "Don't."

"But—"

"No, I don't care what excuse you give. You're out of control. It's like you're physically incapable of keeping your mouth shut."

"Adam, come on, I had no idea Sarah—"

"Danielle," he corrects me.

"*Danielle*, sorry. I had no idea she was going to mess with Millie's playlist."

"That's not the point."

I know that's not the point. The point is I told an entire room full of people that Millie's food tasted like rancid possum. I also ruined an opportunity to show Adam I can be the woman he wants me to be. And now I'm wondering if I ever could be that woman. Do I want to be?

"I messed up. I'm sorry. But this isn't worth fighting over. I've done worse."

"Yeah—*exactly*."

"My unpredictability is part of my charm, right?"

I'm clutching at straws here, grasping for something, anything, that will inject levity into the conversation, but Adam ignores my pathetic attempts at humor.

"Not anymore," he says. He lays his glass on the counter and wipes his brow with the palm of his hand. "You know I want a career in politics. And things at the office have been going really well lately. The partners have started talking promotions. I have more important things to worry about when I socialize than your big mouth."

"Adam, I told you. You don't have to worry about me."

"Is that what tonight was? Me not having to worry about you?"

I toss the blanket off my lap and walk hesitantly toward the opposite side of the kitchen counter. "In the scheme of things, it wasn't a big deal. No one cared."

"Millie cared."

"Millie doesn't count. She hates me."

Adam sighs. "Whatever—this isn't even about tonight."

"Then what is this about?"

"You."

I clear my throat. "Me?"

"You're never going to be The One, Hannah. I had fun for a while, but fun isn't enough. I need someone more . . ." He trails off.

"More what?"

"Gracious. Subdued. Serious. Take your pick."

My vision blurs. I blink to fight back the tears. "Oh really?"

He nods. "Yes, really."

"And you decided this, when? Tonight? Last week? Three months ago?" Adam doesn't respond. "Because I haven't changed. I'm the same person you met at Millie's party fifteen months ago, and the same person you asked to move in with you. The same person you fell in love with. I'm your little firecracker, Adam."

"More like a bomb," he mutters.

"You want a bomb? I'll give you a bomb." I grab his water glass from across the counter and throw the water in his face. "*Boom, motherfucker!*"

Adam stares at his soaked shirt. "What the fuck, Hannah?"

"This is who I am, Adam. This is the full package right here. Take it or leave it."

Adam wipes the water off his face with a flick of his hand. "I'll leave it."

His declaration—so firm and unequivocal—sucks the air out of the room, and whatever chutzpah I conjured up moments ago vanishes. The words rattle around my brain until they are drowned out by a hollow ringing in my ears.

This is not how this was supposed to go. When I said *Take it or leave it*, I didn't really mean *Adam Prescott, you can either (a) Take it, or (b) Leave it*. Takeitorleaveit. It's an expression. The correct choice is implied, like in Eddie Izzard's "Cake or Death?" routine.

"Hang on a sec," I say. "I didn't mean—"

"Yes you did. And you're right—you are who you are, and I am who I am, and those are two very different people."

"But . . . I can change." I realize I'm reversing myself on the principles of individuality and nonconformity I espoused moments ago, but apparently principles are for homeless, boyfriendless losers.

"If you want to change, that's your choice," Adam says. "But you're going to have to do it without me."

"I don't understand. I thought you loved me. I thought we were in love."

But as I say the words, they don't sound true even to me. We were in love, months ago, but at some point we fell out of love and neither of us bothered to notice. Or, more likely, we both noticed but were too afraid to do anything about it. And, what's worse, it's increasingly clear that what I've been clinging to these past few months isn't a relationship; it's an apartment and a lifestyle.

I study Adam's face: his square jawline, his soft eyes, his sharp cheekbones and perfectly plump lips. It's a face that could make a woman do stupid, reckless things, a face I had called mine for more than a year. But now his face seems as distant and detached as the ones on the TV screen, as removed as Will or Grace, and I wonder if his face had ever been mine at all.

"I can stay with Millie until you find a new place," Adam says.

"With *Millie*? Are you kidding me?"

Adam shrugs. "She's an old friend."

"Who wants to fuck you."

"Hannah, stop. We're just good friends."

I roll my eyes. "Then why don't you move in with her permanently? If you're such good friends."

"We both know you can't afford this place on your own."

He's right, of course, the jerk. But his patronizing tone pisses me off. I hate that he gets to keep this apartment. I hate that he plans to stay with Millie. And, most of all, I hate that he is the one telling me the relationship is over, even though, deep down, we've both known that for a while.

Adam makes his way into the bedroom, and I follow him like a puppy—more precisely, like a puppy dog-paddling through a river of shit. Just because I know we're wrong for each other doesn't mean the pain of rejection hurts any less. Yes, this relationship is ending because we aren't compatible, but it is also ending because Adam doesn't want me anymore.

Adam throws some clothes and toiletries into a Kipling bag and gives one last look around the bedroom. "Let's try to sort out your living situation in the next week or two. If I forgot anything, I'll try to swing by while you're at work—so it's not awkward."

Adam searches my eyes, but I look away. He comes closer and grabs my chin between his fingers and tilts my head until we are looking at each other. Out of nowhere, he brightens and flashes his signature smile, as if he suddenly realizes parting on bad terms could cost him a vote in a future election. "I'd love to stay friends," he says.

"Screw you."

Adam winces. At this point, I don't care. I just want him to leave.

"Well . . . bye." Adam leans in and wraps his arms around me, as if somehow this will counteract any feelings he may have hurt, and then he turns and walks out the door. The door crashes shut, creating a bang that echoes off the concrete floor and walls.

I stagger over to the freezer, wanting nothing more than to fill the emptiness inside me with something rich and disgustingly caloric, anything to erase this feeling of being so completely alone. But, as I dig out a fist-size spoonful of cookies and cream ice cream, for the first time in my entire life, I cannot bring myself to eat.

CHAPTER

six

I look down at the address scrawled on the paper in my hands, then up again: 1774½ Church Street NW. I guess this is it.

The town house, the last on the block, stands three stories high, with bright red painted bricks, a large bay window, and a yellow door. The bright colors fit with the character of the street, where the multicolored houses look like a collection of Easter eggs, their facades dyed butter yellow, pale peach, navy blue, dusky gray, and mint green. Oak trees dot the sidewalk from end to end, stretching so high and wide they nearly touch each other across the street, creating a shady canopy. There is a distinct calmness to this stretch of Church Street, even though it sits only one block east of the bustling traffic circle that gives Dupont Circle its name.

The circle itself is the neighborhood's heart, and Connecticut Avenue is its aorta, piercing the circle from northwest to southeast and teeming with restaurants, coffee shops, and boutiques. On more than one occasion, I've found myself strolling up and down Connecticut, picking up a Salty Oat Cookie and steaming cup of chai from Teaism and a new cookbook from Kramerbooks, before ending up in the grass around the Dupont Circle fountain, relishing my newly acquired loot. It's one of my favorite ways to spend a Sunday.

Church Street lies to the east of all of that activity, but 1774½

Church Street sits on a block bounded on its other side by Seventeenth Street, another major thoroughfare and the epicenter of DC's gay scene. And yet, even situated so close to Seventeenth Street, this block manages to feel completely separate from the hustle and bustle of the neighborhood. There is a charming brick theater slipped between the row houses and a small church at the western-most end, but otherwise, the shaded street is filled only with houses and trees. Tucked away as it is, the street feels private and quiet and low-key—in other words, everything I'm looking for in a new neighborhood.

In front of me, a black wrought iron stairway leads to the front door of the main town house, which bears a shiny gold placard for 1774 Church Street. To the right of the stairway, a narrow flight of steps tucks beneath the entryway and descends to the basement door, the entrance to 1774 ½ Church Street, the English basement apartment I saw advertised on Craigslist. I look at my watch: eight o'clock in the morning. Right on time for the open house.

"Please," I mutter under my breath. "Let this one be okay."

This is the tenth apartment I've looked at in three weeks. Or the twelfth. At this point, I've lost track. All I know is I've been scouring Craigslist and *Washington City Paper* for the past three weeks and have nothing to show for it but a bunch of apartments that smelled like mildew or cat pee or both. This one claims to be an English basement apartment with "character" and "charm," which probably means it's the size of a closet with plumbing that hasn't been updated in half a century.

I knock on the basement door, which is shiny and black and has a small peephole and a brass knocker. No one answers. I knock again, louder this time, but still, nothing. I peer through the small sliver of a window to the right of the door, but I can't see anything because the entire apartment is pitch-black. On the day of an open house? What the hell?

It occurs to me I may have misread the ad—a very real possibility, since I have been operating on minimal sleep and maximum stress for the past three weeks. Maybe the landlord wants to meet in his town house first before showing the apartment.

I march up the steps to 1774 Church Street's bright yellow door and press the doorbell, which instead of making the familiar "*Ding*-dong," chimes with an ascending "Dong-*ding*." A stocky man in a faded Georgetown T-shirt and jeans opens the door.

"Uh, hi," he says, running his fingers through his wispy brown hair. "Can I help you?"

I reexamine the piece of paper in my hand. This is the right address. Unless I wrote down the wrong one. Which is entirely possible. "I'm here for the open house?"

The man looks down at his watch, and his lips curl into a goofy smirk. "You're twelve hours early."

I slump against his doorway. "You're kidding."

Of course he isn't kidding. Who the hell would hold an open house at eight on a Sunday morning? I guess he figured any rational person would know 8:00 meant 8:00 P.M. But I've lost all sense of time since Adam and I broke up. The days and weeks have melted together, where the breakup and today feel as if they occurred along the same continuum but on two different planes, like a lonely and depressing Möbius strip.

The man shrugs his broad shoulders. "No worries. I can give you a tour of the ship if you want. I'm up anyway. Come on in."

I ignore his reference to the apartment as a "ship" and decide, what the hell? As long as I'm here, I might as well get the grand tour. He ushers me into the house, past the Lichtenstein print hanging in his foyer and along the shiny hardwood floors in his hallway. His home is cool and clean and smells like freshly pressed cotton. To my right, a broad doorway at least six feet wide leads into the living room, which, with an open floor plan, flows directly into the dining room in the back right corner of the house. We pass the doorway and continue straight ahead, toward an archway at the end of the hall.

"I'm Hannah, by the way."

"Blake Fischer," he says, grabbing my hand and shaking it firmly as he leads me through the archway.

We enter the kitchen, which resembles something out of *House Beautiful* or *Architectural Digest* or my wildest fantasy of what my kitchen might, maybe (possibly), look like someday. Creamy granite countertops crawl along the left perimeter of the room and cover a large center island featuring a six-burner Viking range and a breakfast bar. A stainless steel hood descends from the ceiling like an intergalactic transporter, hovering over the stove top. To the right, an open entryway leads into the dining room, allowing for an open flow from the living room into the dining room and finally into the kitchen. There's a double oven to my left, a Sub-Zero refrigerator to my right, a wine cooler along the back wall, and a backsplash made of translucent gray tile. I take slow, deep breaths to keep myself from gasping or crying because, quite honestly, I'd like to do both.

I caress the smooth granite counter with my hand and imagine myself standing in front of this stove, caramelizing onions while I wait for the cookies in the top oven to finish baking and for the beef tenderloin in the lower oven to reach a perfect medium rare. The house is filled with the smells of toasted brown sugar and onions and rosemary, and I call to my gorgeous boyfriend in the next room, who runs in and scoops me off my feet and twirls me around before putting me down and kissing me and presenting me with a new puppy, one that looks exactly like the dog in those toilet paper commercials. I tell him he shouldn't have, and he says of course he should have because I am amazing, and I deserve all the happiness in the world. Surely not *all* the happiness in the world? But he tells me yes, *all* the happiness in the world. Because I am that special.

And then I wake up.

"Can I get you something to drink?" Blake asks.

I clear my throat and nod, my fingers still fondling his countertop. "That would be great. Your kitchen is gorgeous, by the way."

He removes two Duralex glasses from one of the cupboards. "Thanks. After nine months, the renovations are finally finished." He rolls his eyes. "Contractors."

"Ha," I say. "Tell me about it." I say this because it sounds right, not because I have any idea what I'm talking about. I've never renovated anything in my life, unless you count my Barbie playhouse when I was six, and I did that myself.

And, frankly, I can't imagine owning a town house, much less renovating one. That's something adults do, people who have careers and nest eggs, people who buy wrinkle creams and wear sensible shoes. None of those descriptors apply to me. And yet, at twenty-six, aren't I an adult? I'm not a girl anymore; that much I know. But a woman? No, that doesn't sound right either. Women don't have parents who swoop in to fix all their problems. Women know what they want out of life. Women have direction.

Blake, on the other hand, is definitely an adult—a youngish adult, maybe thirty-five, but an adult nonetheless. He has a few wrinkles around his eyes, a receding hairline, a mortgage, and a contractor, all attributes that scream *adult, adult, adult*. How long do I have until I reach his stage of life? Nine years? Ten? Somehow I doubt I'll have a mortgage or a contractor by then, though whether or not I'll have wrinkles and alopecia is still up for grabs.

Blake hands me a glass of water, almost dropping it as he hands it to me. "Whoa—hot potato!" He blushes. "Why don't we go downstairs so I can show you around?"

He leads me outside and escorts me down the steps to the basement door, which he informs me is one of two entrances to the apartment, both of which lead to the outside; there are no stairs connecting the basement to his part of the house. I follow him into the darkened basement, and he flicks on the light.

"Here you have it," he says.

I swivel my head to take in the entire apartment: a small room with beige Berber carpet and white walls in a space slightly larger than Mark's office. The crisp and slightly chemical scent of fresh paint permeates the room. There is a tiny kitchen in the corner with an oven, a sink, and a narrow refrigerator; it is smaller than my parents' powder room.

"It definitely has . . . character," I say.

"It looks small, but you can fit the basics in here—a bed, a couch, and a dresser. Depending on how you arrange things, you could even fit a queen in here. It would be tight, but doable."

Not a problem, I think. Adam owns all the furniture in our apartment, and thus none of it will be coming with me.

"And if you like the outdoors . . ."

Blake opens the door leading to the backyard. Well, "yard." It's more like a patio with a few tufts of grass. But it does have a small vegetable garden and a grill. I could do worse.

We walk along the back patio, half of which is covered by a large wooden deck that connects to his kitchen upstairs.

"I've had some issues with the gutters in the past," he says, pointing up to the rainspout, "but I think I fixed the problem." He smiles. "At least I hope so."

I trail behind him as we go back inside to check out the bathroom (tiny) and closets (even tinier). He follows me as I inspect all of the surfaces (cracked laminate countertop, mildly dingy sink), as well as the locks on the front and back entrances.

"This neighborhood is really safe," he says as I inspect the dead bolt on the back door.

"I know, but with two entry points . . ."

"Honestly, it's really safe here. I paid for a fancy security system for the whole house, and I never use it."

"Never?"

"Well, I mean, if I'm going away for more than a week, then yeah, I use it. But anything less than that and I don't bother. You'll be safe down here. I promise."

Once I've checked the doors and inspected the heating vents, Blake suggests we leave this furniture-less space and go over the rest of the details upstairs—or, as he calls it, the "upper deck."

When we reach the so-called upper deck, I settle into the chestnut-colored leather couch in his living room, from which point I can stare directly into his dining room and out his back windows. Blake sits across from me in a plush, beige recliner, pressing his back into the cushion and resting his ankle on his knee. His face reminds me a little of a chipmunk's—wide at the temples, narrow at the chin, with big eyes and a buttonlike nose.

"So," Blake says, "what brings you to the area?"

"I've lived here for three years, actually. The only reason I'm moving is because I'm being forced out of my old place."

"Could I ask why? Sorry to pry, but as a landlord I have to ask."

"I'm not being evicted or anything, if that's what you mean. It's a long story involving a live-in boyfriend and a breakup."

"Ah, gotcha. Sorry." He scratches one of his ruddy cheeks. "So . . . where are you from originally?"

"Philadelphia. The suburbs, technically."

"Cool. My dad grew up in Philly." He pauses and loses himself in a thought, as if he is looking at me and through me at the same time. "My grandpa still lives there."

"Oh. That's nice." I'm not sure how I'm supposed to respond. He looks caught up in some memory of which I clearly am not a part.

"Anyway," he says, shaking himself out of his reverie, "a few more quick things about the apartment. Like the ad said, the rent is twelve-fifty a month, including utilities. I'll need one month's rent as a security deposit, but you'll get that back if and when you decide to move out, assuming you haven't trashed the place. Oh, and I'll need some sort of proof of income, so that I know you can make the rent."

I do the math in my head. On my $35K salary, I can barely afford this place. God knows where that security deposit will come from. But of all the places I've seen, this is by far the best. It's clean, it's three blocks from my office, and the landlord seems moderately sane. And, almost as important, the place is five blocks from Adam's apartment in Logan Circle: far enough to avoid frequent run-ins, but close enough to engineer run-ins if I choose to do so. And anyway, Adam can't lay claim to the entire Dupont-Logan neighborhood; these are my stomping grounds, too.

"I'm anxious to rent this place out," Blake says. "We're still in the August recess, and I have to head back to my congressman's district next week. The sooner I can secure a tenant, the better."

"You work on the Hill?"

He nods. "Communications director."

"For . . . ?"

"Congressman Holmes," he says. I stare at him blankly. "Florida's eleventh district? Big on immigration?"

"I'm not really up to speed on the immigration debate. Sorry. Is he up for reelection or something?"

"Congressmen are *always* up for reelection." He smiles. "But no, this is an off year. He isn't on the ballot again until next year. But given the political climate, we're holding a bunch of town halls on immigration reform, so I'm going to be in Tampa for most of the time between now and Labor Day. If you want the apartment, I'll give you first dibs, but you have to let me know in the next twelve hours. After that, it'll be available to anyone at the open house."

I jump up from the couch and extend my hand toward Blake. "No need to wait. I'll take it." I grab Blake's hand and, taking a cue from Martin Prescott, shake it firmly.

He smirks. "Okay then, Ms. . . ."

"Sugarman."

"Sugarman. Sweet." He chuckles, apparently amused by his own joke, which tells me everything I need to know about this guy's sense of humor. He lets go of my hand and gives me a sailor's salute. "Welcome aboard," he says. "How soon can you move in?"

"I'd like to board ASAP, if that's okay." Why we are speaking like sailors I do not know, but I am now participating in Blake's awkward nautical metaphor. I sound like an idiot.

"If you can get me the paperwork by this afternoon, I can run a credit check and work on getting you in by Saturday. Cool?"

"Cool."

He shakes my hand a final time and smiles. "Well . . . anchors aweigh," he says with a wink.

Shiver me fucking timbers. What have I gotten myself into?

CHAPTER

seven

after two weeks of blissful peace and calm in my new apartment, I awake the Tuesday morning after Labor Day to what sounds like an earthquake rumbling over my head.

I sit straight up, my eyes cast at the ceiling. *Thump. Thump. Thump, thump, thump!*

What the . . . ?

Thump!

Either my landlord is back from the congressional recess, or an elephant is stomping through his living room. As someone hoping for a prolonged period of undisturbed sleep, I am kind of hoping for the latter. Also, it would be pretty cool to see a live elephant in the middle of our nation's capital.

I collapse back onto my pillow as the thumping increases in its intensity, all of it seemingly concentrated directly above my head.

"*Shut uuuuuup*," I groan into my pillow. But Blake (or maybe the elephant?) does not shut up, and so I let out a resigned grunt and roll out of bed—or, rather, out of AeroBed, since I no longer own a bed and cannot afford a new one. At this point, the only "furniture" in my entire apartment is this air mattress and an oversize beanbag. I've been scouring Craigslist and Freecycle for a dresser, but I don't have one yet, so for now my clothes sit in the closet, in boxes, or in small piles around the periphery of the room. I've tried to make the place look like less of a crack den, but my progress has been minimal.

Moving out of Adam's apartment was generally traumatic and terrible, or at least as traumatic and terrible as disentangling your life from someone else's is bound to be. I couldn't afford movers, and since I wasn't bringing any furniture with me, I didn't really need them. But I don't own a car, so moving day involved me carrying box after box the five blocks from my old apartment to my new one, alone. Adam offered to help, saying it would give us "closure," but I basically told him to get lost. The only closure I want at this point is the closure of a door in his face—his *and* his sometime roommate Millie's.

The one upside to being kicked out of an apartment where I owned very little is that I brought with me only the stuff I care about: clothes, toiletries, books, and kitchen gear. I may not have a dresser, but my kitchen drawers are lined with measuring cups and mixing bowls, citrus zesters and Kugelhopf pans. Any other random crap I collected—the kind of stuff that gets shoved in a junk drawer and forgotten about—is Adam's problem, not mine. I hope he enjoys his drawer of nonfunctional pens.

As I rub the sleep from my eyes, the *Knight Rider* theme song blares from beneath a pile of pants. My cell phone. I jump up and rummage through the stack of denim, wearing nothing but an old Cornell T-shirt with a large coffee stain down the front. For the first time, I appreciate my apartment's few windows.

I glance at the screen on my cell phone and see a very long series of numbers. An international call. My parents.

"Hello?" I say, my voice scratchy with sleep.

"Hi, sweetie, it's Mom. I got your e-mail. How are you?"

I sent my parents an e-mail a few days ago telling them Adam and I split up and sending them my new address. I didn't want to bother them all the way in England over something as silly as a breakup, but I figured they'd want to know I moved. I also secretly hoped they'd send money. They didn't.

"I'm okay. Settling into my new place and everything."

"What happened? I thought things with you and Adam were going well."

"Obviously not." My tone is snarkier than I intended, but I'm tired of telling and retelling this story. The breakup has been hard enough without having to relive it twenty times. My mom never cared for Adam anyway. She was convinced he would always promote his own career at the expense of mine—that his intense ambition would inevitably stifle my own. I'm not in the mood to listen to her gloat.

"I'm so sorry, sweetie. I know how you must feel. But you are beautiful and brilliant, and anyone who can't see that must be an idiot."

"I'm the idiot. Or at least the one who can't keep her mouth shut."

"Listen—any man who is looking for a submissive wallflower is living in the wrong era!" I pull the phone from my ear to keep from going deaf. "Do you think I became a prominent and tenured professor by not speaking my mind? You are a strong woman with something to say. Some man isn't going to muzzle you—I don't care who he is!"

If she knew my "something to say" was not about economic theory or civil rights, but about leg of lamb and beef satay, she might change her mind. My mother has always regarded my interest in food as a trivial hobby, an unfortunate pastime I picked up from her mother-in-law. If she's said it once, she's said it a hundred times: "My friends and I didn't break down all these barriers so that you could end up back in a kitchen!" So, needless to say, cooking isn't something over which we bond.

"I appreciate that, Mom. I'm doing okay. Don't worry."

"Well, just so you know, your father and I talked last night, and he's going to wire a couple hundred dollars into your checking account to see you through the move."

"Oh, Mom, you don't have to do that . . ." My halfhearted protest doesn't convince even me. I've already spent hundreds of dollars I don't have on an air mattress and new bedding.

"It's only two hundred dollars," she says. "We insist. Anyway, how's work going?"

Ugh, work. Let's see. Between my intensive apartment search and looking for free furniture, I am massively behind schedule. I've barely done a thing about Mark's December conference. I've also run into Millie almost every day since Adam and I broke up, where I've been forced to engage in stilted, awkward conversations that make it clear Millie still hasn't forgiven me and possibly never will. So that's been a treat.

"It's been . . . a little exhausting lately."

"I could put in a call to Mark. You know we have a good professional rapport."

"No, Mom. Things are fine. Just busy." The last thing I want is my mother running to Mark on my behalf, especially when the most intensive work I've done recently has involved monitoring Adam's Facebook relationship status (for the record, he is still "single").

"Well, before I let you go, I've been meaning to tell you about a wonderful fellowship opportunity I came across. Princeton is offering an economics fellowship perfect for someone your age."

"Princeton?"

"Yes, sweetie, Princeton. I think you should apply. I know Mark would write you a good reference, and I have some connections there as well. I'll send you the link."

"You can send it, but I'm not making any promises," I say.

"What do you mean by that?"

"That I'm not really fellowship material."

"Of course you are. Why would you say that? Of course you're fellowship material. They'd be lucky to have someone like you."

"Assuming I'd want to apply to a fellowship like that. Which I don't."

"You haven't even seen the description of the fellowship! Just read it over. Then decide."

I have no interest whatsoever in applying for an economics fellowship, but this is how we work, my mother and I: she suggests an activity I should pursue, I push back, and she takes my resistance as further evidence I am too naïve and inexperienced to know what is in my best interest. The pattern persists, I suppose, because up to this point, I've done most of the things my parents wanted me to do—everything from bassoon lessons to SAT prep to a job at a Washington think tank. The main reason I pursued those activities was because I knew I *could* do them, and doing so would be an easy way to win my parents' approval. Sometimes I feel as if I've been chasing their approval my whole life.

That's part of the reason I've stayed at NIRD so long. I don't love the work, but I'm smart enough to do a better-than-average job, and working at NIRD is my way of holding my parents' attention, of making the Professors Sugarman proud of their only child. The first time Mark listed me as a coauthor on one of his policy outlooks, my parents both wrote me enthusiastic and commendatory e-mails. Two Ivy League professors! Impressed! By me! For the first time, I felt as if I might be something other than a disappointment to them. But lately, I'm finding it harder and harder to pretend my job fulfills me when it doesn't even come close. Signing up for an economics fellowship would take me further down a path I no longer have an interest in exploring.

My mom outlines the benefits of various fellowship programs but is interrupted by a knock at my front door. "Coming!" I shout, covering the phone with my hand. "Hey, Mom? I have to run. And anyway, this call is probably costing you a fortune. But thanks for checking on me. I love you."

"I love you too, honey. We'll be home in a few weeks. Oh, and let's talk soon about Thanksgiving. Your father and I can't decide what to do."

"Thanksgiving is more than two months away."

"I know, but your aunt Elena wants to reenact the first Thanksgiving in upstate New York, and we're trying to get out of it. It sounds like a total nightmare. I am *not* wearing a bonnet." She sighs. "Anyway, take care of yourself, okay? And please read up on that fellowship."

I hang up and rush to make myself presentable. As it stands, I have not brushed my teeth and am not wearing any pants.

"Just a sec!"

I quickly throw on a pair of sweatpants, gargle some Scope, and splash some water on my face. It's no use. I look like a bag lady.

I hustle to the front door and open it to a gust of Blake's woodsy aftershave.

"Good morning," he says with a smile. He adjusts his blue-and-white-striped tie and fiddles with the buttons on his gray suit jacket. He looks nice—professional. I might even say dapper, if it weren't for the blood-soaked hunk of tissue hanging off his jaw-line.

"You're back," I say, trying to mask the disappointment in my voice. I really enjoyed those two weeks of quiet. I was also really rooting for that elephant. "I thought you'd be tanner after two weeks in Tampa."

"With this skin? Are you kidding? If I didn't wear SPF forty-five, I'd be red as a strawberry." He rubs his jaw, and as he plucks off the piece of bloody tissue, his cheeks flush. "Or possibly as red as I am right now. Yikes."

He tucks the piece of tissue into his pocket and shakes his head. "Anyway," he says, "sorry to bother you so early, but I have a quick favor to ask."

"What's up?"

He holds out a set of three keys on a bright yellow plastic key chain. "Would you mind holding on to an extra set of keys for me?"

"If you want me to . . . sure."

"Awesome. The immigration debate is going to get crazy this fall, so I'll be traveling to the home district a bunch. I'd feel better knowing there was someone around to keep an eye on the place. 'Manning the ship,' if you will." He smiles awkwardly as he makes air quotation marks.

More nautical references. Who is this guy, Jack fucking Sparrow?

"So . . . what, you want me to water your plants or something?"

He shakes his head. "No, no, nothing like that. Just, you know, if something were to happen to the house while I'm away—a pipe explodes or something—I want you to be able to let the repairman in to fix it." He smiles. "And if you want to clean my oven, by all means . . ."

I smile awkwardly.

"Sorry," he says. "Bad joke."

I shrug, smiling for real this time. "I've heard worse. How long will you be away?"

"Not that long. Mostly just a few days at a time, over the fall recesses—the last two weekends of this month, and then over Columbus Day weekend next month. With any luck, we'll adjourn October thirtieth, and that'll be that."

"Doesn't the congressman have an office in Tampa? Why do you have to go back with him?"

He shrugs. "Hand-holding, mostly. As his communications director, it's my responsibility to handle the press—interviews, questions, press releases, stuff like that. Given how heated the immigration debate is becoming, he wants me there to grease the wheels."

I reach out and take the keys from Blake's hand. "I'll keep an eye on the place. Not a problem."

"Oh, and I've been meaning to ask you . . ." He reaches into his inside jacket pocket and pulls out a piece of paper and a pen. "Now that you're living in the neighborhood, would you mind signing my petition for the Dupont Circle ANC?"

"ANC?"

"Advisory Neighborhood Commission. They basically serve as the voice for the Dupont community. They're having a special election this fall, and I'd like to run. It's an unpaid position— something to do on the side—but I thought I'd give it a whirl."

"Oh. Sure."

I grab the pen from his hand and scrawl my signature on the page.

"Excellent," he says. "Thanks."

I hand the paper and pen back to him. "My pleasure."

I expect him to jump in with one more sailing reference (something about "learning the ropes" or "getting my sea legs"), but mercifully he does not. Instead he gives a small salute, marches up the front steps, and heads down Church Street, disappearing from my line of sight.

I lock the door and amble back into my apartment, heading straight for the kitchen to deposit Blake's keys in my take-out menu drawer. Before dropping them inside, I hold the key chain by its yellow plastic tag and dangle the three keys in front of me like a little wind chime, studying the notched grooves as they clang back and forth against each other. Then I shrug, drop the keys in the drawer, and slam it shut. Me and a set of my landlord's keys. What's the worst that could happen?

eight

i rush down Church Street toward Eighteenth Street, stumbling across the cracks in the pavement as I try to avert yet another late arrival at the office. NIRD's building sits along Dupont Circle's southern border, only three blocks from my apartment, but its proximity has done nothing to abate my rampant tardiness. This morning I could blame my mother's call or my landlord's surprise visit, but really, I still had a good forty-five minutes to shower and throw myself together. And yet, somehow, I've managed to both run late *and* look disheveled. My mastery of wasting time should impress one and all.

As I hurry along Eighteenth Street, passing the glorious Andrew Mellon building with its ornate stone balusters and wrought iron balconies, I brush past other workers equally as rushed as I. Washington always bustles with energy the Tuesday after Labor Day as Congress returns and the city comes alive again after the hot, sleepy days of August. A grown-up "back-to-school" feeling permeates the city, and there is a renewed sense of hope and optimism. September heralds a fresh start. A blank page. An opportunity to set things right for the rest of the year.

Yes, I decide, September is when I will turn it all around. Things will get better from now on.

And then I enter the office and find Millie hovering over my desk, leafing through my papers in her tight black sleeveless turtleneck and gray pencil skirt. If this is the start of a better day, I haven't bought nearly enough vodka.

"Can I help you?" I ask.

Millie throws one of my folders back into the pile on my desk—the folder, I suspect, that I use to hide all my recipes, so that it looks as if I'm reading about interest rate policy when I'm actually reading about the best way to cook a turkey or how to make homemade mozzarella.

"Well hello to you, too." Millie stares at my white button-down top. I look down to see one of the small pearlescent buttons hanging by a thread, pulled to its limit thanks to a few too many batches of triple-fudge brownies and homemade Twix bars. Marvelous.

"Susan wants to know how you're coming with the December conference," she says. "I thought maybe I'd find some notes on your desk."

Millie works for Susan Jenkins, who runs NIRD's economics department and is, by default, Mark's direct boss. Susan resembles Condoleezza Rice, if Condi wore skirts several inches shorter and heels several inches higher, and she is both a fierce gossip and a fearsome manager. A total ice queen, she once made a research assistant cry simply by staring him down in silence after he turned in a substandard report. She also fired an intern for lacking intellectual vigor, but we all suspect the real reason was because the intern was thinner and prettier than she was. And, according to an e-mail somewhere in my in-box, Susan is cohosting Mark's economic recovery/financial risk conference—the event I am supposed to be helping with and for which I have done almost nothing.

"I'm still waiting for a confirmation from the last speaker," I say.

This is true. What is also true is that Mark sent me a memo with a little more information on the conference, as well as what I should ultimately include in the handouts and on the PowerPoint slides, and that memo is still floating somewhere in my in-box, unread. I would have read it, but I had more pressing matters to attend to, such as cropping Adam out of all my Facebook photos.

Millie scowls. "Susan wants an update sooner rather than later, so you'd better hurry up."

"Relax, I'm on it. The conference is three months away."

Millie purses her lips and lingers behind my desk, tapping her fingernails against the surface, as if she is stroking the keys on a piano.

"Is that all?" I ask.

"How's the new apartment? Adam has been sleeping at his place for a while now, so I assume you moved out."

Hearing Adam's name makes my stomach somersault, and if I thought my mood couldn't get worse, it already has. "The new apartment is great," I say. "Amazing, actually. A real find. I totally lucked out."

"Glad to hear it." She probes my eyes, as if she is expecting them to well up with tears. "Anyway, Susan wants to coördinate her slides with Mark, so you'd better hurry up with all the conference stuff. I turned in an outline to Susan a week ago."

Well la-di-da. Does she want a prize? "Will do," I say. "Now, if you don't mind?" I gesture toward Millie's desk, and taking the hint, she stomps off in a huff.

I plop down in my chair and boot up my computer. I am taken through about eight security screens before I can check my e-mail, and when I finally do, I see I have sixty-five unread messages, several of them from Mark.

But before I can read any of Mark's messages, the man himself emerges from his office and appears in front of my desk. He wears a rumpled tweed jacket and navy blue bow tie, this one studded with large yellow currency symbols, almost none of which I recognize. He is also barefoot.

"Ah, there you are," he says. "Did you see my e-mail?"

"Um . . . yes," I say, lying.

"Good. Because I really think we will need to talk about Greece come December."

"Right. Greece."

"Also, the dollar. The dollar will be very important."

I pull out my pen and begin jotting on my notepad. "Greece . . . and the dollar. Got it." Except that I don't. "So . . . what would you like me to send you? About Greece . . . and the dollar."

"I think I made that pretty clear in the e-mail."

"Right. The e-mail." That I haven't read.

"Also, did you see the article I left you? I stuck it in one of your folders . . ." Mark reaches for my undercover recipe folder and lifts it from my desk.

"No!" I shout, snatching the folder from his hands. Mark recoils. "No, sorry, I haven't seen it."

"Well, you should find it and give it a quick read. Could be useful background for my presentation. Susan has been on my case since last week, so I need to send her a rough outline ASAP."

"The event isn't for like three months, right?" He frowns. Apparently that was the wrong thing to say. "Don't worry—I'm on it."

He disappears back into his office, and I frantically pull up all the e-mails he has sent me in the last month and print them out sequentially. I will get organized, I will figure out what I'm supposed to be working on, and I will forge ahead. I will triumph. But first, I will check my favorite food blogs.

"Hannah!" I jump as Mark pops out of his office. "One more thing. Did you send me anything on the pee pip?"

"The what?" I rack my brain. The pee pip. The pee pip. What the hell is the pee pip?

He sighs. "The pee pip, Hannah." As if any *idiot* knows what the pee pip is.

I stare at him blankly.

"The *P-P-I-P*? The Public-Private Investment Program the Treasury is running with the FDIC and the Fed?" he says. "Did you send me a status update or not?"

"Oh, no—I didn't. Or, not yet at least." Was I supposed to? Was that in one of his e-mails?

"Okay, good, because ultimately I may want to feature the PPIP on a slide with the TALF and the TIP, and so it would be more helpful to have a condensed status update on all three programs. Something short and snappy."

I grab my pen. "Short . . . and . . . snappy . . ." This means nothing to me.

"In fact, we may want the PPIP, TALF, and TIP on the same slide as the TARP. To simplify it."

Right.

"I don't know, Mark. Don't you think that's a little . . . 'alphabet soup-y' for one slide? All those acronyms?"

Mark scrunches up his face in disapproval. "If these people don't know a TIP from a TALF, they probably shouldn't be coming to this conference."

And, in a single sentence, Mark sums up why I do not belong at a place like the Institute for Research and Discourse and why I never should have started working here in the first place.

After lunch, Rachel sidles up to my desk, her graceful figure slinking between the rows of filing cabinets and bookshelves. She wears a cream vintage shift dress, striped with alternating horizontal bands of brown and baby blue. According to her latest Facebook update, Milk Glass won some award for "Best New Design Blog," a distinction I might begrudge if she weren't so damn deserving. Every photograph she takes and posts on her site looks like it belongs in *House Beautiful* or a Martha Stewart magazine, and she manages to keep her entries fresh and interesting. All this on top of her day job at NIRD. It's impossible for me to resent someone who brings such a zest for life to everything she does.

Rachel parks herself on the edge of my desk as she sucks on a Jolly Rancher. "How are things?"

"Generally crappy, but what else is new?"

Rachel rolls her eyes. "Whaa, whaa, whaa."

"Well it's the truth."

"You know what you need?"

"A winning lottery ticket and a plane ticket to Capri?"

Rachel clicks her tongue. "No. You need a diversion. Something to take your mind off of recent events."

"I've been at NIRD for three years. My job isn't particularly recent."

"That's not what I'm talking about."

I know it's not. She's talking about Adam. But I don't what to discuss him. And anyway, my job is responsible for at least 50 percent of my misery. Adam can't claim all the credit.

"You've lost your joie de vivre," she says, "and we need to get it back."

"And how do you propose we do that?"

Rachel bows her head and stares at the tip of her chocolate round-toe pumps. She presses a finger to her lips and sighs. "You know what you *could* do . . ."

"Oh, here we go . . ."

"You could start one of those supper clubs you're always talking about. Now that Adam is out of the picture."

I laugh. "Nice try."

I spent most of our relationship begging Adam to let me hold an underground supper club out of his apartment before we lived together, then out of our shared apartment once we did. Combining the novelty of a restaurant experience with the intimacy of a dinner party sounded exciting and offbeat and, above all, *fun*. I loved the idea of hosting a secret dinner in an undisclosed location. It was edgy. It was different. I wasn't ready to start my own catering company, but I figured I could try my hand at an underground restaurant and see how it went. Adam put the kibosh on the idea immediately. I believe his exact words were, "I'm not going to ruin my reputation by running a speakeasy out of my home." Rachel used it as one of her many examples of Adam putting his own interests before mine.

"I'm serious," Rachel says. "It'll keep you busy. You've always wanted to do it, and now there's nothing holding you back."

"Nothing but a dwindling bank account. Where am I going to get the money to put on a dinner for twelve? I can barely afford a dinner for one—even with my parents' help."

"That's why you charge an entrance fee. Thirty-five bucks a head or something. And I can help. My grandmother just unloaded some cash on me. Something to do with the estate tax. I can decorate and feature the table setting on my blog."

"I don't know . . ."

But we both know I'm warming up to the idea. The investment and risk of holding a stand-alone dinner are minimal, and since I'd be doing it on the side and in secret, I could save the one-hour lecture from my parents about how I'm throwing away my future.

There is, however, the minor issue of my living space: an efficiency apartment with no furniture and enough plates and cutlery for precisely one guest. Rachel assures me these are obstacles we can work around.

"Besides, your apartment is underground. How perfect is that? An underground restaurant that is, in fact, underground."

"It is tempting . . ."

"Oh, come on, you should do it. This can be for you what Milk Glass is for me—your creative outlet. Trust me, you won't regret it. And I'll help." She smiles and raises her eyebrows. "Say yes. You know you want to."

I consider it. What do I have to lose? My boyfriend already dumped me, and I am stuck in a job I increasingly hate. And my landlord is away a bunch of weekends this fall, so I could hold the dinners while he is away and not have to worry about bothering him with the noise. If ever there was a time to give the whole supper club thing a try, this is it.

I look at Rachel, who is still smiling and has begun twiddling her fingers excitedly. I bite my lip and take a deep breath.

"What the hell," I say. "Let's do it."

i n what is perhaps an indication of how pathetically boring my life is at the moment, I haven't been able to think about anything—*anything*—but this underground supper club since Rachel and I talked on Tuesday. We've e-mailed back and forth all week about dates and menus and guest lists while my brain has spun like a pinwheel, dreaming up appetizers and entrées and swanky cocktails. Each correspondence between Rachel and me has used the code word "DCSC," in reference to The Dupont Circle Supper Club, the tentative name for our underground venture. I'm sure much of the allure of putting on this event stems from how unadventurous I usually am, and thus organizing something secretive—with code words and undisclosed locations—feels really badass, which probably only demonstrates how badass we are not. By charging money for a meal without the DC health department's stamp of approval, we are also possibly doing something illegal, which only adds to the air of mystery and intrigue.

After a week of planning, we decide to launch The Dupont Circle Supper Club next Saturday, the third weekend in September and the first weekend my landlord is back in Tampa for a series of town hall meetings. Rachel creates a Facebook page called The Dupont Circle Supper Club, which bears little information other than a teaser about Saturday night's dinner:

Unique dining experience awaits adventurous eaters
with interest in creative cooking and stimulating
conversation. Twelve diners will meet at a secret
location on Sat. 9/19 at 8:00. Five-course meal, $45
sugg. donation. Get in touch to reserve your spot now!

While Rachel handles the logistics, I promise to spend the rest of
the week firming up the menu, which, as far as I'm concerned, is
the most important part. Who cares if a supper club is secretive
and fun if the food isn't any good?

On Friday, I rush home after work, foregoing the usual after-
work happy hour with my coworkers, and plop down on my air
mattress with a glass of wine and my laptop. I have one week to
nail down all of the details, which means it's officially crunch
time.

I grab three of my favorite cookbooks—Julia Child's *Mastering
the Art of French Cooking*, Marcella Hazan's *Essentials of Classic
Italian Cooking*, and Alice Waters's *The Art of Simple Food*—along
with my four-inch stack of archived loose recipes from *Gourmet*,
Bon Appetit, and *Food & Wine*. Tonight I want to nail down the
main course, so that I can build the rest of the meal around it. I
need something special, something spectacular. I want to blow
people's minds—or, at the very least, convince them they got their
money's worth.

As I dog-ear pages and jot down menu notes on my computer,
I hear a loud crashing sound outside my front door, followed by a
thumping down my front steps. I freeze.

I tiptoe toward the front door and peer through the peephole,
where I see Rachel, dripping in sweat, lugging a large folding table down my stairway from the sidewalk above.

"What the hell is this?" I say, leaning against my doorframe.

Rachel pauses and wipes her forehead with the back of her
hand. "A table," she says, panting.

"I can see that. Where'd it come from?"

"Don't worry about it."

I narrow my eyes. "What does that mean?"

"It means I took care of it. We have a table for the party. And there's another one on the way. That's all you need to know." She grins as I spot the IRD logo at the bottom of the table.

"I'm sorry, do I know you? Since when do you steal furniture?"

Rachel rests her hand on her hip. "Do you want the table or not?"

I roll my eyes. "Like I have a choice. Come in."

Rachel wrestles the table into my apartment, and I shake my head as she nearly bashes through my wall. Her wily antics should come as no surprise. This, I have learned, is how Rachel Cohen operates. She's a Chicago girl through and through. If she wants to make something happen, it will happen, and god help anyone who stands in her way. You want a table? She'll get you a table. Just don't question her methods. She possesses an unexpected mix of refined elegance and gutsy determination, a powerful combination that will likely result in her taking over the world someday. I, on the other hand, will be lucky if I take over my own life. I talk a good game, but backing up words with action isn't usually my forte.

I watch as Rachel gently leans the table against the far wall. "Dare I ask about chairs?"

"I've taken care of that, too," she says. "I'll have them to you by Monday."

"Who are you, Tony Soprano?"

"What? No. You know I'd never wear a tracksuit." She places her hands on her hips and surveys the piles of clothes encircling my air mattress, which altogether takes up most of the space in my tiny studio apartment. "You'll have to do something about this mess."

"Relax—the air mattress deflates. I'll just shove the clothes in my closet."

"Is that your long-term storage solution? Leaving your clothes in piles around your bed?"

I shrug. "I've been busy."

Rachel arches her eyebrows. "There's always time to work functional aesthetics into our daily lives."

"Thanks, Martha."

A labored sigh. "*Anyway*, I got another reservation request today. We're up to eleven. We'll definitely be able to get one more person by next Saturday."

Rachel, the social media junkie, has been recruiting guests using Twitter, Facebook, and whatever social media tool she is into at the moment. How she managed to amass eleven guests in one week is beyond me, but I'm guessing it has something to do with her three thousand friends on Facebook and five thousand followers on Twitter. That, and the fact that she undoubtedly oversold my cooking experience.

"Well, gotta run," she says. "I have forty-five minutes to shower and change before I'm supposed to meet my date at Cork."

"Your date, huh? Anyone I know?"

She bites her lip. "Don't think so."

"There's a new person every week. I can't keep track."

"What would be the point?"

That pretty much sums up Rachel's position on men and dating. When she was twelve, she walked in on her father, a ne-phrologist, kissing his research nurse, and from what I gather, she now views relationships and monogamy through a highly skepti-cal lens. There is always a man in her life, but she never keeps him around for very long because, she says, eventually he'll leave her for someone else anyway. She always says this as if she is entirely comfortable with the disposable nature of the men in her life, but I know there is more pain beneath the surface than she cares to admit.

"By the way, any thoughts on the menu?" she asks.

"A few. I haven't made any decisions, though. Maybe a slow-roasted pork shoulder?"

Rachel grimaces. "You can't serve pork."

"Why not?"

She gently raises an eyebrow. "Uh, because it's Rosh Hasha-nah? What kind of Jew are you?"

Apparently, a very bad one. "Wait . . . next weekend is Rosh Hashanah?"

She laughs. "Why do you think Congress is in recess? Duh."

"Well . . . whatever. It's not like I keep kosher. Neither do you, for that matter."

"Hey, just because I'm not flying back to Chicago for the Rosh doesn't mean I'm okay with serving pork on one of the holiest Jewish holidays. It just feels . . . wrong."

I sigh. "Fine. I'll come up with something else. Maybe I could work Rosh Hashanah into the theme—resurrect some of my bub-be's old recipes, explain the symbolism and history of the food."

Rachel brightens. "That sounds like a great idea, actually. It gives the dinner a hook."

And it is becoming abundantly clear a hook is definitely something we need. In all the excitement of planning an under-ground supper club, Rachel and I may have overlooked one minor detail—a teensy little factoid, really—and that is the fact that I have no official cooking credentials whatsoever. Sure, I like to cook, and I'd like to think I'm quite good at it, but I am not a professional chef and, as it stands, I do not own my own catering company. I did enroll in a part-time cooking class after I gradu-ated from Cornell, which I took in secret while I waited tables and lived at home, but that is the closest I've come to being a professional cook. I've never had to run my own kitchen, nor have I cooked for payment, which means Rachel and I need to forestall a possible riot when people realize they've paid forty-five dollars to eat in a cramped basement apartment.

"Call me tomorrow," she says, giving me a quick hug. "We can discuss the details."

I lock the door behind her and scurry back to my computer, suddenly excited by the prospect of a unifying theme. My bubbe's holiday dinners were legendary, the tables overflowing with platters of brisket and tzimmes, stuffed cabbage and potato knishes, blintzes and kugel and fat loaves of challah. Ever since she died eight years ago, our holiday celebrations have splintered into quiet, nuclear affairs, and this year, with my parents in London, we aren't even getting together. But I miss her cooking, the way her tender brisket melted on the tongue, the way her stuffed cabbage hugged the fragrant beef filling tightly and always tasted both a little sweet and a little sour. Cooking was an act of love, a way of providing for her family. She always said she saw a lot of herself in me.

I glance at my computer screen and begin jotting down notes in a new blank document:

Brisket/tzimmes
Stuffed cabbage (mini)
Potato/apple tart?
Apple cider challah—honey!
Apple cake? Honey cake? Both?

As I dream up more ideas—potato and celery root kugel! chopped liver toasts! Hungarian walnut torte!—my cell phone rings. My parents. The second time this week. This can't be good.

"Mom? What's up? Is everything okay?"

"It's your father."

"Oh, sorry, Dad. What's wrong?"

"What do you mean, 'What's wrong'? Can't a man call his only child every once in a while?"

I picture my dad's face as he says this—his lip curling up at the side, rumpling his fuzzy, bearded jowls. When I was a baby, I used to love grabbing his beard with my little fists, rocking his head from side to side as I screamed with delight. He shaved it once when I was in high school, but my mom and I begged him to grow it back; I told him he looked as if he didn't have any lips, and my mom said she felt as if she were kissing a stranger. He hasn't messed with it since, even though gray hairs seem to be taking it over like crabgrass.

"Isn't it after midnight in London?" I ask.

"You know me—always the night owl. And besides, I wanted to talk to my daughter. So sue me."

"You can give a call whenever you want," I say. "It's always good to hear your voice."

It is always good to hear his voice. That said, given that my mom called three days ago, I am not convinced this call is without an agenda. Before the last call, I hadn't spoken to my parents on the phone in two weeks, and with all their work-related travel, that's about how often I've spoken to them for the past two years. As professors who study the economies of Brazil, Russia, India, and China (so-called BRICs specialists), they're always flying to some exotic place, and their travel has become more frequent in recent years. Our main form of communication is e-mail, which usually involves my parents sending me updates on their travel and links to articles or papers they think I should read. We e-mail every few days and occasionally Skype, but when they travel, calling tends to be a twice-a-month affair. Why the sudden urgency?

"I heard about Adam," my dad says. "What a shame. He seemed like a nice guy." Unlike my mom, my dad admired Adam, though he never expressed his thoughts in any detail in front of my mother.

"Yeah, well, live and learn."

"True, true, kiddo." He pauses. "Listen, Mom and I were wondering—well, it came up in the context of that Princeton fellowship and some other issues we were discussing. Are you planning to take the GRE exam this fall?"

Bingo: the real reason for this call. "Um . . . not sure."

I've thought about taking the GREs, but every time I attempt to sign up for the exam, I back out, driven by the intense nausea I experience every time I contemplate a career in economics.

"Well don't you think you should sign up for a course? Mom and I were talking about it. Those courses fill up pretty quickly."

"I don't think so, Dad. If I decide to take the exam, I'll be fine studying on my own."

"I'm sure you will, but a course would definitely give you an edge."

"Maybe," I say, "but I'm not sold on taking the exam."

"I know, but when you think about it, kiddo, you have absolutely nothing to lose. The test is good for, what, five years? Might as well take it now and get it out of the way—even if you decide not to use it. Trust me. I speak from experience. Better to get it over with while you can."

As my dad speaks, I resume typing on my laptop and flipping through my recipe file. I don't want to talk about the GREs. I don't want to talk about fellowships or research journals. I don't want to talk about any of those things because they all point to a future completely divorced from what I'm actually interested in— namely, food and cooking, the two subjects my parents assure me aren't serious or worthy of my time.

"Hannah, are you typing?"

I stop. "No."

"Oh. I thought I heard tapping. Must be the connection."

"Probably." I stare at my computer screen. "Actually, I'm sorry, Dad, but I have to go. I'm . . . meeting up with friends."

"Okay. I'll let you go. Oh, but before I do—have you made plans for Rosh Hashanah?"

I clear my throat. "Yeah. Kind of."

This is true. What is also true is that my parents would kill me if they knew that instead of going to temple, I plan to host a questionably legal dinner out of my apartment.

"Good," he says. "You're mother and I like to know you're keeping up the tradition. Anyway, have fun tonight. Love you."

"Love you, too."

"And keep us posted on the GREs," he says. "Taking them this fall would be a very good idea."

I hang up and lie back on my air mattress, staring up at the ceiling as the bed rolls beneath me like a pool of water. My life, in some ways, would be a lot easier if I hated my parents—if they were awful, annoying people whose sordid reputation hovered over me like a dark cloud. But I genuinely like my parents. I think they're great. And yet, it's times like these, with their talk of fellowships and GREs and professional advancement, that I wish they'd hear me when I said no. That, for once, they'd realize I might know what I want and need better than they ever could.

Maybe they're afraid to let me figure out what I want to do with my life. Or maybe it's easier for me to see things that way—my anxious, overprotective parents as the barriers preventing me from moving forward—rather than admit the only fear standing in my way is my own, and it always has been.

CHAPTER

ten

a weekend of planning and recipe testing flies by, and before I know it, Sunday morning arrives, which means one thing: it's time for the Dupont Circle farmers' market.

The market opens every Sunday year-round, stretching north along the pie-shaped block from Dupont Circle up to Q Street. The circle itself is like the hub of a wheel, with streets radiating outward like spokes, and the market is wedged between the northwestern spokes, crawling up Twentieth Street. Each Sunday the street fills with vendors who display baskets filled with fresh breads and pastries and crates teeming with seasonal fruits and vegetables. The market spills over into a large parking lot to the east, which overflows with more farmers and tradesmen, selling everything from handmade soaps to lamb chops. Needless to say, I consider this market one of the happiest places on Earth.

I usually start with a practice lap, where I survey the offerings and compare prices and realize my NIRD salary will allow me to buy precisely three things, maybe four if I'm feeling *wild*. This Sunday, however, is different. With The Dupont Circle Supper Club debuting in less than a week, I have a license to buy.

I show up at 8:45 A.M., fifteen minutes before the market opens—a strategic move on my part. Arrive too late and the market will be picked over and crowded, filled with throngs of food enthusiasts and farmers' market tourists who do little more than clog the main artery of the market. But now, fifteen minutes before the bell rings, the market is calm and the tables are fully stocked, giving me a chance to bookmark what vendors I want to revisit and what products I want to buy first.

Rachel promised to meet me here when the bell rings at nine because, well, she knows me: with a license to buy and no one to stop me, I would inevitably spend way more than I should, which would no doubt involve the purchase of several gourds and leafy greens for which we'd have no use whatsoever. What can I say? Some women melt at the sight of Prada shoes or Gucci bags; I go crazy for free-range eggs and organic kale. It's how I'm programmed. Adam never understood that. He bought me a Coach wallet for my birthday last May, when all I really wanted was a basil plant.

Ambling through the market, I spot baskets of purple and orange cauliflower, bundles of Swiss chard and collard greens, and crates of Honeycrisp apples and Italian prune plums. The tables at the market always feel a little schizophrenic this time of year, as piles of fat summer tomatoes rub shoulders with apples and knobby winter squash. Just as the late-summer fruits and vegetables are celebrating their last hurrah, the autumn harvest makes its timid debut, competing for the attention of market-goers who may have tired of the surfeit of corn on the cob and tomato salad, but who may not be ready to commit to six months of gourds.

I pass an impressive display of apples and an intriguing array of leafy greens, but before I can finish my practice lap, I feel a tap on my shoulder. I whip my head around and recognize Shauna, one of the owners of Open Meadow Farms.

"Hannah, Hannah, bo-bana," she says with a smile as she fastens her mousy hair into a twist with a large plastic clip. "I have your brisket on the truck. Ready to pick it up?"

"Mind if I wait until the end? I don't have a freezer bag."

Shauna shrugs. "Fine by me. You might want to stop by the tent, though. We have some amazing lamb today. We're offering a special on pork chops, too."

"Alas, no pork today."

She raises her eyebrows and shakes her head. "Big mistake. Finest pork in America."

A few years back, the *New York Times* called Shauna's pork the "finest pork in America," and she has never let anyone forget it. Admittedly, her pork is fantastic—rich and flavorful, with the perfect amount of fat. Most of the charcuterie shops in town buy her meat and turn it into pâté and prosciutto and pancetta—all of which, Shauna will remind you, are so good because they start with the "finest pork in America."

Shauna pats me on the back and heads back to her stand, and a portly blonde in khaki shorts and hiking boots rings a large cowbell up and down the market thoroughfare. The market is officially open.

Unfortunately, Rachel is nowhere to be seen. I stand by the gate to the parking lot on Massachusetts Avenue, tapping my foot as I check my watch every thirty seconds, becoming increasingly anxious that someone else has already bought all the parsnips and sweet potatoes, as if that's even possible at 9:08. Rachel and I haven't spoken since she dropped the table off Friday night, but I sent her multiple texts reminding her we were meeting at 9:00 this morning. And, unlike me, Rachel is never late. This is very unlike her.

After ten minutes of waiting by the entrance, I give up. I don't have all morning to wait around for her. My time is just as valuable as hers, and she shouldn't waste my time like this, and this is very annoying, and how dare she—and so on. As the queen of tardiness, I fully appreciate the hypocrisy of my outrage, but never mind. There are vegetables to buy and free apple slices to sample.

I wind my way through the market, picking through bunches of parsnips here and crates of apples there. I toss a few pears into my bag, followed by a head of cabbage and a skinny eggplant, shaped like a carnival balloon, because it's so damn cute. By the time I reach Shauna's tent, my bags overflow with an excessive amount of produce, including a bundle of Swiss chard and a mess of zucchini, neither of which I plan to use for the party. If Rachel's role was to rein me in, she has failed spectacularly.

"Finest pork in America!" Shauna bellows from her green-and-white tent, shouting at no one in particular. "Come and get it!"

In front of her, dozens of vacuum-sealed packages of chicken and pork and beef and lamb sit atop an ice-filled tray, with packages of sausage and bacon stuffed into round coolers. An open carton of brown eggs sits to the right of display, in front of a huge sign that says FARM FRESH EGGS—GET YOURS TODAY! Every time I visit Shauna, I want to buy everything she sells, until I see the price tag and realize I cannot justify spending ten dollars on a single chicken breast.

Shauna smiles when she sees me staring at a beautiful rib-eye steak. "Hey—Sam! Go get Hannah's brisket off the truck, would you?" She points to the vacuum-sealed sirloin and strip steaks nestled into the ice tray, each piece bright red and marbled with streaks of fat. "Interested?"

"Got any of it ground?"

Shauna points to the corner of the ice tray. "Tons. How much you want?"

"About two pounds?"

She grabs two packages and sets them aside. "Done. Anything else? What about the lamb?"

I glance at the price tag on the lamb chops. Too rich for my blood today. Then again . . . "Throw in one packet of chops," I say. "I'll freeze them until I figure out what to do with them."

"We have one wild boar chop left. Any interest?"

"Um . . ." No. There is no reason for me to buy wild boar. I don't need it. It's totally unnecessary. On the other hand, I've never cooked wild boar before. And, really, I should probably learn how. Buying it would basically be *educational.*

"It's great marinated in lemon juice and olive oil with a little garlic and rosemary," she says. "I'll knock a dollar off the price."

"Sold!"

And just like that, I manage to spend more than a hundred dollars on meat.

The hundred-plus dollars on meat wouldn't be such a huge problem if I hadn't already spent thirty dollars on fruits and vegetables, twenty dollars on bread, and another twenty dollars on cheese, yogurt, and milk. But now I've bought more groceries in a day than I sometimes do in a month. This is all Rachel's fault.

As I lug my three thousand pounds of groceries through the market, I finally see Miss Classyface Stylewonk herself walking down Massachusetts Avenue toward the market, in no apparent hurry whatsoever. Guess who's going to give her an earful in front of Dupont's most passionate locavores? That's right: this girl.

When Rachel turns toward the market entrance, I notice she is walking next to a tall Asian man with broad shoulders and a strong, chiseled jawline. They both stop right before the entrance, and he turns toward her and reaches down and kisses her on the lips while resting his hand gently on her shoulder. I am beyond confused.

Rachel waves good-bye to the mystery man and marches up the market thoroughfare, meeting me in front of the mushroom stand.

"Hey!" she says. "Sorry I'm late."

I look at my watch. "It's nine-forty-five. We said nine."

Her cheeks turn pink. "I know. I'm sorry. I overslept."

"With the muscular Asian dude?"

The pink in her cheeks deepens to a dark red. "His name is Jackson."

"Ah, yes, another suitor you can pump and dump."

"Hey!" Her indignation yields to her usual feistiness. "Listen to you—'pump and dump.' You do realize that's a stock-trading expression. It has nothing to do with dating."

"It does now."

"Well, I'll have you know, Jackson is very cool and very interesting, and if I get a few fun dates out of him, then I don't see anything wrong with that."

I roll my eyes. "Whatever you say, Jezebel."

She whacks me in the shoulder with her purse. "Prude."

"Tease."

"Blabbermouth."

"Etsy addict."

Rachel bursts into a fit of laughter. "You are ridiculous," she says, wiping the tears from her eyes with the back of her hand. She collects herself and glances down at my grocery bags, which I've laid on the ground to prevent myself from herniating a disk. "Is all of that for the supper club?"

"Some of it is. The rest . . ." I shrug. "Impulse purchases."

Rachel shakes her head. "You're the only woman I know for whom an impulse purchase involves a bunch of Swiss chard." She reaches for two of the bags and grunts as she lifts them to her shoulders. "Come on, Julia Child," she says. "Let me help you walk these home."

Once we've put away all the groceries and drafted a shopping list for our last-minute Whole Foods run on Thursday, Rachel flips open my laptop and signs into the dedicated e-mail account she created for The Dupont Circle Supper Club.

"Check it out," she says. "Five more e-mails."

I glance over her shoulder at the screen. "But you said we only have one more spot available."

"Exactly. We're drumming up interest for supper club number two."

I reach out and slam the laptop cover shut. "Why don't we see how supper club number one goes before we commit to a number two? I may have burned the house down by then."

Rachel rolls her eyes. "Whatever. So, let's go over the menu again. Break it down for me. Tell me a story."

"I'll do you one better." I reach beneath my stack of cookbooks and hand Rachel a sheet of paper.

Rachel drags her eyes down the sheet of paper, studying its contents:

Red and white wine/Manischewitz cocktails
Apple cider challah/homemade date honey
Potato and apple tart with horseradish cream
Old-Fashioned braised brisket with tomatoes and paprika
Tzimmes duo: Honeyed parsnips with currants and saffron,
    sweet potatoes with dried pears and prunes
Stuffed cabbage
Mini Jewish apple cakes with honeycomb ice cream

"What's the difference between 'Jewish apple cake' and regular apple cake?" Rachel asks.

I shrug. "Not sure. Maybe the fact that it's made with oil instead of butter? I think it's a regional thing. My grandmother used to make it all the time."

Rachel nods and runs her finger down the menu one more time. "Mind if I hang on to this?"

"Go ahead."

She jumps to her feet. "Cool. Might be useful for our future Web site."

Leave it to Rachel to worry about a Web site. She always works ten steps ahead, planning the next supper club or the next vacation or the next ten years of her life. I'm hardly a carpe diem type of gal—my modus operandi tends to involve agonizing over my future with little follow-up action—but Rachel's groundless optimism over the success and future of this supper club unnerves me.

"Let's not get ahead of ourselves," I say. "One secret dinner at a time."

Rachel wraps her arm around my shoulder and walks with me to my front door. "Yeah, yeah, yeah," she says. "I know. But I have a good feeling about this."

"I'm glad someone around here does."

"Stop worrying. You're a fabulous cook, and we've been planning like crazy, and there's no way this dinner will be anything but a success." She gives my shoulder a squeeze. "You, my dear, are going to be DC's next big thing."

I smile nervously and feel my stomach rumble because, if I'm being perfectly honest, I'm not ready to be "DC's next big thing," and I'm not sure I ever will be.

eleven

the day before the supper club, I rush into work full of energy. We've set the menu, we've bought all the ingredients, and we've cleaned my apartment from top to bottom. I plan to scoot out of work a few hours early to start prepping everything for tomorrow, but as far as I can tell, we're right on schedule.

As soon as I get into the office, I swing by the top-floor conference room in search of free bagels and coffee, part of my daily routine since I moved to 1774 ½ Church Street. I've been on a tight budget, and with all the money I spent at the farmers' market, I am officially in full-fledged cash preservation mode.

I grab a poppy seed bagel and pot of cream cheese and fill a paper cup with very dark, very strong coffee. For some reason, catering has decided we need to serve caffeinated jet fuel at NIRD conferences. I'm not sure what that says about the events we host, but it isn't a ringing endorsement.

I quietly slip out of the conference room and head downstairs to my desk, where I see a large yellow Post-it note tacked onto my computer screen. It's from Mark.

NEED EDITS ASAP!

Last week, Mark sent me a rough sketch of a paper on the future strength of the dollar and asked me to fill in the blanks. Suffice it to say, the paper had more blanks than a toy gun, so I've spent the past week frantically researching currency markets. Susan has been on his ass all week to submit this paper to the publishing department for her Economic Outlook series, one of our think tank's flagship publications, which means he's already on her shit list. I finished pulling together a decent draft yesterday, so all I need to do is give it a final polish before sending it off to Mark. From what he says, it will be one of his most important papers of the year.

I slather my bagel with cream cheese while I wait for my computer to boot up, but as I take a bite, my computer lets out a long, deep drone like a dying lawn mower. The droning gets louder, building in intensity, and then abruptly stops. The computer screen flickers and turns black.

I press the POWER button and nothing happens. I press it again and again, pressing it quickly, then holding it down for ten seconds at a time. Nothing happens. I press every key on my keyboard. Again, nothing. My stomach seizes, contorting violently from the potent mixture of coffee and anxiety.

I don't know much about computers, but I know this does not bode well.

Poppy seeds fly everywhere as I drop the bagel on my desk and run to find Rachel. I scan her desk for a Starbucks Venti Latte, the telltale sign she is somewhere in the office. The latte isn't there, and neither is she. Crap.

I scurry back to my desk and along the way encounter Millie typing furiously at her computer. I slow my pace. Was she there the whole time? And, more to the point, do I ask her for help? The thought nauseates me. But so does the thought of losing Mark's paper. I take a deep breath and sidle up to Millie's desk.

"Yes?" she says, her eyes fixed on her computer screen.

"My computer won't start."

"So call IT," she says, banging away on her keyboard.

"Sean doesn't get in until nine-thirty . . ." I pause. "I was wondering if you might be able to help."

Millie stops typing and looks up at me. I realize how ridiculous my request sounds. Millie probably knows even less about computers than I do. And, as far as I know, she does not possess magical powers that will somehow restore my computer's functionality.

"Help you?"

"I figured . . . maybe this has happened to you before. Maybe you'd know what to do." I force a smile.

Millie clicks her mouse and looks back at her computer screen, smirking. "That's never happened to me. And besides, I don't see what I could do."

I clench my jaw. "Millie, for once in your life, could you do something to help someone else?"

"What, like join the Peace Corps? Oh, wait. I already did that."

Oh my god, I'm going to kill her. "Never mind," I say. "I'm sure you couldn't fix it anyway."

Millie snaps her head around. A challenge. "Or maybe I could," she says. "Let's have a look, shall we?" She lifts herself from her desk. "By the way, you have poppy seeds in your teeth."

The two of us walk over to my desk, and Millie presses the POWER button.

"I already tried that," I say. "For some reason it won't turn on, no matter what I do."

Undeterred, she presses a few more buttons on the computer tower and keyboard, grimacing as she observes the mess of papers and poppy seeds on my desk. Nothing happens.

"I don't know what's wrong with this thing," she says. "You'll have to call Sean and have him fix it." I let out a frustrated sigh. "What, is there something you need on there right away?"

"Mark's paper," I say as I bury my head in my hands. "The one for Susan."

"You backed it up somewhere, right?" I stare at her blankly. "Right? You must have saved the paper on a flash drive or the server or something. You wouldn't forget to back up all your work."

"Well, actually . . ." I trail off.

Millie's eyes widen. "How could you *not* back up your work?

Haven't you seen the *Sex and the City* where Carrie forgets to back up her computer? That was, like, a *decade* ago!" Her voice echoes down the hallway.

"Shhh," I say, motioning with my hand to keep her voice down. "Yes, I've seen that episode. I'll . . . I'll figure something out. We still have a week."

"Yeah, but Susan wants that paper *now*. Yesterday, actually. How am I supposed to do my job if you won't do yours?" Millie sighs and stomps off, her mop of curls bouncing off her shoulders.

Fantastic.

I press the POWER button on my computer one last time. Nothing. I look at the clock: 9:29. I pick up the phone and dial Sean's extension, hoping he has arrived. He has not. Why am I surprised? Sean never shows up on time and consistently lacks a sense of urgency. Part of me thinks he enjoys the control. We're all at the mercy of the IT guy.

I leave Sean a frantic voice mail and run upstairs to scout the ninth and tenth floors, hoping to find someone—anyone—who can help me. But the only people I encounter are the ones even more technologically incompetent than I am.

I run back downstairs. "Please, please, please," I mutter to myself. "Please let Sean be there."

But, of course, he is not. Why is this happening? Maybe it's a sign. Maybe the universe is telling me I never should have taken this job to begin with, and this is my punishment for doing so. Or maybe it's a sign that this supper club is a terrible idea, and I should cancel the whole thing. What was I thinking, trying to juggle my work with an underground supper club? I'm not Rachel. I can't shift seamlessly between two demanding ventures. I let out a whimper and collapse into my chair.

"What seems to be the problem?" I whip my head around. It's Mark. And, once again, he isn't wearing any socks or shoes.

"My computer—it died. Or at least I can't turn it on."

"Did you call Sean?"

"Yes," I say. "He's not in yet."

"Hmm. Let me take a quick look."

At the moment, I'm willing to believe almost anything if it means my computer will start working again. The existence of unicorns or vampires, for example. But believing Mark possesses the competence to fix my computer? That's a bridge too far. He can't even create his own PowerPoint slides.

"Oh, Mark, you don't have to . . ." He starts banging at my computer tower and keyboard, his arms flailing as he randomly pushes buttons. He looks as if he has cerebral palsy. If anything, he is making things worse.

"Hmm," he says, "I'm not sure what the—"

"Maybe we should wait for Sean," I say. He kicks my computer tower with his bare foot. Oh, god. Someone make him stop.

As Mark kicks my computer, I see Sean at the end of the hall-way, meandering slowly toward my desk in his blue-and-white paisley shirt and dark-wash jeans.

"Sean!" I run to meet him halfway down the hall. "Oh, thank god. I have major computer problems. I need your help."

"Dude, what is Mark doing over there?" I look up to see Mark lifting my computer screen over his head, like Moses at Mount Sinai.

"Who the hell knows. Please . . . help me."

Sean walks to my desk and pushes Mark out of the way. Like Mark, Millie, and I, he presses the POWER button and nothing happens. Does he think we haven't tried that? Do we look like idiots? I look up at Mark, who is wringing his hands and has bro-ken into a sweat. Okay, never mind. The POWER button is fair game.

Sean tries a few more combinations of buttons, but nothing works. He scrunches up his face and sighs.

"There's a problem with your hard drive," he says. "I'll need to send out for a replacement."

"A replacement?" I ask in horror. "But . . . what about all the stuff I saved on there?"

"You mean you didn't back it up?" Mark and Sean ask in unison. Apparently I am the big asshole who, in the twenty-first century, forgets to back up her work.

"I backed up . . . most stuff. But not everything." Mark doesn't need to know the truth. Not yet. I still have time to fix this.

"There are ways to retrieve the data, but it could take a while," Sean says.

"A while as in . . . ?" Please say a few days. Please say a few days.

"A couple of weeks, at least," Sean says. "In the meantime, I can hook you up with a spare computer so you can get online and stuff."

"Good, because I'm going to need that paper by noon," Mark says, turning to face me. "Oh, and I also need you to type up a summary of the latest IMF reports on Greece, Latvia, and Spain before you leave as well. I'd like that by five, please."

That gives me two hours to rewrite a fifteen-page paper on currency markets, and then five hours to read and summarize three IMF reports. No way. No way I can make that happen. And now, it has become abundantly clear, there is also no way I can leave early to start working on the supper club. Which means all of my carefully constructed plans are about to fall apart.

twelve

i grab my keys and rush over to Rachel's desk. Her eyes widen as she spots me charging down the hall.

"Whoa, slow down, lady," she says, leaning back in her chair. "What's going on?"

I slam my keys on her desk. "Can you sneak out early today?"

"I guess? I don't know. Why?"

"My computer died. I have five hours to write up some report on Greece, Latvia, and Spain and rewrite Mark's currency paper."

"But didn't you—"

"No, I didn't back up my work. And yes, I saw that *Sex and the City*."

"Oh."

"I was going to leave early to start braising the brisket and pulling stuff together for tomorrow, but there's no way I can do that now. I need your help."

Rachel snaps to attention. "You need me to cook?"

Rachel doesn't cook. Well, that's not fair. She cooks, but most of her recipes involve the microwave and Duncan Hines. I keep encouraging her to branch out, but she suffers from a profound lack of confidence in the kitchen—surprising, since she possesses an abundance of confidence in every other area of her life. I blame her mother, Barbara, whose kitchen philosophy resembles that of my mother and Sandy Prescott.

"Rach, you can do this. All you need to do is start some of the prep work. The recipes are sitting on my counter."

Rachel bites her lip. "Okay . . . If you think I'm up to it . . ."

"I have total confidence in you. I'll send you an e-mail explaining what I need you to do, and I'll get home as soon as I can to help. Cool?"

She hesitates. "Yeah, okay. I can probably get out of here by three." She takes my keys and shoves them in her bag. "Good luck," she says.

"You, too."

I hurry back to my desk and find Sean plugging a spare computer into my power strip. "All set," he says. He digs into his pocket and pulls out a blue-and-white flash drive. "And, uh, take this. You know, to back up any new documents you start on this computer." He knows my shame.

I turn on the computer and download Mark's sketchy outline of his paper. I stare at the page.

"Oh, what am I doing?" I groan as I massage my temples. The question is all-encompassing: hosting a supper club, not backing up my work, working at NIRD in the first place. What am I doing?

I never should have taken this job, although when I accepted the position, it was this job or nothing. When I started at Cornell, my sneaky plan was to transfer into the Hotel School and focus on a career in the food industry, but my parents caught wind of this idea during my freshman year and nearly shit themselves. So, after several heated phone calls and threats to cut off my tuition payments, I let go of the Hotel School idea and ended up majoring in American studies, a discipline that prepared me for nothing in particular in the real world. Thus, after spending four years at Cornell, I was both highly educated and unemployed. In my parents' warped view, unemployment was preferable to a career in the restaurant industry.

And yet, in an ironic twist, entering the restaurant industry is exactly what I did. After graduation, I moved back into my parents' home in the Philadelphia suburb of Jenkintown and waited tables at a nearby restaurant called Cedarwood to make some cash while I looked for a job. No one prepared me for how grueling waitressing would be—the dull, persistent pain that would extend from my spine and wrap itself around my midsection, the nonstop disrespect from customers—but after a few weeks, I got into a groove and, to my surprise, started to enjoy it. That's not to say I wanted to waitress for the rest of my life. Far from it. But the chef started sharing cooking secrets with me, and I soaked up everything he would teach me, and before long I wasn't just waiting tables—I was helping in the kitchen, too, chopping onions, slicing carrots, and making vinaigrettes.

One evening, the sous chef slipped a piece of paper in my pocket, and as he headed back to his station, he winked. "You've got talent, kid," he said. "Check that place out."

The paper listed the contact information for a local cooking class, which met three days a week and wasn't too expensive. I signed up without telling my parents. Waiting tables was exhausting on its own, but juggling my job with a bunch of secret cooking classes sapped all of my energy. Many a night ended with me falling asleep on top of my comforter, fully clothed. And yet, although most of my memories from that period blur together, what I remember most is how happy I was. The kitchen environment felt right. I fit in there.

My parents, however, were having none of it. After watching me work at Cedarwood for a year, they sensed a diminished intensity in my search for a "real job." One night they confronted me. They sat me down on their living room couch and told me, point-blank: "College-educated girls don't wait tables." I pointed out that apparently they *do* because I *was*. Needless to say, that comment did not go over well.

After much yelling and many tears, my parents shamed me into seeing things their way—that I was wasting my time, my intellectual potential. And I have to hand it to my parents: they're good salesmen. I started to believe them; I started to doubt my own happiness. After all, I'd spent years studying until my eyes ached so that I could get A's and the occasional B+. I'd worked hard, I'd learned, I'd achieved. Surely I hadn't done all that to land a job a high school dropout could do.

My mother mentioned she had a favor to call in with a former colleague named Mark Henderson at the Institute for Research and Discourse. These are the kinds of favors my parents call in. Some parents know important business people or Hollywood producers or congressmen. But no, my parents have connections in places of no use to the general populous. They know people in academic departments and at think tanks. So that's where I ended up.

And now, here I sit, with a few hours to work magic in a subject area where my lack of insight is outpaced only by my lack of interest. The only way I could forestall my imminent failure is if, by some miracle, I managed to remember the intricacies of the structure and prose I assembled over the past five days. This, I believe, is on par with asking me to speak Hindi, or fly. But, much to my surprise, as I flip through the notes Mark sent me on his paper, all the details start rushing back to me. Global asset price bubbles. The carry trade. The euro. The yen. I can do this. I can finish this by noon. And the report on Greece, Latvia, and Spain by five. This won't be as difficult as I thought. I'll skip lunch and work straight through, and no one will be the wiser.

Apparently the whole "skipping lunch" idea was wishful thinking. I know other people do it, like Simon Wellington in NIRD's foreign policy department. He has trained his body to eat once a day, which explains his high productivity and toxic halitosis. But I can't concentrate when my stomach starts gurgling. As soon as I type the words "credit crunch," all I can think is "mmm, crunch." And then I want a bag of potato chips and a plate of nachos.

What I'm saying is, the idea of working straight through

doesn't go exactly as planned. I finish the currency paper by noon, so on that front I'm right on schedule. But when I print out the IMF country reports on Greece, Latvia, and Spain, I discover I have more than two hundred pages of text to (a) read, (b) understand, and (c) summarize in a way that is useful to Mark. For some people, five hours would be more than enough time to do that. I am not one of those people.

Fueled by NIRD coffee and jelly beans, I race through the reports. Well, maybe not race. Claw. I claw my way through the reports. But by five I at least have some notion of their substance. By six I have a rough outline of a summary for Mark, and by six-forty-five I finish. An hour and forty-five minutes later than my deadline, but it's a freaking miracle nonetheless.

Mark hasn't left yet, so I march into his office and drop the report on his desk with a loud thud. "The IMF summary," I say.

He pushes his glasses up the bridge of his nose and flips through the pile. "Remind me—what is this?"

"The summary of the IMF reports. On Greece, Latvia, and Spain."

He frowns. "Oh. Right. I'll take a look Monday morning."

Are you kidding me? "I thought you needed it before you left today."

"Did I say that?"

"Yes. You said that."

"Hmm. Interesting." He rubs his chin. "Well, I appreciate your hard work, Hannah. Have a nice weekend. We can discuss the report Monday afternoon."

"Monday afternoon? What about . . . Monday morning?"

"Unfortunately, my youngest daughter is visiting me this weekend. Have I told you she's finishing her PhD in American history at Yale? Anyway, I want to spend as much time with her as possible this weekend, so I won't have time to read your work until Monday morning. But thank you again for getting it all together. Good effort, as always."

He adjusts his glasses and returns to reading an article in *The Economist*, oblivious to the fact that I am now foaming at the mouth.

I grab my bag and stomp to the elevator, seething as I descend the eight floors to the lobby. I hate this place. Un-freaking-believable.

I stalk through the lobby and stop abruptly when I reach the door. It's raining—and not a minor drizzle. A torrential downpour. Sheets of rain beat against the glass doors, the long metal handles rattling with each gust of wind. I reach into my bag for my umbrella and discover I left it at home. Fantastic.

"Take this, honey," says the security guard behind the desk. She hands me a copy of today's *Washington Post*.

With the newspaper over my head and my bag pressed against my body, I bolt out the door and start running up Eighteenth Street. The rain saturates the newspaper, which quickly dissolves into a mound of pulp. My flats fill with water and refuse to stay on my feet, and by the time I reach Massachusetts Avenue, I am holding them in my hand. Drenched, cold, and barefoot. Could this day get any worse?

In fact, it could. Rachel is in my kitchen right now, attempting to cook something more complicated than a Lean Cuisine. There's a high probability she has overcooked something, and a slightly lower probability she has set something on fire.

I walk into my apartment and find Rachel wiping off my kitchen counter, her hair soaked in sweat, and her slender face bright red. She jumps when she sees me enter the apartment.

"Don't be mad," she says.

"Mad about what?" I ask. "What did you do?"

I move gingerly toward the kitchen in my bare feet, but I stop abruptly as something sharp and pointy pierces my toe. I shriek in pain.

"Shit!" Rachel cries. "I didn't realize you were barefoot!"

She rushes over and helps me limp over to my air mattress. I lift up my foot and pull out a tooth-size shard of glass. "What the hell is this?"

Rachel clears her throat. "You know how you're supposed to brown the brisket before braising it?"

"Uh-huh . . ."

"Well . . . I didn't realize you weren't supposed to put glass on the stove top . . ."

"You used a glass dish on the stove? Are you *crazy?*"

"But it was Pyrex—the glass is supposed to be tempered."

"That doesn't mean you can put it directly on an open flame!"

"Well I know that *now*." She sighs. "Anyway, the glass kind of . . . exploded. It burst into a billion pieces. Glass shards flew everywhere. I started crying. And the thing is . . . I had all the food laying out, so there were bits of glass in the dates, in the horse-radish sauce, and, of course, in the brisket."

"The brisket? Tell me you're joking. That brisket cost more than fifty bucks."

Rachel bites her lip and wrinkles her brow. "Sorry."

I run my fingers through my hair. "Shit. Shit, shit, shit."

"Listen, I'm really sorry, but we need to throw out all the food I made or touched. There's glass in all of it, which is pretty much a lawsuit waiting to happen. We need to buy new stuff and start over."

"But I special ordered that brisket, and the Dupont market is only open on Sundays."

"Doesn't Open Meadows sell at the Arlington market tomor-row morning?"

"Yeah, but the cooked brisket needs to rest overnight. It's al-ways better the second day. That's, like, the number one rule of brisket making."

"Brisket making has rules?"

I narrow my eyes. "Are you seriously questioning me right now? After you just detonated a brisket bomb in my apartment?"

"Sorry." She smoothes the sheets on my air mattress and shrugs. "Well, there's always Whole Foods."

I sigh and cradle my head in my hands. "Great. Another hundred some dollars down the drain."

I try to come up with a silver lining for this situation, but I can't find one, and that's because a silver lining does not exist. The only lesson I can glean from this incident, other than never letting Rachel alone in the kitchen again, is that whenever I think I've hit rock bottom, I should wait a few minutes, because something will almost always happen to send me plummeting to a new low point. I can only hope tomorrow's dinner will be the exception, and not the rule.

thirteen

a s predicted, the situation deteriorates from moderate compli-
cation to total catastrophe. The next morning I awake with
a start to the shrill beeping of my alarm clock and, in an unfortunate turn, the distinct smell of mildew.

I fumble for the off switch on my alarm and roll over, fixing
my eyes on the ceiling. My body feels heavy and stiff, as if, in my
sleep, someone replaced my bones with thick lead pipes. The act
of rising from my mattress poses a far greater challenge than I
expected, and so instead of moving, I continue to stare at the ceiling, willing myself to get out of bed. This is what happens when
you spend seven hours shopping and cooking with a friend who is
now afraid to boil water.

I rub the sleep out of my eyes and take a deep, calming breath,
when—once again—a rotten smell fills my nostrils, a sour mix of
moldy leaves and raw clay. What *is* that?

I push myself up from my mattress and scan the room. That's
when I see it: a shallow pool of muddy water creeping in from the
front and back doors to my apartment.

Rainwater. From last night's storm. Shit.

My mind races. How did this happen? *When* did this happen?
I retrace my steps, from the time we started cooking to the moment I collapsed into bed at 3:12 A.M. I don't remember seeing any
water last night. After the drama following the Pyrex explosion, I
would have noticed a small lake in my apartment.

I pick up my phone and dial Rachel. "Rach—we have a major problem."

"Hey," Rachel yawns into the phone. "What time is it?"

"Eight," I say.

"Could I call you back in like an hour? I can't function on five hours' sleep."

"Too bad. I need your help. My apartment flooded."

"What?"

"From the storm. There's water leaking in from the front and back doors. My apartment smells funky and moldy, and there's water everywhere."

"Uh-oh."

"This is a total disaster. I can't ask people to pay forty-five bucks to sit in a flooded apartment."

"But we've already cooked, like, half the dinner."

"I know." I run my fingers through my knotted hair. "We'll have to move the location."

"Not to my place," she says. "Lizzie is studying for some big law school exam. I promised she could have the apartment to herself tonight."

"Crap."

I have no idea what to do. I can't cancel, that much I know. I've already spent more on this dinner than I should have. Thanks to Rachel's glass explosion, I needed to spend another $100 on replacement groceries and another $50 on cleaning supplies and a new baking dish for the tzimmes. If I have a prayer of making this month's rent, I need to recoup at least some of my costs.

"This was a dumb idea," she says. "I pushed you into this. It's my fault."

"No it's not," I say, although I do blame her, just a little. But I'm not going to let this fall apart like everything else in my life. I've looked forward to this supper club for almost two weeks.

And then, through a fog of sleeplessness and desperation, an idea comes to me.

"You know what we could do . . . ?" I say.

"Donate the food to a soup kitchen? Because I know some people at Miriam's Kitchen and could hook that up."

"That's not what I was thinking," I say. "But thank you for making me feel like a really bad person."

"Sorry."

"What I was thinking is, my landlord is away for the congressional recess, and I have the keys to his apartment. We could use his dining room and kitchen. We've already cooked a chunk of the meal anyway, and as long as we leave everything the way we found it, he'll never know."

Rachel is silent. I gather she is uncomfortable with this idea.

"Well?"

"I don't know," she says. "Isn't that . . . illegal? Trespassing or something?"

"He gave me a set of keys. He told me I could let a repairman upstairs. As far as he knows, maybe I needed to let someone in because of the flooding."

"I guess."

"And why are you suddenly worried about the legality of all this anyway? This whole enterprise is basically an unlicensed restaurant. And you stole two tables. And twelve chairs."

"First of all, supper clubs aren't illegal, per se. It's kind of a gray area. And I *borrowed* that furniture, thank you very much."

"Whatever—you're missing the point. Are you in or not?"

She hesitates. "Yeah, okay. I'm in. What do you need me to do?"

"Get over here as soon as you can," I say. "And bring as many rags as you can find."

Rachel arrives twenty minutes later with a huge tote slung over her shoulder and a heap of rags in her arms.

"Whoa," she says as she examines the apartment. "You weren't kidding about the smell."

"Here—give me some of those rags. We can pile them at the

front and back doors to sop up as much water as possible. I'll deal with the rest of the cleanup tomorrow."

We line the floor with old towels and T-shirts and haul all the ingredients and food from my refrigerator to Blake's kitchen. Rachel stares at the ingredients lining Blake's kitchen island.

"Maybe you should start cooking while I decorate the dining room," she says, tugging at the tote on her shoulder.

"Sure, whatever." After last night's debacle, I'm happy to keep her away from food and flames.

We spend the next eight hours pulling everything together in a rushed frenzy. I try to focus on the positives, rather than the negatives, of which there are many (that Rachel shattered one of my dishes into all of the food last night, for example, and that we are now hosting a dinner in my landlord's house). So, the positives: our menu is solid. Rachel's Pyrex snafu notwithstanding, every component of tonight's meal has turned out even better than expected. Last night I baked the Jewish apple cakes, and each one came out moist and fragrant and dense, bursting with apples I caramelized with Calvados and a touch of rosemary and then folded into a vanilla-and-cinnamon-scented cake. We braised the brisket in a tomato sauce so rich and garlicky I can still smell it on my fingers, and the honey ice cream came out silky smooth and tastes like a spoonful of creamy honey, with crunchy chunks of honeycomb toffee.

Another positive: Blake's kitchen is a magical, glorious place. I would kill for a kitchen like this, and even though I know that, technically speaking, I shouldn't be cooking in here, our dinner will be ten times better for using this space.

As Rachel bangs around the dining room, I plow through my morning prep work. I proof the yeast for the challah and toss all the ingredients into Blake's KitchenAid mixer because, well, the mixer is there, and it seems silly not to use it. While the dough hook slaps the rich, tacky dough against the sides of the metal bowl, I toss the chopped onions into a frying pan on Blake's six-burner range, filling the house with the fragrant smell of sautéing onions. I toss in the celery and carrots and eventually dump the mixture into a bowl along with the ground beef, rice, and seasonings. Later, Rachel will help me roll the filling into previously frozen cabbage leaves, which we'll then braise in a pot of sweet-and-sour tomato sauce—assuming, of course, Rachel doesn't have a total meltdown at the prospect of helping in the kitchen.

When the challah dough is smooth and glossy, I set it aside to proof and move on to the tzimmes, cutting the parsnips into coins and the sweet potatoes into paper-thin medallions. Rachel calls to me from the dining room as I finish slicing the parsnips and chopping up the dried pears, and I wipe my hands on my apron, a red-and-white-striped smock I bought at Anthropologie a few years ago. Adam used to joke that it makes me look like a 1950s housewife. I was never sure whether he meant that as a compliment or an insult.

I walk through the doorway and find Rachel arranging votive candles in the middle of Blake's dining room table, tucking the candles among sprays of dried leaves, clusters of pomegranates, and antique honey jars. A large chalkboard leans against the far wall, the menu scrawled on the board in Rachel's bubbly handwriting.

"Well, I'll be damned," I say. "When did you buy all this?"

"Over the past few weeks. I picked up decorations when I was out buying groceries and stuff."

She says this as if it's nothing, as if putting together a table setting worthy of *Martha Stewart Living* is akin to breathing, or blinking. I guess this is what it means to have style: to make beauty and class seem effortless, despite how much effort is actually involved.

Rachel scatters a few more candles around the table and stands back to snap a few photos of the table setting with her Canon Rebel. "We're actually going to pull this off," she says as she shifts one of the honey jars slightly to the right.

I scan the table, with its honeypots and tiny votives and sprays of autumn leaves, and for the first time today, I think she might be right.

But what if she isn't right? And, really, isn't it more realistic that she wouldn't be? I have no business doing what I am about to do: charging people forty-five dollars to eat a meal prepared by me, an enthusiastic home cook, in a house that isn't my own. I am an imposter—a wannabe—and I am beginning to doubt whether I can do this.

Which is why, thirty minutes before the guests arrive, I start to lose it.

My hands shake as I slice the apples and potatoes, the razor-sharp edge of the knife fluttering wildly above the cutting board, dipping and diving perilously close to my fingertips as I try to prepare the savory tart. All of my limbs take on a life of their own, thrashing and flailing in the air, spilling olive oil all over the counter and knocking an entire jar of peppercorns on the floor. My elbow jabs its boney tip into Rachel's ribs on two separate occasions, and my feet have forgotten how to work together and keep getting in the way. I am a total mess.

But I can't help it. I feel like one of those jerks who starts a blog, claiming authority on a topic without any credentials whatsoever—the gym teacher who decides he has an opinion on financial regulation everyone needs to read. What makes him think he's an expert? The fact that he cares? Well, swap out the blog for a whisk and a ladle, and I'm doing the same thing: acting as if my interest in cooking qualifies me to run a restaurant out of my home. Correction: my *landlord's* home. Who am I kidding?

But before I can voice any of my misgivings to Rachel—before I can tell her how utterly unprepared I feel, how we've bitten off way more than we can chew—a loud "Dong-*ding*" echoes through the house. I look at my watch. Eight o'clock on the dot.

"Ready to do this thing?" Rachel says, wiping her hands on a dish towel.

I nod and smile because, ready or not, here they come.

to my infinite delight and surprise, the night doesn't begin as a total disaster. As soon as people arrive, they pile into the candlelit living room and start talking and drinking and playing the name game. The volume of their chitchat rises and falls like crashing waves, with a constant low-level buzz maintained by the jazz music humming through Blake's speakers. The yeasty smell of freshly baked challah wafts through the house as the guests nibble on my last-minute menu addition of chopped liver canapés with date puree and pomegranate seeds, with the group standing as far away from Blake's leather furniture as I can manage.

The group is a typical Washington mix: a lawyer, a journalist, some nonprofit workers, a teacher, some Hill staffers and lobbyists, all in their twenties and thirties. Some are Republicans, some are Democrats, and some are Independents, which means the dinner table could either be fertile ground for lively conversation or a Grade A disaster.

Once everyone settles in, I gently tap the side of a wineglass with a pair of steel tongs to get everyone's attention. "Before Rachel and I get back in the kitchen," I say, "we should probably introduce ourselves."

I bumble my way through an introduction, making a mockery of the English language in the process, but somewhere in the middle of my spiel I notice a man at the back of the room staring at me, his ice blue eyes fixed steadily on mine. A light dusting of stubble covers his angular jawline, and his mesmerizing jewellike eyes peer from beneath a mess of dark, tousled hair. He wears an Old 97's T-shirt and dark-wash jeans, and when I hold his gaze, his lips curl into an impish smile as he subtly winks and raises his cocktail glass. My face grows hot, and I look away, but when I look back he is still boring into me with his stare, giving me no choice but to freeze midsentence.

". . . and so we hope all of you have a great time tonight," Rachel says, jumping in. "Please make yourself at home and enjoy your drinks."

As soon as she finishes, Rachel yanks me by the arm and pulls me into the kitchen. "What was that about?"

"What?"

Rachel raises an eyebrow, but I ignore her and begin to fumble through Blake's kitchen drawers.

"Have you seen the thermometer? How is the tart coming along? Where is the horseradish sauce?"

Rachel slides up behind me and grabs my shoulders. "*Relax.*"

But how can I relax? I'm up to my elbows in brisket juices and horseradish sauce, and there is a seriously good-looking guy standing in my living room. Sorry, Blake's living room. *Blake's.* But if I am trying to calm my frazzled nerves, that guy's presence isn't helping.

I turn on the heat below the pot of stuffed cabbage, and within a few minutes, my anxiety melts away, and food becomes my primary focus. Getting each course to the table in order and on time requires a disciplined system, one that allows no room for distraction and panic. I organize my *mise en place*, and once I get my bearings, Rachel and I fall into a rhythm, like two workers on an assembly line. I slice the cooled challah; she arranges the slices in a basket and buses the basket to the table. I pull the tart out of the oven; she plates it. Back and forth, back and forth.

Just as I pull the brisket from the oven, the meat supple and richly seasoned in a bubbling scarlet tomato sauce, Rachel shuffles into the kitchen from the dining room, carrying an empty platter and a stack of twelve plates—Blake's plates, which we decided to use because they were much nicer than the ones Rachel "borrowed" from the NIRD dining room.

"Apparently people loved the tart," she says.

I nod solemnly, acting as if I am too preoccupied with cooking to bask in the glory of a compliment, but really, I'm basking. Nothing thrills me more than hearing people enjoyed my food, and tonight the positive feedback kicks my adrenaline rush into high gear, which is exactly what I need to see this dinner through until the end.

Rachel rinses the dishes in the sink, but as she grabs one of the plates with her soapy hand, she loses her grip and sends the plate crashing to the floor. The plate cracks into dozens of irregular hunks and shards, and the dining room erupts into facetious applause at the explosive sound.

"Jesus, Rachel."

She scurries to sweep up the broken plate. "Sorry, sorry, sorry."

"My landlord is going to kill me."

"I doubt he'll even notice. One plate out of twelve? He'll probably figure he broke it himself or misplaced it somewhere. Or we can replace it. No biggie."

I shake my head as I give the tzimmes a stir. "Whatever you say, butterfingers."

"Hey!"

"Let's try to make it through this dinner without shattering any more glass or ceramic objects. That's all I ask."

Rachel dumps the broken plate into the trashcan. "Fine. Point taken."

Once I've coated the parsnips in a honey-saffron glaze, Rachel helps me plate them alongside the brisket, stuffed cabbage, and sweet potato tzimmes, and we carry the plates out to the dining room together.

"Let me explain a little about tonight's dinner," I say, addressing the softly lit faces around the table, which is covered with flickering votives and tapered candles. I launch into a description of the Jewish New Year and the symbolism behind all of the food: how the honey represents the hope for a sweet new year, how the challah is round instead of braided to represent the circle of life, how my grandmother used to make stuffed cabbage on every possible occasion because it reminded her of her Hungarian mother. I tell them lots of things—about food, about my bubbe, about me—and, to my surprise, they actually pay attention. They hang on my every word and ask intelligent questions and make thought-provoking points of their own. And I realize, hey, these are people who get it, people who love to eat and talk about food and culture as much as I do. Most of them aren't Jewish, but that doesn't matter. Every family has its traditions. Every family has a story to share. That's the point of this dinner—to swap stories and histories and see how food can bring people together.

"Everything has been awesome," says a voice from the middle of the table. My eyes land on the source: the same guy who was staring at me earlier, the one with the blue eyes and Old 97's T-shirt.

"Thanks," I say. He grins, revealing a set of shockingly white teeth. His eyes soften, which has the dual effect of raising my heart rate and making me feel as if I might pee my pants. I try to think of something witty to say, something about brisket or the Old 97's, but my mind goes blank. All I can come up with are platitudes and stupid puns that would make me sound as lame as my swashbuckling landlord. The last thing I need is to sound like a moron, or a pirate.

So, in the end, I say nothing and retreat into the kitchen.

At this point, we're over the hump. One more course to go, and that's the easy one: cake and ice cream. Guaranteed hits.

"What's the deal with that guy out there?" Rachel asks as she scrubs one of Blake's frying pans.

"What guy?"

"Oh, shut up. You know exactly who I'm talking about."

But before I can answer, "that guy" walks into the kitchen. He stuffs his hands in his jean pockets and scrunches up his shoulders. "The bathroom . . . ?"

"Down the hall and to the right," I say.

When he shuts the door, Rachel turns to me and raises an eyebrow.

"Don't," I say. "We'll talk about it later."

She purses her lips and continues scrubbing the pan. A few minutes later, Mr. Old 97's emerges from the bathroom and sidles up to the kitchen island, watching me as I lift the lid off the honeycomb ice cream.

"Oooh, what's that?"

I wipe my hands on my apron without looking up. "Honeycomb ice cream."

"Nice." He raps his hands against the counter, like a timpanist beating on a pair of bongos, and his eyes land on the tray of apple cakes in the corner of the kitchen. "Hey, are those cinnamon buns?"

"What?" I glance over my shoulder. "Oh, no. Individual apple cakes."

"Ah, got it. I must have cinnamon buns on the brain. I visited my family last weekend, and my mom makes a mean recipe for cinnamon buns. The best in the world, as far as I can tell."

Like a Siamese fighting fish flaring its gills, I roll back my shoulders and look him in the eye. "I make excellent cinnamon buns."

He laughs. "I'm sure you do, but I don't know—my mom's are pretty spectacular. I think her recipe won some award."

"I use homemade brioche dough. Does your mom do that?" Rachel subtly elbows me in the side because, apparently, I sound like a competitive jerk.

"I don't know what she does. Maybe we should have a taste test sometime."

"Yeah, maybe." I hustle over to the corner of the kitchen and grab the tray of cakes, my way of suggesting, *Thank you for your time, but in case you hadn't noticed, I am working my ass off; this conversation is over now.*

"So how long did it take you to pull all this together?" he asks as I dump the tray on the counter. I can see my attempts at subtlety have failed.

"A while," I say.

He stares at me as I begin transferring the cakes to the dessert plates, carefully lifting each one with a wide metal spatula. I pause halfway through and look up at him.

"I'm sorry—do you need something?"

"Oh—no. Sorry. I just wanted to say hi. But I guess I'm in your way."

Rachel jumps in. "You're not in our way. We're—"

"We're plating dessert," I say. "Now isn't a great time."

His smile fades. "Oh. Gotcha. Sorry."

It is clear from his expression that, once again, my remarks came out bitchier than I'd intended, and now I feel guilty because . . . well, this guy is very good-looking. "I promise I'll be a lot nicer in about thirty minutes," I say. "When things calm down."

"Yeah, okay. That sounds good." He walks toward the dining room and turns around halfway to the door, flashing a quick smile as he runs his fingers through his hair. "My name is Jacob, by the way."

I bite my lip to keep from smiling. "Jacob," I say. "Reaser, right? I remember your name from the list. Nice to meet you."

He bows his head without saying anything, and then he turns around and joins the others in the dining room.

Dessert is an even bigger hit than I expected, and when Rachel and I finally make it into the dining room from the kitchen, the guests welcome us with a boisterous round of applause.

"Bravo," says a blond woman at the end of the table. "I'd do this again in a heartbeat."

Rachel casts a sideways glance and smiles, and then she sneaks out of the dining room into Blake's living room. She returns a minute later, clutching a bottle of Fonseca port in one hand and a bottle of Macallan scotch in the other.

"Scotch or port, anyone?"

Ten hands shoot up around the table, and Rachel pulls me into the kitchen to grab some glasses.

"Where did you get the booze?" I ask.

"Where do you think? Your landlord's liquor cabinet."

"Have you lost your *mind*?"

Rachel shoos me away with her hand. "It'll be fine. We have plenty of time to replace it."

"I thought you were worried about the legality of all this."

Rachel shrugs. "Eh. I got over it."

We portion out the port and scotch and carry the glasses back into the dining room on a large silver tray. Rachel passes the glasses around to the guests, who are chatting and laughing like old friends, even though most of them never met before this evening. I catch a man and a woman in the corner swapping numbers, and in my mind I imagine they are setting up a future date, which will evolve into a romance that will lead to a fifty-year marriage, and one day they will look back and realize all of it started right here at my dining room table. Sorry, Blake's dining room table. *Blake's.*

By midnight, the party winds down, and the guests start gathering their coats and purses and hats before saying their good-byes. Rachel stands by the door with a large, decorated hatbox, the receptacle for our forty-five-dollar fee—though Rachel emphasizes the guests can give as much or as little as they like. I reemphasize the "as much" part.

The guests shuffle out the door one by one, each tossing a wad of bills into the hatbox. A lawyer in a pink-and-white-striped Oxford shirt drops fifty-five dollars into the box. "That stuffed cabbage was like Proust's madeleine," he says. "Reminded me of my grandmother's—only better."

A trade analyst from New Zealand nods her head. "For me it was the honeycomb ice cream. We called it 'hokey pokey' back home, except with vanilla ice cream instead of honey. I would pay you to make that for me every week."

The praise continues, each person highlighting a favorite part of the experience, from the food to the relaxed atmosphere to the lack of pretense. Eleven guests pass through the front door, and finally Jacob makes his way through the foyer, sauntering toward me with his hands tucked into his jean pockets. He stops when he reaches the box and looks inside. He looks back up at me and grins.

"Maybe if you leave them alone tonight, they'll make lots of baby dollars," he says. He tosses a hundred-dollar bill into the box. "That should help."

"Oh—no, Jacob, that's way too much. Really. You don't have to do that."

"I insist."

I grab the box from Rachel and shove it toward Jacob. "Seriously, take back some change. Forty, fifty, sixty—whatever you want."

He stares at me for a few seconds, curling his lips to the side in a mischievous grin. His eyes twinkle in the light from Blake's foyer, and only now do I notice the flecks of sapphire in both of his irises and the tiny sesame-seed-shaped scar along his left temple. He reaches into his pocket and pulls out a business card and drops it into the box. "Why don't you bake me a batch of cinnamon buns sometime, and we'll call it even."

Then he winks and walks out the door.

i awake the next morning at the ripe hour of 11:00 A.M., at which point I realize I spent the night sleeping on my landlord's leather couch, fully clothed in my jeans, T-shirt, and apron, minus one shoe. At the moment, an explanation for this behavior escapes me.

Rachel and I spent two hours cleaning up last night, and I vaguely remember the involvement of Blake's Fonseca port, which we drank in celebration of The Dupont Circle Supper Club's success. Thanks to some generous tipping by our guests, we took in $750 last night, and after expenses, we cleared about $400. I suggested we split the $400 down the middle, but since I did most of the cooking, planning, and shopping, Rachel insisted we split the proceeds 75/25. As I recall, Rachel poured us each a generous glass of port after we tallied up the cash and then possibly poured another glass (or two?) after that, and at some point I ended up on this couch and decided to stay here.

As I pull myself upright, I hear the muffled sound of my phone ringing from somewhere in the kitchen—where, exactly, I could not say. I scour every surface, every drawer and cabinet, but although I hear the low hum of the *Knight Rider* theme song, the source evades me. I eventually find it in the refrigerator, on top of a plate of chopped liver toasts.

"Rach, hey, what's up?" I say as I pull the leftover canapés from the refrigerator.

"Are you near your computer?"

"Not really. I'm still in my landlord's house." I nibble on one of the toasts. "Apparently I slept here."

"Oh. That's weird."

"Really? I hadn't realized."

Rachel clicks her tongue. "Always with the sarcasm. Anyway, when I woke up this morning, I checked the e-mail account I set up for The Dupont Circle Supper Club, and guess what? I had ten new e-mails asking about future dates and reservations."

"Already? Seriously?"

"Yep. Word gets around. I guess one of our guests writes a local food blog, and she already posted a review: 'The food managed to both comfort and surprise, with complex flavors, artful preparation, and beautiful plating.' She threw in a few photos, too."

I yank the piece of toast from my mouth. "Photos?"

"Of the food and stuff, yeah."

"Crap."

"Who cares? It's good publicity."

"Not when we've used my landlord's house without his permission. What if he sees the photos online and recognizes his house?"

Rachel sighs into the phone. "You really think Long John Silver reads some obscure DC food blog?"

"Probably not."

"Exactly," she says. "We're fine. How much longer is he away?"

I lick a blob of date puree off my finger. "He gets back tomorrow morning. But he's away again next weekend, and then again over Columbus Day. He's on the town hall circuit thanks to the immigration debate."

"Perfect. We can hold another dinner in his house next weekend, and another one in October."

"In *his* house?"

"It's bigger and nicer than yours," she says. "Smells better, too."

"That's because mine flooded."

"My point exactly."

"Weren't you the one warning me about trespassing and all that?"

Another sigh. "Let's just say it worked out better than I expected. I really don't think it's a problem."

"That's probably because you're not the one who would face eviction."

"You're not going to get evicted," she says. "Face it—you're a hit. People are clamoring for a seat at your table. Why would you want to pass that up?"

Of course I wouldn't want to pass that up. Who would? Last night was like a dream, where I could finally immerse myself in the sort of career I've always wanted to pursue—running my own kitchen, letting my imagination run wild, satisfying a group of patrons I could call my own. I spent the night fearing I would wake up and realize none of it was real, that I'd been hit on the head, like Dorothy in *The Wizard of Oz*, and all of these people were figments of my imagination. But it was real, and I want to relive the thrill of last night again and again, if only to prove to myself that I can.

There is, however, the issue of my landlord's house, the main issue being . . . it isn't mine. To be fair, we cleaned his place from top to bottom and left it in even better condition than when we arrived. And, when you think about it, he invested so much time and money and effort into renovating his kitchen, it's almost like we're doing him a favor. If he isn't around, *someone* should be using his kitchen. Letting a Viking range sit around like a piece of art? That doesn't even make sense.

Besides, now that I've actually hosted a supper club, I see Friday's flood was a blessing in disguise. There's no way I could have pulled off last night's dinner in my tiny apartment. No way. And now that I know what's involved in making The Dupont Circle Supper Club a success, I can't imagine ever hosting one of these dinners in my apartment—which, no doubt, still smells like a bat cave.

"Fine," I say. "Let's meet for coffee and discuss the details. If we're really careful, we can probably make this work."

Rachel squeals into the phone. "Awesome. I'll meet you at Kramerbooks in, what, an hour?"

"Make it two," I say. "First I need to hit CVS and deal with the mess in my apartment."

The line at CVS stretches down aisle three, and I am forced to wait as two clerks with no sense of urgency ring up one customer after the next. As I inch my way forward, I suddenly hear the whine of an unmistakable voice.

"Ugh, could this line be any *longer*?"

I whip my head around and see Millie standing right behind me. And standing next to her is Adam.

His dark brown eyes spring open. "Hannah! Hi!"

My stomach flip-flops. It's been two months since Adam and I spoke. Two months since the breakup. I've tried not to think about him since then, but I haven't been very successful. As much as I want to erase him from my memory, I can't, and I find myself thinking about him at the oddest times, like when I roll over on my air mattress and find myself lying on a chilled strip of cotton, the side of the bed where he used to sleep. Some days the thought of him sneaks up on me when I walk by our old apartment, or when I hear a song by Maroon 5, a group Adam always pretended he didn't like but would listen to at home all the time. Other days I think I hear his laugh or see his face, and when that happens I think about what I would say if I ran into him. But of all the scenarios I've run through in my head, none of them have adequately prepared me for seeing him in person—for being so close I could touch him. Seeing his face and hearing his voice knock the wind right out of me.

Adam scratches his jaw with one hand as he awkwardly sticks the other into the pocket of his Diesel jeans; I could swear he had been touching the small of Millie's back.

"Hi," I say, trying to seem as relaxed as possible. "What brings you all the way to Seventeenth Street?"

This is a lame attempt at a joke. Neither of them lives far away. Adam's apartment—my old apartment—is about three blocks from here.

"We were having brunch in the neighborhood," Millie says. "What about you?"

"I live a block away."

Millie eyes my basket, which is filled with bleach, carpet cleaner, air freshener, and a pair of rubber gloves. "Growing pains in the new apartment?" she asks.

"Something like that."

I look down at the items in Millie's basket: antibacterial hand wipes, three protein bars, a jug of Listerine, and a box of condoms. Adam catches my glance and shifts his weight from one foot to the other.

"By the way," Millie says, "I'm impressed you were able to turn in that currency paper Friday. I know how difficult that must have been to pull off, considering you lost all of your work."

"Thanks."

Millie is being pleasant. This scares me. I am half expecting her to reach in for a hug, at which point her jaw will snap open, and she will eat me.

"Mark and Susan will probably agree the paper needs some serious tweaking, but at least you've given them something to work with," she says.

Ah, there's the Millie I know and love: never passing up an opportunity to make me look painfully average.

I rummage through my purse in search of my wallet, not wanting to waste any time when it's my turn at the register. All I want to do is pay and get the hell out of here, and staging an intense exploration of my bag's interior is a good excuse not to talk to Millie or Adam.

"Hannah?"

A third voice calls my name, one that isn't Millie's or Adam's.

I look up and see Jacob Reaser standing right in front of me. He threads his thumbs through the belt loops on his jeans and smiles. I drop my wallet on the floor.

"Jacob—hi," I say, bending down to pick up my wallet. "Wow, it's like a party in here today."

If they had parties in *hell*.

Jacob and Adam look each other up and down. Adam studies the washed-out New Pornographers T-shirt tucked beneath Jacob's moleskin blazer.

"Sorry," I say, shaking my head. "Adam and Millie, this is Jacob. Jacob, Adam and Millie."

Jacob gives a friendly hello as he shakes both of their hands. "Nice job last night, by the way. That brisket was killer."

"Oh . . . thanks." I cast a sideways glance at Adam and Millie, since they clearly have no idea what Jacob is talking about, and I don't want them to.

Adam knits his eyebrows together. "So your brisket is making the rounds, eh?"

"Not really." My eyes shift between Jacob and Adam. "It's a long story."

"We have time," Millie says.

If there is one person in the world who I don't want to find out about last night, it is Millie. She has an uncanny ability to wring the joy out of pretty much anything. I pray for a sudden natural disaster—an earthquake or a tornado—to interrupt this scene and terminate this conversation. Either that, or The Rapture.

"Really," I say, waving my hand. "It's not worth explaining right now."

I look at Jacob. This time, I think he gets the hint.

"Next customer!" shouts the man behind the register. That's me. Oh, thank god.

"Great running into you," Jacob says. I start to move toward the register, but he rests his hand on my shoulder and stops me in my tracks. "And hey, don't forget—you still owe me a batch of cinnamon buns. Call me sometime."

I smile nervously, something I'm sure Adam notices. "Yeah, okay," I say. "I will."

Jacob offers a half-wave good-bye, one of those hip-height gestures that falls somewhere between a peace sign and the number three. Not everyone can pull that off, but Jacob can. He seems to pull off a lot of things.

I walk up to the register to pay, and when I look over my shoulder, I see Adam clenching his jaw and staring at Jacob with narrowed eyes.

And even if it's only the tiniest bit, I have to admit, I suddenly feel better.

sixteen

i show up at Kramerbooks fifteen minutes late because, let's be honest, I'm me, and punctuality evades me on a regular basis. As expected, the place is a mob scene. Kramer's sits on Connecticut Avenue just north of Dupont Circle and is a Washington institution of sorts, functioning as a bookstore, restaurant, and bar all in one. The front always swarms with people perusing the book displays, which overflow with stacks of paperbacks and hardbacks, everything from political memoirs to the juiciest works of fiction. Some of the people browsing through the books are bookworms, but many are waiting for tables in the store's Afterwords Café, particularly at brunch time on the weekends, when the throng almost doubles in size. At the moment, I can barely move through the store without unintentionally groping someone's ass.

I peer around the corner toward the bar area and spot Rachel sitting at a small round table, scrolling through her BlackBerry. She perks up as she spots me heading her way.

"Six more reservation requests," she says. "Word travels fast."

I slide into the wooden chair across from her and sling my purse over the back. "So that puts us up to what? Sixteen?" I do some hazy math. "We can't fit sixteen in that dining room. At least not comfortably."

"I know," Rachel says, nodding. "That's why I've come up with an idea. Blake is away from Friday until Tuesday morning, right?"

"Yeah . . ."

"So we can hold two or three dinners in one weekend."

"*Three?*" I snort loudly. "No way."

Rachel furrows her brow. "Why not?"

"Because there's no way I can make that work."

She purses her lips. "Well, sure, not with that attitude."

"You don't get it. Aside from the fact that we're talking about holding dinners in *my landlord's house*, I can't front that kind of money—at least not yet. We made a decent profit last night, but not enough to bankroll the shopping for three dinners in a row."

Rachel sighs. "Fine. I see your point. What about two dinners? Saturday and Sunday? You'd have twice as much stuff to prep, but we'd use the same menu both nights, so you'd only have to do it once."

"I still don't love the idea of using Blake's house."

"Hannah, it'll be fine. The place was spotless when we left last night. I thought cooking was your passion—I thought you wanted to give this a shot."

"It is. I do."

"So? Let's do this. Two dinners, Saturday and Sunday."

I stick out my jaw and tap my foot nervously against the floor. "Maybe."

She grins. "I know that tone. That means yes. Yes?"

"I . . ." I watch as the smile on Rachel's face grows. "Okay, yes. Fine. Yes."

Rachel claps her hands together and pulls out a tan moleskin notebook. "Great. Let's start with the menu. We need a new theme. Any ideas?"

"Actually . . . yes."

Ever since we came up with the last dinner's theme, I've been brainstorming other ideas that might work with a group—concepts that would bring together the notion of culture and tradition and would allow me to share my stories and encourage others to share their own. I started thinking about my favorite foods and what I miss since moving to Washington, and that brought me to my hometown: Philadelphia. I thought about cheesesteaks and hoagies, tomato pie and roast pork sandwiches, water ice and Philly-style soft pretzels and black cherry Wishniak soda. All of those foods are woven deeply into the fabric of my childhood, and I haven't been able to find a decent version of any of them since I moved away from home. So my latest idea—the one Rachel, the taskmaster, has yet to endorse—is to base a menu around Philadelphia's favorite foods, which I'll deconstruct and reinvent and whose origins I'll explain to our guests. Sure, the motivation is a little selfish, but I want to deconstruct a cheesesteak, and by god, that's what I'm going to do.

And selfish or not, I think people will connect with the idea behind the dinner: the way food tethers us to our personal history. For me it's Philadelphia, but for someone else it's London or Boston or Nashville. You move somewhere new and suddenly you can't find the foods you grew up with. It's the sort of experience that makes you feel like you're from a place—mentioning a favorite food and having everyone look at you as if you're crazy, not because they don't like that particular food but because they've never even heard of it.

Rachel brightens as I describe my idea and go through the possible menu options. "Love it," she says. "Fantastic."

She starts scribbling in her notebook, outlining ideas for table decorations and lighting options. As I rattle off menu ideas—pretzel bread, mustard sauce, lemon water ice, cheesesteaks—she makes bullet points and annotations, noting what colors the menu might involve and how that might play into the overall color scheme. As someone to whom "color coordination" means wearing all-black, I am at a loss.

Rachel jots down a few more notes, and I glance at what she's written down under MENU. "By the way, I'm making pork this time," I say. "Like it or not."

"As if I could stop you. Do whatever you want. You're Hannah Sugarman. You're in charge."

And for the first time in a long time, I smile with pride at that pronouncement. "That's right," I say. "I am."

By the next morning, The Dupont Circle Supper Club's in-box is overflowing with requests. Even with two dinners in one weekend, we can't keep up with the demand. Other bloggers have posted about our underground venture, and soon the DC food blogosphere is alight with news and reviews and information about The Dupont Circle Supper Club. The e-mails pour in faster than we can read them, and Rachel finishes cobbling together an official Web site to field the many questions from prospective guests. We can't tell people too much about ourselves, and our schedule is a moving target, subject to Blake's travel schedule and the congressional calendar, but we dangle enough bait to satisfy people's curiosity. And yet, even with a Web site and FAQ section, the volume of e-mails continues to explode, at a rate that is both exciting and completely overwhelming.

I barely focus on my work all day Monday, spending most of my day drawing up shopping lists and preparation timetables and cooking schedules. I print out and squirrel away a few more recipes in my secret recipe folder, and each time Mark comes out of his office, I minimize my screens for Epicurious and *Food & Wine* and *Saveur* and instead bring up screens from Bloomberg and the *Financial Times* and Reuters. Luckily, Mark is too busy humming his regular rotation of Verdi and Puccini arias at full volume to notice I even exist.

When I return from work on Monday, I stumble into my still-damp, still-smelly apartment and, as soon as I do, Blake calls.

I stare at the screen, debating whether or not to pick up the phone. If I pick up, he might scream and shout and tell me he knows all about the supper club and, after more yelling, evict me. If I don't pick up, my apartment might smell like a bat cave until the end of time. How to decide?

"Hey, neighbor," Blake says as I pick up the phone. The smell, I conclude, is too much to bear. "How's the apartment?"

"Um . . . still a little wet and stinky, actually."

"That's why I wanted to talk," he says. "I saw your e-mail and checked it out earlier today. You did a good job with the bleach and towels, but you need to use a dehumidifier for a while."

"Okay . . ."

Blake laughs into the phone. "Don't worry. I'll hook you up. And a guy is coming out later this week to fix the gutters—for real this time."

"Great. Thanks."

My ceiling creaks as Blake paces back and forth above me. "No problem," he says. He suddenly stops moving. "By the way, did you leave some ice cream for me in the freezer?"

My stomach flip-flops. "Sorry?"

"There's a container of homemade ice cream in my freezer." I hear him smack his lips. "It tastes a little like honey? With something crispy in it?"

The ice cream. Shit. How is that still in there? Rachel told me she double-checked everything. "Um . . . maybe . . ."

"Maybe? The container has SUGARMAN written on it."

I clear my throat. "I mean yes. It's a . . . gift. For you. For the Jewish new year."

Blake pauses. "It's half eaten."

"Right. Yes." *Fuuuuck.* What is happening? "I . . . originally made it for myself," I say, the words flying out of my mouth faster than I can control them. "But I couldn't stop eating it, so instead of gaining twenty pounds I thought I'd give it to you instead."

What? Does that even make sense? No. No, by any measure, my explanation makes no sense at all. But, as usual, my mouth works faster than my brain, the result of which is sure to be disaster.

He chuckles. "Okay . . ."

"Sorry. I shouldn't have done that."

"No, no—it's fine. I mean, don't make a habit of wandering through my house while I'm away, but I appreciate the gesture. The ice cream is amazing, actually. Some of the best I've had."

"Thanks . . ."

I hear Blake swallow on the other end of the phone. "No, wow, this is really good." He takes another bite. "For real. You should pack this up and sell it. Have you ever considered going into business?"

I gulp loudly. "I've thought about it."

"You should. Although not out of that apartment. That's the last thing I need."

"Oh . . . ?"

He laughs. "Haven't you read my election platform? We're having major problems in Dupont with undocumented restaurant workers and restaurant owners not paying their taxes. A bunch of frustrated restauranteurs are supporting my campaign. I don't need someone running an unlicensed ice cream operation out of my basement."

He laughs again, louder this time, obviously amused by the absurdity of this scenario, and I attempt to join in, but what comes out is a halfhearted, "Haaaaa . . . aaa . . . *aaaah* . . ." which is really code for "*shit, shit, shit!*"

Blake pulls himself together and sighs. "Sorry. I'm just teasing."

"That's okay. It was . . . funny."

He chuckles. "Yeah, right. Anyway, I'll get that dehumidifier to you ASAP. And in the meantime, thanks for the ice cream. Semi-weird trespassing aside, I think you might be the best tenant I've ever had."

"Somehow I doubt that."

"No, seriously. My last tenant almost burnt down the house, and the one before that stole my grill. But you," he says through a smile, "you make me ice cream. Really *good* ice cream. I think you're a keeper."

I laugh nervously as the floor creaks beneath Blake's feet, the floorboards sounding old and weak, as if they could break any second. "Oh, I'm a keeper, all right," I say. "That's for sure."

Paging Lucifer: save me a seat. I'm headed your way, sooner than either of us expected.

seventeen

almost burning down the house is much worse than respectfully, cautiously holding a secret supper club in that house while the landlord is away. Right? Right. And stealing a grill—that's definitely worse. We haven't stolen anything. Except the port and scotch, I guess, but we were borrowing those, really. We're going to replace them. So, in that context, I am a good tenant. Well, maybe not good, but decent. Ish. Decentish.

The point is, we've already taken twenty-four reservations for this weekend, so we can't back out now. Or we could, but we'd risk ruining our supper club's reputation just when it's on the rise, and I'd lose the one thing that makes me happy these days, the one thing I look forward to more than anything else. And, dehumidifier aside, my apartment is small and cramped and generally unpleasant, meaning Blake's house is the only location that makes sense. To me. As for the general public . . . Whatever. This supper club is the only bright spot in my life at the moment, and we're not calling it off. End of story.

Thursday afternoon, I sneak over to Rachel's desk, making sure Millie and the other research assistants are out of sight. "Could you cover for me for an hour or two?" I ask.

Rachel tosses a folder into her desk organizer, a vintage two-tiered oak box she bought on Etsy. "Sure. Where are you off to?"

"Penn Quarter farmers' market."

"Near Chinatown? That's kind of a schlep for groceries. You're sure you don't need my help?"

I shake my head. "I'll be fine. If Mark or Millie asks . . . say I'm at the dentist or something."

"The gyno," Rachel says. "Always say the gyno. No one can argue with that."

"I'd rather you not share my gynecologic goings-on with Mark and Millie."

She shrugs. "Suit yourself."

I slip out of the office and scurry up Eighteenth Street toward the southern entrance to the Dupont Circle Metro stop, which sits smack on the circle, right next to an outpost of Krispy Kreme. That I manage to board the escalator without being sucked in by the smell of fresh, hot doughnuts is a testament to my willpower— of which, admittedly, I have almost none.

"I'll be back," I whisper over my shoulder at the Krispy Kreme sign as the escalator descends into the black pit below. Riding the escalators at Dupont Circle always feels like plunging into the great abyss. The daylight suddenly disappears at the start of the tunnel opening, and the stairs plummet downward into the darkened tunnel, at an angle that makes it nearly impossible to see where the downward journey ends. At 188 feet, the north entrance is steeper and scarier, but the south entrance nevertheless feels like an amusement park ride, albeit one lacking any sort of amusement whatsoever.

Metro pass in hand, I charge through the turnstile and down another set of escalators and manage to squeeze through the doors to a red line train just before it leaves the station. Clutching one of the metal poles with one hand, I glance down at the piece of paper crumpled in the other, on which I've written a brief sketch of the menu for Saturday and Sunday:

Red and white wine (TBD)
Victory Brewing Company Prima Pilsner
Soft pretzel bread/spicy mustard sauce

Cheesesteak arancini/homemade marinara sauce
Deconstructed pork sandwich: braised pork belly, sautéed
    broccoli rabe, provolone bread pudding
Lemon water ice
Commissary carrot cake

I'm particularly proud of my riff on the pork sandwich, one of Philadelphia's lesser-known specialties. Everyone presupposes the cheesesteak is Philadelphia's best sandwich, when, in fact, my favorite has always been the roast pork. Juicy, garlicky slices of pork are layered with broccoli rabe and sharp provolone on a fresh roll, the rich juices soaking into the soft bread while the crunchy crust acts like a torpedo shell, keeping everything inside. The flavors explode in your mouth in each bite: the bitter broccoli rabe, the assertive cheese, the combination of garlic and spices and tender pork. That's what I'm going for with my deconstructed version, and if all goes according to plan, the dish will be a knockout.

I jump off the train at Gallery Place–Chinatown and rush up the escalator, heading through Chinatown toward the market. To be fair, Washington's Chinatown is more like Chinablock. The "Chinese" part only takes up approximately one city block and generally lacks the Chinese character of Chinatowns in other cities like New York and San Francisco. There is a red Chinese gate over Seventh and H streets and a handful of average Chinese restaurants, but that's about it.

The surrounding area, however—the East End of downtown Washington known as Penn Quarter—is studded with upscale restaurants and art galleries and houses everything from condos and office buildings to the Verizon Center and the FBI. Unlike Dupont Circle and Logan Circle, Penn Quarter is all high-rises and pavement, a full-fledged business district, with the odd museum and government building thrown in and no town houses or backyards to speak of. Every Thursday, a farmers' market opens from three until seven on a tucked-away stretch of Eighth Street, filling with lawyers and government workers from nearby offices.

Today I've made the four-Metro-stop trek because this is the only place I can buy "the best pork in America" before our dinners this weekend.

As soon as I turn onto Eighth Street, I spot Shauna's tent, already swarming with customers at three-fifteen.

"Well, look who it is," she calls out, waving to me from behind her well-stocked ice tray as I approach her table. She reaches across and gives me a hug. "My favorite customer. You ready for your bellies?"

I pull a folded-up cooler bag from my tote and shake open the top. "Yes, ma'am."

Shauna digs through one of the coolers behind her stand and comes back with an enormous plastic bag filled with vacuum-sealed pork bellies. "Look at these beautiful babies," she says, pulling one of the packages out of the bag. She glances at the price tag and scrunches up her lips. "You know what? I'll give you the employee discount today. You've been good to me lately."

I'm about to tell Shauna she doesn't have to do that, but when I see the thirty-dollar price tag on one of the packages, I decide to keep my mouth shut. "Thanks," I say. "I appreciate that."

"I'm looking to move a few sirloin and strip steaks today, too. Any interest?"

"Yeah, actually. I could use them for my cheesesteak arancini."

Shauna's face twists into a skeptical frown. "Your what?"

I shake my head. "Never mind. Another course for the party this weekend. Same idea as cheesesteak spring rolls."

"Sweetie, I don't think 'cheesesteak' and 'spring roll' are supposed to be used in the same sentence."

"Trust me," I say. "It's better than it sounds."

I first tried a cheesesteak spring roll ten years ago at my cousin's wedding at the Four Seasons in Philadelphia, and though I wasn't as unconvinced as Shauna, I had my doubts. That Philadelphians could bastardize a menu item didn't surprise me—this is, after all, the city that invented The Schmitter, a sandwich made of sliced beef, cheese, grilled salami, more cheese, tomatoes, fried onions, more cheese, and some sort of Thousand Island sauce—but the fact that the Four Seasons found it worthy of their fancy-pants menu intrigued me.

One bite and I knew I'd struck gold. The cheesy meat and onion filling oozed out of the crisp, fried wonton wrapper, enhancing the celebrated cheesesteak flavor with a sophisticated crunch. This weekend, I'm doing a similar riff, but instead of spring rolls, I'm using arancini, the Sicilian fried risotto balls that are usually stuffed with mozzarella and meat ragu. Instead, I will stuff mine with sautéed chopped beef, provolone, and fried onions and mushrooms. The crispy, saffron-scented rice balls will ooze with unctuous cheesesteak flavor, and I will secure my place among the culinary legends.

Shauna grabs three steaks and tosses them in my cooler bag before pulling out her calculator and punching in some numbers. "That'll be . . . let's make it an even eighty bucks."

I sigh as I dig through my wallet. "Thank god I'm making money at this, right?"

Shauna frowns. "Making money at what? I thought this was for a party."

I catch myself as I hand her a stack of twenties. "Right. It is. Sorry. Never mind."

Shauna chuckles and stuffs my cash into her cashbox and gives me another hug across the table. "Same time next week?"

"Two weeks from now," I say. "But don't worry. I'll be in touch."

I scamper away from Shauna's stand and swing by Nature's Harvest, where I pick up a few large bundles of broccoli rabe. I grab some prosciutto at Terrine, the charcuterie stand, and a bag of mushrooms from the mushroom lady, all of which I stuff into one of my reusable bags. The only other ingredient I need is a loaf of bread for my savory bread pudding, and then I can head back to the office.

Or so I think. As I inspect the loaves of bread—the country French and the Italian Pugliese and the English Pullman—I feel a tap on my shoulder. I whirl around, half expecting to see Shauna standing there with some meat product I forgot to toss in my bag, but instead of Shauna, I see Blake.

"Ahoy," he says, a geeky grin painted on his face.

"Hey . . ."

Blake stares at the twenty pounds of groceries dangling from my arms and shoulders. "Wow, someone's hungry."

I glance down at the pork bellies and mounds of broccoli and let out a nervous laugh. "You know me."

"Not well enough, clearly," he says with a grin. "You hosting some big party this weekend?"

My stomach drops. "What? Party? Noooo. No, no, no. I was just passing through the market and got a little carried away."

"You work around here?"

"No, I work in Dupont Circle."

Blake furrows his brow. "Oh. Then what are you doing in Penn Quarter?"

"Just, you know . . ." You know . . . what? That I'm a big fat lying liar? "I was at the National Archives. Looking up some information for my boss. Happens all the time."

Blake nods, looking a little surprised. "You know what's funny—I've worked in this town for more than a decade, and I've never been in that building. Maybe you could give me a tour sometime."

"If you're ever in town," I say, my voice dripping with sass. What am I doing? He could evict me. He could also change his travel schedule. Now is not the time to bust out Hannah the fire-cracker.

He grins. "Yeah, well, I'm sorry to say, with the immigration debate going the way it is, our travel schedule is only going to get worse."

My ears perk up. "Really?"

"Unfortunately, yes. We're trying to adjourn by October thirtieth, but I don't see that happening. And on top of that, when I am in town I need to press the flesh for the ANC election, which is coming up fast." He sighs. "Anyway, speaking of work, I should get back to it."

"Yeah, what are you doing in these parts? Shouldn't you be on the Hill, getting chased down by reporters?"

"They chased us all the way downtown today," he says, nodding over his shoulder toward H Street. "We had an event with the Migration Policy Institute over at the Grand Hyatt. Speeches, press conference—the usual. But I figured I'd pick up a few cookies for the office on the way back."

"By all means," I say, gesturing toward a basket of chocolate chip cookies. "The last thing I want is to interfere with your sugar consumption."

His lips curl to the side as he pats his stomach. "Thanks for looking out for me, ice cream lady." His smile grows, the skin around his eyes crinkling like tissue paper. "And good luck with all those groceries. If you have any leftovers, you could always leave them in my freezer."

"Ha! Yeah . . ."

I force a smile, gripping my grocery bags tighter in my clenched fists, and wonder how much longer I can keep this up before I crumble under the weight of these increasingly preposterous lies.

eighteen

I've never been good at keeping secrets. This is an established fact. And yet, for someone who claims to lack the necessary skills for trickery and deception, I've managed to squeak through two encounters with Blake without exploding on the spot. This, I believe, is progress. Either that, or a total deterioration of my moral compass.

The following Saturday morning, once we're sure Blake has left town, Rachel shows up outside Blake's house at nine, dressed in boyfriend jeans and a loose linen sweater and carrying two tote bags filled with decorations. I meet her at the bottom of the wrought iron steps, holding two paper grocery bags in my hands, dressed in yoga pants and a faded Cornell T-shirt.

I jiggle the key into Blake's lock, and Rachel and I storm through his hallway, dumping our bags on his breakfast bar and launching straight into our prep work for both tonight's dinner and tomorrow's. Rachel heads for the dining room with one of her bags and begins arranging the table while I lay out the ingredients for the pretzel bread, risotto, and arancini filling. With the exception of the pretzel bread, I can make most of the components for both tonight's and tomorrow's dinners, which will save me a lot of time tomorrow morning. Last night I braised the pork belly in my own apartment, and tonight I'll simply reheat half the recipe and sear the crackling under the broiler to crisp it up. I also baked two carrot cakes, both of which I will fill and frost today.

Before I start with the cakes or arancini, I decide to get the bread pudding out of the way, since the bread needs to soak for at least a few hours. I tear up one of the stale loaves of bread and scatter it into a rectangular baking dish, dousing the hunks of bread with a savory custard of cream, eggs, herbs, sharp provolone, and salty wisps of prosciutto. I press my hands into the dish, making sure each piece of bread is saturated with custard, and then I stick the whole thing in the refrigerator to steep until dinner.

Moving on to the risotto, I quickly chop up the onions and dump them in the cast-iron pot, the tiny squares dancing and sizzling in the hot oil. As the kitchen fills with the smell of frying onions, Rachel comes in for her second bag and glances at the copy of the menu I left lying on the counter.

"I meant to ask," she says. "What's 'Commissary' carrot cake?"

I tell her how The Commissary was a popular Philadelphia restaurant in the 1970s, a café that was, in essence, an upscale cafeteria. There were multiple food stations, manned by students of the arts, and the place was packed from morning until night, with lines out the door. All of their food was top quality, but their carrot cake was legendary. The restaurant folded, but the catering arm still exists, and they still make their carrot cake for everything from weddings to office parties.

"Ah, so it's not really *your* carrot cake, is it?" she says.

I shrug. "Technically, no. I cribbed the idea from them. But it's still damn good."

"Agreed." She plays with the handle on her tote bag as I dump the rice into the risotto pot. "So . . . have you been in touch with that guy from our first dinner? Jacob?"

My cheeks flush, and I take a whiff of the toasting rice, foisting the blame for the redness in my face onto the heat from the stove. It's been nearly a week since I ran into Jacob at CVS, and I still haven't e-mailed or called him. I came very close—starting to dial his number, beginning the draft of an e-mail—but each time I chickened out. I guess I figure if I set up a date, then all of this becomes real. And in reality, Jacob may decide he doesn't like me as much as he thought. He may not like me at all. Or he may decide, after dating me for fifteen months and living with me for three of them, that he doesn't find my quirks endearing anymore. And so what happens then? I'm tossed away like an outdated cell phone. It's more fun to live in a fantasy world where I'm sought after but untouchable. I'm in control. It's harder to get hurt that way.

That's not to say I haven't been thinking about Jacob. I have. But I haven't been *obsessing* over him. My thoughts are like the hum of a refrigerator: constant low-level noise, just sort of . . . there. If the humming went away, that would mean something was broken. Having it there tells me I am, in fact, alive.

"Not yet," I say, the insecurity in my voice masked by the hiss of the white wine hitting the hot pan.

"You're waiting for . . . what, exactly?"

I ladle in the first cup of broth and begin stirring the risotto with one of Blake's long wooden spoons. "I've been . . . busy."

"So have I, but I've still managed to call and e-mail people."

"Well, I'm sorry I'm not as naturally social and outgoing as you."

Rachel clicks her tongue. "That's not what I meant. I just think it would be good for you to get out there again. Take a risk."

"Holding an underground supper club in my landlord's house isn't risky enough?"

"All I'm saying is this Jacob character seems friendly and interesting and hot, and you'll probably kick yourself in a few months if you let him slip through your fingers. That's all I'm saying."

I pour in another ladle of broth and give the pot another stir. "Fine. I'll e-mail him on Monday. Okay?"

"Okay," she says, pulling her bag off the counter and tossing it over her shoulder. "You'll thank me later. Trust me."

Thirty minutes before our guests arrive, I arrange the slices of tomato pie on a big platter, the three-inch squares of pizza crust and tomato sauce looking like a red checkerboard against the white porcelain plate. Rachel grabs the platter from my hands and lays it on one of the side tables in Blake's living room, across from the table where our stromboli will sit.

"You like?" Rachel asks, gesturing around the room as she spins slowly in place. The room is filled with votives and little twinkle-light replicas of the Philadelphia skyline, and the bottles of microbrewery beer are artfully arranged in an ice-filled metal tub.

"I like," I say.

"Wait until you see the dining room."

She waves me into the next room, where she managed to decorate the table with miniature oars and rowing boats, slipped between a series of paper luminaria bags cut to look like Philadelphia's Boathouse Row. In different hands, decorated white paper bags could look cheesy or cheap, but with Rachel's touch, the entire table looks sophisticated and classy and perfect for the occasion.

I pat Rachel on the shoulder. "You have a gift, my dear."

She knocks into me gently with her hips. "So do you."

We head back into the kitchen, where I finish baking off the pretzel bread and pull one of the carrot cakes from the refrigerator to let it come to room temperature. Mounds of toasted coconut cling to the side of the cake, held in place by the fluffy cream cheese frosting. Beneath the frosting lies a moist and fragrant cake bursting with carrots and cinnamon and golden raisins, stuffed with a gooey caramelized pecan filling. It is, in my eyes, a dessert approximating perfection.

"A thing of beauty," Rachel says, twirling the cake stand by its base.

We scurry around the kitchen as the final countdown approaches, pulling the stromboli from the oven, warming the pan of marinara sauce on the stove, and bringing the tall pot of frying oil to 350 degrees. Rachel shuttles back and forth between the kitchen and dining room, making last-minute adjustments to the table arrangements and laying the pots of mustard sauce in the appropriate locations.

Just as I pull a sheet tray of stuffed risotto balls from the refrigerator, the doorbell chimes with its signature dong-*ding*.

"Here we go again," Rachel says, raising her eyebrows. "Break a leg."

I do not, thank Christ, break a leg, nor do I break anything else in Blake's kitchen—a small miracle after last weekend's rampant clusterfuckery. In fact, now that I've done this once before, the entire evening proceeds without a hitch. The jitters I experienced last weekend—the flailing limbs, the two left feet, the utter lack of coherence—have all evaporated, and I now run The Dupont Circle Supper Club like a seasoned chef de cuisine. Courses fly out one after the other, and Rachel clears and cleans plates in mere minutes. We have this operation down to a science, as if this were a professional kitchen and not a Dupont Circle town house—one that, incidentally, happens to belong to someone else.

After I serve up the cheesesteak arancini, each ball golden and crispy and swimming in garlicky marinara sauce, a woman with a brown bob and a pointy chin slips into the kitchen.

"Are you Hannah?" she asks, tucking a lock of her pin-straight hair behind her ear.

"The one and only."

She adjusts her black-rimmed glasses and smiles. "I'm Cynthia Green. With the *Washington Post*? I was hoping I could ask you a few questions after dinner."

My stomach churns. "Questions?"

"I want to write a little feature about your supper club for next week's food section. Nothing major, but I thought it would be a fun below-the-fold piece."

I heat the flame under the sauté pan for the broccoli rabe, and as I do, the timer goes off for the bread pudding. "What did you want to talk about?"

"Your background, where the idea came from, what sort of food you cook. That kind of thing."

I grab a pair of pot holders and pull the bread pudding out of the oven, the crisped top bubbling with provolone and Parmesan cheese and studded with flecks of salty prosciutto. "Um . . . maybe . . ."

"I won't give away your identity in the article, if that's what you're worried about. And we can keep the location a secret." She watches as I toss the broccoli rabe into a pan of garlic-and-red-pepper-laced olive oil. "Think about it."

I give the pan a flip and a swirl and meet her eyes across the counter. "Why don't you meet me in the living room after dessert," I say. "I'll see if I can help you out."

If possible, this weekend's dinner is even more successful than the last one, and the table hangs on my every word as I put the dinner in context. I tell them about Philadelphia's Italian neighborhoods and how they gave rise to the famous cheesesteak and lesser-known roast pork sandwich, and about the Pennsylvania Dutch and how they introduced the pretzel to North America. I talk about water ice and The Commissary, Tastykakes and South Philly, the ongoing cheesesteak rivalry between Pat's and Geno's and my personal preference for Delassandro's Steaks over either one. One diner originally from Chicago jumps in with his own stories about Lou Malnati's pizza and Chicago-style hot dogs, and another from New Haven talks about white clam pizza at Pepe's and burgers at Louis' Lunch. Before long, everyone at the table is talking about the foods they grew up with as kids and crave whenever they visit home. In my mind, it doesn't get much better than this.

As the crowd digs into their slices of carrot cake, Cynthia

Green nods toward the living room and steals away from the table. I undo my apron and lay it over the back of one of Blake's kitchen barstools.

Rachel grabs me by the elbow before I leave the kitchen. "Remember—if it starts to get weird, just tell her you need to aerate the scotch."

"Rach, we've been over this. Under no circumstances would I need to aerate the scotch. That doesn't even make sense."

"To *you*."

"To anyone."

"Hey," she says. "I'm only trying to help."

"Yeah, well, why don't you focus on not burning down the kitchen? I'll handle the interview."

Rachel rolls her eyes. "Whatever you say . . ."

I slip into the living room and find Cynthia sitting on Blake's leather couch, her legs crossed as she scribbles in her slim reporter's notebook. She looks up as I walk into the room. "Don't worry," she says. "I'll make this quick. Like I said, this will only be a small feature."

I park myself on the edge of Blake's recliner, my back straight and tense as I watch her flip to a blank page.

"So how long have you been cooking?" she asks.

"Ever since I can remember," I say. "My grandmother used to babysit me a lot when I was a kid, and when I was seven or eight, she taught me how to make scrambled eggs. Then she upgraded me from eggs to brownies, then on to more complicated stuff like bread and strudel and brisket. By the time I was twelve, I was making my own pie dough. From there, my interest in cooking sort of took on a life of its own."

She smiles as she scribbles notes in her notepad. "Excellent. Do you have any professional training?"

"A little. I took a short course after college."

"And where was that?"

I blink rapidly as she flashes a friendly smile. "I'd rather not say, if that's all right."

She sticks up her hands defensively. "Fair enough." She pauses. "Was it a certificate or a degree?"

"Um . . . a certificate." She doesn't need to know the certificate was printed off the instructor's computer using Microsoft Word.

"So what inspired you to start an underground supper club? Other than your general enthusiasm for food and cooking."

That's easy: a boyfriend who dumped me and kicked me out of our shared apartment, and parents who would poop their pants if I ever became a chef for real. But I can't say that. Not to a *Washington Post* reporter, anyway.

"It's something I've always wanted to do," I say. "And the timing seemed right."

Cynthia glances around the room, at Blake's leather furniture and framed artwork and marble fireplace. "What's your day job, then? I'm guessing these supper clubs aren't paying for this house."

I gulp loudly as my face grows hot. "I . . . work in public policy."

"Lobbying?"

My heart pounds in my chest. "Kind of. Something like that."

"And how long have you lived here?"

I peek at my watch as I tap my foot rapidly against the floor. "You know what? I really have to get back to the kitchen."

"Just two more questions," she says, flipping to a fresh page. "What other themes can we look forward to? What's on the schedule?"

"Not sure. Maybe diner food. Or carnival treats. When we set the menu, it'll be on the Web site."

"And how often will The Dupont Circle Supper Club hold dinners?"

I fiddle with my ponytail. "Every few weekends. The next one is over Columbus Day. It depends on our schedules."

"Whose schedules?"

I clear my throat. "Mine. And . . . my assistant's."

"Speaking of which—"

"I'm sorry," I say, cutting her off before she can continue. "I really have to go."

She folds her hands together and nods. "I understand. If I have any follow-up questions, could I send an e-mail to the supper club e-mail account?"

"Sure." I jump up from my seat and start heading back to the kitchen, but I spin around before I reach the doorway. Cynthia is still sitting on the couch, furiously scrawling notes in her notebook. "You promise not to use my name and address, right? Or anything about my appearance?"

She looks up as her hand continues writing. "Hmm? Oh, yeah. Sure. No, nothing like that." She looks down again and flips to the next page in her notepad.

"Promise?"

But this time she doesn't answer and keeps writing, and as I disappear into the kitchen, I can't shake the feeling that I just made a terrible mistake.

nineteen

Under normal circumstances, the Cynthia Green interview would trigger an angst spiral of hideous proportions. I would bite my nails down to the quick and suffer from insomnia and descend into an abyss of stress eating and drinking. But with the demands of a second dinner Sunday night, I don't have time to indulge my anxiety. I need to make the second dinner as successful and seamless as the first, and, in an unexpected stroke of luck, I do.

The stories are different the second night—the hometowns of note now including Mumbai and Austin instead of Chicago and New Haven—but the spirit is the same. The guests swap stories and compare food notes and wolf down their helpings of pork belly and carrot cake. By the time the weekend is through, Rachel and I are relaxed and exhausted and, combined, approximately $1,220 richer. Thanks to Shauna's discount and some leftover ingredients from the Rosh Hashanah dinner, we had fewer expenses to cover this time, which means a larger chunk of the proceeds end up in our pockets—$305 to Rachel, $915 to me. Combined with the profits from last weekend's dinner and my parents' $200 contribution to my back account, my take will cover almost all of my moving expenses and make up the deficit created by September's rent and my security deposit. That's enough to make me forget about an inquisitive *Washington Post* reporter and her supper club feature.

Until Wednesday. Wednesday morning, Rachel slams a copy of the *Washington Post* food section on my desk. "Check it out."

I run my finger down the page to a small headline in the bottom right corner, which reads: "Shhhh: Dinner Is Served":

In a city known for classified documents, situation rooms, and top secret reports, there's a new covert operation in town: The Dupont Circle Supper Club. Featuring luscious fare and lively storytelling in a secret Dupont Circle town house, guests are greeted by the young hostess, a buxom twenty-something with a penchant for pork sandwiches and carrot cake . . .

I gasp. "Carrot cake? She mentioned *carrot cake?*"

Rachel grabs the paper from me and has another look. "Yeah, so?"

"I told her not to reveal anything about me."

Rachel throws the paper back on my desk. "You do realize there are other people in town who like carrot cake, right?"

"Not as much as I do." I glance down at the paper again. "And 'buxom'? Really?"

"Have you seen your boobs lately?"

I jab Rachel with my elbow. "She wasn't supposed to reveal anything about me. That was our deal."

"Yeah, well, since the article came out, fifty more people have e-mailed about reserving a spot over Columbus Day. So I wouldn't get too worked up."

"Fifty?"

She nods. "Fifty."

I sigh and rest my chin in my hands, stealing a quick look at Jacob Reaser's business card, which I've taped to the bottom of my computer screen. Rachel follows my gaze and clicks her tongue.

"Have you e-mailed him yet?"

I grab an economics paper Mark left on my desk and pretend to leaf through it. "Not yet."

"It's Wednesday."

"I know it's Wednesday."

She throws her head back and rolls her eyes toward the ceiling. "Stop being lame and e-mail him. I'll stand right here and talk you through it."

"I don't need you to talk me through it."

"Apparently you do."

"Just—go back to your desk. I'll handle it. See? I'm clicking 'compose message' right now. Happy?"

Rachel lets out an exaggerated sigh and disappears from behind my desk, and I start writing Jacob a message:

SUBJECT: (none)
Hey stranger . . .
Great running into you at CVS the other week. Sorry if it
got a little awkward, but that guy you met was my ex-
boyfriend, and the whole situation is still a little raw.

Why am I telling him about Adam? Am I insane? Do I want this guy to run away screaming? No. No Adam. Also, no calling Jacob "stranger." He almost is a stranger. No need to dwell on that. Start over:

SUBJECT: Hey!
Hey there!
Great running into you the other week! I didn't realize
we lived in the same neighborhood! That's so funny!

Seriously, what is wrong with me? There is nothing funny about running into someone at CVS. Also, why am I suddenly ending every sentence with an exclamation point? God, I suck at this.

Maybe I shouldn't have told Rachel to leave me alone. I

haven't sent a flirty e-mail in . . . years, I guess. And I was never any good at it. Why is it so hard to write a friendly e-mail without seeming desperate or crazy? Probably because, by its very nature, an e-mail is a snapshot of yourself, a glimpse into your wit and desirability. I wouldn't send an ugly photo of myself to a potential date, would I? No. I'd find the best one, the one where the lighting was just right and I maybe didn't even look fully like myself, but I nevertheless looked approachable yet sexy, the way I'd *like* to appear rather than how I actually do.

But I have to create this snapshot from scratch, and the more I do to punch up the color, the more I sound like a total lunatic. I should keep it short and sweet. Get in and get out:

SUBJECT: Cinnamon buns
You pick the date and the location, and I'll bring the cinnamon buns. Warning: your mom's reigning title is in danger.
   Hannah

I take a deep breath, click SEND, and launch the message into cyberspace.

No more than ten minutes later, I get a reply from Jacob:

RE: Cinnamon buns
Why don't we meet up tonight? Your place?

Okay, *whoa*. So many things wrong with that plan. Number one, I live in a basement apartment the size of a shoe box, in which the only furniture is an air mattress, a beanbag chair, and some secondhand drawers and shelves. Also, the room still smells like rusty ass. Also, Jacob doesn't realize I don't live in the house upstairs. Number two (or are we up to four?), I was running late this morning and didn't have time to shower, which is gross, period, but also means I look as if I dipped my head in a tub of olive oil. And, on top of all that, it's almost lunchtime, and I don't get out of work until six. How am I supposed to whip up a dozen cinnamon buns in an hour or two? And shower?

No. I will push him off until next week:

RE: Cinnamon buns
   How about next Tuesday? And why don't we say your place?

I click SEND and shuffle through the stack of papers on my desk, in search of another report Mark asked me to read, when my cell phone rings. A 202 area code. A local call. A number I recognize as the one on the card hanging off my computer.

"Hello?"

"So you're playing hard to get, huh?"

My heartbeat quickens. "Who is this?"

"Who do you think? It's Jacob."

"How did you get this number?"

"It's in your e-mail signature."

"Oh. Right." I really need to change that.

"Anyway, I saw the article in the *Post* today. Now that you're an unnamed minicelebrity, you're too good to go on a date with me?"

"No—I didn't mean . . . it's just . . ."

Jacob chuckles into the phone. "Relax. I'm kidding. I totally understand if you already have plans tonight. But I'd love to see you, and I'd rather not wait until Tuesday if I don't have to."

I cup my hand over my mouth and the phone, not wanting everyone else on the eighth floor to bear witness to my social ineptitude. "Well . . . um . . . the thing is . . . this is kind of short notice. For me to bake, I mean."

He laughs. "You know what? I'll give you a free pass on the baking. We can just hang out."

"Right. Okay. But . . . it's still a little . . . complicated."

"Listen, if you're not interested—"

"No!" I shout into the phone. "Sorry, no, it's not that. I am interested. It's that . . . well . . ." *I haven't showered today and look like a greaseball.*

"How about this," he says. "I have to work a little later than normal tonight, so why don't you meet me on the corner of Fifteenth and F at eight o'clock? We'll have one drink, and if you decide I'm totally lame, you can leave, and I'll never call you again. Does that sound reasonable?"

"Um . . . okay . . ."

"Good. See you soon."

Jacob hangs up, and I scurry to get myself organized so that I can leave work early because, apparently, I have a date tonight.

twenty

for the first time in many years, I am early. Well, not early in the sense that I've arrived before eight o'clock, because I haven't. But I've arrived before Jacob, so I am early in a relative sense. I stand on the corner of Fifteenth and F in front of the W Hotel, facing the Treasury Building on the other side of Fifteenth Street. The vast Ionic columns shine brightly up and down the street, regal white pillars set against the darkness of the evening sky. The building towers over the sidewalk, as if an ancient Greek temple fell from the sky and landed smack in the middle of a city block.

I check my watch and cell phone for the twentieth time, and when I look up I see Jacob crossing the street toward me. He wears dark gray pants, a white button-down, and a narrow black tie, with a black messenger bag slung across his body, and his face is again covered with a smattering of stubble. He struts across the street with a cool confidence, gripping the strap of his bag with one hand and offering a nonchalant wave with the other. I wave back, pleased I had time to shower and change after work. Rather than wearing a pair of matronly wool slacks and a shirt with a mustard stain on it, I am now wearing a pair of skinny black pants, flats, and a silky jade tunic. I also managed to whip up and scarf down a small *fines herbes* omelet, since I wasn't sure if tonight's date would involve food and, as always, am perpetually afraid of missing a meal.

"Hey," he says as he reaches my side of the street. "Sorry I'm late. My editor needed me to file one more blog post before I left for the day."

"Don't worry about it. I'm never on time anyway. I just got here."

He points up to the large W sticking out from the hotel behind me. "Shall we?"

"Oh—is this where we're going?"

He laughs. "Yeah, is that okay with you?"

"Of course. I'm surprised, that's all. I assumed we were going to Old Ebbitt Grill or something."

"Nope, I got us a reservation at the POV Lounge." He winks. "I know people in high places."

Whatever that means. I follow Jacob through the lobby, treading along the black-and-white checkered floor until we reach an elevator, in front of which stands an enormous bald man wearing a black suit. He holds a clipboard and wears an earpiece and looks completely out of place.

"Name?" he asks.

"Jacob Reaser. Eight o'clock reservation for the POV Lounge."

The man utters something into his jacket sleeve, as if he is a member of the Secret Service, and then he checks off something on his clipboard and ushers us into the elevator. The doors close, and we ascend to the top floor.

"Talk about taking yourself too seriously . . ."

Jacob furrows his brow. "What do you mean?"

"This place is located in Washington, not New York or LA. What's with the clipboard and the earpiece? Washington isn't that cool."

"What? Washington is totally cool!"

"My boss's briefcase has wheels. My colleagues regularly wear tweed and sweater vests. My landlord talks like a pirate. Washington is not cool."

The elevator doors open, and we walk into the bar's reception area. "You live in Washington, and I think you're pretty cool," he says with a smile. "Very cool, actually."

And I decide there's nothing I can do with that but giggle stupidly and shrug my shoulders and try my hardest not to wet myself.

The POV Lounge pulses with a chic Euro-trash soundtrack, administered by a man in the corner wearing oversize headphones and a very tight T-shirt. The room is dark and sultry, with bright red couches and zebra-striped chairs and a bar that glows like a light box. Jacob and I sit down on one of the red couches in the middle of the room.

"What do you think of the view?" he asks. He points over my shoulder toward the window, and I turn around to see the Washington Monument looming so close I swear I could touch it.

"Wow. I mean, *wow*." I jump up from my seat, and Jacob trails behind me as I walk over to the window, from which I can see the monument, the Treasury Building, and the East Wing of the White House. I can even see the snipers on the White House roof. "This is insane. I could spy on the treasury secretary from here. Or the president."

"Pretty cool, right?" He rests his hand on my shoulder. "What can I get you to drink?"

I turn around quickly to shake his hand off me because touching, I don't know what to do with touching yet. "Um, not sure. Let me look at the cocktail menu."

We head back to our big red couch, and I scan the menu of overpriced cocktails and choose one involving elderflower liqueur. At fifteen dollars a pop, it's a good thing he's buying. Jacob flags the waitress and orders, and soon she returns with thirty dollars' worth of alcohol, which apparently includes fancy glasses and custom-crafted ice cubes, specially shaped and designed for each cocktail on the menu. Jacob's ice is fashioned into large cubes, whereas mine is shaped into small spheres.

"Cheers," Jacob says as he clinks his glass against mine.

"Thanks for the drink," I say as I take a sip. "Do you come here a lot?"

He shakes his head. "Not really. I've been here once, I guess. Maybe twice."

"I figured you for more of a U Street guy. Or Columbia Heights. Not so much the downtown scene."

"What, I don't look like a connoisseur of the power lunch?"

"Not really. No offense."

He smiles, his pearlescent teeth shining in the glow from the bar across the room. "None taken. And you're right. This isn't my usual scene. But it's more private here. We can actually talk, instead of being shoved into a corner and having to shout over a crowd."

Jacob and I plow through the first-date basics: where he went to college and when he graduated (Tufts, three years ahead of me), where he grew up (Ohio), how long he's been in DC (three months) and where he lived before this (Brooklyn then Boston). He worked for the *Village Voice* and then the *Boston Globe*, but after the *Globe* went through some "restructuring," he lost his job. He eventually got an offer from *Reason* magazine and jumped at it, even though he didn't want to move to DC. Apparently these days journalists can't afford to be picky.

I tell Jacob about my job and my interest in food, and though I catch his eyes wandering every now and again and can't always tell if he's actually listening, he keeps finding an excuse to brush up against my leg or touch my arm, so I must not be boring him too much.

Jacob knocks back the rest of his drink and flags the waitress for another round. How he can afford sixty dollars' worth of drinks on a journalist's salary is beyond me.

"So who was that guy standing with you at CVS a few weeks back?" he asks. "Adam or something?"

I take a long, slow gulp of my drink as I nod my head. Do we have to talk about Adam? Really?

"Yep, Adam, that's right," I say as I put my empty glass on the table. "My ex-boyfriend."

Jacob nods knowingly. "Ah, I thought the vibe was a little off. Got it. Was this a recent thing?"

"We broke up two and a half months ago. So yeah, pretty recent."

"Well he's the one who lost out," Jacob says, grabbing his fresh cocktail off the table.

"It's never black and white." I roll the ice cubes around in my glass. "Relationships are complicated."

Jacob follows his drink with his eyes as he brings it to his lips. "Tell me about it . . ."

"Were you dating someone in Boston?"

"Something like that," he says. "It was a long time ago, actually."

"Then you know how messy it can get."

"That I do." He stares into the bottom of his glass. "Anyway, enough talk about ex-boyfriends and girlfriends. Kind of a downer."

"Agreed."

Jacob scans the room and pauses as he lays eyes on someone or something at the bar. I follow his stare, but with all of the up-lighting and down-lighting, I can't make out who or what he is looking at. "Sorry," he says. "I can't get over that bar. The lighting is cool, right?"

"Very."

He lays his hand on my knee. "Want to go outside and check out the view from the roof deck?"

"Sure," I say.

He grabs his drink and his jacket, and we walk outside together and spend the rest of the night chatting and drinking in the glow of the U.S. Treasury.

"No," I say, swatting Jacob's hand away from his back pocket. "I've got this. You paid for the drinks."

"Are you sure?"

An eight-dollar cab ride versus sixty dollars in drinks? "Yeah, I'm sure."

I pay the cabdriver and stumble out of the cab onto Seventeenth Street. Jacob grabs my elbow to keep me from falling to the ground. "Easy, girl."

I'm still a little tipsy from my fancy elderflower drinks, and whereas earlier I would have rebuffed Jacob's advances, I now welcome them, the way he holds me up and presses his fingers into my arm. His fingers are slender but strong, like a rock climber's, and suddenly I want nothing more than to be touched by them, to have them run along my lips and shoulders and the inside of my thigh. I lean into him, rubbing my arm against his as we walk down Church Street.

I slow my step as we reach the front of Blake's house. "This is me."

"Let me walk you to your door," he says, rubbing my shoulder.

Jacob begins walking up Blake's front steps, but I grab his arm before he reaches the top. "Wait."

I contemplate making up some elaborate story as to why we need to enter the house through the basement, but I decide there's no point. I don't know where we're headed, Jacob and I, and I would hate to start a relationship on a lie. And as I've established over the past few months, my lies lack both plausibility and common sense.

"I actually live in the basement," I say.

"The basement? My memory is a little fuzzy these days, but I'm pretty sure I ate dinner upstairs about a week and a half ago."

"You did." Jacob rumples his eyebrows together beneath his side-swept bangs. "I borrowed my landlord's house for the supper club."

"Borrowed?"

"Yes, borrowed." I look into Jacob's eyes, hoping this explanation will be enough, praying he doesn't ask me to what extent my landlord was complicit in this "borrowing."

Jacob shrugs. "Okay. Then let me walk you to the basement."

Jacob wraps his arm around me and walks me down the steps, and when I get to the bottom, he grabs me by the waist and presses me into the door and kisses me. His mouth tastes like whiskey, and he kisses with intensity and desire, his hands running along my hips and up my back. I feel myself begin to sweat beneath my jacket.

"Maybe we should take this inside?" he whispers into my ear.

My initial instinct is to say *yes, yes, yes*, but then I realize taking things inside will involve making out on my Aerobed, the mechanics of which are far beyond anything I can probably handle.

I pull away and bite my bottom lip. "I'm not sure that's the best idea."

"What? It's a great idea," he says, nibbling at my neck. "A genius idea. The best I've had all week."

"Right. Except my apartment isn't exactly . . . set up for that sort of thing."

"You'd rather stay out here?"

"Well, no, but . . ."

"Because that might be kind of kinky. Getting it on in a basement entryway."

It might, if I weren't Hannah Sugarman, the least kinky, most uptight girl in all the land.

"That's not what I was thinking . . . ," I say.

"Listen, what if I took sex off the table? I just want to hang out with you a little longer. No strings attached."

The intensity in Jacob's ice blue eyes renders me weak and helpless, as if Jacob's will has somehow swallowed me whole. And so, despite my misgivings and against my better judgment, I unlock the door and let him inside.

CHAPTER
twenty-one

"Okay, out with it."

Rachel holds out a Tall Starbucks coffee and parks herself on the edge of my desk. I grab the coffee from her hands and take a sip and can already feel the caffeine starting to pump through my veins. After last night, I need it.

"Thanks," I say, smacking my lips.

"Blah, blah, blah. You're welcome. Now tell me about last night. Did you have fun?"

"I did. He took me to POV, and then we hung out at my place for a while."

"Hung out?" Rachel pinches my chin between her thumb and index finger and examines my face. "You look tired. Your under-eye circles are bigger than normal. And . . . is that a *hickey* on your neck?"

I smack her hand away. "*No.* Okay, maybe."

"What are you, twelve?"

I didn't even kiss a boy until I was sixteen, so this question confuses me. "You were getting hickeys when you were twelve?"

"Yeah, so?" Rachel shakes her head and sighs. "Anyway, what happened? Did you have sex with him?"

"No!"

"Thou doth protest too much . . ."

"No, seriously, Rachel. We didn't have sex. Honest."

This is true. Jacob and I did not have sex. What is also true is that the not having sex was more Clintonian in nature than something that might please the pope. I didn't intend for events to go in that direction, but Jacob was a superlative kisser—smooth, passionate, strong—and under the influence of two strong cocktails, I couldn't help but surrender.

"You obviously fooled around at least a little bit." Rachel points to the spot my upturned collar is now covering. "That thing didn't come from nowhere."

"We messed around for a few hours. No big deal."

"On your air mattress?" She laughs as I nod my head. "How'd that work out?"

"Not as bad as I thought. A little wobbly, but nothing I couldn't handle." I take another sip of my coffee and shrug. "I don't know, Rach. I like this guy."

Rachel rests her coffee cup on my desk and rubs her hands together. "How do you feel about a little Facebook stalking?"

"I'm not going to stalk him."

"Come on. A little stalking never hurt anyone."

Under pressure from Rachel, I pull up Jacob's Facebook page. His profile picture is a black-and-white photo of him sitting pensively in front of his laptop as he scratches his chin. Other than that, there isn't much to see. All of his information is private.

"I'm not adding him as a friend," I say. "It's too soon."

"No it's not. You've made out on an air mattress. It's not too soon."

I let out a huff. "Am I to assume you 'friend' each of your many suitors?"

She blushes. "Not all of them. The ones with potential."

"Potential for what? More than two dates?"

"Hey, that's not fair."

I sigh and lean back in my chair. "Sorry."

"That's okay." She fidgets with the chunky gray beads on her necklace. "Actually, I've been meaning to talk to you . . ."

"Do you really think I should add him?"

Rachel stares at me, her expression unexpectedly serious, and then she nods her head and smiles. "Yes. I think you should add him."

I look back at my computer screen and hover my mouse over the words ADD FRIEND on Jacob's profile. "Okay, fine. I will. But I still think this could be a big mistake."

Rachel glances over her shoulder as I click the button. "I should get back to work," she says, her voice soft and a little distant.

I meet her eyes and scrunch my eyebrows together. "You okay?"

She opens her mouth to say something, but as she does, she spots her boss, Ruth, heading down the hallway in our direction.

"Never mind," she says. "I'll talk to you later."

Then she spins around and heads back to her desk without saying anything more.

Five minutes later Mark comes barreling into the office, zigzagging through the labyrinth of bookshelves at high speed with his wheely briefcase. As long as I have worked here, Mark has used this suitcaselike apparatus to haul his scholarly belongings, never once having thought that in addition to the rumpled blazer, tortoiseshell glasses, and occasional bow tie, perhaps a briefcase on wheels would be overkill.

"Good morning, Hannah!" he says as he approaches my desk. Someone's in a good mood this morning.

"Good morning, Mark."

"I had a bit of a breakthrough last night."

"Oh . . . ?" This is never good. The last time Mark had a breakthrough, I needed to read through fifty pages of footnotes in search of an obscure Swedish research paper.

"Yes. I am going to e-mail you some links, and I want to see what you can do with them."

"What project would these links pertain to?"

He yanks off his glasses and massages the bridge of his nose. "My research paper on IMF intervention?"

Mark speaks as if this is obvious—as if an IMF research paper is the only thing he could possibly be referring to.

"Okay. Send me the links and I'll have a look."

"Great."

"Oh, and Mark," I say, stopping him as he wheels his brief-case into his office. "CNBC called and wants to interview you this afternoon. You don't have anything on your calendar, but I wanted to see what you think, since you have a lot on your plate right now."

"What do they want to discuss?"

"Something about the Treasury's currency report that came out today? The producer I spoke with mentioned 'the dollar,' so I thought you might be interested. They'll send a car."

Mark holds his chin in his hand. "Okay, fine, but I haven't read the report, so you'll have to print it out for me, along with any related articles. I won't have time to read it until I'm heading to the studio. What time is the interview?"

"They're aiming for a live shot at three-thirty."

"All right, set it up," he says. "Good thing I wore a clean tie today."

Before he turns around, I take a look at his tie. It's navy with a bright green pattern that, upon further inspection, involves a series of economic equations using the Greek letters Σ and Π and Δ.

The man is nothing if not consistent.

A half hour before the car is supposed to come for Mark, I print out the currency report, along with articles from the *Wall Street Journal*, *Washington Post*, *New York Times*, and *Financial Times*. I even print out a Google-translated version of a piece in the Frankfurter *Allgemeine Zeitung* to add a little international perspective. I'm still using the temporary computer Sean gave me two weeks ago, though he assures me I'll have my computer back and in working form by Monday. I'm not holding my breath.

The printer next to my desk whines like a wounded cat, cranking out page after page of text, reminding me that I sit in the absolute armpit of the Economic Policy department. While I wait for the documents to finish printing, I check my e-mail no fewer than six times to see if Jacob has accepted my friend request on Facebook. He hasn't.

Instead of continuing to obsess over Jacob and the status of our social networking relationship, I decide to click on my Google Reader to see if any of my favorite food blogs have updated over the past two hours.

Jackpot.

I find ten new recipes I want to try and print all of them out: pistachio cake, meatball lasagna, salted caramel popcorn, caramel mousse, deep-fried potato croquettes, and on and on. If I am honest with myself, there is no way I will end up making all of these dishes, but I keep printing anyway. At the very least, the recipes will provide inspiration for our next supper club.

I grab my dedicated recipe folder off my desk and pull out a fresh folder for Mark from the supply cupboard. I hustle over to the printer and stick the recipes in my folder and the Treasury articles in Mark's, and when I return to my desk I place the folders next to my computer and see Jacob still hasn't accepted my friend request. Which shouldn't bother me, because I vowed not to let myself get swept away by this. But it does bother me. And that, in turn, bothers me more.

To put Jacob and his twinkly blue eyes out of my mind, I turn to the *Food & Wine* Web site to peruse the latest recipes. But before I manage to read even one entry, Mark comes flying out of his office, carrying his wheely briefcase by the handle.

"The CNBC car is here! Where is the currency report?"

"Oh!" I jump up from my desk. "I—they're early."

"Yes, Hannah, I know they're early!"

"I was just—"

"Where is the report?"

"It's—"

"The *report*, Hannah!"

"Here!" I throw Mark's folder at him, and he shoves it into his briefcase, extends the briefcase handle in one swift motion, drops the wheels to the floor, and flies down the hall.

My chest heaves as I grip the edge of my desk and try to catch my breath. I can feel my heart pounding in my chest, racing wildly in the wake of Mark's panicky fit, and I fear I am moments away from undergoing a major cardiac episode—all of which raises the question, how is this my life?

Between reading about food for half an hour and burning a thousand calories out of sheer stress, I'm starving. Mark won't be on air for another forty minutes, so I grab my wallet and head to Firehook Bakery for a quick snack before the interview, figuring I'll be ten minutes, tops.

At least that's what I think before I see the line. A hungry and impatient queue snakes around the store, and there is one borderline comatose woman working behind the counter. I rock back and forth on my kitten heels, debating whether or not I should forget it and go back to the office.

Then I see the towering stack of two-inch-thick fudge brownies sitting behind the glass pastry case, and I'm a goner. I'll wait in this line as long as it takes. And I do.

When I get back to the office, it's already three-fifteen—fifteen minutes until Mark appears on CNBC. I return to my desk, licking the fudgy crumbs off my fingers, and find the red light on my phone flashing furiously. My voice mail.

As I pick up my phone to listen to my messages, I notice I also have five missed calls and two voice mails on my cell phone, which I left on my desk while I popped down to Firehook.

"You have three new messages," the automated voice on my office phone tells me. Five voice mails on two different phones? Weird.

The first message on my office voice mail is from Mark. "Hannah, I am in the car reading through this folder you left for me, and none of this is what I asked for. Salted caramel popcorn? *Lasagna*?? Where is the information I asked for? Please call me back right away."

Uh-oh.

As I press on to the next message, I spot a manila folder on my desk. I open it. The Treasury report. The *Wall Street Journal*. The Frankfurter *Allgemeine Zeitung*. It's all right here. I gave him the wrong folder. The one with my recipes. The one that has nothing whatsoever to do with the work I'm being paid to do.

The second message is also from Mark. His tone is sharper this time. "Hannah, it's Mark again. I also left you a message on your cell phone, but for some inexplicable reason you still have not called me back. I'm at the studio now. I need the language in that report. Call me immediately!"

Message three. Also Mark. "Hannah! Where the hell are you? I'm live in twenty minutes! This is unacceptable! CALL ME IMMEDIATELY!"

I call my cell phone voice mail. More of the same. In one message I swear I can hear steam pumping out his ears. The gist: Hannah, you fuckup, where the fuck are you and why the fuck am I looking at a recipe for pistachio cake?

I'm screwed.

I look at my watch: 3:23. I still have seven minutes until Mark is live on the air. I pick up the phone and call Mark. Straight to voice mail. Shit.

I rummage through the papers on my desk until I find the number for the CNBC producer I talked to earlier. Joanne Gerber. I call. Straight to voice mail for her, too. Crap! Crap, crap, crap!

I scroll through my in-box and find our e-mail exchange from earlier. Mark doesn't have a BlackBerry, but a producer for CNBC would. Maybe she could even print these documents for him. Or tell him to call me.

I shoot off a quick e-mail:

> Joanne—could you print these documents out for Mark Henderson? Had a problem with our printer.

And then I wait. And wait. And wait. Until it is 3:29, and I realize there's no point in waiting anymore.

I am officially 1,000 percent screwed.

twenty-two

Just as the clock is about to strike three-thirty, I run up the emergency staircase to the tenth floor, taking two steps at a time and wheezing like a ninety-year-old invalid by the time I reach the top. Dorothy, NIRD's receptionist, has a small television on her desk that carries cable. I have to watch the interview. I have to see what happens.

"Dorothy!" I pant, barely able to catch my breath. "I need . . . to watch . . . Mark . . . on . . . C . . . NBC."

My fitness is an embarrassment to mobile people everywhere.

"Sweetie, calm down," Dorothy says, apparently troubled by my profuse sweating and wheezing. "You wanna watch Mark on TV?"

"Yes." I exhale loudly. "Please."

She flips through the channels with her small remote until she lands on CNBC, where I see Mark sitting in front of a shot of the Capitol. Wisps of his brownish orange hair jut from either side of his head, and his wild eyebrows sit in a position of consternation on his forehead. His glasses are crooked.

The monitor moves to a four-way split screen. In one box sits another analyst in front of a set of bookcases, whose graphic informs me he works for a group called Economics Anomalous. In another box, a gray-haired male reporter paces on the trading floor of the New York Stock Exchange. And in the third box, a brunette named Erica Eckels—who looks as if she could moonlight at Hooters—sits behind an anchor desk. Her hot-pink top scoops dangerously close to her nipples, displaying breasts that are pushed together like two large grapefruits. She leans seductively over the news desk.

"Why can't the administration grow a pair and call China a currency manipulator?" she says. "Are you actually telling me you think China *isn't* manipulating its currency?"

"Now wait a second," Mark says, visibly flustered. "What I *said* was we're in a difficult position right now where we need China to buy our debt. And calling the Chinese currency manipulators might make the administration seem pushy."

"I'm sorry, what did you just call the administration?" She looks wide-eyed at the camera.

"*Pushy*," Mark says. "The administration might seem pushy."

"Oh, okay, for a second there I thought you said something else." She smirks. "But doesn't the administration risk seeming like a bunch of pushovers? That's the sense I got in reading the report."

"Well, certainly the language in the report isn't . . . as . . . strong as perhaps it could have been . . ." Mark trails off.

Crap. The report. The report that is sitting on my desk. The report that Mark hasn't read because I handed him a pile of recipes instead.

"Let me jump in here for a second, Erica," says the reporter on the floor of the stock exchange. "Mark, how would you say the report compares with past reports? How is this report different from anything the administration has said before? Is there anything new here?"

"It . . . depends what you mean by different . . ."

I can tell Mark is bumbling his way through this. I wonder if other people can tell, too.

"Are we even talking about the same report?" asks the Economics Anomalous analyst. "The language in this report is *much* harsher than past years. Much more frank."

"And you disagree, Mark?" Erica asks, her lips pursed in a shiny pout.

Mark blinks wildly as he stares into the camera. "Well, no, not entirely." He pauses. "But the bigger issue here is what impact all of this will have on the value of the dollar."

"Interesting," Erica says, leaning even farther over the desk, her breasts nearly toppling out of her shirt. "Explain."

This is Mark's way of fudging it—shifting the conversation to a topic he can control, one that relates to the subject at hand but doesn't require his intimate knowledge of a report he hasn't read. A report I failed to give him.

He and the three other talking heads jockey back and forth on the dollar, exchanging barbs and talking over one another so loudly it sounds like a bar brawl. I am impressed with how skillfully Mark is able to navigate his way through the interview. I guess I shouldn't be surprised. He spent fourteen years on the Fed's Board of Governors and writes about all of this for a living.

After a few more minutes of verbal sparring, the interview draws to a close. Erica Eckels tosses her hair over her shoulder. "So, Mark, final word."

Mark bumbles his way through a statement about China and the dollar, a statement I do not fully understand and that, apparently, his host doesn't either.

"I don't know, it's like all four of us read a different report today," Erica says. "But anyway, thanks for being with us. That's Mark Henderson, of the Institute for Research and Discourse, and Eric Stall, of Economics Anomalous."

The camera cuts away from the other boxes and focuses in on Erica, who moves on to another story. The interview is over.

Which means I have about twenty minutes until Mark rips me to pieces.

I hear Mark hurrying down the hall before I see him, the wheels on his briefcase screeching in an agitated fury as he moves toward his office. Toward my desk. Toward me.

When I finally see him approaching my desk, the menacing

look on his face sends a sharp pang to my gut. He looks like a man capable of eating puppies or killing babies. I have never seen him like this. Not even when the Federal Reserve bailed out AIG.

As soon as he reaches my desk, he throws the folder on my desk with a loud *thwack!*

"What in god's name is all this?" he shouts. "Was this some sort of joke?"

"Mark, I'm so sorry."

"Where were you when I tried to call? Where were you for thirty minutes?" His face swells until it resembles a big, fat tomato.

"I must have been . . . in line at Firehook . . ."

"For *half an hour?*" he roars. "Hannah, this is unacceptable. Absolutely unacceptable."

"I'm so, so sorry. I promise it will never happen again."

"No, you're right, it won't," he says. "I don't have time today, but tomorrow we need to have a long talk in my office. We need to talk about your future in this organization."

My future? "Uh . . . okay. I'd be happy to talk."

"I'm sure you would," he says. "You always are. In the meantime, can I count on you to finish tweaking my PowerPoint slides? Can't I at least count on you for *something?*"

"Of course," I say, my voice thin and raspy.

Mark storms into his office and slams the door, a sound that echoes down the corridors of the entire eighth floor.

Great. Now Mark is going to fire me.

twenty-three

i return home after a day of record-breaking crappiness at the office to a refrigerator whose interior mocks me. Nothing but half an onion and a nearly empty carton of milk. Excellent.

Over a dinner of Honey Bunches of Oats, I make a list of the Pros and Cons of getting fired:

> Pros: Don't have to work at NIRD anymore (no Mark, no Millie, no Susan); can focus on supper club; can (possibly) move closer to goal of running my own catering company
>
> Cons: Won't be able to pay rent; won't be able to pay bills; might not be able to find new job or start company; will have to tell future employers I was fired; will have to tell my parents I was fired; parents will go postal

I'm no mathematician, but it strikes me that, at this point, the cons significantly outweigh the pros.

My phone rings, and—speak of the devil—it's my parents. But this time it's a domestic number. I do the math and realize they flew back last night. I've been so caught up in my own drama I forgot they were coming home.

"Welcome home," I say, trying to shake myself out of my funk. "How does it feel to be back in the Motherland?"

My mom lets out a labored sigh. "Your father and I are beyond jet-lagged. You'd think we'd get better at this after all these years, but we seem to get worse and worse. Old age, I suppose."

"You're not old," I say. "You're not even sixty."

"We're not as nimble as we used to be, that's for sure." She covers the receiver with her hand and mumbles something to my dad about not putting her black cardigan in the dryer because *oh my god, how many times does she have to tell him?*

"Anyway," she says, talking to me again, "how are things in the nation's capital? How are things at work?"

"Um . . . well . . ." I pause. Might as well temper expectations while I still can. "Not that great, actually."

"Oh?"

"I don't want to get you all worked up, and I know this probably isn't the best time to talk about this, but my job . . ." I trail off. I can't tell them about my imminent firing. Not yet. "I don't think this job is a good fit for me."

"How do you mean?" she asks, trying to sound gentle and motherly but sounding typically tense and serious and concerned. I imagine her anxiously tugging at her fluffy auburn bob, twirling a frizzled strand around her index finger.

"I've worked at IRD for three years, and I still don't fit in. I'm not sure I'm cut out for think tank work. I feel as if I'm constantly faking it."

"Listen. On some level a job is a job. And in this economy, you should be thanking your lucky stars you have a job at all."

"I know. I am thankful. But I also feel so . . . stuck. Like I'm trapped in a job that has nothing to do with anything I care about and isn't leading anywhere either."

"Oh, Hannah." She sighs. I hear her cover the phone with her hand and whisper to my father: "She's having another one of her breakdowns . . ."

"Tell her to go for a walk," I hear my father say.

"She needs more than a walk . . ."

"I can hear you, Mom," I say. "I can hear both of you."

"Let's not talk about this now, okay?" she says, redirecting her voice back into the phone. "We just got back from three months in England, and I haven't talked to my baby in a while. I don't want to fight. Let's talk about this when we see you next weekend."

I fumble with my phone. "Next weekend?"

"Your father and I were thinking of making a trip down to DC. We haven't seen you in so long, and we figured you'd have Monday off."

Visiting next weekend? No. No! This is a terrible idea. Next weekend is Columbus Day weekend—the weekend in which Rachel and I will hold two more installments of the supper club.

"I . . . don't think next weekend is going to work."

Her voice tenses up. "Oh?"

"We . . . some friends and I rented a cabin up in the Blue Ridge Mountains. I'll be out of town."

"Can't you drop out?"

"I don't think so. We made the plans a while ago." I fiddle with the tip of my ponytail. "Let me look into it, and I'll get back to you."

"Please do. In the meantime, maybe I can talk to Mark about carving out a better role for you at work."

"No! Mom, please—don't call Mark. I'll handle it. It's fine."

"Okay, if you say so," she says, using the singsong voice she assumes when she doesn't believe me. "Anyway, if you want to advance and move on, you should send out those grad school and fellowship applications ASAP. I know your father talked to you about enrolling in a GRE course. Have you signed up for one yet?"

"No."

"Don't you think you should?"

"Not really?"

"Well I think it would be a very good idea."

And this, more or less, is how the rest of our conversation goes. Ten more minutes of planning my future, or rather, my future according to my parents. I hang up feeling more confused and conflicted than ever. They have always been this way—trying to fit me, the square peg, into a very round, very narrow hole—and because I've spent most of my life trusting their instincts more than my own, I've tried to jam myself into that hole, too.

My choice in musical instrument is a perfect example. In middle school, I wanted nothing more than to play the flute. It was shiny, it was pretty, and it sounded like a tweeting bird, and, by god, I wanted to play it. But, according to my mother, flute-playing girls were a dime a dozen. Playing the flute would *not* get me into Harvard. So what did I end up playing? The fucking bassoon. And did the bassoon end up getting me into Harvard? No. Why? Because I didn't give a crap about that instrument because deep down it was never what I wanted to play.

That isn't to say my parents somehow ruined my life. Thanks to them, my life so far has been categorically easy, my every step mapped out, from Little League to Cornell. I learned French and Hebrew, traveled around the globe, landed a job at one of the top think tanks in the country. I learned to write a good research paper and successfully answer an essay question.

What I didn't learn, however, is how to forge my own path. And now I have to wonder: am I really ready to throw myself into the great unknown? Am I ready to struggle? Am I ready to fail?

No. I don't think I am. Not yet, at least. I don't want to get a PhD, but I also can't bring myself to close that door entirely. Not until I explore all of my options. I flip open my laptop and stare at the screen, which is open to The Dupont Circle Supper Club Web site. Then I type "GRE Registration" into Google, click on the link, and sign up for the November 7 exam.

Sometime later in the evening, I awake with my face pressed against my keyboard to the sound of someone banging at my door.

I snap upright and smooth my hair into place, running my fingers along my cheeks, which bear the imprint of my computer keys. With every passing day, I take the art of looking terrible to new and unexplored heights.

"Coming!" I shout, dusting the flakes of Honey Bunches of Oats off my T-shirt.

I pull open the door, in all likelihood resembling an alien shar-pei, and find Blake standing in my entryway with his hands tucked into his jean pockets.

"Hi . . . ," he says, eyeing the right side of my face. "Sorry—I was coming down to check on the dehumidifier. Did I . . . wake you?"

"No. Yeah. Kind of." I touch the side of my face. "I fell asleep on my computer. Sorry."

Blake swats away the gnats and mosquitoes, both of which I'm convinced are breeding in my entryway. "I can come back later, if that would be better."

"No, no—now is fine. Come on in."

I let Blake inside, and he inspects the dehumidifier and the overall state of my apartment, giving particular attention to the areas surrounding the front and back doors. I pretend not to notice his facial expressions when he observes the disgraceful trifecta of my air mattress, beanbag chair, and pile of rumpled clothes.

"Looks like you're back in business," he says. "And I finally— officially—fixed the drainage problem, so the apartment shouldn't flood again."

"Cool."

Blake tucks his hands back into his jean pockets and leans back on his heels. "So . . . what did you end up doing with all those groceries? I noticed my freezer was disappointingly empty when I got back from Tampa."

Thank god.

"I . . . braised some of the pork belly. Sautéed the broccoli rabe. Nothing special."

Blake raises his eyebrows. "Nothing special? I don't think I'd know how to cook pork belly if you paid me."

"It's not hard. You could handle it."

"No, seriously. I don't even know what the word *braise* means."

"It means cooking something in liquid. Super easy."

He smiles. "You're quite the cook, huh?"

I shrug. "I'd pretty much cook constantly if I could."

"I'm telling you—you should start an ice cream business. Or a pork belly business. Whatever floats your boat."

I force a smile. "I'd love to. Maybe someday."

Blake rubs his chin and nods his head, scrunching his lips together as he studies my face. "In that case," he says, tapping his finger against his bottom lip, "I have a proposition for you."

I arch an eyebrow. "Okay . . ."

Blake surveys my apartment, and his eyes land on my Aerobed. "Want to come up to my place to talk about this? Not that there's anything wrong with your place, but . . ."

"You have more furniture than an Aerobed and a beanbag chair?"

He grins. "Exactly."

I follow Blake up to his house and pull up a seat along his breakfast bar. He grabs a bottle of Vouvray from his refrigerator and points it in my direction.

"Wine?"

I stare at the bottle and consider his offer, which seems a little weird and forward but also very appealing after my day from hell.

"Sure," I say. If I'm not going to drink after a day like today, why drink at all?

Blake grabs two wineglasses and fills them both halfway, pushing one glass across the table toward me. I take a long sip of wine and let the chilled, fruity Vouvray trickle down the back of my throat.

"So," he says. "My proposition. I'm having a huge Halloween party on the thirty-first. How would you feel about catering it?"

I spit the wine back in my glass. "Sorry?"

"When it comes to food . . . let's just say I'm much better at the eating part than the cooking part. But I want this party to be awesome. I could use a helping hand from someone who knows her way around a kitchen." He sips his wine. "Not that you know your way around *my* kitchen, but I'm sure you'll figure it out."

Right. Because why would I know my way around his kitchen? That wouldn't make any sense at all. The bigger problem, of course, is that I'd planned an entire Halloween menu for The Dupont Circle Supper Club and hoped he'd be out of town that weekend.

I grab my wineglass and take another swig. "Won't you be in Tampa that weekend?"

He shakes his head. "Nope. I'm taking the weekend off."

"Any particular reason . . . ?"

He widens his eyes, bewildered by my ignorance. "Uh, because it's *Halloween*."

"I didn't realize Halloween was a holiday requiring devout observance."

"It is if you're me. My costume parties are legendary."

"Oh, yeah?"

He flashes a geeky smile. "Like, major. Get ready for it."

Great. I can only imagine the levels of geekdom this party will achieve.

"And anyway," he says, "it's the weekend before the ANC election, so I should be in town. The party will build momentum leading into the election."

"How many people are we talking? For the party, I mean."

Blake waves his hand back and forth. "About fifty, maybe?"

Fifty? *Fifty?* I've never cooked for fifty before. Holy crap. On the other hand . . .

"I assume there would be some sort of compensation involved," I say, fiddling with the stem of my wineglass.

"Oh—sure." Blake's smile fades, and he bites his bottom lip. "Although . . . I need to check on whether or not that's legal."

"Why wouldn't it be legal?"

"Well, usually to operate as a caterer you need to obtain a catering license. But I think there's an exception if you're cooking at the home of the person who's paying you." He pauses. "Let me check it out. I'm sure it'll be fine."

"You could always pay me under the table. No one would have to know."

He chuckles. "Ha, right. Nice one, Sugarman. That'll do wonders for my campaign."

I laugh nervously as I grab the wine bottle and refill my glass. "It's just a volunteer position, right? I mean, it's not like you're running for mayor."

"Just because the commission doesn't have legislative authority doesn't mean the members don't have to follow the law. We represent the neighborhood. Plus, if I ever run for higher office, I need a clean record. Hiring an illegal cleaning lady, paying an unlicensed caterer—I don't need anything like that hanging over my head."

I gulp down my entire glass of wine. "You want to run for higher office?"

Blake's cheeks flush, and he waves me off. "That's a conversation for another time." He glances down at his watch. "Anyway, I should get to bed soon. Congressman Holmes has back-to-back live shots on MSNBC and CNN tomorrow morning, and then he's meeting with a reporter from the *New York Times*, before heading into a markup of the immigration bill." He smiles. "And that only takes us to ten A.M."

I let out a drawn-out sigh. "I have a big day ahead of me, too."

The difference being, my big day will involve me getting fired.

"Remind me what you do again? You're a think tank person, right?"

I nod. "Institute for Research and Discourse."

"Wow, don't sound *too* excited. You say it like working there is some sort of punishment."

"Some days I'm not so sure it isn't."

He slaps his hands against the counter. "Well then maybe my party can be your launching pad to a new career."

I let out a huff as I play with the base of my wineglass. "Wouldn't that be nice . . ."

"Again with the lack of enthusiasm. From what you said, I thought you'd love to cook for a living."

"I would. My parents . . . not so much."

"What, they aren't fans of your cooking?"

"They're not fans of cooking as a career." I look up at Blake, whose eyebrows are scrunched into a knot on his forehead. I shrug. "Cooking isn't a serious profession."

"That's not true," he says. "Any profession is serious if the person doing the job takes it seriously. Who cares what they think?"

"They're my parents. There's a lot of history there." I push my glass back and forth across his granite counter, holding it by the base. "What, you don't care what your parents think?"

"Well, my dad is dead . . ."

"Oh. I didn't realize."

"But, yes, of course I care what my mom thinks, and what my dad thought when he was alive. That doesn't mean I let them dictate my entire career path. There's a fine line between respecting your parents and letting them control your life."

"What about the line between asserting your independence and pissing off your parents for all eternity?"

Blake laughs and looks down at the counter, his hands gripping the edge of the granite countertop. When he looks up, a broad smile still painted across his face, I am struck by the color of his eyes. They are a pure, deep gray—not quite blue, not quite green, with a dark gray rim around the iris.

"Listen, at some point, you've got to fish or cut bait, right? That's what growing up is all about."

Another nautical reference. At some point I need to address this.

"I guess." I let out a heavy sigh. "No one told me growing up would be such a huge pain in the ass."

Blake smirks. "Deciding between a job at a prestigious think tank and a catering career—yeah, life is hard."

"Oh, shut up, Long John Silver."

I slap my hand over my mouth and feel the blood rush to my face because, *oh my god*, I just told my landlord—whose house I am using for an underground supper club—to *shut up, Long John Silver*. What is wrong with me?

"Sorry," I say, my hand still over my mouth. "I didn't mean that."

Blake chuckles, his eyes wide. "Long John Silver? Where'd that come from?"

"I . . . it's something my friend and I say sometimes. Never mind."

"What, is that like cockney rhyming slang or something?" He swings his arms back and forth as if he is marching in place. "'That bloke's a Long John Silver.'"

I start shaking with laughter at Blake's absurd English accent and even more absurd pantomime. "I don't even think that's how rhyming slang works," I say. I glance up at the clock on his oven. "Anyway, don't you need to get to bed?"

He looks at his watch. "Yeah, I think I said that twenty minutes ago. But you somehow managed to derail me with your cute smile and first world problems." He blushes. "I take that back. Your smile isn't *that* cute."

I purse my lips and arch one eyebrow high while furrowing the other.

"Now that's a much better look," he says, grinning.

Blake walks me to the front door, and when I don't hear the door close behind me by the time I reach the bottom of his steps, I turn around and see him standing in his doorway.

"Don't worry," he says. "You'll figure it out. Your career, I mean."

"I guess."

He shrugs. "It'll happen. You'll do what you have to do to maintain your sanity."

Somehow those few words make me feel better—not because my future is any clearer or because Blake is suggesting my sanity is still intact (although I do appreciate that), but because for once someone has faith in my ability to chart my own path. What's surprising is not that I feel better, but that the person who made me feel this way isn't my best friend or my parents or anyone I've known for more than two months. It's my landlord, a man to whom I've been lying for nearly a month and whose political career I could, with just one misstep, easily ruin.

twenty-four

the next day I arrive at the office a good forty-five minutes before Mark does. This is a strategic move on my part, though
the specifics of my strategy elude me. I suppose I want enough
time to collect my thoughts and organize my desk before Mark
fires me. As if, somehow, that will soften the blow.

I power up my computer, and the first e-mail I see is one from
my mother, with the worlds "Visiting DC!" in the subject line. I
cannot see how this e-mail will contain anything but bad news:

> Any word on canceling your trip to the mountains? Your
> father and I would LOVE to see you next weekend. If you
> cannot change your plans, we'll understand, but please
> give us some alternate dates. Otherwise it will be Thanks-
> giving before we see you! Speaking of which, we really
> need to discuss our Thanksgiving plans. Aunt Elena is
> still keen on the reenactment idea, but there is no way in
> hell that's happening.
>
> Hugs and Kisses,
> Mom
> p.s. How is the GRE prep going??

I don't know what deluded me into thinking a lame excuse about a
trip to the Blue Ridge Mountains would stave off my mother. It's as
if, deep down, she knows I'm lying, and by gently applying pressure

through a series of innocent and inquisitive calls and e-mails, she will ultimately break me. That's how she operates. In high school, when Alex Greenberg threw a wild, unsupervised party and I lied and told her Alex's parents were there the whole time, she casually kept asking and asking and asking about it. Had Dr. Greenberg's ankle healed? Did Mrs. Greenberg mention whether or not she'd be attending the parents' reception next week? How was their trip to Bermuda? Finally, I caved under the stress and started crying and told her everything. As my mother, she knew keeping secrets was my weakness, and she knew just how to play me.

But she won't play me this time. I'm not going to tell her about The Dupont Circle Supper Club, and I'm not going to cancel. Rachel and I have already booked two seatings for The Dupont Circle Supper Club next weekend, and people continue to flood our in-box with more requests. We're running what is arguably the most popular hot spot in town, and my parents can't know anything about that. Another thing they can't know anything about? The termination of my employment at NIRD, an event that will take place in approximately thirty minutes.

Correction: five minutes. I already hear the wheels of Mark's briefcase squealing down the corridor. Great.

My hands start shaking. I need more time to . . . what? Prepare? What could I possibly say to change his mind? Off the top of my head, I can think of at least ten ways I could become a better employee. The question is whether I want to do any of those things. The answer is no.

Instead of stopping at my desk like he normally does, Mark breezes past me toward his office. "Give me five minutes," he says without looking at me. "Then let's talk." He walks through his door and slams a book on his desk.

It appears my hopes for leniency were in vain.

I spend five minutes nervously stacking and restacking the piles of paper on my desk. I shoot a quick e-mail to my parents telling them I cannot get out of my trip next weekend and need to take a closer look at my calendar before I suggest any alternate dates. I swallow three Tums. Then I arise from my chair, smooth my brown woolen skirt, and creep toward Mark's office. Mark looks up from his copy of the *Financial Times* as I knock on his door. He folds the paper into a crinkled mass and dumps it on the floor.

"Come in," he says. "Close the door. Sit down."

Three explicit commands in a row. This spells trouble. Mark is never this straightforward.

I wade through the mounds of old newspapers on Mark's floor and sit on the only chair in his office not covered by piles of papers and stacks of economic journals. The chair is awkwardly located directly behind his computer monitor and positioned so that, when seated, I cannot see his face. All I can see is the gray plastic back of his computer screen, with all its vents and screws. I feel like I'm being fired by Darth Vader.

"I'm sure you've heard the latest on my CNBC interview," Mark says from behind his computer screen.

There's a *latest*? "No," I say. "What happened?"

"The whole interview is making the rounds on YouTube." Beneath the computer screen, I see his hand grab for the ecru handkerchief sticking out of his blazer pocket. "Honestly, Hannah, the whole situation is very embarrassing."

"I'm—I'm sure it has nothing to do with you. People probably want to gawk at Erica Eckels's breasts."

At the word *breasts*, Mark's goes silent for an uncomfortable period of time. Part of me wonders if he is embarrassed because he has never actually seen a female breast, but then I remember he wears a wedding ring and has two grown daughters, a fact that astonishes me daily. I can't keep a boyfriend for much more than a year, and yet someone voluntarily made babies with Mark Henderson. The universe makes no sense at all.

"Yes, well, maybe that is the reason, but nevertheless, I am still *quite* displeased with how the interview went."

"I know, and I promise nothing like that will ever happen in the future."

Mark shifts in his chair. "Then you would agree that your performance lately has been lacking?"

"Yes," I say, craning my neck to catch a glimpse of Mark. He does the same, but in the opposite direction, so that I am left talking to the back of his chair.

"Then the question is what we should do about this. What is your future at IRD? Do you *have* a future at IRD?" He pauses. I pick at the little balls of fuzz on my seat cushion and wait for him to continue. I wonder what he is looking at while he speaks to me. I picture him staring at big, fat currency symbols on his computer screen—dollars and pounds and wons and rupees.

"Well?" he says.

"Sorry?" Was there a question in there I was supposed to answer?

"What is your future at IRD?" Mark repeats. "Perhaps I should rephrase the question: do you *want* a future at IRD?"

"Um, I guess?"

My answer is neither true nor is it the first thing that comes to my mind. But I'm not quite sure how to tell my boss that, no, I don't want a future here; I just want an income stream until I come up with a better plan. So, instead, I give the most equivocal answer I can muster. *I guess* isn't yes and it isn't no; it's, *Does it really even matter?*

"Okay then," Mark says. "Since you *do* want a future here, let's establish some ground rules. I have always said one must be challenged to be satisfied with one's work. And, given how talented I know you are, your behavior lately indicates I am not challenging you enough. So I will involve you more in the work I am doing, in particular having you take on more sophisticated research."

Mark clears his throat. My stomach contracts violently. As it stands, I can barely maintain an interest level in the subjects Mark has assigned me. Increasing the complexity will not help.

"I also believe strongly in incentives," Mark continues, "and so for my upcoming book, I am putting together an outline and would like you to draft a few chapters on the history of Federal Reserve intervention. And assuming you've done an adequate job, I will list you as a coauthor on the book. How does that sound?"

In a word: horrendous. I do not know what changed in the course of our conversation, but I entered this room terrified Mark might fire me, and now I am devastated he hasn't. The thought of drafting full chapters on the Federal Reserve makes me want to set my hair on fire. I have no idea how this conversation spun so wildly out of control, to a place where getting fired is the preferable option. All I can do is stare at the back of Mark's monitor, thankful he cannot see the dumbstruck expression planted on my face.

"Hannah?" Mark says from behind his computer screen.

"Sorry, um, it's just . . . I'm having trouble seeing you from where I'm sitting," I say, trying to buy myself time. I have no idea how to respond; I have been preoccupied with not letting the words *horrendous* and *awful* and *what the hell* fly out of my mouth.

I scoot my chair a few feet to the left. Mark's floor is covered with old newspapers, photocopies of journal articles, and random bits of clothing, and so my chair now tilts backward, the front left leg bolstered by a pair of maroon argyle socks and what may or may not be an old pair of boxers.

"What do you think? Coauthoring a book is quite a big deal. I thought you'd be pleased."

"I'm honored, Mark. Absolutely. And on such a substantial topic." I gesture wildly with my hands as I talk, hoping Mark will mistake my animation for genuine enthusiasm. "The Federal Reserve—wow."

On the word *wow*, I throw my hands forward and lean back in my lopsided chair—a massive misjudgment that throws off my balance and sends me flying backward onto the floor. My head hits a pile of newspapers as my legs thrash above me in the air. I deeply regret my decision to wear a skirt today.

"Oh, dear," Mark says as he rushes to my side of his desk. He approaches my chair and bends down to lift me up but jerks his head away when he realizes he is looking right at my crotch.

He fumbles around like a blind person, feeling for my hands and in the process grazing my right breast, at which point he lets out a high-pitched yelp.

"What is going *on* in here?"

From my current location, I cannot see anything but the back of Mark's head and the ceiling, but the voice sounds like Susan's.

"Could someone please help me up?" I say as I flail on the floor.

Susan's face appears above me, the whites of her eyes widening as she watches me squirm like an overturned beetle. She pushes Mark out of the way and extends her arm, and I grab on as she lifts me to my feet. I smooth my skirt and brush my hair off my face. Mark faces the wall, barefoot and unable to look at me.

"Thank you," I say to Susan.

"You're welcome," she says, eyeing Mark and me suspiciously. Her expression reminds me of the one my mother had the time she caught Scott Kraut kissing me on my living room couch senior year of high school. Scott and I were going over lines for the school play, but my mom assumed we were up to the usual teenage mischief and gave me a look similar to the one Susan is giving now: arms crossed, lips pursed, an eyebrow raised. Which raises the question: does she think Mark and I were . . . ? Oh, *gross*.

"I lost my balance," I say, trying to explain. "My chair was resting on a pair of socks."

"A pair of *socks*?" Susan raises one of her thin, black eyebrows and glances at Mark's bare feet, then drags her eyes across Mark's floor until she reaches the boxerlike article of clothing. "Is that *appropriate*?"

Great, now she thinks I was undressing him. I might throw up.

"Never mind," I say. "Mark, thank you for the opportunity with the book. I look forward to working on it."

I rush back to my desk, wondering how this day has already managed to surpass my most horrific expectation, and it's only eight-thirty.

———————

By lunchtime, I am still in a daze, as if I've fallen down the rabbit hole into an alternate reality. On one side, I was a research assistant moments away from being fired, and on the other I am a research assistant with even more responsibility and less free time, whose boss has seen her crotch.

I cannot face Mark or Susan or anyone else in the lunchroom and decide to buy a sandwich and eat at my desk. In my current state, I am not fit for human interaction.

When I am about halfway through my gyro, my cell phone rings. I lick the tzatziki off my fingers and grab my phone, when I see the caller in question is Jacob. We haven't spoken since our rendezvous two days ago.

"How's my favorite think tanker?" he says.

I blot a trickle of gyro juice off my chin. "I've been better."

"Why, what's up?"

"Long story. Office drama."

"Ah. Fun times." He snickers. "Don't worry. Whatever it is, it'll blow over in a day or two."

Considering I've been tasked with researching the history of Federal Reserve intervention, I somehow doubt this is true. "Here's hoping," I say.

"So . . . I was wondering . . . what are you up to next weekend?"

"Over Columbus Day?"

"Is that next weekend?" He pauses. "Then, yeah. Over Columbus Day."

Given the near nonexistence of my social life, I cannot understand why everyone wants to spend time with me over the one weekend where I have other obligations.

I sigh into the phone. "I'm busy that weekend. Supper club duties."

"Ah, got it. That's too bad."

Too bad? Surely we can work out an alternate plan. I glance at my calendar in Outlook. "What about this weekend?"

"As in tomorrow?"

I squeeze my phone between my ear and shoulder and wipe the grease from my fingers. "Or Sunday."

Jacob goes silent for a few seconds on the other end, and I suddenly fear I've shown my hand too quickly. We just saw each other two days ago. I probably seem needy and overly eager.

"Sorry, I'm out of town this weekend, and I'm busy most of next week," he finally says. "What about the week after Columbus Day?"

I scan my calendar and see I have nothing going on that week, nor do we have a supper club planned for that weekend. "Sure. Works for me. What day?"

"Maybe Wednesday night? Let me see how my work schedule is shaping up that week. This immigration debate is screwing up everything. We might need to wait until the weekend."

"Oh. Okay." I'd rather not wait two weeks to see him again, but I will if I have to.

"Great. I'll give you a call in the next week or two, and we'll work out a plan. I already have something in mind."

"Oh?"

He laughs. "When the time is right, I'll let you know. Until then . . . good luck with the work drama."

"Thanks," I say. "Although I think I'll need more than luck."

I hang up with Jacob and spot Rachel gliding down the hallway toward my desk, her silky, brown hair tied into an off-center chignon. As soon as she gets within five feet of me, Millie jumps out from a side hallway and latches onto Rachel's side.

"Hey, ladies," Millie says, smoothing the front of her characteristically tight red button-down top, which is tucked into a pair of skintight black pants.

Rachel and I wave passively, trying not to engage her, hoping she will go away. She doesn't take the hint. She never does.

"What's up?" she asks, taking a seat on the far side of my desk. "Hannah, I heard you talking on the phone. New boyfriend?"

Rachel and I exchange a look: *The Hemorrhoid.*

"He's not my boyfriend," I say.

Millie rolls her eyes. "Whatever, it sounded to me like you were planning a hot date."

"Not really."

As I say this, I pretend to organize papers on my desk, as if to say, *I could not be less interested in this conversation. Please go away.*

"Well, if you're looking for a fun restaurant, I highly recommend Central. Adam and I went last week and loved it."

I stop shuffling papers when I hear Adam's name. Rachel stiffens. "Oh?" I say, trying to sound casual. The gyro churns in my stomach.

"He got a big promotion at work, so we went out to celebrate. He totally deserved it. You know how driven he is."

Of course I know. I dated the guy for more than a year. Why she thinks it's appropriate to bring up Adam in this context, I do not know. I assume it has something to do with her status as the most annoying woman in all of Washington.

But, Millie's irksome nature aside, hearing about Adam's success stirs up a hot pot of emotions. On the one hand, I am genuinely happy for Adam. I know how hard he worked for this promotion, and I know it's what he wanted. And though a small part of me wants his career to crash and burn in a spectacular fashion so that he will regret the way he broke up with me, the rational part of me knows that won't happen. Adam doesn't "do" regret. What I feel most of all, I suppose, is bitterness. Adam's promotion is yet another story of a friend moving closer to his or her dream job, while I get sucked further into a job I increasingly cannot stand. As Gore Vidal once said, "Whenever a friend succeeds, something in me dies."

"Good for him," I say, trying my hardest to seem genuine. "Tell him I say congrats."

Millie sighs loudly. "Like he doesn't talk about you enough already . . . *Anyway*, I should get back to work. I have so much on my plate right now. Susan wants my help writing some book."

I grunt. "Join the club."

Millie narrows her eyes. "What?"

"Mark offered to add me as coauthor on his book if I help him with a few chapters."

Millie jerks her head back. "Really? Wow. That's . . . surprising. Good for Mark."

Rachel raises an eyebrow. "I think you mean good for Hannah."

"Sure, whatever," she says, lifting herself off my desk. "Good luck with your work. My guess is you'll need it."

As she stalks away, I look up at Rachel and plead with my eyes, trying to communicate that if this is what it means to stay employed here, I want her to take my pen and stab me in the throat immediately.

But she doesn't. And I'm still here. Still here, and stuck, stuck, stuck.

CHAPTER

twenty-five

there is only one way to bring myself out of a funk of this magnitude, and that is to cook my ass off. And, with a week to go until the next installment of The Dupont Circle Supper Club, that's exactly what I do.

I spend the weekend sifting through my recipe files, trying to come up with a suitable theme for our next two dinners. If the food blogosphere is to be believed, The Dupont Circle Supper Club specializes in gourmet comfort food, and so whatever menu I come up with should align with our growing reputation, inadvertent though it may be. After jotting down nine potential themes, I settle on a winner: diner food.

Growing up outside of Philadelphia, I never wanted for diner food, whether it was from Bob's Diner in Roxborough or the Trolley Car Diner in Mount Airy. The food wasn't anything special—eggs and toast, meat loaf and gravy, the omnipresent glass case of pies—but I always found the food comforting and satisfying, served as it was in those old-fashioned, prefabricated stainless steel trolley cars. Whenever we would visit my mom's parents in Cranbury, New Jersey, we'd stop at the Claremont Diner in East Windsor on the way home, and I'd order a fat, fluffy slice of coconut cream pie, which I'd nibble on the whole car ride back to Philly.

I'm not sure why I've always found diner food so comforting. Maybe it's the abundance of grease or the utter lack of pretense.

Diner food is basic, stick-to-your-ribs fare—carbs, eggs, and meat, all cooked up in plenty of hot fat—served up in an environment dripping with kitsch and nostalgia. Where else can you get scrambled eggs and toast all day long? Where else are a jug of syrup and a bottomless cup of coffee de rigueur? The point of diner cuisine isn't to astound or impress; it's to fill you up cheaply with basic, down-home food.

My menu, however, *should* astound and impress, which is why I've decided to take some of the diner foods I remember from my youth and put my own twist on them. So far, this is what I've come up with:

Sloe gin fizz cocktails/chocolate egg creams
Grilled cheese squares: grappa-soaked grapes and Taleggio/
    Asian pears and smoked Gouda
"Eggs, Bacon, and Toast": crostini topped with wilted spinach,
    pancetta, poached egg, and chive pesto
Smoky meat loaf with slow-roasted onions and prune
    ketchup
Whipped celery root puree
Braised green beans with fire-roasted tomatoes
Mini root beer floats
Triple coconut cream pie

The menu is longer and slightly more involved than my previous supper clubs, but now that The Dupont Circle Supper Club has started turning a slight profit, I can afford to splurge on some extras here and there. Plus, due to the surge in our popularity, we've increased the price per head from forty-five to fifty-five dollars, giving me a little more wiggle room. These decisions hardly make me the Warren Buffett of supper clubs, but I'm beginning to grasp the business end of this operation in a way I hadn't appreciated before.

My greater concern, however, is that due to the surge in demand, we increased the number of available seats each night.

Now, instead of hosting twelve guests a night, we're hosting twenty-four, catching the overflow in Blake's living room with the folding table Rachel borrowed from NIRD. That amounts to forty-eight heads a weekend. I'm a little concerned as to how, exactly, this will work, but with three dinners under my belt, Rachel assures me I can handle it.

The Friday before the dinners, Rachel and I sneak out of work early and head to Whole Foods to pick up our last-minute ingredients, slipping out before Mark, Millie, or Susan spot us leaving the building. The local Whole Foods sits one block away from my old apartment, where Adam still lives and where the temperature is probably still five degrees too cold. I would worry that I might run into him, but given Millie's big news about his promotion, I'm guessing he is either at work or in Millie's pants.

Rachel grabs a shopping cart and pushes it into the Whole Foods produce section, leaning her weight into the handle as she steers around the displays of apples and pears.

"So . . . have you seen the paper today?" she asks.

"I scanned the digital version. Why?"

She reaches into her purse and pulls out a ripped-out page from the Letters to the Editor. "Here. Read this."

I grab the paper from her hand and begin skimming the page as Rachel fills a plastic bag with green beans:

I was disappointed with Celia Green's feature last week on The Dupont Circle Supper Club ["Shhh: Dinner Is Served," Sept. 30], which glorified an operation that is, at best, irresponsible and, at worst, illegal. The Dupont Circle corridor already suffers from an overabundance of restaurant and food establishments, some of whom employ illegal workers and owe back taxes to the DC government. The last thing our neighborhood needs is yet another shifty restaurant operation. While the secret nature of The Dupont Circle Supper Club may sound exciting and fun to some, the complete lack of regulation and accountability creates a risk for patrons and for the neighborhood at large. I would encourage the carrot-cake-loving hostess of this supper club to do the responsible thing and terminate her operation immediately. She should play by the rules, just as I, as candidate for the Dupont Circle ANC, am encouraging all restaurants in the neighborhood to do. There is no point in having rules if some people don't have to follow them.

Sincerely,

Blake Fischer, candidate for Dupont Circle ANC (Ward 2B07)

"*Whaaaaaaat?*" My voice fills the entirety of the Whole Foods produce section.

Rachel snatches the article from my hands. "Shhh. Don't shout."

"This is five thousand percent terrible, Rachel. Five thousand percent!"

Rachel grips the shopping cart by its handle and pushes it toward the baking aisle. "It isn't that bad." She casts a sideways glance. "Okay, yeah, it's pretty bad. But this feels to me more like a 'concerned citizen' letter. He's leaving the responsibility in your hands. Besides, ANC members have no legislative authority whatsoever. So even if he does get elected, he doesn't have the power to shut us down."

"Uh, he does as the owner of the house in which we operate."

Rachel frowns. "True."

"We can't do this in his house anymore. We have to call it off."

"Hannah, you're overreacting. Blake is out of town for the entire weekend. Let's get through this dinner and figure out the rest later. Okay?"

I sigh. "Okay. But you are taking some of the blame if we get caught."

Rachel takes a deep breath, her eyes tense as she stares into the distance. "I'm sure everything will be fine. I wouldn't worry."

She pushes the cart speedily along the linoleum floor, and I race to catch up with her, now more anxious than ever because although Rachel says I shouldn't worry, the tone in her voice says the opposite.

Saturday morning, we meet outside Blake's front door and launch straight into our prep work in his kitchen. Rachel unloads a bunch of double shot glasses onto the counter, which we'll use for our mini root beer floats, and unpacks a few vintage diner napkin holders that are painted a pale robin's egg blue.

"Where did you find these?" I ask, twirling one of the napkin holders in my hand.

"Etsy. Aren't they great? I'm going to showcase them on my blog after the dinners are over."

"How's the blog going?"

She flashes a confident smile. "Great, actually. The *Post* listed me as one of the top ten local bloggers to watch."

"Rach—that's fantastic."

"Thanks. Although I've been a bit of a slacker ever since I started helping you with the supper club. And there have been . . . other distractions."

Rachel looks as if she is about to continue, but before she can say anything, my phone rings.

"Oh my god," I say, staring down at my phone. My heart races. "It's Blake."

"Answer it," Rachel says.

"I can't answer it! I'm in his house."

"He doesn't know that. He can't magically see you through the phone."

"But what if he can tell by the sounds in the background?"

She furrows her brow. "Because the silence sounds different here than it would in your own apartment? You're being crazy. Just answer it. If it's important, he'll just keep calling anyway."

I pick up the phone and press it to my ear. "Hello . . . ?"

"Hey, Hannah? It's Blake."

"Hi." *I'm in your house, I'm in your house, I'm in your house.*

"You're going to think I'm a little OCD," he says, "but I'm in Tampa, and I can't shake the feeling that I left the lights on in my kitchen. Would you mind running up to my house and checking for me?"

I gulp loudly. "You want me to go . . . into your house?"

"Yeah, if you don't mind. I don't set the alarm or anything, so you should be fine. Sorry. I know it's a weird request, but my electricity bill was insane last month, and I can't figure out why, since I was away so much. The only explanation is that I'm leaving lights on by accident while I'm away. Either that, or I'm totally losing my mind."

Those aren't the *only* explanations . . . "O-okay. Sure. I'll run upstairs and let you know."

"Great. Thanks." He laughs. "Sorry to make you do this. I know you have better ways to spend your Saturdays than wandering around my house."

"Ha," I say, my eyelids batting at one hundred miles an hour. "Right."

Of course I do.

I can't keep up this charade forever. Can I? No, I can't. But that's fine because I never intended to run this supper club out of Blake's house *forever*. Frankly, I never intended to run it out of his house at all. But now that I have . . . No. I'll get through this weekend, and then I'll find a new location, and that will be that. The only reason I've continued to use his house is because my apartment is too small and I haven't found a better place to host these dinners. But I'll start looking. Soon. As soon as this weekend is over.

By the time our guests arrive that night, I'm already a sweaty mess. All six burners on Blake's Viking range are firing like mad, and both ovens are cranking at high heat. In two huge skillets, I am frying up the grilled cheese sandwiches, the buttered brioche sizzling in the pan as the Gouda and Taleggio melt into the slices of pear and grappa-soaked grapes. A huge skillet of water bubbles away in the back corner, ready to poach the eggs for the bacon-and-egg crostini. My braised green beans are hanging out in the other back corner of the stove top, swimming in a sauce of fire-roasted tomatoes and sweet fennel seed, and on the middle burners sit a pan of frying pancetta and a bowl of celery root puree atop a bain marie. Two weeks ago, the mere sight of all of these pots and pans and total strangers would have been enough to send me into cardiac arrest, but now, aside from shedding a few gallons of sweat, I'm fine. Although, admittedly, Adam's subzero apartment doesn't sound so bad right about now.

Rachel buses the grilled cheese squares out to the living room like a pro, and in what feels like no time at all, the guests are seated at the tables in the living and dining rooms, working their way through their bacon-and-egg crostini and hunks of smoky-sweet meat loaf. As usual, I give a little background about myself, as well as some background on the history of the diner, this time standing along the invisible dividing line between Blake's living and dining rooms and speaking to two tables at once. I tell them how the first diner was invented in 1872, when a guy named Walter Scott decided to sell food out of his horse-pulled wagon, and how diner cuisine varies by region, depending on whether you're in Pennsylvania or Michigan or New Jersey. Everyone jumps in with stories about their own diner experiences, many of which involve postdrinking binges, and once again, the dinner takes on a life of its own.

Rachel and I slip back into the kitchen to prepare the mini root beer floats, and as Rachel pulls out the shot glasses, she clears her throat. "I'm going to slip out a little early tonight, if that's okay."

I grab the quart of homemade vanilla ice cream from the freezer and toss it on the counter. "Yeah, sure. Any reason?"

Rachel nervously bites her fingernail. "Um . . . well . . . actually . . ."

As Rachel stutters through an answer, a slender Indian woman with almond-shaped eyes and long, delicate fingers wanders into the kitchen.

"Sorry to bother you," the woman says, interrupting Rachel. She tucks her jet-black hair behind her ear. "I just wanted to thank you for everything so far. Dinner has been fantastic."

I offer a friendly smile and begin to line the shot glasses along the edge of the counter. "Thanks."

She plays with one of her dangly, silver earrings, staring at me intently as I make my way along the counter. "I've also been meaning to ask . . ." She pauses and gives her earring another flick. "Do you guys know Blake Fischer?"

Rachel coughs violently, and my palms begin to sweat until I nearly lose my grip on the remaining glasses. "I—sorry?"

"Blake Fischer? I think he used to live here. He was friends with my ex-boyfriend. We only hung out once or twice, but I could swear his house looked just like this."

"Nope," I blurt out, too quickly and too loudly. Rachel sidles up next to me and gently steps on my toes. "Never heard of him."

"Huh," she says. "I guess I'm thinking of a different house."

"Guess so."

She glances around the kitchen. "Now that I look around, this kitchen looks different than his did." She shrugs. "Oh, well. I hadn't thought about those guys in ages, but this house brought back a wave of nostalgia."

I force a smile as I fidget with one of the shot glasses. "It's probably all the diner talk. Trolley cars, meat loaf—diners are all about nostalgia."

"That's probably it." She gives the kitchen another once-over, narrowing her eyes as she studies the back windows and granite counters. Something about her expression tells me she isn't entirely convinced, but eventually she refocuses her gaze on me and smiles. "Anyway, sorry to bother. I'll let you get back to work."

She starts to head back into the dining room, but I stop her before she leaves. "Sorry—I didn't catch your name."

"Geeta," she says. "Geeta Kapoor."

Congratulations, Geeta Kapoor: you have earned a premier spot on The Dupont Circle Supper Club's blacklist. "Nice meeting you, Geeta," I say.

"Likewise." She flips her hair over her shoulder and rubs her lips together, smoothing out her shiny raspberry lip gloss, and then disappears into the dining room.

As soon as Geeta is out of sight, Rachel turns to me with raised eyebrows. "Ruh-roh," she says with a frown.

"That's all you have to say? *Ruh-roh?*"

"What do you want me to say?"

"That this is horrible? That this is a total freaking disaster?"

"It isn't a disaster."

"Oh, really? Tell me how this isn't a disaster." Rachel has no response. "What if Geeta says something to Blake?"

"She isn't going to say anything to Blake. And, anyway, when would she say it? She said she never sees him anymore."

"Yeah, but what if she runs into Blake or one of his buddies and mentions this dinner?"

Rachel offers a conciliatory shrug. "It's possible, I guess. But think about all the acquaintances you have in this town. How often do you run into any of them?"

I stare at Rachel with arched eyebrows. "Hmm, let's see. Oh, that's right: three weeks ago, I ran into Adam, Millie, and Jacob at CVS, all at the same time."

"True."

I let out a deep groan. "This has disaster written all over it. What are we going to do?"

Rachel grabs one of the bottles of root beer, pops off the cap, and slides the bottle to me across the counter. "The only thing we can do—finish this dinner, clean up the house, and hope for the best."

Because, of course, nothing could possibly go wrong with that plan.

i don't like close calls. I never have. In tenth grade, I made the colossal mistake of throwing a party while my parents were in Boston for a conference. My friend Gabby convinced me the party would be my ticket into the cool crowd, but instead, the popular kids showed up, drank all my parents' liquor, and trashed my house before ditching my party for something better. I spent the entire weekend scrubbing vomit and mud off the floor. I vowed never to tempt fate again.

But what am I doing now? I'm more than tempting fate. I'm pole dancing in front of fate in a leopard thong. Topless. Doused in Love Potion No. 9. What is *wrong* with me?

Okay, yes, the rest of the weekend went off without a hitch, and we made our biggest profit yet: a whopping $2,600 after expenses, $1,950 of which ended up in my pocket. But still. Between the run-in with Geeta and Blake's call Saturday morning, this whole operation is getting uncomfortably dicey. I need to explore other locations. I suppose I could call off the entire supper club, but . . . No. No, I couldn't do that. I made a killing last weekend, and for the first time, I've realized I could make money doing what makes me happier than anything else. I can't give that up. Or, more accurately, I don't want to.

Resolved: I will find a new location for The Dupont Circle Supper Club. As soon as I think up our next menu. And talk to Rachel. And call Jacob.

Jacob. I haven't heard from him since our conversation more than a week ago, and I'm beginning to wonder if he forgot about our plans for a date this week. He did say Wednesday, didn't he? And that he already had something in mind? Or did I make that up? Maybe I misheard. It wouldn't be the first time.

Tuesday morning, I peer into Mark's office, and when I see he has stepped out, I pick up my phone and call Jacob, after briefly hyperventilating into a brown paper bag under my desk. He picks up after the second ring. "How's it going, hot stuff?"

I crumple up the brown paper bag and toss it into the trash. He called me hot stuff. The hyperventilation was overkill, I see.

"Pretty much unchanged since the last time we talked," I say.

"Gotcha." I hear him type a few strokes on his keyboard. "So what's up?"

"I was just wondering if we're still on for tomorrow night . . . ?"

"Ah, right," he says. "I've been meaning to call you about that. One of my colleagues is out on maternity leave, so work has been insane. I'm covering for both of us. Unfortunately Wednesday isn't going to work."

I slump back in my chair. "Oh."

"Hey—you're not getting off that easy. How about Saturday?"

I perk up. "Sure—Saturday is great. What time?"

"Let's say . . . four-thirty?"

"In the afternoon?"

"No, in the morning." He laughs. "Of course in the afternoon."

Who goes on dates at four-thirty in the afternoon? That's friendville. Platonic station. Nonsexual junction. I am the mayor of those towns. I know them well.

"Sure. Okay. I guess four-thirty works."

"Excellent. Meet me outside the Federal Triangle Metro stop, and we'll go from there."

"Go . . . where exactly?"

He chuckles. "Patience. You'll see."

"But I mean . . . Federal Triangle? Are we taking a tour of the

EPA or something?" Talk about the least romantic atmosphere ever.

"Relax. I've got something special planned. Just take a deep breath and roll with the punches."

I titter like a drunken sorority sister and fiddle with a loose thread on my sweater. "Right. Roll with the punches. I can do that."

As if I've ever been that kind of girl.

Late Saturday afternoon, I put the finishing touches on my cinnamon buns, drizzling the silky white icing on top of the feathery, cinnamon-filled coils. My grand plan: to bring Jacob back here after whatever uber-platonic date he has planned and make him fall for me. Hence, the cinnamon buns.

I wrap the tray of buns in foil, throw on the outfit Rachel picked out for me (black V-neck wrap cardigan, dark jeans, black boots), and work my way through the appropriate combination of mascara, eye shadow, and lipstick. Given that our date begins at four-thirty, I don't want to look overdressed, but I also don't want to look frumpy or completely asexual. For me, this poses a great challenge and explains why I needed to call on Rachel for advice.

Once I've put a sufficient amount of effort into making my style look effortless, I hustle down Eighteenth Street toward the Farragut West Metro stop and board an orange line train, which bumps along for three stops until we reach Federal Triangle. I hop off and ride two short escalators toward the exit until I reach the top, which empties onto an airy portico within the Environmental Protection Agency's complex. The building is neoclassical, with grand columns, broad archways, and a sweeping semicircular edifice made of pale gray limestone.

As soon as I step off the escalator, I spot Jacob standing beneath a sign for the Post Office Building, which is what I imagine this used to be before it became the EPA. He wears dark jeans, gray-and-yellow Adidas sneakers, and a black-and-white Arcade Fire T-shirt, broadcasting once again his undying support of indie music.

"Don't you look like a million bucks," he says as he notices me walking toward him.

"A million might be a little generous," I say.

He grabs me by the hand and pulls me toward him. "I'm a generous guy."

I'm not sure whether I find that comment sexy or unspeakably cheesy, but he looks so adorable with those mesmerizing eyes and that tousled mop of hair that I have trouble finding fault with anything he does. Jacob, I am learning, is the type of guy who makes you feel cooler simply by spending time with him—the kind of person who follows a band two years before anyone else has heard of them and who has probably dabbled in a little bit of everything, from women to drugs to unnecessarily complicated sexual positions. He skates right up to the line of trying too hard, with those aggressively hip T-shirts and that carefully unstyled hair, but he somehow manages to glide along without devolving into a total poseur.

He pulls me closer and plants a kiss on my cheek, at which point I have to make a conscious effort not to start making out with him right in the middle of the EPA complex. How is this guy so freaking smooth?

"Shall we?" he says, gesturing down a long arcade toward the Mall.

He leads me down the covered passageway, which hugs the curved side of the building all the way down Twelfth Street. The walkway is peppered with alcoves and hidden recesses, and a series of lanterns dangles from the arched ceiling.

"So where are we going?"

He casts a sideways glance, smirking. "You really want to know?"

"Is there a reason why I shouldn't?"

He grins. "Nah, okay, I'll tell you. We're going to the Museum of American History. It closes at five-thirty, which is why we're meeting so early."

"Oh. Okay." I don't know what I was expecting, but by the tone of my voice, it sounds as if I expected something else.

Jacob slows his step. "We don't have to go there. It was just an idea."

"No, no—it'll be great. I used to love that museum. I haven't been there since I was a kid."

"Exactly. When you move to a city, all the tourist attractions become dead to you. I hate that. It's like, we have all these free museums right on our doorstep and never bother to visit them. It's crazy."

"You're right. In the three years I've lived here, I've been to the Spy Museum, and that's it."

"And that one isn't even free," he says. "Come on. Let's get cultured."

He grabs my hand and whisks me through the doors to the Museum of American History, which sits on the northwest corner of the National Mall and takes up an entire block. I first visited this museum with my parents as a child, and I remember pressing my face against the glass case holding Dorothy's ruby red slippers and wondering if they were really as magical as they were in the movie. Did they really help Dorothy get back to Kansas? Could I try them on? My dad proceeded to tell me that in the book on which the movie was based, the ruby slippers were actually *silver* slippers, which some of Daddy's colleagues believed was a populist allegory about the gold standard and the move to a bi-metallic monetary standard in the late 1800s, a time of great social and industrial change, but Daddy wasn't convinced. I was six.

Jacob and I work our way through the security line in the vast marble lobby, and as soon as the guard inspects my bag, I spot an old powder blue "Detroit Jewel" stove top in one of the artifacts cases to the right.

"Check it out," I say, running over to check out why a big blue oven is on display at one of the nation's preeminent museums.

"Uh-huh," Jacob says, grinning. "I knew you'd like this. And now you have an idea why I brought you here."

I wrinkle my eyebrows together. "To look at old cooktops?"

"Exactly. Come on."

He pulls me into the West Wing, toward the exhibit for Science in American Life, when I suddenly see what he's talking about.

"Julia Child's kitchen!"

"Ding, ding, ding!" Jacob laughs. "As Washington's supper club doyenne, I thought you'd appreciate this."

We wind our way into the curved alcove housing Julia Child's kitchen and collection of utensils, the entire kitchen preserved as it appeared in her Cambridge, Massachusetts, home: the blue cupboards, the Peg-Board walls, the central table, now covered by a laminated tablecloth. Along the walls of the exhibit bay, the curators have hung collections of her pots and pans and cooking utensils, everything from her copper saucepans to her meat tenderizer.

"Don't tell me you actually know what all this stuff is," Jacob says, pointing to a pair of poultry shears.

"Of course I do. Most of it, anyway."

"Okay, then what's that?" He points to a tapered knife with a funny jagged underbelly.

"Shrimp knife," I say.

"And what about that?"

"Cherry pitter."

"And that?" He points to a strange clamp that looks like medical forceps.

"I . . ." I glance at the explanatory key next to the objects. "A lamb bone holder? Okay, in all fairness, I've never seen that one before."

"Ha! Well at least there's something you don't know."

"Oh, there's plenty more where that came from. Trust me."

"I hope so. Otherwise you're like freaking superwoman. She cooks! She bakes! She writes about quantitative easing and currency valuation! You put me to shame, girl."

He grabs my hand and pulls me out of the exhibit to the escalator, and as he does, I feel as if I'm flying. No one has ever spoken about me that way. No one has ever called me superwoman. Even in our early days of dating, Adam wasn't nearly as impressed by my cooking abilities. That's probably because he was an asshole.

As we land on the second floor of the museum, I see a huge sign for the First Ladies exhibit, which features gowns, accessories, and household trinkets of the nation's First Ladies.

"Ah, what could have been," I say, sighing as I gaze at the placard.

"You wanted to be a First Lady?"

I shake my head. "No. But my ex-boyfriend wants to be president someday, I think. I wasn't exactly the First Lady type."

"Let's see about that, shall we?"

We enter the exhibit, and I immediately stumble upon Helen Taft's inaugural ball gown from 1909, the white silk chiffon glittering with rhinestones and beads and metallic thread. I remember coming across this dress on my first visit with my parents twenty years ago. I gazed at the dress and told my mom I wanted to be a First Lady so that I could wear a dress like that someday. My mom then proceeded to give me a five-minute lecture on how the institution of the First Lady was sexist and dated and how I should want to be the next *president* instead. And so began my years of occupational dysfunction.

We meander through the exhibit until we end up in the room with the inaugural gowns and corresponding archival photos. The first dress I see is the sleeveless off-white dress Jacqueline Kennedy wore to the inaugural ball in 1961, the silk chiffon top encrusted with sparkly stones and glittery thread. Next to the dress is a photo of her walking arm in arm with JFK as they leave the

White House, both looking radiant and classy, like two Holly-wood stars.

"You don't think you could've handled that role?" Jacob asks, pointing at the photo.

"Poise and grace aren't exactly my thing."

"You were totally gracious at the dinner I went to. And any-way, poise and grace are overrated. I'll take sexiness over poise any day."

"Jackie Kennedy was incredibly sexy," I say, nodding toward her photo.

He wraps his arm around my waist and gently squeezes my side. "Not as sexy as some people I know . . ."

I pull away slightly and gently nudge him with my elbow. "Well, well, well. Don't you know all the right things to say, Mr. Smooth Talker?"

Jacob pokes me in the side with his finger and flashes a wry smile. "How did you manage to turn a compliment around and make me look like a bad guy? You really are superwoman."

"I guess I am."

He laughs and pushes me along by the small of my back. "Come on, then, superwoman," he says. "Time to fuel your super-powers. Let's grab something to eat."

Jacob and I manage to snag a bar seat at Central, the local bistro run by renowned chef Michel Richard, and given our early six o'clock arrival, there are only about six other people at the bar. We each order a burger and fries, and as we wash the juicy burgers down with a hearty zinfandel, we talk about his career—how he started writing for newspapers in high school and how he hopes to launch his own digital news outlet someday. He tells me about the band he toured and played with in college and his thoughts on the current music scene. When I try to get more personal, ask-ing about his family and his past relationships, he clams up, and I notice he keeps things a little close to the vest, not wanting to open up or expose too much. But the more he talks, the more I want to know about him and the more willing I am to wait until he's ready to tell me everything.

"So what about you?" he asks. "What's your game plan?"

"In terms of . . . ?"

"Life. Career. Yada yada."

I shrug. "Not exactly sure. I'm waiting to see what happens with this supper club. If it continues along this trajectory, I might give the cooking thing a try for real."

"You'd quit your job?"

"With any luck, yeah."

He presses his eyebrows together. "Why would you do that?"

"So I could cook full-time."

"Can't you do both? I mean the supper club is awesome, but so is working for someone like Mark Henderson."

I feel the burger churning in my stomach. Why does everyone think my work is so great? My parents, Adam, Jacob—they all value my career a thousand times more than I ever have. Maybe I'm missing something. If this many people support what I do, maybe I'm the one who has it all wrong.

"We'll see," I say. I fiddle with my napkin. "I signed up for the GREs. I'm taking them in three weeks."

"Right on. See, I thought you had a game plan. You can be the chef-scholar-baker-economist. It'll be awesome."

I force a smile as Jacob signals for the check. I wish the idea sounded half as awesome to me as it does to him.

Jacob pays the bill, and we wander back toward the Federal Triangle Metro stop, strolling beneath the arches and lanterns, which now light the dusky walkway of the EPA building. When we turn around a bend, Jacob pulls me by the arm and ducks behind a hidden archway and presses me against a cool, limestone column. He runs his hand down the front of my cardigan and brings his face close to mine.

"Hey there, superwoman," he says. He kisses me, softly at first, then more forcefully, pushing against me with desire as he moves his lips down my neck. When he pulls away briefly, his eyes glittering in the light of the lanterns, he smiles in a way that turns me into a puddle of goo.

"There are a dozen fresh cinnamon buns waiting back at my apartment," I say.

He grins. "There's only one set of buns I'm interested in tonight."

I start shaking with laughter, unsure how to respond to a comment that is both totally sincere and totally cheesy. Truthfully, the buns I'm interested in tonight don't involve cinnamon either.

Jacob plants another kiss on my lips and then grabs my elbow and pulls me toward the escalator.

"Come on," he says, nibbling at my ear as we approach the escalator steps. "Let's give that air mattress another try."

twenty-seven

i am not the kind of girl who sleeps with men on the first date. I'm not even the type of girl who sleeps with men on the second date. But since I met Jacob at the first Dupont Circle Supper Club, the museum night is almost like our third date, and so sleeping with him isn't so bad. At least that's what I tell myself.

When we return to my apartment, Jacob and I have sex twice on my Aerobed—sweaty, aggressive sex, the kind Adam and I used to have after having a big fight or after he spoke on the phone to his parents. Jacob kisses my shoulders and rubs my thighs and whispers in my ear that I am hot and sexy and wild. I'm tempted to inform him that, deep down, I'm not any of those things, but if I learned anything from my past relationship, it's that showing my hand too soon will ruin everything. And so I pretend I am hot and sexy and wild, or at least as wild as my self-conscious, uptight personality will allow.

Around 4:00 A.M., Jacob rouses me awake with a kiss on my shoulder. "Hey," he whispers. "I'm going to head out."

I glance at my alarm clock. "It's four in the morning. You really have to go now?"

He nuzzles me with his chin. "Busy day ahead of me. I have to file a story for Monday."

"Oh. Okay."

He kisses my shoulder again and then looks into my eyes,

which crinkle at the edges as he smiles. "I'll call you next week, okay?"

I smile back. "Okay."

"I had a great time tonight," he says, grabbing for his clothes.

"Me, too."

He smirks. "Sounded that way." I throw his boxers in his face, and he laughs. "I'll talk to you soon, superwoman," he says.

Then he throws on his clothes, runs his fingers through his hair, and gives me one last kiss before he heads out the door.

Jacob does not call all week. Correction: Jacob does not call for two weeks. I consider sending him a text or calling him instead, but he specifically said he would call me, so I don't. I tell myself I am taking the high road. Consequently, I have no contact with Jacob for two full weeks and am plagued by feelings of self-doubt and insecurity. Apparently the high road is for losers.

I hate that he hasn't called me. What I hate even more is how much I care—how much I want him to call me and kiss me and shower me with displays of affection. After dating Adam, I feel as if I've opened some sort of Pandora's box. I'm Relationship Sensitized, and now when a man so much as buys me dinner I'm ready to hop into bed with him and make him my boyfriend. This is why I never dated anyone seriously before Adam. I was protecting myself. But now I'm ruined, and so instead of spending the past two weeks finding a better location for our next supper club or studying for the GREs, I've spent nearly every waking hour obsessing over Jacob and why he hasn't called me. Well, that and helping Blake with his stupid costume party.

The Friday before Halloween, my phone rings as I flick through some documents for Mark, and I quickly grab the phone before the call goes to voice mail. Much to my dismay, it isn't Jacob. It's Blake.

"Hey—what are you up to right now?" he asks.

"Immersing myself in the life and times of Nelson Aldrich," I say, leafing through a stack of papers festooned with neon yellow Post-its.

"Who?"

"Republican Senator in the early 1900s. He wrote up a plan that became the basis for the Federal Reserve Act."

"Wow, that sounds . . ."

"Mind numbing?"

"I was going to say specific."

"Yeah, that, too." I stop flipping through my papers and click the cap back on my highlighter. "So what's up? Why are you calling me at work?"

"I was wondering if you could get out of work early today. Maybe leave after lunch or something?"

"Not sure. Why?"

"I need some help picking up stuff for the party."

Here we go again. I've spent all week getting ready for his Halloween party—making blood orange sorbet, baking and freezing dozens and dozens of cupcakes—and yet Blake continues to interrupt my flow by coming to me with his inane requests. Tuesday he wanted to discuss serving pieces and paper goods, a conversation that should have taken fifteen minutes, tops, but that Blake managed to stretch out to a full hour. Wednesday night he asked me to come along to pick up a bunch of cases of wine and beer and hard liquor, which involved mainly moral support on my part, since I neither own a car nor possess the strength to carry cases of booze more than a few feet. All I did was sit in Blake's passenger seat and talk to him for a while. Then yesterday, he asked me to help him hang decorations, an activity I actually enjoyed, but one that, again, Blake managed to draw out for an extensive period of time. All of this togetherness would be only mildly annoying if Blake weren't Enemy Number 1 of The Dupont Circle Supper Club. By spending time with him, I am forced to continue lying to his face.

"Yeah . . . I don't know, Blake. My boss needs me to get going on this book research."

"Aw, come on. What's a few hours on a Friday afternoon? You probably wouldn't get much work done anyway."

This coming from the workaholic who allegedly hasn't taken a day off in six months. "Don't you have stuff to do on the Hill?"

"My boss is letting me take off early. My deputy will cover for me until close of business, and then I'm off for the weekend."

I lean back in my chair and sigh. "Okay, fine. Where should we meet?"

"Can you swing by my office around two-thirty? I'm at 327 Cannon."

"Remind me which building Cannon is again? I always get the three House buildings confused."

"Easy—it's the one right across from the Capitol South Metro stop. Can't miss it."

"Okay. See you at two-thirty."

"Great. Oh—before I let you go, what are you wearing today?"

"Excuse me?" This conversation has taken an uncomfortable turn.

"Are you wearing a skirt or pants?"

"Pants. Gray ones."

"Good. Pants are good."

"Yes, generally speaking I'd say pants are good. And in case you were wondering, I'm also wearing a cream V-neck sweater and white underwear. Are we done here?"

"We're done here," he says, through what I can tell is a smile. "See you soon."

I hang up the phone and lean back in my chair and wonder where the hell Blake is taking me.

As I'm on my way to meet Blake, Millie accosts me in front of the elevator with her signature blend of nosiness and gall.

"Where are you off to?"

"I haven't been feeling that great," I say, faking a cough. "I'm heading home to rest up."

She looks me up and down. "You seem okay to me."

"Tell that to my tonsils," I say. *You nosey biatch.*

"Well, I hope you feel better by tomorrow. It would suck to be sick on Halloween. Speaking of which, if you're feeling better, give me a call. Adam and I are throwing a Halloween party at my place."

She and Adam are hosting a party? Together? I refuse to acknowledge what this could mean—that, after all this time, Millie's wish has come true, and the two of them are actually an item. No, I'd much rather live in denial and believe they are throwing the party together as friends. I will do what I must to forestall a rapidly descending spiral of self-hatred and McFlurries.

"You're welcome to come," Millie says.

"I'll let you know," I say. Like I'd ever attend that party. I'd rather walk barefoot on a bed of flaming hot coals. Naked. While being stabbed.

"You should come! It's going to be a blast. Adam is dressing up as the secretary of defense, and I'm going to be a sexy soldier."

"I've never thought of female soldiers as being particularly sexy."

"They are when they wear camouflage rompers," Millie says, winking.

"Soldiers wear rompers? Since when?"

Millie scowls. "Since now. God, Hannah, you're so literal. It's Halloween. Loosen up a little."

And it is in this moment, when Millie Roberts—tension personified—is telling me to loosen up, that I realize how dire the situation at NIRD has become, and how desperately I need to leave this place.

The escalator at the Capitol South Metro stop dumps me out directly across from the Cannon House Office Building, where the smooth, white marble and limestone facade towers five stories above the street, the narrow windows arranged in perfect lines, as if someone pricked the side of the building with the tines of a fork. I scurry across the intersection and make my way up the marble steps to the First Street entrance, pushing my way through the double doors and into the security line. I lay my black nylon tote on the conveyor belt and pass through the metal detector, noting the unapologetic prominence of the handgun sitting in the holster of the Capitol Hill police officer in front of me.

I grab my tote and move toward the building map posted on the wall. The map informs me "You Are Here," which, given my appalling sense of direction, means absolutely nothing to me. All I know is that Blake works in 327, an office I can only assume is on the third floor. I push through the doors to the elevator bay, a cavernous, trapezoidal cove that houses two elevators and a broad staircase with a brass and wrought iron banister. The alcove smells sweet and chalky, like old books and sweet tea, and the cool air makes the hair on my arm stand upright. Men and women wearing suits in varying shades of gray, black, and navy pass in and out of the elevators, carrying stacks of papers and typing furiously on their BlackBerrys.

Instead of waiting for the elevator, I ascend the two flights of stairs to the third floor and meander in the direction of room 327. The hallway ceiling rises twenty feet, dotted with textured globe lights, and the stark white walls are peppered on either side with American and state flags. After passing an office for a congressman from New Jersey and a congresswoman from California, I come upon room 327, which bears a plaque for Congressman Jay Holmes. An American flag hangs to the left of the door, and the white-and-red Florida state flag hangs to the right, beside a sign that says WELCOME, PLEASE COME IN.

I open the door to the office, which is lined with plush blue carpet, and find myself standing right next to a young woman's shiny mahogany desk, which takes up most of the space in the cramped office reception area.

"Hi," she says as she finishes jotting a message onto a pad of paper. "Can I help you?"

"I'm here to see Blake Fischer?"

"And you are?"

"Hannah Sugarman."

She gestures toward a small seating area to my right. "Have a seat."

I sink into the blue-and-gold-striped couch, which is nestled in the corner of the room, in front of a small windowed office at the back of the reception area. The woman watches as I hug my tote against my side and offers a faint smile. At least she didn't ask why I'm here because, quite frankly, I have no idea why I'm here. To help my landlord with his grocery shopping? To let him torture me with inane Halloween tasks? Not exactly the kind of thing I want to share with some congressional receptionist.

As I pick a piece of black fuzz off my cream sweater, a camera crew and a woman dressed in a red suit emerge from the door behind the receptionist's desk. A strikingly tall man with salt-and-pepper hair follows behind them. He wears a gray pinstripe suit, an American flag pin, and a navy tie with small red polka dots.

"Thank you so much for your time, Congressman," the woman says, shaking the man's hand. "The story will air on *The Situation Room* tonight."

"My pleasure," the congressman says. "This issue isn't going away anytime soon."

Blake emerges from behind the congressman and beams when he sees me sitting in the waiting area.

"Hannah—hey," he says, coming toward me. "Sorry, we just wrapped up an interview with CNN. Do you mind waiting one sec while I hand stuff off to my deputy?"

"No problem."

He waves me up from my seat. "Come here a sec."

I fumble with my bag and cautiously follow Blake across the room.

"Jay, this is Hannah Sugarman," he says, pushing me forward by the small of my back. "Hannah, Congressman Holmes."

Congressman Holmes breaks into a smile and reaches out his hand. "Pleasure to meet you, Hannah."

I shake his hand, my palms slick with sweat. "Nice to meet you, too."

"Hannah works over at the Institute for Research and Discourse," Blake says.

"Wonderful, wonderful," the congressman says. "They do good work over there. Who do you work for?"

"Mark Henderson."

"Sure, sure, sure. Mark Henderson. Monetary policy, right? And isn't his daughter Emma getting a PhD in American history from Yale?"

"I—yes. Wow. Good memory."

Congressman Holmes smiles. Then he turns to Blake. "Hey, make sure you get Susie up to speed before you take off. Jim will take over once I get to Tampa."

"Will do," Blake says.

The congressman heads back into his office, and Blake slips into the windowed minioffice behind me. He leans over the desk of a young blonde, whose straight hair is pulled into a tight ponytail. They gesture back and forth at each other, nodding their heads and exchanging stacks of paper. Finally Blake emerges from his office and sighs.

"Okay," he says, loosening his bright blue tie. "Let's go."

He escorts me down the long, marble hallway and out the same entrance I used earlier, and as we walk down First Street, he shimmies out of his jacket and throws it over his shoulder.

"So you and the congressman are on a first-name basis, huh?" I ask as we saunter across C Street.

He grins. "We keep it pretty casual."

"And how does he feel about your ANC run?"

Blake shrugs. "He gets it. He knows you have to get your start in politics somewhere. But he's also glad being a neighborhood commissioner wouldn't require a lot of my time. It's a pretty low-key commitment."

I head for the Metro entrance, but Blake grabs me gently by the shoulder and steers me toward a parking lot across from Cannon. "Easy, there," he says. "I drove today."

"Oh." I grab my sunglasses from inside my tote. "Where are we heading?"

Blake scrunches his lips together and wiggles them from side to side. "Not sure yet, actually. Haven't made up my mind. I think I'll make the decision on the fly." He grins. "We'll see what inspires me."

Great. That's just the answer I was hoping for.

Somewhere past the Air and Space Museum we have a change in course. As we zipped down Independence Avenue, I figured he was heading back to Dupont Circle so that we could shop at Whole Foods or one of the stores in our neighborhood. But then, suddenly, Blake veered into the left lane at the corner of Seventh Street, indicating he planned to head south instead of north, and that's when I knew the plan had changed. To what, exactly, I could not say.

"Uh, so Blake. Care to tell me where we're going?"

He turns to me and grins. "You'll see."

Blake rounds the corner onto Seventh Street and chugs past the Federal Aviation Administration in his shiny white Volkswagen SUV. I've always thought this was one of the least attractive parts of the city. Most of the federal agencies hover around Independence Avenue between Second and Fourteenth streets, and it looks as if God shit huge cement blocks from the sky, and this is where they landed. Each building takes up an entire city block, and there is little else around them. I cannot imagine why Blake is taking me this way.

We continue through the agency wasteland, where we pass the sweeping, concave curvature of the Department of Housing and Urban Development, which, with its pale concrete facade and repetitive rows of dark square windows, looks like a cross between the Watergate and the Starship *Enterprise*. I don't think I've ever driven past this building before, and I officially have no idea where we are—not in some sort of metaphysical "where is anyone in this world?" way, but in the very physical sense of "I cannot, for the life of me, figure out where we are in the context of this city."

"Blake. Seriously. Where the hell are we going?"

Blake smiles and says nothing. We ride across the overpass above I-395 and follow the curve of Seventh Street around a bend until we reach the intersection with Maine Avenue, at which point I can see a series of small boats in the distance and a sign for the Southwest Waterfront. A pale blue roof looms just above the tree line, with *Zanzibar Nightclub* scrawled across the top in bright red cursive letters.

Blake speeds across Maine Avenue and turns right onto a small road called Water Street, which is sandwiched between Maine Avenue to the right and the city's southwestern waterfront to the left. As we crawl along Water Street, we pass a ramshackle series of run-down restaurants and shuttered buildings, none of which seems to be open, and I cannot help but feel as if I'm starring in some mobster movie, where Blake is taking me down to the waterfront to put a bullet in my head before tying me in chains and dumping me in the river. It is clear I need to watch fewer *Sopranos* reruns online.

We bump along the narrow road until we reach a bottleneck surrounded by more run-down buildings and shacks, and my confusion is supplanted by the unnerving sentiment that something is very, very wrong. The small hovel to my left looks as if someone constructed it from warped baking sheets and jungle gym pieces, and I have seen a total of two people since we turned onto Water Street. Unless these passing minutes are meant to be my last, this strikes me as an unfortunate way to spend a Friday afternoon.

Blake maneuvers the car through the narrowed opening at the end of Water Street and pulls into a small parking lot, which opens up to a series of shops, with people milling along the sidewalk. I am relieved to see signs of life. I am also thoroughly confused.

As Blake rolls his car into a parking spot, I peer through the front windshield and spot a vast sign for CAPTAIN WHITE'S SEAFOOD CITY perched atop a steep turquoise roof, the white block letters punctuated by metal replicas of crabs and lobsters and shrimp, each of which is approximately the size of Blake's car. Smack in the middle of the sign sits an enormous image of a bearded sailor gripping an old-fashioned spoke steering wheel.

"You've got to be kidding me," I say.

"What?"

I study Blake's face and recall all the times he has used the phrases "ahoy" and "going overboard" and "anchors aweigh." Now we are at some sort of fish market, in front of a huge image of a bearded sailor. And, apparently, I am the only one in this car who sees the humor in any of this.

"Never mind," I say. "What is this place?"

"The Maine Avenue Fish Market. I figured you'd never been."

He figured right. In three years of living in Washington, I have never even heard of this place. Frankly, even though there are fifty state-named streets across the city, I never encountered Maine Avenue before today. The location's novelty does not, however, explain our reason for being here.

We hop out of the car, and immediately the stench of raw seafood slaps me in the face. "Lovely," I say, covering my nose with my hand.

Blake sticks his buttonlike nose in the air and takes a deep breath. "You don't like it?"

"Not particularly."

"Yeah, I guess most people don't. But I love it. It reminds me of my dad."

"I'm not sure how your dad would feel about that . . ."

"It would probably make him smile." Blake's cheeks flush, and that's when I remember his father is dead. Well done, Hannah. "We used to go fishing all the time when I was growing up," he says, rolling up his shirtsleeves. "We called ourselves the Fischer Men."

"The Fischer Men—wow. So many things about you are starting to make sense . . ."

"What's that supposed to mean?"

"Nothing . . ."

"Hey, Fischer Men is a lot better than some of the names my dad got called in the navy. Apparently *Fischer* was an easy target for dirty puns. Although the Fischer Men do like a good pun now and then."

"You don't say . . ."

Blake smirks and gently elbows me in the side. "Anyway, I saw you had some seafood on your shopping list for the party, so I thought I'd take you here as a little surprise. Given how much you like to cook, I thought you might get a kick out of it."

We wind our way past one of many seafood shops, and at this first one, the seafood sits on ice below foot level, with a bunch of men standing in the pit behind the seafood and shouting up at passersby to ask what they want. No wonder Blake asked what I was wearing earlier. Some of these fishmongers would have an X-rated view if I'd worn a skirt today.

The combination of seafood and commotion reminds me of the Pike Place Fish Market in Seattle, which I visited a decade ago when my parents dragged me across the country for the World Trade Organization meeting. While they were off talking about trade imbalances and domestic subsidies, I snuck off from our room at the Crowne Plaza and hopped on a bus down to the fish market. The place was a cook's dream come true—fish everywhere, all different kinds, right off the boat. I'd never seen anything like it.

I spent an hour strolling around the market, watching the fishmongers toss slick, silvery king salmon across vats of ice while shouting back and forth to each other over the bustle of the crowd and the drifting guitar music. I bought a tub of cooked Dungeness crab as a souvenir, not fully appreciating the mechanics involved in transporting fresh seafood on a five-hour flight across the country. When my parents spotted the container in our hotel mini-fridge, they—not without justification—thought I'd lost my mind, but I told them Pike Place offered such a staggering selection of seafood that I had to buy something. Unfortunately, my parents forbade me from bringing fresh seafood on an airplane, and I was forced to wolf down what I could before throwing the rest of the container in the trash.

This place on Maine Avenue lacks the energy of Pike Place, and it's definitely grungier than Seattle's famous market, but they carry an extensive selection of seafood, everything from whole snapper to grouper filets to octopus, and every kind of shellfish, including live lobsters and crabs.

Blake leads me over to Captain White's, and I survey the shrimp and crab's legs. "You're sure this stuff is fresh?"

"Well, I should be honest," he says, lowering his voice and turning his back to a tattooed fishmonger who looks eager to make a sale. He comes in close and whispers in my ear. "Most of the fish is trucked in from Maryland. And some of it's frozen. But it's still pretty good, and for the amount of seafood you have on your list, you can't beat the price."

Blake calls over the tattooed man and points to the extra-large shrimp. "We'll take ten pounds of those guys, and five pounds of the oysters over there."

I point to the jar of shucked oysters. "Why don't we buy the shucked kind? I don't need them in the shell. I'm cooking them anyway. It'll save me time."

"Aw, come on. Fresh is the only way to go."

"Are you planning to shuck them for me?"

He bites his lip. "How about this—you cook with the jarred oysters, I'll do my own thing with the fresh ones. There's nothing quite like a freshly shucked oyster."

"Fine."

Blake calls to the tattooed man. "Make that three pounds of the oysters in the shell, and a jar of the shucked oysters."

"And throw in four pounds of squid," I add.

Blake offers me an approving grin and then turns back to the fishmonger. "Whoa—hey, we don't want any of the shrimp with the spots on them. Or the milky eyes. Put those back. Only the fresh ones." The fishmonger nods, scoops out the objectionable shrimp, and tosses in some fresher ones.

"Someone knows his seafood," I say.

He shrugs. "What can I say? I'm more than just a beautiful face."

Blake surveys his order and hands the man a wad of cash.

"By the way," he says, "all this cash reminded me—I checked it out, and when it comes to catering my party, it's totally legal for me to pay you."

Frankly, I'd forgotten it might not be. That's probably because the finer points of what is legal and what is not no longer seem to enter the calculus of my daily behavior.

We trudge back to the car, weighed down by about twenty pounds of seafood. Blake opens his trunk and lifts off the lid to an enormous blue-and-white cooler, which is nestled among a bunch of red-and-white fishing rods, a rusty tackle box, a pair of beat-up Adidas sneakers, and a set of jumper cables. We dump the food in the cooler, seal it up, and hop back in the car. Blake pulls out of the parking lot and slowly turns onto Maine Avenue.

"Three more places I want to take you," he says.

He flicks on a compilation of '80s tunes and skips forward to a song by Flock of Seagulls, and as he starts crooning the lyrics, his wildly off-key tones filling the car, I realize this day is going to be even weirder than I thought.

twenty-eight

after Blake stops off at a cheese shop in Alexandria and a butcher in Arlington, he pulls into the parking lot of a wine emporium in McLean, fist-pumping all the while to Def Leppard. Considering this is a man I should, theoretically, be avoiding, I somehow have managed to spend more time with him over the past week than I have with my parents over the past three months, and the hours of quality time show no sign of abating.

"Didn't we just buy wine the other night?" I ask.

Blake sighs. "Yeah, I know. But I checked my liquor cabinet last night, and it looks like one of my buddies put a serious dent in my supply of port and scotch."

Port. And scotch. The port and scotch Rachel and I forgot to replace. Shit.

"Oh. I see."

"It's weird, though, because I haven't had friends over in months, so I'm not really sure when someone would have drunk all my booze. But between work and the ANC election, I've been operating on very little sleep for months, so who knows. Anything is possible."

I smile uncomfortably. "Isn't it always?"

We hop out of the car, and Blake points his finger between the wine shop and an ABC liquor store across the street. "Want to stick with me, or divide and conquer?"

We have been shopping for more than two hours. I do not need to prolong this day any longer. "Let's split up."

"Cool. If you run across the street to the ABC and find the scotch, I'll grab some port over here and meet you."

Blake heads one way, and I dart across the street to the liquor store. Once inside, I wander down the aisles, searching for the shelves housing the whiskey and scotch. I can't believe Rachel and I forgot to replace his booze. How could we be so stupid? As if he wouldn't notice both bottles were empty. Then again, I managed to leave a container of homemade ice cream in his freezer with the name SUGARMAN on it. Stealth is not a personal strength.

I scan the display and spot the bottle Rachel and I used at each of our supper clubs: the Macallan eighteen-year scotch. I pluck the bottle off the shelf, and as soon as I do, I notice the price: $149.95. Holy shit.

"Hey, how did you know Macallan is my favorite?"

I turn around and find Blake standing directly behind me, his lips curled into a playful smirk. "Lucky guess," I say.

He grabs the bottle from my hand. "Hey there, high roller. The eighteen-year?"

Isn't that what he already owns? I'm so confused. "Not okay?"

"No, it's fine. Just a little pricey, that's all. Eighteen is what I have at home, but I got it as a gift for my birthday last year. I usually buy the twelve-year if I'm just buying it for me."

Great. Now I feel even worse. "Then let's buy that instead," I say. "It's cheaper."

Blake waves me away with his hand. "Nah, don't worry about it. I'm just bitching. It's not your fault someone drank my booze." He smiles. "The eighteen-year tastes better anyway. I shouldn't skimp on your first catering gig."

He hands the bottles to the cashier, grabs his wallet, and drops his credit card on the counter.

I am pretty much the worst person alive.

We get back to Blake's house around six-thirty, and I help Blake unload what feels like one thousand pounds of groceries into his kitchen, finding space where I can in his already overstuffed refrigerator. As I unload the last of the seafood, Blake rubs his hands along the granite countertop.

"You hungry?" he asks.

"I could eat," I say, a statement that is true both now and always.

"Any interest in sharing a pizza? I could eat a whole one on my own, but I probably shouldn't."

I stuff a bag of shrimp between two bottles of Dogfish Head Ale and shut the refrigerator door. "Um, I don't know . . ."

What I really want to do is call Jacob and have him (a) apologize for not calling me and (b) offer to come over and make out with me. I also do not relish the idea of fostering a friendship with the one man I should be avoiding.

"Aw, come on," Blake says. "Don't make me eat a pizza all by myself. Do it for my waistline."

I sigh. "Yeah, okay. Pizza sounds good."

Blake leaves to pick up a pizza from Pizzeria Paradiso, the only place in Dupont Circle to get authentic, Italian, wood-fired pizza, and I plop down on his living room sofa and let my back meld into the soft leather cushions. What the hell am I doing? With every passing day, I manage to dig myself into a deeper hole. I can't become *friends* with Blake. Friends don't lie to each other and sabotage each other's political careers. Friends don't steal each other's liquor and use each other's kitchens without permission. I shouldn't even be here. I should be out somewhere fun with Jacob. I should be getting laid.

Whatever. Jacob will call me when he's ready. In the meantime, I need to get my head in the game and prepare for tomorrow night. This party will be my first nonsecret, paid catering gig, and as such, I can't afford to make any missteps. If I play this right, I could get requests for other events, and soon I could have enough buzz around my name to start my own company. Then I could quit my job and cook anywhere for anyone, without worrying about who might find out. I wouldn't have to use my landlord's house. Behind his back. While he runs for neighborhood commissioner and pays me to help with his parties.

For the party to be a launching pad to a new career, however, the food has to be perfect. So far I'm off to a good start. I pawned the menu for tomorrow night from my ideas for The Dupont Circle Supper Club, where I tied each dish into the Halloween theme. There will be curried deviled eggs and barbecued "skeleton" ribs, blood orange sorbet and devil's food cupcakes. Tomorrow morning, Blake will help me with my last-minute prep work, and from there . . . well, I guess the rest is up to chance.

Unfortunately, Rachel was mysteriously unavailable to help with the decorations, and so I was left to my own devices and those of Washington's resident pirate. Despite that significant handicap, I must say, the rooms look pretty great. I strung yards of cobwebs across Blake's living room walls and strategically pinned a bunch of plastic black widow spiders into the cottony strands. Then I unwrapped six packets of bat clusters, minimobiles that flap and squeal when a gust of air moves through the room, and hung each cluster in the perfect location along the ceiling in both the living and dining rooms. After searching through Blake's storage closet, I rustled up a lifelike witch, one covered with warts and wrinkly skin and brittle gray hair, and stuck her in the corner of the living room next to the fireplace.

Admittedly, the longer I sit here without Blake in the house, the scarier all of these decorations become, but thankfully I'm smart enough to know they are only decorations. As in, they're fake. And it's not like witches even exist. So I'm fine. Halloween is stupid, anyway. I never bought into ghosts and goblins or any of that spooky stuff. Someone else might be frightened by my exemplary decorating skills, but not me. Nope. I'm just impressed with what a good job I did.

———————

One of the spiders just moved. It was sitting to the far right of the cobweb, and now it's more toward the center. By a centimeter, I think. And something is scratching inside the walls. And the ceiling. Holy shit, that witch is scary. Why does she keep looking at me? *Stop looking at me.* And those bats. They won't shut up. *Someone make them shut up.*

Just as I'm about to search for a pickaxe and a garlic cross, Blake returns with a large pizza. I run to the front door and grab the pizza from his hands.

"You're back! Great! Let's eat!"

Blake follows me into the kitchen. "Someone's hungry . . ."

"There's something crawling in your walls," I yell over my shoulder. "I thought you should know."

"Oh, that's just the pipes. They make noises sometimes. Don't worry about it."

The pipes. I knew that.

Blake opens the cupboard and grabs two plates, but then he picks up the top plate and flips it upside down. "That's weird," he says.

"What?"

He stares at the writing on the bottom of the dish. "This isn't my plate."

Christ on a cracker. "You sure about that?"

He scrunches his lips together and rubs his chin. "Yeah. My plates are from Williams-Sonoma. This plate is some brand called Tuxton."

"Maybe a friend left one of theirs?"

"But then I'd have thirteen." He quickly counts the plates in his cupboard. "I only have twelve."

"Maybe you broke one and forgot."

"I don't think so . . ." He shrugs. "Or maybe I did. Like I said, I feel like I'm going crazy these days. I guess sleep deprivation will do that to you."

"It will," I say. "Definitely."

Blake lays the plates on the counter and serves up the pizza—

the Atomica, with tomato, salami, black olives, and pepper. I can smell the charred crust and fiery salami from across the counter. Blake opens two bottles of beer and pulls up a stool along the breakfast bar.

"*Bon appetit*," he says, clanking his beer bottle against mine.

I swallow a hunk of pizza and wipe the grease from the corners of my mouth, quickly mulling over a way to change the subject to something other than the mystery surrounding Blake's plates. "So . . . that was a pretty fragrant afternoon, no?"

Blake furrows his brow. "How do you mean?"

"The fish market? The smell of fish entrails?"

"Oh, come on, it wasn't that bad," he says, taking a swig of beer. "Trust me, you don't know from bad fish smells."

"But I'm sure you do, Santiago."

Blake pauses, his beer hovering before his lips. "Is that a Hemingway reference?"

"It is—well done."

Blake laughs and shakes his head. "So I'm into boats and fishing? So what?"

"So nothing," I say. "It's your hobby. I get it."

"A hobby makes it sound so trivial."

"That's not what I meant."

Blake smiles. "I know. I guess it's hard for me to explain sometimes. Being around boats and the water—I don't know, it brings back a lot of good memories. I spent a lot of time around boats growing up as a navy brat, and my uncle ran a restaurant in Tampa. Every spring break we'd pay my uncle a visit, and he and my dad would take my brother and me fishing almost every day. That's where I got hooked—no pun intended."

I raise an eyebrow as I bite into my pizza.

"Okay," he says, "you got me. Pun intended."

"Thought so."

"But what I remember most about those trips to Tampa is how happy I was—fishing with my dad, helping Uncle Jack in his restaurant, getting into trouble along the harbor. It was this amazingly innocent time, where the most I had to worry about was getting sunburned or eating too much fried shrimp. Everything was so much simpler then." He picks at the label on his beer bottle. "Sorry, I don't know why I'm telling you all this. The point is, boating and fishing—those things are more than hobbies. They symbolize one of the happiest times of my life."

Well, aren't I the asshole?

"Sorry," I say. "I didn't mean to trivialize your interests."

"Nah, you didn't trivialize anything. Don't worry about it." He grabs another slice of pizza from the box.

"Is that why you represent a congressman from Tampa? Because of your uncle?"

He nods. "I moved around a lot as a kid before we finally settled in Annapolis when I was a teenager, so I never really felt like I was from anywhere. But I always had a connection to Tampa because of my uncle. Plus, after my dad died, we got a lot closer, so it's nice to have an excuse to visit him every once in a while."

"Have you ever considered moving there?"

He shakes his head. "To be honest, after going to Georgetown and working in DC for more than a decade, Washington feels like home more than anywhere else. That's why I'm trying to get more involved in local politics. Working on the Hill is great, but I feel like I could make more of a difference here, at the local level."

By shutting down underground supper clubs like mine . . .

I nibble on my pizza crust. "Why get involved with politics at all? Isn't it just one big power trip?"

"It doesn't have to be. I just want to make my neighborhood and city a better place to live. The Advisory Neighborhood Commission is a good start." He smiles as he glances at his watch. "T minus four days until the election. You could be talking to a future Dupont Circle Neighborhood Commissioner. How does it feel to be this close to a future celebrity?"

"Wow. Do you think if you signed this napkin it might be worth something someday?"

He chuckles. "At *least* fifty cents. Maybe a dollar if I work a few miracles."

I take a swig of my beer. "Yeah, well, if you could throw a few miracles my way, I'd appreciate it."

"Hey, I'm letting you cater my Halloween party, aren't I? That may not be a miracle, but it's a step in the right direction. Who knows? Tomorrow could be the start of a new career for you." He fixes his gray-blue eyes on mine. "I hope it's the start of something great."

I smile softly as I take another sip of beer. "Thanks. I hope so, too."

Blake is right. Tomorrow could be the start of something wonderful, a chance for me to parlay my experience from The Dupont Circle Supper Club into something new and meaningful and legal. Tomorrow could be the moment when I finally go legit.

Of course, that assumes everything tomorrow night goes as planned. Which, if I'm being honest, it rarely does.

twenty-nine

i show up at Blake's front door the next morning at our appointed time of nine o'clock to keep plugging away at the party prep. Blake whips open his door, holding a steaming mug of coffee. His pin-straight hair sticks out in all directions, a haphazardness outclassed only by his red Teenage Mutant Ninja Turtles pajama pants and a faded orange T-shirt. A gust of fishy air floats past my nostrils.

"The olfactory extravaganza continues," I say.

Blake smiles. "Come on in."

He lures me back into the kitchen, and the smell intensifies as we make our way down the hall. "I'm a pretty fearless cook, but I'm not gonna lie—the smell of raw seafood is a little much for a Saturday morning."

Blake shrugs. "The shrimp aren't going to peel themselves, right?"

"Unfortunately not."

He points to the heap of shrimp sitting next to the sink. "Why don't you start with those, and I'll start prepping the oysters."

Peeling ten pounds of shrimp: an activity slightly more enjoyable than gutting a fish or de-feathering a chicken. These are the moments where I wish I had a kitchen assistant or sous chef, but alas, this morning it's just me and a thirtysomething Teenage Mutant Ninja Turtles fan.

I start peeling the shrimp, tossing the shells in a big container for stock, and slipping the black veins out of their backs. Blake stands on the other side of the sink, scrubbing the dirt and grit off the oyster shells with a stiff-bristled brush. He dumps the cleaned shells into a big bowl lined with damp paper towels.

"So," Blake says, plucking another oyster from the pile, "anyone special in your life at the moment?"

I shoot him a sideways glance as I slip another shrimp from its shell. "You mean like a boyfriend?"

"Sure."

"Not really."

No one except Jacob, who hasn't called me in two weeks and, in a bothersome development, still hasn't approved my friend request on Facebook. I would say my request simply got buried somewhere in his in-box, but considering how plugged in he is, I doubt that's the case. However, last night I noticed we have a friend in common: Becca Gorman, a friend of mine from Cornell who seems to know pretty much everyone in the universe. And, because I have turned into an obsessive stalker, I sent Becca a message through Facebook to see what she knows about Jacob. Her status update from a few days ago said she'd be AWOL until next week while she travels around Cambodia with her sister, but with any luck, she'll be able to shed some light on Mr. Reaser when she returns. Maybe she can explain why he's been such a flake.

"What about you?" I ask, tossing another peeled shrimp into the bowl. "Any girlfriends to speak of?"

Blake shakes his head. "I don't exactly have the best luck with the ladies."

I look up at him, with the intention of making a joke about his Ninja Turtles pajama pants, but I clam up when I see the sad, lonely look in his eyes. I know that expression, more intimately than I'd care to admit.

Blake plows his way through most of the oysters, and then he throws on a pair of gloves and plucks one of the oysters from the cleaned pile. With gloved hands, he jabs a small oyster knife into the side of the shell and, with a gentle sawing motion, pries it open, like a thief jimmying a locked door. He runs the knife around the oyster meat and tilts the shell up to his lips, slurping down the oyster in a single gulp.

What I can't get over, aside from Blake's willingness to knock back oysters before ten in the morning, is how quickly Blake does this. His movements are almost balletic, prying the oyster meat from its shell in one graceful movement. I always thought Blake was a little on the doughy side, but watching him shuck that oyster, I realize he's more muscular than I thought. Between the button-downs and pajama pants, I guess I never noticed.

Blake catches me staring at him and smiles. "Want one?"

"No thanks. It's a little early for raw seafood. For me at least."

"Ever shucked an oyster before?"

"Believe it or not, I haven't."

"Wanna try?"

"Oh—no. I'm fine. I was only watching to see how you do it."

"Aw, come on," he says, waving me over. "I'll show you. If you're going to be a famous cook someday, you'll need to know how to shuck an oyster."

Blake offers me a pair of gloves, which I slip on as he grabs my shoulders and gently positions me in front of him at the sink. "Hold down the shell with your hand like this," he says, pressing his broad hand over mine as I hold the shell against the counter, "and stick the knife in the hinge of the shell. Like that." I dig the knife into the oyster and start rocking the knife back and forth. Blake grabs my wrists. "Careful—you're going to cut yourself. You don't want to rock the knife. You want to twist it until you hear the shell snap. There. Better. Now start carving around the outside."

He lets go of my wrists and rests his hands on either side of me against the counter, poking his chin over my shoulder as he watches me pull the knife around the oyster shell until I feel the top release. I pop the shell open and look over my shoulder at Blake, my nose nearly touching his. "I did it!"

He pulls away and chuckles. "I had no doubt you would."

I inspect the slimy, gray blob nestled in the shell. "My dad always says oysters look like big boogers."

"Wow. That's gross."

"I know. But I've never been able to shake the visual."

"So you don't eat them?"

"Oh, I eat them. Just not at ten in the morning. And I kind of feel like I'm eating big boogers. Which sort of detracts from the experience."

Blake laughs and grabs the shell and knife from my hands. "I'll stick to the boogers then. You stick to the shrimp."

I scoot back to my station next to the sink and carry on with the eight remaining pounds of shrimp.

"So take me through the menu again," Blake says.

"Okay, first there are the angels on horseback and devils on horseback."

Blake shakes his head. "Remind me what those are?"

"An English thing. Angels on horseback are baked oysters wrapped in bacon. Devils are the same thing with dates instead of oysters."

Blake nods. "Got it. What else?"

"I'm going to slow-cook the barbecued ribs and serve them as 'skeleton ribs,' and I'll serve up the calamari tentacles as 'deep-fried spiders.' Then I'll roast the shrimp and arrange them in glasses of ice to look like claws or fingers, which people can dip into a 'Bloody Mary' cocktail sauce. And I'll scatter platters of deviled eggs around the living and dining rooms."

"Think that'll be enough food?"

"Definitely. I'll throw some cheese and crudités into the mix, too. Oh, and dessert—spiced devil's food cupcakes and blood orange sorbet."

Blake leans his back against the counter and crosses his feet. "Well aren't you the most creative cook I know?"

I shrug. "Like I said, food is sort of my thing."

I rinse my shrimp-covered hands under the kitchen faucet and wipe them on one of Blake's dish towels, and then I grab a sheet pan from one of Blake's cupboards, along with a pair of tongs and a spatula from one of his drawers. I dump the shrimp onto the sheet pan, sprinkle them with salt and pepper, and toss them with some of the olive oil from Blake's pantry. When I look up, Blake is staring at me with raised eyebrows.

"Wow," he says. "You really know your way around this kitchen, huh?"

I freeze. "Beginner's luck, I guess."

Blake smiles, pulling a new roll of paper towels from beneath his kitchen sink. "That or a sixth sense."

"Yeah," I say. "Something like that."

"Well, let me know if you have any questions about where I keep pans or ingredients or whatever. But for now it seems like you have a good handle on things."

I smile politely and nod and think, *You don't know the half of it.*

Blake and I finish prepping the food by four o'clock and arrange to meet back in his kitchen in two hours. I will need to take at least three showers to wash off the smell of raw fish, which has embedded itself into the fabric of my clothes and my entire earthly being.

"Oh, but don't worry about what you wear," Blake says. "I've got you covered. You can get dressed in the guestroom upstairs."

"Sorry?"

"I already took care of your costume. For the party."

"You . . . took care of my costume." I hope my tone adequately conveys my skepticism.

"It's part of my costume, so yeah. I'm going to be Sweeney Todd, and you're going to be Mrs. Lovett."

"Mrs. Lovett?" As I recall, Mrs. Lovett is Sweeney Todd's accomplice, who chops up Todd's victims and bakes them into pies. She was portrayed most recently on film by a psychotic-looking Helena Bonham Carter.

He grins. "Yup."

"But I'm the caterer. I don't need to dress up."

"Of course you do."

"But . . . Mrs. Lovett is supposed to be hideous and freaky."

"It's Halloween. You're supposed to be hideous and freaky on Halloween. Unless you're a college girl, in which case you're supposed to dress up like a slut."

I hate to break it to Blake, but that is what women of all ages do on Halloween. The holiday serves as an excuse to wear as little clothing as possible, where all creatures—from rabbits to schoolgirls—exist only in their "sexy" forms. This year Millie will don a "sexy soldier" ensemble, and last year Rachel dressed as a "sexy crayon," bestowing sexiness on burnt siena for possibly the first time in history.

"Thanks for looking out for me," I say, terrified as to what this costume will look like. Regardless how good the food is, no one will want to hire a caterer who looks like a serial killer.

"Don't worry," Blake says. "It'll be great."

I somehow doubt that. But as I watch Blake's eyes crinkle around the edges with excitement, I realize I don't need great. I'll settle for decent. Or even mediocre. Because, as much as I hate to admit it, I like being part of a duo again, and I'll take it in whatever form it comes.

CHAPTER
thirty

i stare at my reflection in Blake's full-length mirror and cannot believe what I see.

"You've got to be kidding me," I say, tugging at the black corset strings around my waist. "Where the hell did you get this thing?"

Blake comes to the doorway and immediately hunches over in a fit of laughter. "Oh my god, it's perfect."

"Stop laughing. I look ridiculous."

"No you don't. Okay, maybe a little bit, but it's Halloween. Seriously, it's perfect."

Perfect is not how I would describe this costume. Hideous, maybe, or highly flammable, but definitely not perfect. The black gauzy sleeves fall about an inch below my knuckles, and the tiered skirt cascades to the floor in a way that guarantees I will trip at least once during the party. And while I appreciate the slimming effects of the corset, I do not enjoy the supreme boost it gives to my breasts, which are now so perky they distract even me. Perhaps that was Blake's intention.

Blake grabs my shoulders and spins me around to face him. He pulls a strand of hair away from my face. "I have a can of hairspray in the bathroom, and a big bag of costume makeup." He digs into his pocket. "Oh, and here's a photo of Mrs. Lovett from the latest *Sweeney Todd* movie. You can use it as a guide."

I take the picture from Blake and inspect Helena Bonham

Carter's white face and black, sunken eyes. "Please tell me you're joking."

"Of course I'm not joking. What's wrong with that picture? Her makeup looks cool."

"She looks insane. Can't I mess up my hair and be done with it?"

"No," he says. "That's lame. There's no point in dressing up if you only go halfway."

"So then why don't I not dress up at all?"

He sighs. "Because it's Halloween. Everyone will be dressed up. Everyone will look ridiculous. Trust me."

"Fine," I say. "But don't blame me when no one wants any food or drinks because I scare everyone away."

Blake ruffles my hair with his fingers and steals a quick glance at my chest. "I assure you, my friend. That won't happen."

Thirty minutes before Blake's friends show up, I march back into the kitchen, my hair teased into a frizzy mass atop my head and my makeup a near facsimile of Helena Bonham Carter's. When Blake sees me, he gives me an enthusiastic thumbs-up. I interpret this to mean I look absolutely hideous.

However ridiculous I look, Blake's outfit gives me a run for my money. Let's just say he's no Johnny Depp. Aside from the puffy shirt and ornate cravat, his ratty wig puts the whole ensemble over the top. He looks like Don King.

"Blake, is that a pirate shirt?" I ask, pointing at his torso.

He looks down at his sleeves, which balloon from the arm-holes of his gray, button-down vest. "What, you don't like it?"

"It looks a little, I don't know . . ." I swoop my arm like a pirate. "*Argh, matey!*"

"Listen, Sugarman, I don't know what you're talking about. This is a Sweeney Todd costume." He rolls up his sleeves and washes his hands in the sink.

"You probably *should* have dressed as a pirate. It would have been much more appropriate."

"Because I like boats?"

"That, and the fact that you talk like a pirate half the time."

"No I don't. Do I?"

I dip my head and stare at him with widened eyes. "Are you kidding?"

"No. What are you talking about?"

I smack my forehead and shake my head. "Blake, I've been meaning to address this for weeks. You use sailor and fishing expressions *all the time*. 'Welcome aboard.' 'Fish or cut bait.' 'Anchors aweigh.' I could go on and on."

He blushes and scratches his temple. "Really? Sorry. Sort of a throwback to childhood, I guess. When I was a kid, my dad used to call me First Mate, and I'd call him Skipper. It was a running joke between us—the Fischer Men, remember? I guess I still talk that way sometimes when I get nervous."

"Not just when you're nervous," I say. "You do it all the time."

"Around you," he says, turning his back to me as he opens the refrigerator.

"Right. All the time . . . around me."

Before I can ask Blake to explain what he means, he hands me a container of marinated artichokes hearts and a box of toothpicks. "I had an idea."

I poke a toothpick into an artichoke and hold it up for Blake to see. "A 'stake in the heart'?"

He smiles. "Exactly."

"Nice. I hadn't thought of that one."

I arrange the artichokes in concentric circles on a big, porcelain platter, occasionally stealing glances at Blake out of the corner of my eye. He does look ridiculous in that wig, but it's sort of endearing, like people who wear knee-high tube socks or super white sneakers without a hint of irony. I want to hug those people and hold them and tell them everything will be okay.

As I stab a toothpick into the last artichoke, I sense Blake standing behind me. "Can I squeeze in there a sec?" he asks. "I need to grab a spatula."

I move to the right, but he grabs me by the waist and moves me to the left. I jump.

"You ticklish?" he asks, smirking.

"No," I say. This is a lie. I am extremely ticklish.

"Oh?" He grabs my sides again. This time I squeal. "You're not? So if I went like this"— he wiggles his fingers under my arms— "you'd be fine?"

I let out a sharp yelp, and he starts poking me in the side and behind my knees, and before I know it I am on the ground and he is kneeling over me, prodding me all over as I giggle and shriek and tell him to stop.

"Bwahahaha, you cannot escape from Sweeney Todd!"

I screech and slap his hands away, and finally he stops when he is laughing so hard he can't manage to tickle me anymore. He wipes the tears away from his eyes, still kneeling over me with his legs straddled across my knees. His expression turns serious, and his gray eyes fix on mine.

"You know, there's something we need to talk about," he says. But before he can finish his thought, the doorbell rings.

"What?" I ask, trying not to let the panic rise in my voice. The supper club. He knows. "What do we need to talk about?"

He presses his lips together and looks away as he tugs at his wig. "Never mind," he says, shaking his head. "Let's get the door."

He grabs my hand and pulls me up from the ground, and he doesn't loosen his grip until we reach the front door.

thirty-one

s the crowd in Blake's living room multiplies, I discover I am not alone in looking like a lunatic. One guy is completely naked, save a pizza box, which he wears around his waist like a tutu. I imagine the box's contents are a special delivery for some lucky gal at the party tonight. Another man is dressed as Borat, clad in a neon yellow V-shaped unitard, which seems dated and unoriginal but, nevertheless, manages to attract the attention of everyone at the party due to its emphasis on this particular gentleman's, shall we say, impressive anatomy. These costumes, combined with a man dressed as a snake charmer (charming his own "snake"), lead me to revise my thesis on Halloween costumes. Girls aren't the only ones who dress like sluts on Halloween; apparently men are enthralled by any costume that showcases their schlong.

The man wearing the pizza box sidles up to the bar, where I am temporarily serving as the bartender while I wait for the crowd to deplete some of the platters. "Whatcha got?" he asks.

"Red and white wine and the usual hard stuff. The beer keg is out back."

He scans the bookshelves behind me, which Blake and I lined with bottles of rum, vodka, and other liquor. "You know what— I'll stick with beer," he says. He eyes me up and down. "Nice costume."

"You, too."

He smirks. "Sausage, baby. Extra large."

I roll my eyes. "The beer is out back."

"Oooh, the surly type. Me likey. Don't worry. I'll be back later. "

"Don't hurry," I call after him.

A short Indian man cloaked in silver Mylar slips in front of the pizza guy and approaches me at the bar, smiling as he watches me stare in puzzlement at his shiny costume.

"You like?" he asks, holding out his arms and spinning around, so that I can take in the whole ensemble. The silver material hangs over him and puffs out in the middle like a balloon.

"Um . . . yeah. . . . What are you supposed to be?"

"Balloon Boy! You know, the kid who supposedly got trapped in that air balloon?"

"A few years back?" I chuckle. "Wow. Hadn't thought about that one in a while."

"Yeah, well, the truth is, I went on Amazon to buy a Mylar blanket to line my sleeping bag for a camping trip, but I accidentally bought a pack of twelve, so I was looking for a way to use a few of them up."

"Nice job. I'd say you used at least three."

"Five, actually. I stuffed a few inside." He grins and extends his arm across the bar. "I'm Anoop, by the way."

I grab his hand and shake it. "Hannah."

"I see you met Wes," he says, pointing to the guy wearing the pizza box, who is now chatting up a woman dressed as Cat-woman. "Don't worry, he's harmless. Just crazy."

"And horny."

Anoop laughs. "That, too. So I hear you've been hanging out with Blake a bit, huh?"

I shrug. "I've been helping him get ready for the party. If that constitutes hanging out."

"Yeah, you made all this food, right? Those bacon-wrapped oysters are killer."

"Thanks."

"And I love the ribs. I ate like five already."

I put on my best smile. "If you ever need a caterer . . ."

Anoop smirks and shakes his finger at me. "I'll keep that in mind. Anyway, Blake is a great guy. One of the best, actually."

"Who apparently is very lucky to have such loyal and complimentary friends."

Anoop lifts his glass and toasts the air. "It's true. He surrounds himself with only the best."

Blake lets out a loud belly laugh from across the room, and I watch as he shakes with laughter. "Would you check out that wig?" I say. "How does he even hold that thing up?"

"With the strength of a thousand bulls." Anoop grins and holds out his glass. "I'll leave you in peace, but before I go, could you hit me with another glass of red?"

"That's what I'm here for," I say as I refill his glass.

"Nah, that's not the only reason you're here."

I scrunch my eyebrows together. "Oh, really? I'm pretty sure it is. I'm the caterer."

"No. There's more to it than that. Trust me." He studies my expression and shakes his head, staring into his wineglass. "Ah, Dionysus. You make me forget myself." He looks back up at me. "I've already said too much. But be good to Blake. He's a quality guy."

"I'll do my best."

Before Anoop can get away, Blake sneaks up behind him and gives him a playful elbow in the side. "What are you two chatting about over here?"

"Hannah's excellent cooking," Anoop says.

Blake grins. "She's pretty great, huh?"

Anoop looks me up and down. "That she is."

"Oh, so get this," Blake says, facing Anoop. "I was talking to Nicole, and apparently she ran into Geeta last week."

"Geeta?" Anoop and I ask in unison.

They turn and look at me. "Anoop's ex-girlfriend," Blake says. "Anyway, apparently she is as crazy as ever."

Anoop shakes his head. "Some things never change. Did she ask about me?"

"Yeah, she asked about all of us." A lithe blonde dressed as a belly dancer approaches the bar with a few of her friends, and Blake nods in her direction. "Hey, Nicole—what was Geeta saying? About that underground supper club?"

My ears perk up, and I feel all the blood rush to my face.

Anoop furrows his brow. "What underground supper club?"

Nicole flicks her hair over her shoulder. "You haven't heard about this? Apparently some amateur chef is running an unlicensed restaurant out of her house. Just Google 'Dupont Circle Supper Club' and you'll find the Web site."

"Oh, *riiiight*," Anoop says. "I read about that."

"Well, Geeta went the other weekend, and according to her, it's right in this neighborhood. One of Blake's neighbors, apparently."

I pull out a glass and two bottles of wine. "More wine anyone?" Everyone shakes their heads. "What about some scotch?" Rebuffed again. "Vodka?"

"Actually," says a black man dressed as a cow, "it's supposed to be really good. I've been trying to make a reservation, but they're completely booked up. Their schedule is a little erratic."

Blake huffs and widens his eyes. "You'd actually *go* to one of these dinners?"

The cow man shrugs. "It sounds fun."

"But the whole operation is totally irresponsible," Blake says. "Not to mention illegal."

"It's sort of a gray area," I blurt out. Everyone turns and stares at me. "It's . . . not legal, per se, but it isn't really . . . *illegal* either."

"Someone is serving food to paying customers without a license from the health department," Blake says. "That's illegal. What if someone gets food poisoning? What if there is damage to the property?"

I clear my throat. "I . . . don't know."

Blake snickers. "I mean, why should some people not have to follow the rules? All the other restaurants in Dupont Circle have to pay for a liquor license and health inspections—and rightfully get in trouble when they don't. Why should this woman get a free pass?"

"I don't think it's that big of a deal," says the cow man.

"Neither do I," says Anoop. "In fact, it's sounds pretty cool. Didn't I read somewhere that this woman made cheesesteak arancini and coconut cream pie? I can dig it."

"No, I see what Blake is saying," Nicole says. "If this woman wants to open a restaurant, she should open a restaurant. She can't have it both ways."

"Exactly," Blake says. He wraps his arm around me and gives me a squeeze. "Look at this lady. She's trying to run an honest catering operation over here. You don't see her running around, flouting the rules, do you?"

I laugh nervously as Blake squeezes me tighter and gives me a quick peck on the forehead, an act that, apparently, surprises everyone else as much as it surprises me. I pretend to ignore the awkwardness and decant a hefty pour of eighteen-year Macallan into a glass.

Nicole taps her fingers on her exposed, toned stomach. "Well, once you're elected you should make shutting down that supper club a priority."

"Once I'm elected, I'll actually have time," Blake says. "Frankly, I have too much going on at the moment to chase down some amateur cook. But once things settle down, I'll look into it." He grins and nudges me in the side. "If only for Hannah's sake."

I gulp down a mouthful of scotch. "Don't do it on my behalf. It doesn't bother me that much."

"No, no—you need a level playing field if you're going to make your cooking dreams a reality. And if I can help you along, well, that would make me a very happy guy."

He gives me another squeeze as I down the rest of my scotch, and I realize there is nothing I can do to make this situation better other than drinking scotch until I am physically incapable of speaking.

I don't drink any more scotch, mostly because I hate scotch, even if it is $150, eighteen-year Macallan. Besides, I have a party to cater, and getting blackout drunk won't ingratiate me with any potential future clients. To my infinite delight, however, I manage to escape any further discussion of supper clubs and campaigns for the rest of the party, and by midnight, I find myself back in the kitchen, where heaps of plates and glasses cover Blake's breakfast bar. Since cleanup is also my responsibility, I decide I'll start now to avoid an onslaught of work later, when I will be twice as tired.

I pull out a large black trash bag and stuff the dirty napkins and plates inside, amazed at the mess fifty people can generate. I rinse out the dirty glasses in the sink, and as I start putting them in the dishwasher, I feel a blunt edge press into my back. I glance over my shoulder and see Wes standing behind me, pushing into me with his pizza box.

"Special delivery," he says. He ogles me with a droopy, drunken smile.

I turn around and look down at the pizza box. "Yeah, okay, I'm gonna go ahead and refuse the package."

"Trust me, you want a taste of this."

"No, I assure you, I do not."

He throws his head back and lets out a slow, lazy laugh, then snaps his head back down and stands there, gawking. "You're hot," he says.

"You're drunk."

He smiles. "You're hot."

"You're drunk."

I'm beginning to think we could go on and on like this, in an endless back-and-forth, a theory Wes proves by adding, one more time, "You're hot."

"Thank you," I say, wanting nothing more than to bring this interaction to a close.

Wes reaches out and lays his broad hand on my shoulder and starts massaging my neck, a move I am certain has worked many times in his favor because, like a puppy being rubbed behind the ears, I go limp. "Yeah, you like that, don't you? Tell daddy how much you like it."

And then I awake from my trance. "You're gross."

"I can be as gross as you need me to be," he says, his left eyelid sagging.

"Listen—I have to clean up. Why don't you join your friends in the other room?"

I try to slip away from him, but he throws both his hands onto the counter, trapping me between them and his pizza box. "Not so fast," he says. "I don't think we're done here."

He leans in and starts slobbering in my ear and on my neck, covering me with the stale, sour smell of his breath. "Stop," I say. I push him away with my hands, but that involves me touching his bare chest, which eggs him on. I start slapping him on the arm.

"Mrrreeeooooww . . . ," he purrs.

"Wes, seriously. Stop."

He releases his right hand from the counter and grabs my breast. "How can you say stop when you're wearing a dress like this?"

"What's going on in here?" Blake ambles into the kitchen from the dining room and moves toward us, clenching his jaw when he sees Wes's hand on my chest.

Wes whirls around to face him. "Hey, man. We're just having a little fun."

Blake's black-rimmed eyes lock on mine, and he reads the panic in them. "Wes, you're drunk. Leave Hannah alone."

Wes puffs up his chest. "What's your problem, man?"

"No problem. I just want you to stop bothering Hannah."

"I'm not bothering her."

"Yes," I say. "You are."

Wes twirls around to face me and runs his hand down the front of my dress, plucking my corset strings in an attempt to undo them. "You didn't seem bothered a minute ago," he says, leaning in again and nibbling on my earlobe.

Blake rushes up behind Wes and grabs the pizza box with both hands, yanking it upward with a quick thrust. Wes screams in pain. "How many times do I have to tell you? Leave her alone," Blake says.

Wes backs away from me, writhing as he tries to pull the pizza box back into place. "Just 'cause you're not fucking her doesn't mean no one else can," he says.

Even the white makeup isn't enough to cover the redness in Blake's face, and he grabs Wes by the neck, tilting Wes's chin toward the ceiling. "Get the fuck out of my house," he says.

Wes coughs violently as Blake releases him and hobbles toward the front hallway, shooting me a hateful look as he passes through the kitchen doorway. "Cock tease," he says. Then he stumbles through the foyer and leaves.

The party winds down around three in the morning, at which point a few stragglers hang out in the living room, drinking Blake's newly purchased port and whiskey while they listen to some guy named Jorge (or Jose?) play the guitar as part of his Carlos Santana costume (though, inexplicably, he plays songs by everyone *but* Santana). I remain in the kitchen, scrubbing sheet pans and rinsing out glasses while I listen to Blake massacre the tune and lyrics of "Hotel California." Don Henley, wherever you are: I am sorry.

Blake's tone deafness aside, the party has been a raging success, although I'm still a little shaken by what happened with Wes. I think Blake is, too. He told me I could go home if I wanted to, but I didn't want to do that, for two reasons. One, I'd still be able to hear everyone thumping around upstairs, so it's not as if I'd be able to sleep, and two, the last thing a girl wants to do after being groped by a stranger is sit in her claustrophobic, basement apartment, alone. So I stayed.

But, on the plus side, I did hand out my contact information to a few inquiring guests, which could lead to future catering gigs down the line. Everyone raved about my light and crunchy calamari and smoky ribs, and I received more than a few requests for the devils on horseback recipe (My secret? Stuffing the dates with honey-laced mascarpone). I realize many of the compliments and requests will amount to nothing, but all I need is one person, aside from Blake, who is willing to take a chance on me. If that happens, tonight could be the beginning of something big.

As I throw the last of the glasses into the dishwasher and add some detergent, Blake waltzes into the kitchen warbling the tune to "Wish You Were Here."

"You might need Pink Floyd's permission if you're going to do that to their song," I say as I wipe my hands on a dish towel.

"What?" he says, playing an air guitar. "You're not enjoying the sweet stylings of Blake Fischer?"

"Is that what you call this?"

He smiles and grabs my hands, placing one on his shoulder and raising the other with his as he holds me by the waist. He leads me in a slow dance around the kitchen, every now and then erupting into song in a key and tone that can only sound good in his head, and probably not even there.

"I'm really sorry about what happened earlier," he says. "With Wes."

I try to shrug it off. "No biggie. He was drunk."

"That may be a reason, but it's not an excuse." He twirls me around and pulls me back in. "We have a history."

"Oh, do you?"

"We were roommates at Georgetown, and after college he got engaged to this girl who was one thousand percent awful. I took him out for a drink before their wedding and told him I thought he was making a big mistake. He got really pissed and cut me out of the wedding party. Then, two years later, they divorced. He and I patched things up, but he's still pretty bitter about the whole situation. I think he's angry that I was right and managed never to say 'I told you so.'"

"I see. So . . . he decides to provoke you by hitting on your tenant? I've heard better plans."

"You're more than my tenant."

"Sorry. Your tenant *and* your caterer."

Blake stops dancing and looks me in the eye, but soon his eyes drift to the doorway. I swivel my head around and see Nicole leaning against the doorframe, tossing her hair over her shoulder. Blake drops his hands to his sides and steps away from me.

"Sorry to interrupt, Blakey," she says. "We're all heading out. Would you mind walking me home? Someone got mugged by my apartment last night, and I'm scared to walk by myself."

"Sure, no problem. Give me a minute."

"Have you talked to her yet?" she asks, nodding in my direction.

Talked to me? About what? Why does he need to talk to me?

He shakes his head. "Not yet. I will."

Nicole gives me a probing look and then struts back into the living room. Blake lets out a long sigh. "I'll be back in about thirty minutes. Make sure you're here when I return. Okay? Can you do that?"

"Sure."

"Good," he says. "Because when I get back, we need to talk."

thirty-two

We need to talk.

What does that mean? I'll tell you what it means: Hannah Sugarman, you are in deep doo-doo.

He must know about the supper club. I saw Nicole and Blake talking all night. I'm sure Geeta came up again—Geeta, the supper club, Church Street. At some point, Blake must have put together the pieces—a missing plate, depleted booze, a tenant who knows his kitchen like the back of her hand. And now . . . Crap. What if he evicts me? No, he wouldn't do that. What am I saying? Of course he would evict me. After burning all of my cookbooks, most likely.

I pace back and forth in Blake's living room, contemplating a way to extricate myself from this mess, when I hear my cell phone ringing from the kitchen. If my parents are calling at three-thirty in the morning, I might actually burst into flames.

My phone vibrates against the granite, and when I pick it up to check the caller ID, my heart races. It's Jacob. *Finally.*

"Hey, stranger," he says, sounding unusually cheery. "Long time, no speak."

My mouth feels as if it's lined with cotton balls. I grab a half-filled glass of water off the counter and throw back a large gulp. "It's been a while," I say, my voice cool and flat.

"Yeah, I'm really sorry about that. I don't know if you've been following the news on the Hill, but I've basically lived at the office for the past two weeks."

"Right. The immigration debate."

"Exactly. Believe me, you are the first person I would have called if I'd had time. I had a great time the other weekend."

My reserve crumbles. "Me, too."

"Listen, I don't know what you're up to, but I'm free now, if you had any interest in hanging out."

I look at my watch. "It's three-thirty in the morning."

Jacob snickers. "Yeah, so?"

"Well . . . I'm at my landlord's place." Also, I look like a Tim Burton character on acid.

"Ah, another supper club?"

"Something like that."

"That's fine. I can help you clean up. I'm only a few blocks away. I could be there in ten minutes. Cool?"

I nibble on my bottom lip and feel my heart thumping in my chest. I want Jacob to come over. I want that more than anything. But in Blake's house? When Blake is about to come home and yell at me? No, I can't have that.

"I . . . now isn't a great time," I say.

"Oh. Okay. That's a shame." He pauses. "I thought you'd want to see me."

"I do—of course I do. It's just . . . I might be in a little bit of trouble with my landlord. He ran out for a few minutes, but if you're here when he gets back . . . let's just say it doesn't bode well for my future."

"Couldn't you leave him a note? Meet up with me and talk to him tomorrow instead?"

I could do that. And, given how long I've waited to hear from Jacob, I probably should do that. But Blake told me to wait here, and I promised him I would, and I can't renege on that now. Lying about the supper club is one thing, but breaking a promise on top of that—that's just bad juju all around.

"I don't think that'll work," I say. "I have to stay here."

"I see. So you'd rather spend time with your landlord than with me, huh?"

A wave of guilt rushes over me, and for a moment I feel as if I've made an unreasonable and foolish decision, one sure to result in my perpetual loneliness. Then I remember Jacob hasn't called me in two weeks and is calling me at 3:30 A.M. on Halloween for what may or may not be a booty call. I am hardly the most unreasonable person ever to exist.

"Of course I'd rather spend time with you. But I need to be here—alone—when my landlord comes home."

Jacob sighs. "Okay, fine. I was hoping to spend time with you tonight, but I guess I'll just go home all by myself." He sighs again.

"I—wait." The guilt returns. There must be a way for me to see him tonight. Surely I can make this work. "What if I called you after I finish talking to my landlord? We could meet up then?"

He pauses. "Okay. Sure. Give me a call, and we'll see if we can work something out."

"Yeah?"

"Yeah," he says.

My shoulders relax. "Great. I'll talk to you soon, then."

"Cool."

I hang up with Jacob and lean back against the counter, letting the cool edge of the granite press into my spine. This night might not end in tragedy after all.

Thirty minutes after I hang up with Jacob, Blake still hasn't come home. After fifteen minutes, I called his cell phone, but the call went straight to voice mail, and now I call a second time, but it goes straight to voice mail again. I peer out the window, but all I see are rowdy Halloweeners cavorting down Church Street, and none of those Halloweeners are dressed as Sweeney Todd. It doesn't seem right, making me wait around like this, while an eminently datable hunk of man sits in his apartment, ready and willing to make out with me. But Blake asked me to stay—he said, "Make sure you're here when I return" because "we need to talk"—so I can't very well leave. Not after he gave me such a huge break and let me cater his party.

But it's just so unfair. I haven't heard from Jacob in weeks, and now that I have, I'm stuck in Blake's house, gazing through the window and checking my watch every five seconds like a lunatic. I don't want to be here. I want Blake to come home, and I want wrap up our unpleasant conversation as quickly and painlessly as possible.

Another fifteen minutes pass, and still no sign of Blake. I don't know what to do. I mean, if I were to add up the pros and cons of waiting around versus leaving, leaving would be the obvious winner. I want to make out with Jacob, I don't want Blake to evict me, and I don't want to have any sort of conversation with Blake that might mention The Dupont Circle Supper Club. But lately, what I want and what is right haven't coexisted in the same sphere, and so I know, deep down, that waiting for Blake is the right thing to do. Even if it results in me being evicted. Even if it means depriving myself of Jacob's smooth, strong hands and impish smile. Waiting is definitely the right choice.

Fifteen more minutes go by, and Blake is still AWOL. If waiting around is right—if waiting is so obviously the nice thing to do—then why, pray tell, am I still sitting here like an idiot with my thumb up my ass? While Blake is off getting his boots rocked by some floozy in a belly dancer costume, I'm sitting here watching infomercials about knives that can cut through tires. I should be the one getting my boots rocked. Not him. Me.

I grab my phone and send Jacob a text message: "You still up?"

Five minutes pass. He doesn't respond. I send another text: "Still waiting for landlord. Should be free soon."

Again, no response. I try again: "Watching lame infomercials. Argh."

Nothing. I contemplate calling him, but I decide that might be overkill. If he isn't responding to my texts, he's probably asleep. Then again, he might not be near his phone, in which case he wouldn't hear a text message alert. He would probably hear his phone ringing, though. So, really, I should call. Definitely.

I bring up his number and call. After five rings, a groggy Jacob answers the phone, his voice thick and scratchy. "Hello?"

"Hey . . . it's me. Hannah."

He yawns. "Oh. Hey."

"Listen, my landlord still isn't back. But . . . after this much time, I think it's okay if I leave a note and meet up with you. It's his fault for taking so long."

Jacob yawns again. "It's been an hour. I fell asleep. I don't think I have the energy to walk all the way to Dupont."

"You don't have to walk here. I'll come to you."

Jacob hesitates. "I don't think that's such a good idea. Not tonight."

I sink back into Blake's cushions. "Oh."

"Hey, you're the one who didn't want me to come over an hour ago . . ."

"That's not fair—I wanted you to come over. But, for a few complicated reasons, you couldn't. That's all."

He snickers quietly. "Calm down, calm down. I'm sure we can work something out. Why don't we meet up next weekend? I'm tied up with work all week, but I could do something Saturday night."

"Saturday—sure. I can do Saturday."

We don't have a supper club scheduled for that night, and the only plans I have for next weekend are taking the GREs Saturday morning (an exam for which I am woefully unprepared due to a complete lack of studying). Seeing Jacob would be the perfect way to celebrate getting the exam over with.

"Cool," he says. "You down with Bistro du Coin?"

"Definitely. Should I make a reservation?"

"I'll handle it. Let's shoot for eight o'clock."

"Great. It's a date then."

"It's a date." He yawns into the phone. "Good luck with your landlord. I expect a full update next weekend. I want to know why you broke my heart tonight—it'd better be good."

I hang up with Jacob and collapse into the pillows on Blake's couch and replay our conversation a zillion times in my head. He wants to see me again next Saturday—he said I broke his heart. I'm back in the game. When he didn't call for weeks, I worried maybe I'd pulled a Sugarman and said something I shouldn't have or put him off with my lack of professional direction, but now we've set up another date and everything is fine. Fine. Or as close to fine as things can be when your landlord is seconds away from coming home and kicking you out of your apartment.

I roll onto my side and stare at the TV. A chef sporting a white toque and red handkerchief wields a bread knife over his head, threatening to use it on a piece of metal piping. As he thrusts the knife at the table and severs the pipe in half, I wonder what the hell I'm doing here and when, for the love of all things holy, Blake will finally come home.

thirty-three

the next thing I know, it's light out, and I'm peeling my face off Blake's leather couch. Apparently I slept here all night. Delightful.

I lift myself up from the couch and stumble toward the kitchen, tripping over the skirt of my dress. Drunk with sleep, I imagine I see Blake sitting at the breakfast bar, sipping his coffee while he reads the Sunday paper. But I quickly realize it's not my imagination; Blake really *is* sitting at the breakfast bar—an exhausted Blake, whose complexion and undereye circles rival Sweeney Todd's, even though he is no longer wearing makeup. He spots me standing in the doorway and folds up his paper.

"Good morning," he says, smiling. "Sleep well?"

His expression, both warm and welcoming, does not suggest he is about to yell at me for using his house as a speakeasy. It also gives no indication that he feels bad for royally screwing me over last night. Confusing.

"Not as well as you and your blond friend did, I'm sure."

"You mean Nicole? The belly dancer?" He shakes his head. "I don't think either of us slept well at all."

"I guess that depends on how you define 'sleep,'" I say, my voice dripping with sarcasm.

Blake furrows his brow. "What?"

"Listen, it's fine. Sometimes you gotta stuff the muffin. I get it. At least one of us got laid."

Blake squints at me, pausing for dramatic effect before he speaks. "I'm going to ignore the crazy talk coming out of your mouth right now and blame it on the fact that you appear to have some sort of eye infection."

I reach up and touch my eye, which is tender and swollen, most likely due to the gobs of Halloween makeup I never washed off.

"That aside," he says, "I want to apologize about last night. I feel really awful that I kept you waiting like that, but there was a fire in Nicole's apartment building. I couldn't leave her there alone."

"Oh my god—you're kidding."

"Unfortunately, I'm not. Apparently some woman in her building threw a Halloween party and lit, I don't know, a hundred candles or something, and one of them set the living room drapes on fire."

"Jesus. Was anyone hurt?"

"Two people were seriously burned, but everyone else got out in time. It was total chaos up there. That's why I didn't come home for hours. I would have called, but my cell phone died."

Well, it's official: I am the biggest a-hole in the universe. Way to go, Hannah. And what's worse, it now seems like I would care if Blake slept with Nicole. Which I wouldn't. Obviously.

"I'm sorry," I say. "That's awful."

"Yeah, her building is wrecked. She had to crash at her friend Emily's place. What a nightmare."

I run my fingers through my hair—or, rather, I try, but my fingers get stuck in the tangled mass matted to my head. "Sorry for falling asleep on your couch," I say. "You should have kicked me out when you got home."

Blake laughs. "And awake sleeping beauty? Nah. You were sleeping so peacefully, I didn't want to bother you."

"I'm amazed I was able to sleep that soundly."

"I've seen your sleeping conditions, Sugarman. The air mattress? If you can sleep on that thing every night, I'm guessing you can fall asleep anywhere."

"Touché." I grab a glass from Blake's cupboard and fill it with water from his Brita pitcher.

"But anyway, I'm really sorry for ruining the rest of your night. I'm sure you had better things to do than sit around on my couch."

Part of me wants to pipe up and tell him I *did* have better things to do, how he ruined an opportunity for me to spend time with Jacob, but I quickly realize Blake is unlikely to care about my failure to make out with a guy who didn't call me for two full weeks. So, instead, I decide to focus on the reason I was in his house in the first place.

"I think the party itself was a success," I say. "I picked up a few potential clients for future events."

"As you should have. The food was fantastic. You're really talented." He tugs on the handle to his coffee mug, pulling the mug back and forth along the counter. "So what are you up to today?"

"Other than untangling my hair and scrubbing this makeup off my face?"

"Yes, other than that."

"Not much."

"How do you feel about taking a little field trip?"

"A field trip?" Why would he want to take me on a field trip? To have the conversation we were supposed to have last night? I don't want to have that conversation. Like, at all. If I could avoid having that conversation for the rest of my life, that would be excellent. "Blake, last time you took me on a field trip I ended up having to smell raw seafood and Gorgonzola for the better part of an afternoon."

"I promise this trip won't involve fish or stinky cheese."

"Rotten eggs? Manure? Rancid BO? Any of that on the schedule?"

He laughs. "Not that I know of. Come on, it'll be fun. I want to make up for leaving you in the lurch last night. No unpleasant surprises. Promise."

I bite my lip and stare into Blake's eyes, which are fixed earnestly on mine. I should avoid this field trip at all costs, but Blake's expression is so sincere and sweet that I can't see how he could possibly want to evict me. Not with those eyes. Not today, at least.

"In that case," I say, "I guess I'm in. But can you at least give me a hint as to where you're taking me?"

Blake flashes a broad smile and winks. "Nope," he says. "It's a surprise."

I'm going to tell Blake about the supper club. Today.

As I rinse the gobs of hairspray out of my tangled mess of hair, I decide this is the only option. I may never know what Blake wanted to discuss last night (the supper club? my rent? something else?), but in the end, it doesn't matter. Last night was a wakeup call. The anxiety, the guilt, the overwhelming sense of betrayal—I can't go through that again. This ruse has gone on long enough. I have to tell him the truth.

When we get to wherever he is taking me, I'll sit him down and break the news. I'll explain about the flooding in my apartment. I'll tell him we'll never use his house again. I'll tell him I'm sorry. Then I won't have to carry this secret around anymore. Blake and I can be normal friends, friends without secrets, two people whose relationship isn't built on a lie. I want that—I want a normal friendship. Blake is goofy and fun, and my mood invariably improves when he is around. He can't find out about the supper club from someone else—from Geeta or Nicole or someone I don't know. He has to find out from me. And if I come clean, he'll be less likely to evict me. You can't evict someone for being *honest*, can you? Not in my warped view of the world.

By noon, Blake and I are traveling down Twenty-third Street in his Volkswagen SUV, heading south until we hit the on-ramp for I-66. Blake pulls onto the interstate, tapping his thumbs rhythmically against the steering wheel as Van Morrison's "Everyone" blares through his speakers. We bump along I-66 and zip across the Roosevelt Memorial Bridge, crossing into Virginia for the second time in the past forty-eight hours. Blake Fischer's Magical Mystery Tour continues.

The car swirls through a disorienting series of loops and exits until I have no idea where we are. A small red-and-white cooler rattles against a brown shopping bag in the backseat. I hope there's food in there. The last thing I ate was a cold bacon-wrapped oyster at one in the morning. I'm starving.

Blake turns off Jefferson Davis Highway onto a virtually empty two-lane road, and through his window I spot a series of white headstones lined up in tightly packed rows. Arlington National Cemetery. The place, I am guessing, where Blake's father is buried.

My palms start sweating. I've never been good with death and mourning and all of that. I never know what to say, and whatever I do say usually comes out wrong. How can I be of any comfort to Blake when I didn't know his dad? If anything happened to my dad, the last thing I'd want is sympathy from some bozo who never met him.

Blake glances in my direction as I wring my hands. "Relax," he says. "We're almost there."

Just as a gated opening to the cemetery appears on our left, Blake turns right onto another narrow road, taking us in the opposite direction. I guess we're not going to the cemetery after all. I peer out the window and read the lettering on the brown-and-white sign at the corner of the intersection: US MARINE CORPS MEMORIAL.

Blake's SUV crawls up the broad hill along a private road, passing a series of tall oak trees whose scarlet and ocher leaves flicker in the midday sun. Given how mild the weather has been the past month, I sometimes forget it's autumn, but even with temperatures hovering in the fifties and sixties, the leaves have finally started to turn. When we reach the top of the hill, an iconic image looms in front of us: six men, cast in bronze, huddling together as they drive a sixty-foot flagpole into the earth. The American flag flaps lazily in the air. The Iwo Jima Memorial.

Blake turns onto the circular drive surrounding the monument and follows it around until we reach the parking lot on the other side. "All right," he says, throwing the car into park. "You ready?"

I nod. I wrack my brain for the possible significance of this particular memorial (from what I gather, Blake's dad was in the navy, not the marines, and he definitely didn't fight in World War II), but I come up dry. I have no idea why we are here.

We hop out of the car, and Blake passes me the cooler. "Can you carry this?"

"Sure," I say.

I grab the handle and follow Blake as he walks around the circle toward the monument. But as we get closer, Blake veers right and starts walking along a small footpath, away from the memorial and back toward the access road we just ascended.

"Uh, Blake? The monument is back there."

"I know," he says and keeps walking.

He leads me toward a giant rectangular bell tower, which soars more than a hundred feet into the air and, with its black steel beams and plates, looks a little like a prison. He passes the bell tower and continues across the brittle grass until he finally stops at the point where the broad, grassy hill begins to descend to the main road.

I drop the cooler to the ground with a thud and wipe my hands on my jeans. "All right, I give up. Care to explain why you took me all the way to"—

And then, as I look over Blake's shoulder, I stop. In the distance, I see the Washington Monument, the Lincoln Memorial, and the Capitol dome lined up side by side, the top of the Washington Monument piercing the sky like a bright white sword. The three buildings reflect the sun, lighting up the horizon with a celestial glow.

Blake lets out a satisfied sigh as he stares out across the landscape. "My favorite view in the city," he says.

I take a deep breath and fill my lungs with the crisp air, thick with the smell of damp leaves and tree bark. "It's . . . spectacular."

Unlike the view at POV Lounge, where the monuments loomed so close I wanted to reach out and touch them, the monuments from this angle look like far-off figurines, part of a skyline etched in white marble.

"You think it's good now—you should see it at sunset," Blake says.

"Oh yeah?"

"Yeah. But I didn't want to wait until sunset. Couldn't risk you coming to your senses and turning down my invitation."

"Well, sunset or no sunset, I've lived in Washington for three years and have never seen the city from this angle. It's special, Blake. Thank you."

Blake breaks into a cartoonish grin and lifts up his index finger. "But wait—there's more!"

He opens the brown shopping bag and pulls out a wool blanket, which he shakes out and lays across the grass. He empties the rest of the bag's contents onto the blanket: fresh bagels, a canister of coffee, two mugs, some napkins, and some plastic utensils. He flips open the top to the cooler and grabs a jug of apple cider, two containers of cream cheese (one plain, one with chives), a package of smoked salmon, a bunch of green grapes, and a fat air-cured sausage.

"Ta-da!" he says. "I thought we could have a little picnic. A little thank-you for your help with the party last night."

"Isn't paying me 'thank-you' enough? Isn't that how hiring a caterer usually works?"

Blake scrunches up his lips and casts a sideways glance. "I guess so." He shrugs. "It's also an 'I'm sorry' for deserting you last night. It's nothing fancy, but it's the best I could do on short notice."

I scan the bagels and cream cheese and fruit scattered across the picnic blanket, a feast haphazard in its display but deliberate in its construction. "Don't apologize," I say. "It's great."

And the thing is, it *is* great. All of it. The food, the weather, this place. There is an indescribable magic in the air, and whether that's due to Blake or me or some intangible wonder, all I know is that right now, among the trees and monuments and colorful picnic lunch, there is, much to my surprise, nowhere else I'd rather be.

But the day is still young, which means I still have ample time to screw it all up. And, if my past behavior is any indication, I probably will. Because that's what I do. I screw things up.

I plow through one cup of coffee and half a bagel before I muster the courage to bring up The Dupont Circle Supper Club, but the powerful combination of caffeine and carbohydrates convinces me this is my moment. I have to say something.

"So, Blake," I say as I smear more chive cream cheese on my bagel. "I have something to tell you."

Blake pours himself another cup of coffee. "Same here—me first."

I stuff a hunk of bagel in my mouth. "Okay . . ."

"Remember Nicole from last night? The belly dancer?"

"How could I forget?"

"Well, it turns out her aunt is on the admissions committee at L'Academie de Cuisine, the culinary school up in Gaithersburg. I told her about the amazing ice cream you made and your cooking ambitions, and she said she could put in a good word with her aunt. Assuming you're interested."

I nearly choke on my bagel and throw back some coffee to wash it down. "Wow, Blake, I don't know what to say."

Blake leans his elbows against his bent knees. "I know there are competing thoughts on whether or not culinary school is worth the cost, but given how talented you are, I thought you should at least consider it."

"I will. Thank you." I pour some apple cider into a mug and take a sip. "Coming up with thirty grand, on the other hand . . . Not the easiest task in the world."

Blake offers a wry smile. "Listen, if you're not interested . . ."

"No—I'm interested. Definitely. It's just . . . complicated, that's all."

"Because of your parents?"

I nod. "And . . . a few other things."

"Well, think it over and let me know. Apparently there's still room in the program that begins in January." He reaches into his bag and pulls out a pamphlet held together by a large paper clip. "Here's the application, if you're interested. You can do what you want, and it's not any of my business, but I think this could be a great step for you. You're really talented, Hannah." He smiles softly. "You're really something."

I stare into Blake's gray-blue eyes, which twinkle in the midday sun, and I feel something inside me stir. "Thanks. That means a lot."

The apples of his cheeks fill with red, and he smiles and looks away as he smoothes the front of his black Patagonia fleece. "So what did you have to tell me?" he asks, looking back up at me. "By your tone of voice, it sounded important."

I meet his gaze, his eyes glittering with sincerity and kindness. He wraps his arms around his bent knees and raises his eyebrows expectantly. From his expression, one thing is clear: Blake believes in me. He cares. He thinks I have what it takes to become a professional cook. And I'm about to ruin everything.

I take a deep breath, about to launch into a lengthy preamble, when I let out a long sigh and shake my head.

"Never mind. Forget I said anything." Then I pour us both another cup of coffee.

CHAPTER

thirty-four

i should tell him. I know I should tell him. But I can't. I try—
several times, actually—but each time I lose my nerve. Blake
is the only person, aside from Rachel, who believes in me. He
doesn't think cooking is a trivial hobby. He doesn't think I should
apply to grad school and cook on the side. He understands how
much cooking and food mean to me. He gets it. And if I tell him
what I've been up to behind his back, I could lose his support. I
don't want that to happen.

So instead of talking about The Dupont Circle Supper Club,
we spend the next few hours lying on the hill behind the Iwo Jima
Memorial, finishing off the food and working our way through
the Sunday *Washington Post*. Once Blake finishes reading through
the Sports section, he looks at his watch and sighs.

"We should probably get back soon," he says. "I have some
last-minute campaign stuff to do. And I'm sure you have other
plans."

I pull the sleeves of my fleece top over my hands. "What time
is it?"

"About three o'clock."

I roll over on my back and stare at the sky. "What time does
the sun set these days? Five-ish? Six?"

"Something like that. Why?"

I push myself up by my elbows. "If you'd be willing to make a
quick run to buy some magazines and snacks, I'd be willing to

stick around for a few hours until sunset. Since you say it's worth seeing."

Blake scrunches up his lips and considers my proposal, obviously torn between working on his ANC campaign and wasting time with me. Imperiling his campaign for neighborhood commissioner isn't my primary goal, but I definitely wouldn't mind if he didn't win on Tuesday. Finally he grabs his keys and jumps to his feet. "Why the hell not? This is the first weekend I've had off in ages. I've earned a little fun."

He drives off and returns twenty minutes later with some chips and pretzels, a bunch of candy, and a stack of magazines— *Food & Wine* and *Us Weekly* for me, *Sports Illustrated* and *The Economist* for him.

As I flip through the latest tales of celebrity woe, Blake throws me a bag of gummy bears. "Some sugar for the Sugarman," he says, laughing at his own joke.

"Oh, Blake. You slay me."

"I try." He lies down on his side and props himself up on his elbow. "So I have a question for you."

"Shoot."

"I've been thinking about this ever since we chatted the other week. Why do you care so much what your parents think?"

I pop a gummy bear in my mouth and chew it slowly, trying to avoid having to answer for as long as possible. How do I explain twenty-six years of history?

"They're both famous professors, for starters," I say.

Blake raises an eyebrow. "So?"

"So . . . I've spent my whole life having people say, 'Oh, you're Alan and Judy Sugarman's daughter? *Wow.*' It's clear from everyone's reaction that my parents obviously made good career choices—the right career choices."

"For them," Blake says.

"Right. For them." I roll a green gummy bear between my fingers. "But every time I talk with my parents about my career, they make a pretty strong argument for why those are the right choices for me, too."

"They really have that much control over you?"

I shrug. "It isn't so much about control. I don't want to disappoint them. They've sacrificed a lot for me."

"But won't they be happy if you're happy?"

"Mmm, yes and no."

"By which you mean . . . no."

"It's complicated." I pour the rest of the gummy bears onto the picnic blanket in a small pile and begin sorting them by color. "My mom used to have this Peanuts cartoon in her office. Charlie Brown is explaining to Lucy that life has its ups and downs, but Lucy is like, 'Why can't life be all ups? I don't want any downs! I just want ups and ups and ups!' That's what my parents want for me: nothing but ups. And as far as they're concerned, the only way that will happen is if I pursue the same things they did. They know how that story ends. They know all the pitfalls. And I think they see my rejection of their choices as a rejection of them."

Blake grabs a piece of candy from the pile. "But you're an adult now. You have a job, an apartment, your own life. If you don't want to get a PhD, don't get a PhD. If you want to be a cook, be a cook. There are no rules. You can do whatever you want."

"Yeah. And I know that, intellectually. Emotionally—that's another story. Plus, my parents don't really treat me like an adult. They still see me as the confused twenty-three-year-old who left their home three years ago and still needs their direction."

"That doesn't mean you have to be that person."

I nod. "I know. But sometimes I look at my parents—how accomplished and successful they are—and think, wow, maybe they have it right, and I'm the one getting it all wrong."

"Don't write off your instincts like that. Give yourself some credit."

"I guess." I take a long sip of apple cider. "Did I tell you I'm supposed to take the GREs next weekend?"

"No. Why would you do that?"

I let out a sarcastic grunt. "I don't even know anymore. I guess because I'm supposed to?"

Blake sits up and wraps his arms around his bent knees. "Do your siblings feel the same sort of pressure you do?"

"That's the problem—I don't have any siblings. My mom couldn't have any more after me, so I'm like their 'miracle child.' Which means all the pressure is on me to become the next great Professor Sugarman."

Blake takes a swig of water and wipes his mouth with the back of his hand. "Then why don't you tell them, point-blank, that's not what you want?"

"Because it's not that simple."

"True. But the longer you wait to talk to them about this, the more difficult it's going to be."

My stomach churns. The same could be said of keeping my supper club a secret from Blake.

He screws the cap back on his water and holds the bottle tightly in his hand. "I know for me, I felt a lot of pressure from my dad to join the military. So what did I do? I said, fuck that, and went to Georgetown and got a job on the Hill. My brother Sam, of course, went to the Naval Academy, where my dad taught. I was convinced my dad was disappointed in me—that he wished I'd done what Sam did. I went along for years thinking that. It poisoned our relationship. My relationship with Sam, too. It wasn't until my dad got sick that he and I ever talked about it. We made amends, but it was too late. I wasted years—good, healthy years— being pissed off and feeling like I had to prove myself to him, when really there was nothing to prove. Now all I have left of him is the stupid town house I bought with the money he left me when he died. Don't make the same mistake. Have faith in your parents. They want you to be happy."

Blake could be right. Maybe. But he doesn't know my parents—how smart and dedicated they are, how they manage to

be right about everything 98 percent of the time. Is there any indication they will accept that my happiness falls within the 2
percent they occasionally get wrong? No. Because, the way they
see it, following their lead thus far has landed me at Cornell and
one of the top think tanks in the country. Their ideas have
worked. What I need them to understand is that *I'm* the one who
brought myself this far. I have ambition and drive, and applying
those characteristics to a job in the cooking industry instead of a
PhD doesn't make me a failure. There are more metrics to success
than the number of degrees after my name. I suppose, on some
level, I have to convince myself of that, too.

Blake stares out toward the horizon, fiddling with the cap to
his water bottle. He looks lost and a little sad, and I wonder if it
has something to do with the talk about his father.

"How did he die?" I ask. "Your dad."

"Cancer. Pancreatic. It's been about five years, but I still miss
him as much as I did the first year."

I run my hands along the blanket, wondering what I could say
that would be of any comfort. "Missing him is better than not,
right? In a way, you're keeping him alive. In your thoughts, at least."

Blake offers a sad smile. "Yeah. I guess that's true," he says.
"But, I don't know, the whole experience made me realize how
unpredictable life can be. There are so many things in life beyond
our control. I could get hit by a car tomorrow. I could get cancer.
We have such a limited time to find happiness, to make a difference in the world. All my dad wanted was for me to do something
good and real and meaningful. It didn't have to be serving in the
navy. It could be anything. It could be running for city council. It
could be finding the love of my life or being a good dad. I figured
all of that out too late. You can't worry about what other people
think you should do. The only way you'll ever be happy or make a
real difference is by pursuing the things that motivate you and
make you excited to be alive. Life is too short to waste years of it
being miserable or asking, 'What if?'"

Blake takes another sip of water, and I feel my cell phone vibrate against my leg. I look down and see the caller ID flashing up at me: Jacob Reaser. A week ago—hell, an hour ago—I would have excused myself and relished an opportunity to talk to him. But something about this place, about listening to Blake talk about his views on life and family and independence, makes me want to stay here in this moment forever. With a few words, Blake has managed to inspire me to take hold of my life and really *live*. My thumb hovers over the buttons on the phone. I press IGNORE.

Blake looks out across the skyline, and his expression softens, his look of somber introspection melting into one of awe. "Check it out," he says, pointing into the distance.

I follow the tip of Blake's finger and shift my attention to the horizon. The Washington Monument soars into the sky like a tall red flame, flickering against the gray-blue sky, a building ablaze in the light of the setting sun.

"It looks like it's on fire," I say. "The Capitol, too."

"Wait," Blake says. "It gets better."

He scoots in closer to me and presses his shoulder against mine, and we sit in silence, our gaze fixed in the distance, as we watch the monuments burn.

CHAPTER

thirty-five

going back to work after a Sunday like that is akin to eating
canned SpaghettiOs after dinner at The French Laundry.
The two experiences cannot compare, and it becomes painfully
clear one event is far more representative of your everyday life
than the other.

But I keep telling myself soon my life *will* be The French
Laundry. Or at least closer to fine dining than canned pasta. First
thing Monday morning, inspired by Blake's pep talk, I cancel my
registration for the GRE exam this weekend. My parents would
spontaneously combust if they knew this, so I've decided not to
tell them until I see them in person—an event I have managed
to put off until Thanksgiving, much to their chagrin. There is too
much going on at the moment, between the supper club and my
ongoing work misery, and though my discussion with Blake bolstered my confidence, it's not as if one good conversation is going
to undo twenty-six years of dysfunctional behavior. Eventually I
will tell my parents everything. Just not yet.

As soon as I cancel my GRE registration, I submit my com-
pleted application to L'Academie de Cuisine, and according to
both Blake and the L'Academie Web site, I should receive a letter
of acceptance or rejection in a few weeks. I wish I could know
now, *today*, but I suppose I can keep my impatience in check for a
few weeks. After all, I've worked at NIRD for three years—three

long and painful years—so it's not as if a few more weeks of uncertainty will kill me. I can handle it.

At least that's what I tell myself on Monday. By Tuesday, I'm starting to lose it.

When I get into the office Tuesday morning, Mark is running in circles like a dog chasing its tail, all atwitter over the election, even though this is an off-year election. Aside from two hot gubernatorial races, there isn't much going on. The only reason Blake is even running for his dinky neighborhood commission is because someone resigned earlier this year.

"Did you vote?" Mark asks, his flame-colored eyebrows bouncing up and down on his forehead.

"Yes, Mark. I voted."

"Well done." He pushes his glasses up the bridge of his nose. "I know it doesn't affect us, but this New Jersey gubernatorial race is fascinating. Absolutely fascinating."

I nod. "Mmm."

"Oh, by the way, did you see the e-mail I sent you?"

"About . . . ?"

He sighs and drops his shoulders in an exaggerated fashion. "Global leverage and asset price bubbles?"

By his tone, he might as well have just said, *DUH*.

"No, I didn't see it. But I'll take a look."

"Good. Because I'd like to write an op-ed refuting certain aspects of Nouriel Roubini's latest report, and I need you to do a little digging on the dollar carry trade. I'd like you to send me a summary and an outline for the op-ed by the end of the day. Oh, and I'm supposed to give a speech on risk management at a conference in New York next week. I'll send you an outline for my PowerPoint presentation. Could you pull that together?"

"Sure."

"Excellent."

He whirls around and heads back into his office, humming "La donna è mobile" at full volume. Ah, yes. Another glorious day at the office.

After eight painful hours of reading through currency reports, I head back to my apartment, and as I round the corner I run into Blake, who is virtually skipping down Church Street.

"Hey!" he says, meeting me in front of his wrought iron steps. "Exciting news! They haven't finished counting the votes, but going by the early results, it looks like I'm going to win."

There was only one person running against Blake, and from what I read on a few local blogs, his opponent was a seventy-five-year-old, borderline senile Libertarian. The contest wasn't exactly heated. Still, his enthusiasm is endearing. "Wow, Blake—congrats. That's great."

"Thanks." He smiles and gently nudges my shoulder. "I couldn't have done it without your vote."

Truthfully, voting for Blake was probably one of the more insane things I've ever done. By voting for him, I endorsed a candidate who would, given the authority and power, shut down The Dupont Circle Supper Club without compunction. But *not* voting for him would have endorsed the idea that holding secret supper clubs in his house without his knowledge was the morally upright thing to do. And not voting at all—well, that wasn't an option. So I voted for him, and I'll just hold our next supper club outside his jurisdiction—something I planned to do anyway, after all the time we've spent together lately. Besides, on Sunday Blake opened my eyes to the possibilities before me—culinary school, a new career, a fulfilling existence. He gave me an entirely new outlook on life. How could I not give him my vote?

"Some friends are coming by in a bit to celebrate," he says. "You're welcome to join."

"I'd love to, but I have a lot of work to catch up on." Work that involves the next installment of The Dupont Circle Supper Club—which, incidentally, will no longer take place in Dupont Circle.

He shrugs. "Well, you know where to find me if you change your mind."

"Okay. Thanks." We linger at the bottom of the steps, an awkward silence hanging between us. "By the way," I say, trying to keep the conversation going, "I submitted the application to L'Academie yesterday."

Blake brightens. "That's awesome. Congratulations."

"Save your congratulations until I actually get in. It's a little late in the application process."

"Nah," he says. "You're a shoo-in. Nicole told her aunt all about you. I sent an e-mail about you, too."

"You did?"

He smiles. "Of course. Between the honeycomb ice cream and the devils on horseback, I told them it would pretty much be a federal crime not to admit you."

"A federal crime? Wow, breaking out the big guns."

"Well, now that I'm part of the Dupont Circle Neighborhood Commission . . ." He smirks as he offers a mock self-important shrug.

"I can already feel the power from where I'm standing," I say.

The skin around his eyes wrinkles as he laughs at my lame joke, and for a minute we just stand there like that, smiling at each other. Then he glances down at his watch. "I'd better get inside and start setting up. But come up anytime, if you want. And remember—I'm looking out for you. No more of these underground supper clubs to ruin your shot at making it."

My cheeks flush. "I'm sure you have bigger fish to fry."

"Hey—who's the one making fish jokes now?" He laughs. "I'll talk to you soon, okay?"

"Sure. And congrats again on the election."

Blake clasps his hands together and shakes them on either side of his head, as if he were just elected president of the United States, and as I watch the smile bloom on his face, I start to think everything would be a lot easier if I'd never started The Dupont Circle Supper Club in the first place.

The week drags on, each day filled with more inane and incomprehensible requests from Mark, and by Friday my week has reached a new level of shitastic. When I arrive at my desk Friday morning, I find a cardboard box bearing the Amazon.com logo sitting to the right of my keyboard. A package for Mark? No. The label on the box is addressed to me. Did I order something from Amazon? I don't think so. And even if I did, I wouldn't have it delivered to the office.

I rip open the box and dump out a collection of goodies: the latest edition of Kaplan's *Get into Graduate School: A Strategic Approach for Master's and Doctoral Candidates*, some sort of self-help book titled *Getting Organized from the Inside Out*, and a detailed Excel spreadsheet outlining acceptable economics PhD programs with coordinating application deadlines, Web site addresses, and GRE codes. I rifle through the box and find a small gift note:

> Chance favors the prepared mind! Thought these might help with your grad school applications. Please note that Harvard's deadline is <u>DECEMBER 1</u>.
> Love,
> Mom and Dad
> p.s. Good luck with your work on Mark's book!

Thought number 1: Shoot me.

Thought number 2: How did they know I was working on a book for Mark? I haven't told them.

I am beyond annoyed, but before I can give the subject any further consideration, my phone rings.

"Mark Henderson's office."

"Is this Hannah?" asks a woman's voice on the other end.

"Yes . . ."

"This is Daphne Curtis. In Human Resources? I was wondering if I could speak with you."

"Okay . . ."

"Is now a convenient time?" she asks.

"Sure."

"Fantastic. Do you know where my office is?"

"Your office? Can't we do this on the phone?"

Daphne hesitates. "No, I'd rather talk in person. If that's okay with you."

She reminds me where her office is and tells me to swing by in the next fifteen minutes, at which point we will discuss . . . I have no idea what. All I know is that when Human Resources gets involved, it's serious: hiring, firing, pay cuts, and benefits.

Ideally I will be told the economic downturn has hit the NIRD coffers hard, and they cannot afford my services any longer, so they're letting me go and offering me an enormous severance package, which I will then use to pay for culinary school or launch my own catering company. Of course the likelihood of this happening is infinitesimal, but a girl can dream.

I take the elevator to the tenth floor and slink down the hallway to Daphne's office. She sits at her desk, stuffed into a leather swivel chair that, set against her plump figure, looks as if it were made for a child.

"Ah, Hannah, come in," she says when she sees me in the doorway. "Please, sit down."

I pull up a chair directly across from her. "What's up?"

She removes her wire-frame glasses and runs her fingers through her feathered, honey-colored hair. "I'd like to talk to you about your relationship with Mark Henderson."

"Okay . . ."

"It was brought to my attention that he has, perhaps, made some inappropriate and potentially threatening advances, some of which may have been sexual in nature."

"I'm sorry, what?"

What, what, *what*?

"Another member of our staff voiced some concern over events that occurred a month ago, though it is unclear if there have been other incidents as well."

"A month ago?"

She looks down at her desk calendar. "Five weeks, to be exact."

Jesus Christ, what is this woman talking about? My mind races. Five weeks ago. What happened five weeks ago? I barely remember what happened yesterday. Five weeks, five weeks. That was around the time of the CNBC interview, right? And the meeting in Mark's office, where he offered to let me help on his book?

And that's when it hits me. Mark's office. The tipped chair. My legs in the air. My crotch. *Susan.*

"Oh, Daphne—no, no, no. This is all a big misunderstanding. Nothing happened. Honestly."

Daphne leans forward and places her elbows on her desk with her hands clasped together. "Hannah, I want you to know this is a safe space. Anything you say in here is between you and me."

Yeah: you, me, and the board of trustees.

"Listen," I say, "I can provide absolute assurance that nothing has happened between me and Mark. He was trying to help me after I fell over in one of his chairs. The leg was propped up on some of his clothes."

"But see that's what's so curious: what were Mark's *clothes* doing on the floor?"

Is this woman on glue? She clearly does not know me at all. If Mark so much as laid a finger on me, I'd scream so loud the whole office would know about it. Is she suggesting I am complicit in this? For Christ's sake, the man is totally insane and looks like a Muppet.

"Daphne," I say. "Look at me. The chair tipped over. That's it. End of story."

"I still need a statement from you, and I will need to take one from Mark as well."

"A statement?"

"Yes," she says. "We will need to keep this on file in case another staff member reports an incident in the future."

"But nothing happened."

"Yes, well, this is protocol. If you don't mind?" She pushes a form across the desk. "Make sure you sign at the bottom."

I grab the pen from her pudgy fingers and write a two-sentence statement explaining what happened. Then, on the dotted line, in a firecracker move that would surely make Adam cringe, I scrawl my signature in grand, swooping cursive: "Bull Shit."

After lunch, Mark stampedes down the hall, dragging his wheely briefcase with one hand and clutching a manila folder with the other.

"Hannah, I just had lunch with someone at the IMF, and I am *very* worried about the situation with Greece," he says. "I'd like to write an op-ed for the *Post* or the *Times*. I need you to summarize this report by the end of the day." He drops the folder on my desk.

"Okay . . . sure . . ."

He cocks his head as he skims the titles of the books on my desk. "I also want to chat about your progress with my book," he says. "Give me a few minutes to settle in, and then let's talk."

Yesterday, I e-mailed Mark a twenty-page outline—per his request—on the origins of the Federal Reserve, with annotations and room for expansion. I don't normally brag about my work, but I must say, I did an excellent job.

Mark calls me into his office, and I pull up a chair behind his desk, dragging it through the detritus on his floor. Out of the corner of my eye, I spot the remnants of a cheese sandwich sitting atop a pile of economics journals. I'm pretty sure I saw the same sandwich sitting there last week.

"So," Mark says, "how are you coming along with the outline?"

"Did you see my e-mail?"

"No. What e-mail?"

"The one I sent you yesterday. With the outline attached to it." *Like you asked me to, you moron.*

Mark presses his glasses up the bridge of his nose and scrolls through his in-box. "Let's see . . . Ah, yes. Book outline . . . from Hannah Sugarman . . ."

He opens the attachment and, as if deciphering ancient hieroglyphics, squints as he skims through the outline.

"I'm sorry, what is this?" he asks.

"The outline you asked for. On the creation of the Fed?"

"But this is a banal compilation of facts. Where's the insight? Where's the analysis?"

"It's . . . an outline. I figured I would add the analysis later."

This is only partially true. I thought I did a fairly good job at putting the history of the Fed into context. Though who knows. Mark's demands and desires are like the wind: erratic and imprecise, changing every few hours. My outline may be exactly what he wanted yesterday, but today he fancies something else entirely.

"Let's hope so," Mark says. "If people want a generic history of the Federal Reserve, they can go on Wikiphilia and get it there."

"Wikipedia," I say.

"What?"

"The site is called Wikipedia."

Mark frowns. "That's what I said. Wikipedia." He pulls at one of his untamed eyebrows. "Anyway, try to send me something a little more substantive by the end of next week. Take a look at that book your parents bought you. It might help with organizing and streamlining the process."

"Good idea," I say. I start to stand up, but I pause. "How did you know that book was from my parents?"

"Because I recommended they buy it for you."

I sit back down in the chair, my shock over the fact that Mark has ever so much as glanced at a book about organization supplanted by the unwelcome news that he has spoken to my parents. "When did you do that?"

"When I talked to them a few weeks ago."

I'm sorry, what?

"You called them?"

"They called me, actually. They sounded very concerned

about how you're fitting in here, and we had a long talk about your work and your direction. We agreed that lately you seem aimless—unfocused was how they put it, I think. That book on organization has helped my daughter Emma a great deal," he says. "I thought it might help you, too."

How can this be true? How could my parents call Mark and discuss my career with him, when I specifically asked them not to do that? I am twenty-six years old. Why are they still treating me as if I'm in kindergarten?

Mark studies my expression and puckers his lips. "Frankly, you should be happy they reached out to me. After the CNBC incident, I was prepared to terminate your position. I didn't think you took this job seriously enough. But they reminded me how valuable you've been over the past few years and convinced me to give you a second chance. That's when we came up with the idea to have you help me with my book. It's all worked out rather nicely for you in the end."

No, it's all worked out rather nicely for *them* in the end. Unbelievable. I could scream. But, before I can do that, I hear the phone on my desk start ringing.

"You should probably answer that," Mark says. "It could be important."

"Yeah. Probably." I shove the chair back and stomp toward the door, clutching my notebook tightly in my hand.

"Oh, and don't forget," Mark says as I leave, "I need the summary for my op-ed by close of business."

The phone has stopped ringing by the time I reach my desk—which is probably a good thing, since right now I'm mad enough to set the building on fire.

Ah, but what luck. The phone rings again. Hey caller? Go *fuck yourself.*

I yank the phone from the receiver and answer in a clipped monotone. "Yeah?"

"Hannah? It's Daphne Curtis again. Listen, I was looking over your statement and, well . . ." She trails off.

"Yes?" I ask, taunting her.

"I'm going to need you to come back and sign another statement," she says.

"And what happens if I don't?"

"Well . . . I . . ."

"You'll fire me?"

"Now, Hannah," she says. "This is a serious matter. I need your cooperation."

"Well, guess what? You're not going to get it."

I suddenly feel reckless. Bold. But, more than anything, angry—at my parents, at Mark, at NIRD, at myself for staying here so long. And I've packed all that anger into a big, ugly emotional bomb that is about to explode.

"Hannah, I need you to sign a proper statement," Daphne says.

"You want a statement? Here's a statement: fuck off."

"I beg your *pardon*?"

"And you know what you can do with that statement?"

"I . . . I . . ."

"That's right, Daphne. You can shove it up your ass." There is silence at the other end of the phone. "And don't worry about firing me," I say. "Because I quit."

thirty-six

i think I went a little overboard with Daphne. Although it's almost not my fault. If it weren't for my parents' meddling and Mark's smug face and NIRD's ridiculous sexual harassment policy and those damn *books*, none of this would have happened. But telling Daphne to fuck off, that was a little much. And the shoving it up her ass part. That wasn't good either.

The thing is, I didn't even want to quit. I need a steady income stream while I figure out my future. I still need to pay my bills. But it's not like I can ask for my job back now—not after I hurled a bunch of expletives at the head of HR.

Whatever, the point is, I quit, and now I have to deal with the consequences. On the bright side, I won't have to deal with Mark or Millie or Susan anymore and can focus all my energy on a career in the food industry without any distractions. This will be good—productive. Silver linings, and all that.

I pound out a one-page note to Mark, march into his office, and hand him the piece of paper. "My letter of resignation," I say, trying not to betray my utter lack of confidence in this decision.

Mark cocks his head. "Your what?"

"My letter of resignation. I'm leaving. Today."

Mark whips off his glasses and folds his arms across his chest. "Hannah . . . I . . . I don't know what to say. Is it because I criticized your outline? Don't you think you're overreacting?"

"It has nothing to do with my outline."

"But what about the conference? You've been instrumental in ironing out some of the details."

I shrug. "I'm sure Millie can pick up the slack. I already spoke with Daphne Curtis and cc'd her on this letter. It's official. I'm leaving."

"Well, I'm very sorry to hear that." Mark puts his glasses back on and skims the letter. "Thank you for letting me know."

I head back to my desk but stop short of Mark's doorway. "And don't even think about saying anything to my parents. I want to be the one to tell them."

"I won't say a word," he says, shaking his head.

"Good," I say, and then I walk out the door.

At five on the dot, I leave the office carrying a box with all my office belongings and head straight for the bar. I told Rachel to meet me after work so that we could "talk." She has been at an off-site conference all day, so she is blissfully unaware of my resignation. Her reaction could go one of two ways: "Congrats, I'm so excited for you!" or "You crazy bitch, what have you done?" Frankly, I've been thinking the latter myself for most of the day.

I burst through the front door of the Bottom Line and scan the barstools and tables for Rachel. When I don't see her, I plop myself down on an empty barstool and slide my box onto the stool next to me.

"Bombay Sapphire martini, straight up," I say, throwing my wallet on the counter. "Extra olives."

By the time Rachel arrives, I am already on my second martini. I wave sluggishly with one hand as she approaches my barstool, using my other hand to guzzle more of my drink, letting the cool, herby gin trickle down the back of my throat. Whoever said alcohol doesn't solve problems was an asshole.

"You have martini dribbling down your blouse," she says as she sticks her mahogany Mulberry tote under the bar.

I look down and see a big wet splotch on the front of my blue button-down. "Huh," I say and let out a small burp under my breath.

"Classy." She slips out of her cream cashmere peacoat and sits on the stool to my right. "So what's going on?"

I nod toward the large cardboard box sitting on the barstool to my left. "I quit my job."

Rachel's eyes spring open. "*What?*"

"You heard me. I quit."

"But . . . why?"

I take another sip of my martini. "Seriously? You're asking why I'd quit my job at NIRD? How long have you known me?"

"I know the general 'why.' I meant, why today? What happened?"

I sigh and shake my head. "Where do I begin?"

Rachel beckons the bartender with her slender, manicured finger and orders a glass of white wine, and I tell her about everything: my parents' Excel spreadsheet, their call to Mark, Daphne Curtis, Blake's pep talk, my application to L'Academie. Rachel stares at me, taking in every word. When I finish, she sits in silence for a good ten seconds, staring at the bar counter as she bites her lip.

I jab her gently with my elbow. "Say something."

She pulls the sleeve of her gray cashmere sweater over her knuckles. "Did you really tell Daphne Curtis to fuck off?"

"Yeah, I know, that wasn't my finest hour."

She shakes her head and sighs. "I'll say."

"But in the end, this is a good thing. Now I can concentrate on culinary school and the supper club."

"Don't you think we should hit the PAUSE button on the supper club, now that Blake won the election?"

"We'll hold it somewhere outside of Dupont Circle. It'll be fine."

"So you've found somewhere else to hold it."

I throw back the rest of my martini in a single gulp. "Not yet."

"With everything you've been through, are you sure you don't want to cancel?"

"I quit my job. I packed up my things and left the building. I officially have no income. Let's just do this one more time, so that I have enough cash to make next month's rent."

"Couldn't you ask your parents for some cash to tide you over?"

"I most certainly could *not*," I say, at a volume that causes the patrons around us to turn in our direction. "I'm not saying anything about anything until I see how the culinary school application plays out. In an ideal world, I'll get into L'Academie, and then I'll tell my parents I'm leaving IRD, and that will be that."

"And if you don't get in?"

I fiddle with the base of my martini glass. "I'll figure something out. For now, I don't want to explain to them why I need the money—I don't want them to think I'm a total failure. We'll do the supper club one last time so that I can make next month's rent, and then we'll take a break while I figure everything out."

"But . . . I mean, even if you do get in to culinary school, won't you need money to pay your tuition? As in, a lot more than one month's rent?"

"That's what financial aid is for, my friend. And that's also when I'll go crawling back to my parents. But I'm not ready to do that. Not yet. At least if I get into culinary school, I'll be able to show them I can succeed at something."

I flag the bartender and signal that I'm ready for another martini, but when he arrives, Rachel jumps in before I can speak. "She'll have a water. Thanks."

I roll my eyes. "Thanks, Mom."

Rachel purses her lips and shakes her head. "Anyway . . . I actually have an idea for another supper club location . . ."

"Oh, yeah?"

"Yeah. But . . . first, there's something I've been meaning to tell you."

"Shoot."

Rachel tucks her hair behind her ear. "There's . . . a guy."

"A 'guy'?" I take a sip of water.

She nods. "We've been seeing each other . . . for a while now."

I start choking on the water and pound my chest with my fist. "I'm sorry, what?"

"I've been dating someone. He's . . . kind of my boyfriend."

"Your *boyfriend*?"

Rachel brings her finger to her lips. "Shhh, Hannah, keep your voice down. You're shouting."

"What the hell? Who is he?" I ask in a drunken whisper, which, by the other patrons' reactions, I gather is not a whisper at all.

Rachel looks sheepishly at the bar counter. "Remember Jackson?"

"The muscular Asian dude I saw at the farmers' market?"

She nods. "Yep. Him."

"So you've been seeing him for, what . . . ?" I try to do some drunken arithmetic. "A month? Six weeks?

"About two months, actually," she says.

"Two *months*? Why didn't you tell me?"

She shrugs. "I tried—a few times, actually—but we kept getting interrupted. And honestly, you never seemed all that interested in following up or asking why I've been preoccupied over the last few months. You didn't seem to care. All you want to talk about these days is you and Adam and Jacob and the supper club and you, you, you."

My face grows hot, and I gulp down the rest of my water. "Oh. I see."

I want to tell Rachel she's wrong—that I *have* wondered about what's been going on in her life, that I *do* care—but the truth is, I've been so focused on my breakup and my career path and my familial dysfunction that I haven't given anyone else much thought. I somehow lulled myself into believing my problems are the only problems that matter. Like a brat. Like a selfish fucking solipsist.

"I'm sorry," I say. "I guess I've been a crappy friend lately."

"You haven't been at your best, that's for sure."

"Why didn't you say something—about Jackson, about me being a crappy friend, about anything?"

"To be honest, I wasn't sure what to say. You've had a lot going on. And I didn't want to rub my budding relationship in your face, so soon after your breakup with Adam."

"But I would have been happy for you," I say.

"Really?"

"Yes—of course." I would have, right? I'm happy for her right now, aren't I? I should be. Maybe I'm too drunk to tell. "Where did you guys meet?"

"At an information session at Johns Hopkins, back in August . . ."

"Wait, you were in Baltimore, looking at grad schools?"

She nods. "You know I've always wanted to get a master's in public health . . ."

"So you didn't tell me about Jackson, and you didn't tell me you were applying to grad school. What else have you been keeping from me?"

Rachel's cheeks flush. "What? Nothing."

I stick out my jaw as I swirl my water glass. "Oh, yeah? Then why do I suddenly feel like I have no idea what is going on in your life?"

She shrugs. "Probably because, in some ways, you don't."

The acidity in Rachel's words stings, but not as much as what the words imply. Until now, I considered Rachel my closest friend in Washington—my partner in crime—but, at some point, I became the friend she can tell only certain things, and I didn't even notice. How could I let that happen? At this point, all of my high school and college friends are spread out around the country, and while dating Adam I let most of my other DC friends drift away. If I lose Rachel's friendship, then I'll really be alone. I'll have nobody.

Rachel looks up and fixes her eyes earnestly on mine. "Sometimes you make it hard for people to tell you things, Hannah. Like, if I say I'm applying to grad school, you start stressing out about your parents and worrying whether you should apply to grad school, too, and suddenly the conversation is all about you. Again."

"But I ask about your blog all the time. And the supper club—we've been doing that together. You're the one who convinced me to start one in the first place."

She swirls her finger around the edge of her wineglass. "I guess that's true."

"Listen, I'm sorry if I've been a bit of an egomaniac lately, but it really hurts to know you've been keeping things from me. Your friendship means a lot to me, and I'd hate to lose that. You're my best friend in town. I don't know what I'd do without you."

Rachel glances down at the bar. "I don't know what I'd do without you either."

I sit in silence, clinking the ice around my glass as I tilt it back and forth. I hate girl drama, and I hate that I've become a part of it. I hate that I've alienated a friend, and I hate that we're arguing right now without really arguing. I just . . . I hate this.

"I'm sorry if I've been a bad friend," I say. "I'll do better—at least I'll try. I don't know what more I can say."

Rachel stares down at the bar. "I'm sorry, too. I should have told you about Jackson and graduate school sooner. I just . . . I didn't know how to handle Jackson, given your breakup with Adam, and then I went so long without telling you that it seemed awkward to bring it up at all, and then I got mad that you hadn't asked about me in a while, and then you started freaking out about life, and then . . ."

I rest my hand on hers. "I get it."

She shakes her head. "Sorry, I didn't mean to make a bigger deal of this than it is. I haven't been a great friend recently either."

"No, I'm glad you brought it up. We're . . . performing maintenance. Friendship maintenance."

She smiles. "Maintenance. I like that."

I shake the ice around my glass and swallow the last bit of water, before the bartender comes back and refills the glass to the brim. "So what were you going to say earlier? About a new supper club location?"

"Oh—right. That's why I brought up Jackson." She takes a sip of her wine and then places the glass back on the bar, holding the stem between her first two fingers. "His friend Hugo is an artist—a real free spirit—and he owns an artist's loft in Northeast that he rents out on the weekends for parties and events. He heard about The Dupont Circle Supper Club, and Jackson said Hugo would be willing to rent the loft out to us for one of our dinners."

"Doesn't renting a loft usually cost thousands of dollars?"

"He usually charges about a thousand bucks or so, but as a favor he's willing to rent it to us for four hundred dollars, since he's Jackson's friend and knows our situation."

"The whole point of next weekend's dinner is to make money, not spend it."

She nods. "I know. But I ran the numbers. His loft has more space than Blake's house, so we could easily fit thirty-six guests in there, and if we bump up the price to sixty dollars a head, we'll more than cover the cost of the loft."

"Can we take a look?"

"Hugo said he could leave Jackson a key so that we could swing by to check it out. Maybe we could stop by Monday on our lunch break?"

"Correction: your lunch break. I no longer have a job, remember?"

She blushes. "Oh. Right."

"But sure, Monday works. Tell Hugo we're in."

"Excellent. What are you thinking in terms of menu?"

"Probably carnival foods—turkey legs, funnel cake, that kind of thing."

Rachel smiles. "Nice. You haven't lost your touch." She swirls her glass and glances down at her watch. "Speaking of Jackson, I'm supposed to meet him at Luna Grille for dinner. Any interest in joining us?"

"Another time," I say. "Tonight I have to start testing funnel cake recipes. But tell him I look forward to hanging out soon."

"Will do."

Rachel drinks a little more wine and then gathers her bag and coat off the bar. I rest my hand on her elbow. "We're okay, right?"

She smiles. "Yeah. We're okay."

She gives me a hug and invites me to a party later tonight, which I probably won't attend, but I tell her I'll try to stop by. Then she walks out the door, leaving me at the bar to sober up over another glass of water before I head home.

The bartender tops me up with a little more water, and I take a slow sip to soothe the lump forming in my throat, fixing my eyes at the bottom of my glass. All the alcohol has made me embarrassingly emotional—about my tiff with Rachel, about the fact that I told the head of HR to fuck off, about the professional challenges I face—and I don't want a bunch of strangers to see me cry. I look up from my glass when a guy with a baby face at the far end of the bar starts singing along to the jukebox.

"Do-on't stop, belie-ving, oo-ooh oooooh!"

He wears a button-down shirt with a loosened tie, and three photo IDs dangle around his neck by a thin metal chain. An intern. He pumps his fist in the air as he takes another swig of his Miller Lite and continues thrusting his fist as he howls to the chorus. His eyes are bloodshot, and he has a wet splotch in the middle of his shirt, even bigger than the one on mine. Nearly everyone in the bar is staring at this guy. He is a total train wreck.

He spots me eyeing him from my perch along the bar and lifts his beer high in the air.

"Fuck yeah!" he screams, his beer spraying in the air. "Mother fucking Washing-ton!"

And, in the midst of his drunken yelps, I allow myself a moment of positive introspection. I'm not as pathetic as this loser, I tell myself. *I'm not that lame.* It's a low bar, I realize, and one that, while sober, I would probably not consider a bar at all. More like a floor. Or a basement, really. But these are the moments in life that keep us going, the nuggets of self-assurance that make us think maybe things aren't so bad after all—or, at the very least, they could be worse.

thirty-seven

here's the problem with having drunken epiphanies in which I decide my life isn't as crappy as it could be: I deny the existence of Murphy's Law and the fact that its principle of "Anything that can go wrong will go wrong" applies to nearly every aspect of my life.

Because the next day, bright and early on a Saturday morning, I find the following e-mail in my in-box:

> Becca Gorman has sent you a message on Facebook
> RE: Jacob Reaser
> Sorry for the delay in my reply—I've been in Cambodia with my sis and have been totally AWOL. But, more to the point . . . WTF?? JACOB REASER? He's engaged to my friend Alexis. She's living in Boston for the year while she finishes her master's, but they've been together for like five years, and they're getting married in June. He's always been a little sketchy, but OMG!! You'd better put the kibosh on this ASAP. I do NOT want to be caught in the middle of this. I'm Stateside now, so call me if you get a sec, and we can discuss.

Murphy's Law. Story of my life.

To prevent myself from falling into a state of despondency and self-loathing, I tell myself Becca must be misinformed. In college, she pretended to know everything about everyone and got it wrong half the time. She'd swear so-and-so was gay and so-and-so failed freshman chemistry and so-and-so had sex in the Olin Library stacks, but there was never any evidence to back up these stories, and I learned to take Becca's declarations with a large grain of salt—something I'd forgotten when I decided to send her a message on Facebook last week. So, to prove her wrong about Jacob, I type "Jacob Reaser + Alexis" into Google and launch a thorough investigation.

The first site I come across is an entry on WeddingChannel .com. Jacob Reaser and Alexis Herrmann. Wedding date: June 12. Damn.

Okay, so he's engaged. Or maybe he was engaged. Or maybe he is *miserably* engaged and I am his one hope for a happy future.

I scour Facebook. I pull up more sites on Google. I even read articles both Jacob and Alexis have published to find out a little more about them. In the movies, this might be the part where I fall for Jacob and discover he is, in fact, my soul mate; his fiancée is a total bitch, and if only we could overcome the hurdle of his engagement, we would join together in eternal bliss.

This is not that story. By all accounts, there is nothing wrong with Alexis whatsoever. Her Facebook profile picture suggests she is a blond-haired beauty on par with Grace Kelly or January Jones, thin and graceful with a delicate smile. Jacob appears in the photo with her, and they both look utterly smitten, broadcasting to the world how in love they are, which I'd find a lot more believable on Jacob's part if he hadn't been naked in my bed three weeks ago.

Not only is Alexis beautiful, but she also seems to be smart and compassionate and driven, at the top of her class as she pursues a master's degree in social work at Harvard. One of her essays I find online, about educating inner-city youth, actually brings tears—*tears*—to my eyes, and everything I read about her leads me to believe she is the kind of person I might have befriended in another life.

But this isn't another life. This is *now*, a life in which I had sex with the man she has dated for five years. Five years! And they are getting married, which means Jacob proposed to her. He spent thousands of dollars on an engagement ring, told her he wanted to spend the rest of his life with her, went through the whole song and dance. Relationships are complex and thorny, but—call me old-fashioned—you don't propose to a girl if you don't want to marry her. Or you break it off when you realize you've made a mistake. You don't have raunchy sex with another woman on her air mattress; you don't lie to that other woman about not being in a relationship. But that's exactly what Jacob did. Which means that even if he is "miserably engaged," he lacks the courage to put an end to it. He is a coward. And I have no time for cowards.

I do, however, have time to wallow in the sorry state of my personal life. And so, for a solid forty-five minutes, that is exactly what I do.

My internal monologue eventually becomes too melodramatic even for me, and so I decide I need to get out of the house. Fresh air. Yes, that's what I need. Also, ice cream.

Before heading into the great outdoors, I send Jacob a quick text message: "Dinner tonight is off. Good luck with the wedding. Don't ever call me again."

I toss my phone in my purse and throw on an old Cornell sweatshirt, trying to ignore the throbbing sensation in my head. Those martinis last night were such a bad idea. My hair is beyond fixing, full of kinks and knots from a combination of restless sleep and hangover sweat, so I leave it alone and grab my purse and keys and trudge up my front steps, an activity that nearly doubles my heart rate. I choose to blame last night's martinis for this and not my acute lack of fitness.

I drag myself to CVS, hating life and pretty much every human being I encounter along the way. What are they all so happy about? Can't they see the world is full of phonies and assholes? Don't they know?

A sign on the CVS freezer tells me they are having a 2-for-1 special on Edy's ice cream, which is pretty much the best news I've heard all week. I buy four quarts: one Cookies 'n Cream, one Mint Chocolate Chip, one Vanilla, and one Caramel Delight, which, incidentally, looks pretty delightful. Four quarts of ice cream. That should get me through the weekend.

I throw a few bags of peanut-butter-filled pretzels into my basket, and as I do, I see a man and a woman holding hands at the end of the snack aisle.

"Get a room!" I groan as I shove them out of my way.

I pay, collect my four bags of snacks, and trudge back to my apartment, where a full day of eating my feelings awaits me. Or that's what I think until I run into Blake on my way down Church Street.

"Hey there," Blake says as he slows his pace and stops in front of me on the sidewalk. He eyes the plastic bags draped up and down my arms like Christmas ornaments. "Uh, so is there anything left at CVS, or did you clean the place out?"

"Two-for-one on Edy's," I say, shrugging, as if this will explain everything.

"I see." He studies my hair, which looks considerably worse than his—quite a feat, I might add, considering he doesn't have much. "So . . . exciting plans for tonight?"

"If by exciting you mean blowing through four quarts of ice cream alone, then yes. Yes I do."

"Alone? You? No way. I'm sure you've had some hot date lined up for weeks."

"The only date I had lined up was with a guy who is engaged to his longtime girlfriend. So no. No hot dates for Hannah."

"Oh. Sorry." Blake scratches his chin. "That's really awful. You deserve better."

I sigh. "Whatever. I can't decide if I'm more bummed about him being a jerk or the fact that I'll miss out on a helping of steak frites tonight."

"Why, where was he going to take you?"

"Bistro du Coin. Alas. I suppose a few quarts of ice cream will have to do."

Blake grins. "Aw, come on, you can't sit home alone all night."

"I'm pretty sure that I can."

"Nope. Not gonna let you sit around and feel sorry for yourself. How about this: I'm supposed to meet some friends across the street at Russia House around nine o'clock to celebrate my election victory. Why don't I rally the troops for a dinner at Bistro du Coin at seven or eight? You can order those steak frites you've been dreaming about all week."

"Really?" Blake nods, smiling. My stomach flutters. "That sounds . . . great, actually. You're sure your friends won't mind?"

"Of course they won't mind," he says. "They'll love you. Who wouldn't love someone who can carry twenty pounds of ice cream on her own?"

I look down at the bags hanging on my arms, the weight of the ice cream bunching up the sleeves of my sweatshirt so that I look like the Michelin Man. A few months ago, if I were forced to choose between polishing off a quart of Cookies 'n Cream on my own or going to dinner with my landlord, I would not have hesitated in choosing the former. But somewhere along the way, Blake stopped being just a landlord. I don't know what to call him now—a friend? a confidant? a mentor?—but what I do know is I want to have dinner with him tonight. I don't want to be alone. And I want those damn steak frites.

"Okay, count me in," I say. "But make no mistake—this ice cream will get eaten at some point. That much I promise you."

Blake smiles as he pats me gently on the shoulder. "Whatever you say, Stay Puft. Whatever you say."

I show up outside Blake's door at seven-fifteen, stuffed by the mercy of Spanx and God into a stretchy black dress and a pair of pointy heels. Dressed in this way, I'd like to fancy myself a poor man's Christina Hendricks or Isla Fisher, though I admit that would be a very, very poor man indeed. Homeless, most likely. But it's a quantum leap from my daily attire, and that's all that matters. I am far from a girly girl, but there is something about putting on a dress and some makeup that makes me feel a thousand times better. Even if I'm still in a funk over the Jacob debacle, at least I'm trying to snap out of it.

Blake rips open his door, and his eyes widen in surprise when he sees me. "Wow. Hannah. You look . . . amazing."

I shrug. "When you set the bar at 'homeless person,' pretty much anything involving a brush and a little makeup is an improvement."

"Oh, please, you never look like a homeless person." He pauses. "The look earlier today was more like 'bag lady.' A slight but important distinction."

Blake grabs a brown leather coat off his coat stand and throws it on, zipping it up over his white button-down shirt and olive green sweater vest. Ah, Blake: even his party clothes are a little geeky. Not that I'm one to talk. This is one of the only dresses I own that doesn't resemble a muumuu.

We arrive at Bistro du Coin at seven-thirty, and I follow Blake as he pushes through the crowd in search of his friends. He can't seem to find them, so we push our way to the bar and order some drinks: a glass of red wine for him and a Kir Royale for me. The dining room buzzes with conversation and clanking silverware, staccato notes that bounce off the tile floors and mirrored bar, and as I nurse my drink I notice at least two guys checking me out. One looks like Bilbo Baggins and the other resembles a shar-pei, but nevertheless, their interest indicates Blake's assessment of my appearance wasn't entirely off base.

A few sips into my drink, Blake waves at someone walking past the hostess's table, a man I immediately recognize as Anoop, the guy dressed as Balloon Boy at Blake's Halloween party.

Anoop strolls up to the bar, dressed tonight in a black button-down shirt and dark jeans, and gives Blake a high five. His eyes briefly shift in my direction, and he does a double take. "Hannah?"

I smooth the front of my dress. "The one and only."

"Wow—I almost didn't recognize you."

Blake smiles. "She cleans up nice, huh?"

Anoop drags his eyes up and down my tightly bound figure. "I'll say."

Anoop orders a gin and tonic, and we sip our cocktails and rehash last weekend's Halloween party. Blake and Anoop mention that one of their friends needs help with a holiday party in December, and after last weekend, they both recommended me highly.

"With any luck, he'll give you a call in the next week or two," Blake says.

Before I can ask more questions about this potential client, a willowy blonde walks into the restaurant, surrounded by two men and two women. The woman looks familiar, and I realize that's because she is Nicole, the belly dancer from last weekend, the one whose apartment building caught on fire and whose aunt works at L'Academie de Cuisine.

"Sorry I'm late," Nicole says, double kissing Blake and Anoop on the cheeks. Her four friends, two of whom I recognize from the Halloween party, offer hugs and waves. "Connecticut Avenue was a nightmare."

Blake pushes me forward by the small of my back. "Nicole, you remember Hannah?"

"Of course. My aunt says she's looking over your application as we speak."

"Really?" Finally, some good news.

"Yep. The admissions department is a little backlogged at the moment, but with any luck, you'll hear something soon. Apparently they have a record number of applications for the January start date." She raises her eyebrows. "The competition is steep."

Great. Just what I wanted to hear.

The hostess leads us to a round table in the middle of the room, and I pull up a seat between Blake and Anoop. A surly waitress tosses a basket of bread on our table, and before she stalks off, Blake orders a bottle of Côtes du Rhône. By the time the waitress returns, everyone at the table is swapping stories and telling jokes, and it becomes clear we won't be ready to order for quite some time.

"So check this out," Anoop says. He launches into a story about one of his coworkers, a woman who dries her wet underwear on the radiator in her office. "So I walk in, and, sure enough, there they are: three pairs of stretched-out underwear and a bra, all lined up behind her desk. And she's acting as if everything is normal—like, oh, doesn't everyone wash their underwear at the office and dry it on the radiator? So I'm like, 'Uh, whoa, isn't that a fire hazard?' And she's like, 'What, that? Oh, no. I've only burnt a pair once.' *Burnt* a pair? Of underwear? What is wrong with these people?"

"Sounds like my office," I say. "Where do you work?"

"The Center for Policy Solutions."

"I work at the Institute for Research and Discourse." I pause. "Or at least I used to. I quit yesterday."

Blake leans forward and rests his hand on my shoulder. "You're kidding. You quit?"

My cheeks flush. "Don't worry. I'll still be able to make my rent." *I hope.*

"Where are you off to next?" Anoop asks before Blake can jump in with more questions.

I grab my wineglass and take a long sip. "Not sure. Maybe culinary school. I'm still trying to figure it out."

Anoop attempts a supportive smile. "I . . . hope that works out for you."

I reach across the table for another slice of baguette, and as I do, I spot Jacob walking into the restaurant. He wears a navy moleskin blazer and jeans, and his hair is carefully styled into its signature haphazard coif. He approaches the hostess's stand, gently resting his hand on the waist of the Asian woman walking beside him, whose glossy, pin-straight black hair reaches all the way to her waist. This woman, his apparent date, is not Hannah Sugarman. She also most certainly is not Alexis.

I try not to let on that I've seen him, but as I rip violently into my piece of bread, shredding the soft interior into smaller and smaller pieces, my blood boils. How is it possible that I consistently fall for the biggest assholes in the universe? Who is this Asian chick? And what the hell is she doing with my reservation—a reservation that, quite frankly, shouldn't have been anyone's because Jacob is *engaged*?

Jacob notices me from across the room but immediately pretends as if he hasn't seen me, turning away and guiding his date through the restaurant as the hostess leads them to their table.

I throw back a swig of Côtes du Rhône, blot the corners of my mouth with my napkin, and lift myself from my seat. "Excuse me," I say, stepping away from the table. "I'll be right back."

I march through the crowded room, the anger and wine pumping through me as I work my way to Jacob's table. Jacob pretends he doesn't see me coming, and his date has no reason to think anything of my presence until I stop directly in front of their table and stand there, staring at the two of them.

The Asian woman's eyes dart nervously between me and Jacob. "Um . . . hi," she says. "Can I help you?"

"I don't think so," I say, shifting my gaze in Jacob's direction.

He offers a casual shrug. "What do you want from me, Hannah?"

The Asian woman furrows her brow. "You two know each other?"

"Oh, I'm sorry—did he not mention me?" I reach out my hand. "I'm Hannah. The one who was supposed to be sitting in your seat tonight."

The woman stares at my outstretched hand. She doesn't shake it. "I thought you said your sister canceled on you," the woman says, glancing up at Jacob.

"His sister?" I let out a bitter laugh. "No, not his sister. Me. But I'm guessing Jacob never mentioned my name. Or Alexis's for that matter."

"Alexis?"

"His fiancée? The woman he's been dating for five years? Her name never came up?"

Jacob opens his mouth to respond, but before he can speak, Blake sidles up behind me and rests his hand on my shoulder. "Everything okay over here?"

"Fine," I say. "I'm just saying hello to Jacob—the guy I was supposed to have dinner with tonight?—and his new friend . . . I'm sorry, I never caught your name."

"Vanessa."

"Vanessa. Well, Vanessa, this is my landlord, Blake." I turn to Blake. "Apparently Vanessa didn't know about Jacob's fiancée either. Isn't that funny?" I let out a protracted brittle laugh.

Jacob lazily places his menu back down on the table. "Hannah, come on . . ."

"Come on, what? You're just lucky Alexis hasn't found out yet. My friend Becca Gorman knows all about us."

Jacob's fair complexion morphs into a color resembling wet clay. He smiles nervously. "Becca Gorman. Got it. Didn't realize you knew her."

"Yeah, well, if it's not me telling Alexis, it'll be Vanessa, and if it's not Vanessa it'll be someone else. How many times can you dodge a bullet?"

Jacob sneers. "Like you're in any position to talk about dodging bullets."

Blake and Vanessa rumple their brows in unison, and my stomach drops.

Jacob narrows his eyes. "Yeah, that's right. What about your little side gig, huh?"

My eyes flit between Vanessa and Blake, and then I glance over both shoulders, as if I am confused as to whom Jacob could possibly be speaking and, with every gesticulation, am broadcasting, *Who, me?*

Blake contorts his face. "What is he talking about?"

"You know exactly what I'm talking about," Jacob says, staring at Blake. "You're the one letting her cook in your kitchen."

My stomach gurgles loudly, and my heart races in my chest, and oh my god I think I might vomit.

Blake grimaces. "Listen, buddy. I checked it out, and what she did was totally legal. The rest is between me and Hannah."

Totally legal? What is he talking about? And how, with every passing second, does this day manage to get increasingly worse?

Jacob cackles. "Legal, huh? I'm not so sure about that."

"Well, you should be," Blake says. "I can pay whomever I want to cater my Halloween party, and it's really none of your business."

Jacob furrows his brow. "Your Halloween party?"

"Yeah, why? What are you talking about?"

"I have absolutely no idea," I say, jumping in loudly as a river of sweat trickles down my cleavage. *Oh god, oh god, oh god.* Confronting Jacob was a terrible idea. My plan is totally backfiring. This is the worst. The worst!

I straighten my posture and slide back my shoulders, narrowing my eyes at Jacob. "All I know is that the rest of our table is waiting for us to order their dinners, and I never want to talk to you again—ever."

Jacob snorts. "Oh, so now you're going to play dumb? Come on, you know you—"

"Hey, guy? Shut up," Blake says. "Hannah has made it abundantly clear she wants nothing to do with you. So why don't you leave her alone and let us get back to our table."

Jacob shoots both Blake and me a cold stare and lets out a huff. "Whatever." He runs his fingers through his hair. "Good luck with your totally effed-up career, Hannah. And by the way, your cinnamon buns aren't that great."

He plucks his menu off the table, and with Vanessa's brow in knots, Blake pushes me back to my seat and orders another bottle of wine.

My cinnamon buns aren't that great? My *cinnamon buns aren't that great?* What the fuck is he talking about? No, I cannot even address this because, quite clearly, Jacob's taste buds are up his ass. Also, I cannot address the fact that I am more upset about him not liking my cinnamon buns than I am about him using me for sex. Because, let's be honest, that makes me sound 100 percent, A-plus crazy.

I will also choose to ignore how close I just came to blowing my cover in front of Blake. If he finds out I *am* The Dupont Circle Supper Club, I'll lose his friendship and support and advice. At least Jacob and I both hold sensitive information about each other. If Jacob rats me out, I will find Alexis and go nuclear on him.

Five minutes after we return to our table, Vanessa storms out of the restaurant, and Jacob follows after her. Once he is no longer in my presence, my stomach gradually disentangles itself, and I manage to enjoy a dinner of steak frites and red wine with Blake and his friends. Every so often, between courses, Blake leans over and whispers, "You okay?" to which I reply, "Of course," which for most of the dinner is only half true. By the end of dinner, however, I'm not lying anymore. I am okay. I'm over it.

After dinner, Blake walks with me down Connecticut Avenue toward his house, his hands stuffed into the pockets of his leather jacket. A chilled wind blows in our faces, and I cross my arms to keep from shivering. After a mild October, November is here, and the weather has finally started to turn.

As we cross Dupont Circle, Blake takes off his coat and hands it to me. "Oh—no. I'm fine," I say, my teeth chattering. "Thanks, though."

"You're shivering," he says. "Take the damn coat."

I pull on Blake's coat, which is about ten sizes too big, and cross my arms over the front to keep it shut. "Thanks."

"My pleasure."

"You could have stayed with your friends, you know. You didn't have to walk me home."

"I know. But I'll feel better knowing you got home okay. I'll meet up with them later."

"Well, thanks. And thanks for taking me out tonight. I'm sorry if I messed up your plans."

"No need to apologize. I had fun. And I'm glad I kept you from drowning in a quart of Edy's tonight."

"There are worse fates . . ."

Blake laughs. "I can't believe you were actually going to spend Saturday night all alone."

"You can go ahead and crown me the least social person you know."

"I—sorry, that's not what I meant," he says.

I smile. "I know. No offense taken."

As we reach our building, I fish out my keys from the bottom of my purse and slip out of Blake's jacket. Blake puts his coat back on and grinds his heels into the pavement while I throw my purse over my shoulder.

"So . . . I was wondering," he says. "I've been invited to a gala next Saturday hosted by the Georgetown Cancer Center. My boss helped pass a bill that increased access to cancer screening, and he's winning an award for that, so I have to go. But I'm allowed to bring a date, so I thought . . . maybe you'd like to come with me."

My stomach sinks. Next Saturday night is the carnival-themed supper club we're holding at the rental loft in Northeast. As much as I relish the idea of re-creating the pumpkin funnel cake I remember from my days in Ithaca, I have to admit: there is a part of me, however small, that would like to accompany Blake.

"I . . . already have plans," I say.

"It's just up the street at the Hilton . . . ," he says, trying to persuade me.

"Sorry. . . . I can't."

Blake presses his lips together and nods, visibly disappointed. "Oh, well. It might have been too much for you anyway. I have to show up at six with my boss for the silent auction, and the gala goes until midnight."

"Wow. A marathon."

He chuckles. "Yeah. Like I said, it probably would have been too much. I'm sure spending six hours with your pirate-talking landlord isn't your idea of a good time."

I look down at the pavement as I rub my hands together to keep warm. "It doesn't sound so bad," I say.

When I look up, Blake's eyes are fixed on mine, his lips drawn into a soft smile, the apples of his cheeks stained with the slightest hint of pink. He searches my face as he removes his hands from his coat pockets and presses them together, tilting them back and forth as he cracks his knuckles.

"Hang in there," he says. "Not all guys are assholes."

"So I hear."

He stops cracking his knuckles and points his finger at me. "Hey—*I'm* not an asshole."

"True," I say, biting my lip to keep from smiling. "At least that's what the evidence so far suggests."

He knocks me playfully on the shoulder. "All right, to bed with you. I'll talk to you sometime next week."

"Good night," I say. "See you soon."

And, as I watch him walk away down Church Street, I hope that I do.

thirty-eight

a t noon on Monday, I meet Rachel outside the NIRD office, and we hop in a cab headed for Hugo's loft in Northeast. We zip down Massachusetts Avenue, passing the Washington Convention Center and NPR's headquarters, as dozens of people wander up and down the sidewalks on their lunch breaks. The cabdriver veers onto H Street and crosses North Capitol Street, taking us from the northwestern quadrant of the city into Northeast, and almost immediately, the landscape changes. The sidewalks become less dense and the buildings are spaced farther apart and the areas around us feel eerily quiet and dead. In the distance, however, I see signs of life, with multicolored storefronts and traffic congestion and signs for restaurants and coffee shops.

I tap Rachel on the shoulder and point through the front windshield. "Have you visited this neighborhood recently?"

"The 'Atlas District'? Not since it gentrified and became a hipster hot spot. But it's supposed to be great—lots of cool restaurants. Kind of the perfect spot for us, actually."

"Except for the fact that the name of our supper club doesn't make sense anymore."

Rachel shrugs. "Details."

Our cabdriver speeds past Ethiopic Ethiopian Restaurant and Sidamo Coffee and Tea, navigating the bumpy road, half of which is being ripped up by a series of large bulldozers, another sign of the neighborhood's ongoing change. He turns right onto Eighth

Street NE, guiding us down a street that, with its blue and pink and white row houses, looks awfully similar to Church Street. Before long, he turns left onto a small side street, at the corner of which sits a tall brick building with a series of modern balconies cascading up its face.

Rachel and I pay the cabdriver and head for the building's front door, which is covered by an angular, brushed metal awning. Using the key Jackson gave her, Rachel buzzes us through the front door, and we stride through the contemporary steel-and-concrete lobby to the elevator bay in the back.

We slip into the elevator, and Rachel presses the button for the third floor. As we wait for the doors to close, I glance over at Rachel, who—with her mustard tweed jacket, gray camisole, and cream pants—appears to be wearing the J.Crew catalog from head to toe. I, on the other hand, am wearing jeans and a plaid button-down because I am unemployed.

"So . . . how is the boy?" I ask timidly.

Rachel's cheeks flush. "Good. He wants to take me to Middleburg next month for a weekend getaway at some B&B."

"Wow. Romantic."

"Yeah, I know, it's crazy. Me and romance? Who'd have thunk it."

I nudge her in the side. "Eh, it gets the best of us."

"I guess so."

She smiles softly, and I search the dreamy look in her eyes, a starry-eyed expression I don't think I've seen on Rachel in . . . well . . . ever. "You really like this guy, huh?"

She presses her lips together and slowly nods. "I think I might even love him."

"Whoa—*love*? Seriously? That's huge."

She shrugs. "It's like I'm a new woman. I don't even recognize myself."

I chuckle as the elevator ticks up to the third floor. "I like this new woman. Tell her to stick around."

The elevator doors open, spitting us out onto a long, narrow hallway with dark concrete floors and bright white walls, which are lined with industrial caged sconces. We tread down the hallway until we reach Hugo's studio, a corner unit at the end of the hall. Rachel jiggles the key into the lock, and as soon as she opens the door and lets us inside, I know the space will be perfect.

The room is open and bright, with a wall of windows on two sides and exposed brick on the other two walls. The studio isn't huge, but it's larger than Blake's dining and living rooms, meaning we will easily be able to fit thirty-six people in here. A small sliver of a kitchen sits along one of the brick walls and includes a refrigerator, a sink, and a gas range. The kitchen is only moderately bigger than the one in my apartment, but I've chosen a menu I think I can manage in a kitchen of this size and will do most of the prep work in advance.

I decided to base this weekend's menu on carnival foods, inspired by the traveling carnivals and amusement parks I visited as a kid. When I was young, my friend Lisa's parents would take a group of us to the June Fete every summer, where we'd gorge ourselves on funnel cakes and sno-cones, after riding the Gravitron and Ferris wheel and getting our faces painted. The tradition continued when friends invited me to their New Jersey beach houses over the summer, and we visited Gillian's Wonderland Pier, where we'd play bumper cars and ride the Tilt-A-Whirl and stuff our faces with hot dogs and boardwalk fries. Admittedly, I always wished I could visit an official state fair, the kind where hogs and cattle are on display and everything—from butter to Oreos—is deep-fried. But growing up in the Philadelphia suburbs, the June Fete and the Jersey Shore were as close as a girl could get.

My menu, however, will pilfer the specialties of other carnivals and state fairs, giving a nod to everything from giant turkey legs to corn dogs on a stick. Rachel managed to find some vintage carnival signs to hang on the walls and will decorate the tables with white-and-red checkerboard tablecloths, antique milk bottles filled with colorful pinwheels, and mock carnival tickets. If all goes according to plan, this could be our best supper club yet.

And, really, it has to be. As it stands, The Dupont Circle Supper Club is my only source of income—my only means of paying my bills and preventing my parents from discovering I am a huge disappointment. If I want our guests to sweeten the sixty-dollar fee with a nice tip, this dinner has to be perfect. I need this money. I need to buy myself time. At this point, my only backup plan is an acceptance letter and financial aid package from L'Academie de Cuisine, and I haven't heard a peep from them yet. Not a promising sign.

Rachel and I inspect the oven and refrigerator, and then I walk the perimeter of the room, peering out the windows and across the city. "I like it," I say.

Rachel beams. "It's great, right?"

"I think it'll be perfect."

We check out the dishwasher, which is considerably smaller than Blake's, meaning we'll be on the hook for a lot more hand washing. But if washing a few more plates by hand means I will save myself Blake's ire, that's fine by me.

Rachel twirls Hugo's keys around her finger. "So we'll hit the farmers' market Thursday, yeah?"

"Yep. And I'll do the bulk of the prep work at my place Friday night, so that we'll have more time to set up Saturday. You'll take care of tables and chairs?"

"Already on it. Thompson at NIRD is hooking me up."

"The kitchen director?"

She nods. "Don't worry, I'll handle the logistics."

She wraps her arm around my shoulder and walks me through the front door, locking it behind her as we head for the elevator. We wait in the cool, stark hallway for the elevator to arrive, and when it does, we step inside as Rachel sighs.

"Back to reality," she says.

These days, I'm not even sure what that means.

The Thursday before the supper club, Rachel sneaks out of work early and meets me at the Penn Quarter farmers' market to pick up the turkey legs, Brussels sprouts, pears, and potatoes. I sneak out of nowhere because I live alone and am unemployed.

"Well, well, well," Shauna says as Rachel and I approach her stand. "If it isn't Washington's favorite carnivore."

"I'm not sure that's a title I even want," I say, eyeing the rows of pork and lamb.

"You put in an order for three dozen turkey legs this week. That's your title, whether you like it or not."

Shauna yells for Sam to grab our turkey legs off the truck, and while we wait, she eyes me and Rachel suspiciously. "What kind of operation are you two running?"

I feign ignorance. "What do you mean?"

Her lips curl into a smirk. "Every week or two, you put in an order big enough to feed a football team. No, two football teams. What gives?"

I shrug. "We have a lot of friends."

She scrunches up her forehead. "No one has *that* many friends."

"We do," Rachel says.

Shauna rolls her eyes, a disbelieving smirk still plastered on her face. "Uh-huh. It wouldn't be for a certain 'supper club,' would it?"

I allow the faintest hint of a smile. "I have no idea what you're talking about."

Rachel and I pay Shauna, who once again gives us a steep employee discount, and we stroll over to the vegetable stand to pick up the Brussels sprouts and potatoes.

"Remind me," Rachel says as I pick through the crate of potatoes, "what are you doing with the Brussels sprouts?"

I reach into my purse and hand her a crumpled-up copy of the menu. "Here."

She skims the menu:

Slushy spiked lemonade/beer
Boiled peanuts/homemade pickles/kettle corn
Mini corn dogs with chili ketchup, curried mustard,
   and cheese sauce
Turkey leg confit
Deep-fried Brussels sprouts
Poker-chip potatoes
Ginger-pear sno-cones and cotton candy
Pumpkin funnel cake

"What the hell are poker-chip potatoes?"

"I'm going to slice the potatoes paper thin—like poker chips or carnival tokens—and line them up in a baking dish, accordion-style, with thyme, shallots, and garlic, and bake them until they're crispy around the edges but tender in the middle."

"Seriously, why aren't you cooking for a living?"

"Uh, at this point, I think I am."

Rachel considers this. "I guess that's true."

She helps me lift my bags of potatoes onto the scale and reaches into her purse for her wallet. "By the way," she says, "I'm going to pick up a small U-Haul van Saturday morning to lug all the tables over to Hugo's loft. We can call Hugo on the way so that he can meet us there and let us in."

"You don't have a key anymore?"

"Jackson had to give it back to Hugo. He and some artist friends paint there Tuesday through Friday."

"Nice life."

She shrugs. "Trust fund baby."

We divide the potatoes and Brussels sprouts between our two bags and saunter up Eighth Street toward the red line Metro stop, the cool November air nipping at my ears.

"You think we'll be okay on Saturday, right? At the loft?"

"Yeah, why wouldn't we be?"

I shrug. "I don't know. New space, bigger guest list, more advanced prep work, higher expectations."

Rachel scrunches up her lips and rumples her brow in deep thought, assuring me, in that very Rachel way, that she is giving my question adequate consideration. Then she relaxes her face into a confident smile. "Nah," she says, shaking her head as we turn onto F Street. "We'll be fine. Trust me."

thirty-nine

We are not fine.

The morning of the supper club, Rachel comes over to my apartment to help me wrap up the thirty-six legs of turkey confit, the vats of trimmed Brussels sprouts, and the dozens of other ingredients we need to transport to Hugo's loft. As I bind my prep pans in swathes of plastic wrap, Rachel picks up her phone and calls Hugo to see when he can meet us. And that's when all hell breaks loose.

"WHAT????" Rachel shouts into the phone. "Are you *joking?*"

I freeze, my hand clasped around a jar of homemade pickles. "What's going on?"

She waves at me to be quiet. "But we told you we wanted it for this Saturday," she says. She listens as Hugo responds on the other end. "Well that isn't my fault, now is it?"

"Rach, what is going *on?* What is he saying?"

She hushes me a second time. "Well what the hell are we supposed to do now, Hugo? Tell me that." She pauses. "Uh-huh. Right. Well that's just awesome. *Awesome.*"

I rush over to Rachel and grab the phone from her hands. "Hugo? This is Hannah Sugarman. The . . . head chef. What's the problem?"

"Hannah, dude, listen, I am so sorry, but I totally mixed up the dates. I thought you guys wanted to use my place next weekend."

"No. This weekend. Not next weekend."

"Right," he says through a lazy laugh. "I get that now."

"Are you laughing?" I say, my rage building. "This isn't funny. We need that loft tonight."

"Right, totally. But see, I already promised another group they could have it tonight—they booked it like two months ago."

"And how is that my problem?"

"Hey, listen, I totally get it. I screwed up. But, like, this other group—they're good people, and they reserved the space months ago."

I clench my jaw. "So what do you propose we do?"

He pauses. "I mean, space is just a construct, right? Like, if you're subverting the food establishment, space and time don't matter. All they do is inhibit us."

What. The. Fuck.

Rachel pulls on the sleeve of my shirt. "What is he saying?"

I cover the phone with my hand. "He's telling me space is a construct. That's what he's saying." I redirect my voice back into the phone. "Hey, Hugo? Forget it. We'll figure out something else."

"Right on," he says. "Good luck with that."

I hang up Rachel's phone and, using all the strength I can muster, throw it onto my air mattress as I shout obscenities that would make Rahm Emanuel blush. What are we going to do? Not only have I spent precious money on enough food for thirty-six people, and not only are thirty-six people expecting me to feed them tonight, but I've also prepared—salted, seasoned, and cooked—thirty-six servings of turkey leg confit. What the hell am I going to do with thirty-six servings of turkey leg confit?

I turn to Rachel, trying to control my panic, which has reached a 10.6 panic on the "Holy Crap" Richter scale.

"Okay, what's our next option?"

"What about your place?" she suggests.

"Take a look around, Rach." I wave my hands across my apartment. "Does it *look* like we can fit thirty-six people in here? It's tight with just you and me. No way. Not going to work. How about your place?"

"No way. Lizzie is hosting some sort of law school study session tonight."

"Can't she have it somewhere else?"

"Have you met Lizzie? She makes Millie look like a stoner. Lizzie won't even let Jackson use our shower because she's afraid he'll contaminate it. Besides, my oven broke last week, and we're still waiting for the electrician to come out and fix it. My place isn't an option."

I rub my temples and let out a long, deep groan. "Throw me a freaking bone, Rachel. What are we going to do?"

She pauses. "What about Blake's place?"

"I told you, he's in town this weekend. And I can't keep using his place—it's too risky."

"But you said you're hitting the PAUSE button after this dinner, right? So it would just be this one last time. Never to be repeated."

"That may be, but I told you—he's in DC this weekend. Not Tampa."

"But isn't he going to a gala or something tonight?"

"Yeah. From six until midnight." I catch myself. I get where Rachel's heading. "You don't think . . ."

"How long do our dinners usually last?"

"About four hours," I say.

"But we could probably pull it off in less than three, right?"

"I mean . . . probably." Rachel raises an eyebrow. "Okay, yes," I say. "We could do it in less than three."

"It isn't ideal, but . . ." Rachel trails off. "You said you need the cash, right?"

"After the amount of money I've already spent on this dinner? Definitely. Even more than before."

Rachel and I lock eyes, and, whether it's due to a profound lack of imagination or an overwhelming sense of defeat, we come to an unspoken agreement: we are holding the dinner in Blake's house tonight, for one last time.

I bite my lip as I tap my foot nervously against the floor. "Okay, here's what we're going to do. You're going to e-mail everyone and tell them the dinner has been moved to seven instead of eight. Send them the new address. I'll do as much of the prep work in my kitchen as I can. As soon as Blake leaves for the gala, we can run up to his house, set up, cook the dinner, and get everyone seated, fed, and out of there by ten. That'll give us an hour to clean up and an hour to spare, in case Blake comes home early."

"You think he'd come home early?"

"No—his boss is getting some award. And given Blake's thumping schedule, he never gets back before midnight on the weekends he's in town."

Rachel goes silent, then nods her head in agreement. "Okay," she says. "Let's do this."

I watch as Rachel scurries out my front door and realize in the history of terrible ideas, this ranks right up there with Olestra and the Pontiac Aztek. And the worst part is, we're doing it anyway.

The minute Blake hops into a cab and peels away toward Eighteenth Street, I grab Rachel by the arm and push her up my stairway.

"Go, go, go!"

We run up the stairs, hustle into Blake's house, and throw our ingredients onto the counter. I immediately dump about two quarts of oil into each of two pots, one for the deep-fried Brussels sprouts and corn dogs and the other for the funnel cake. Rachel runs back and forth between the kitchen and dining room like a madwoman, throwing the tablecloths down, tossing the milk bottles on the tables, and scattering the ticket stubs all over the place in a hurried frenzy. I grab the pan of confit turkey legs, which I prepared last night, and shove them in the oven. All I need to do is reheat them in the oven and crisp up the skin, and they'll be ready to go.

"Pinwheels!" Rachel shouts from the dining room. I grab the

bag and throw it to her, and she catches it in the doorway and races back to finish setting up the table.

Before I start on the potatoes, I shovel the boiled peanuts, kettle corn, and homemade pickles into serving dishes and rush them into the living room, setting them in the area beyond the folding tables Rachel picked up from NIRD and is speedily setting up. I run back into the kitchen, the sweat pouring down my back, and grab a mandoline and start slicing the potatoes into thin, token-size rounds, working at the speed of light.

"Careful!" Rachel snaps as she scurries into the kitchen to grab her chalkboard. "Watch your fingers. The last thing we need is for you to end up in the ER."

"How much longer until you can help me with the slushy lemonade?"

"Two minutes," she says, panting. "I just need to finish hanging the signs."

I quickly arrange the sliced potatoes in the baking dish, aligning them upright in concentric circles, and tuck the shallot wedges among the potatoes. I season everything with salt and pepper and shove the dish into the bottom oven.

"Potatoes are in!" I shout to Rachel. "Ditto the turkey."

Rachel runs into the kitchen. "The living and dining rooms are set up. I've arranged everything so that breakdown will go super fast."

"Great. Could you deal with the drinks?"

Rachel wraps her arms around a dozen bottles of lager and porter and runs them into the living room while I whisk together the corn dog batter and unwrap the mini hot dogs onto a plate. I turn on the heat beneath the pot of oil, slowly bringing the oil to 350 degrees for my deep-frying extravaganza.

Rachel rushes back into the kitchen and grabs the ice, lemon juice, and Absolut Citron and dumps them, with the rosemary syrup and the rest of the spiked slushy ingredients, into the blender. She whirs everything together, tastes and seasons the drink, and then gives everything another whir.

"Look at you," I say. "You look like a real cook these days."

She grins as she pours the mixture into individual glasses. "I learn from the best."

Two months ago, Rachel was exploding glass dishes in my kitchen and balking at anything more complicated than box mix brownies. Now she's whipping up cocktails and helping me deep fry. Granted, it's not as if the woman is throwing together Napoleons and croquembouches in her spare time, but at least she is no longer scared of boiling water.

I glance down at my watch. Twenty minutes to showtime.

"How's the turkey coming?" Rachel asks.

I flick on the oven light. "Good. Right on schedule."

We scurry around the kitchen, lining up plates, arranging the serving pieces, and scrubbing dirty knives and cutting boards. In separate bowls, I whisk together the dry and wet ingredients for the funnel cakes, and I set the bowls away from the stove, next to the sink. We mince, chop, and slice our way through the next fifteen minutes until, suddenly, it's seven o'clock and the doorbell rings.

Rachel brushes her hair off her face with the back of her hand and tosses her dish towel on the counter. "I'll get it."

She scampers down the front hallway and unlocks the front door, and muffled sounds of confusion and surprise and awkwardness begin emanating from the foyer. The thud of footsteps clomping down the hallway echoes throughout the house, and when I look up from trimming the Brussels sprouts, what I see before me causes my heart to race and my stomach to churn and my head to nearly explode.

"Look who it is," Rachel says, flashing a tense and panicky smile.

Standing on either side of Rachel are the last two people I want to see right now aside from Blake Fischer himself—the only two people who could make this night more nerve-wracking than it already is. But they're here, and they're staying, and so there's nothing I can do but force a smile and try not to cry and put on my most professional face as I say hello to Adam and Millie.

forty

"**h**annah?" Millie's eyes pop open when she spots me standing behind the stove. "Oh my God, you're *joking*."

Adam looks startled. "Hannah—hi. Wow. I . . . didn't realize you ran this place."

A zillion questions swirl through my brain, the most recurrent being (a) what the hell is Adam doing at a supper club, (b) why the hell didn't Rachel notice their names on the guest list, and (c) *holy crap, are Adam and Millie actually dating for real?*

Millie eyes the Viking range and granite countertops and narrows her eyes. "This is your house?"

I nod, unable to speak. Their presence has thrown off my entire flow, leaving me disoriented and off-kilter.

"Huh," she says, dragging her fingertips across the counter. "I thought you needed to find someplace cheaper after you guys broke up. This doesn't look cheaper."

"She shares the house with roommates," Rachel says, playing nervously with the collar of her violet boatneck tee.

Adam flashes a toothy smile as he spots the red-and-white apron wrapped around my waist. "So you're the 'buxom hostess,' eh?"

I clench my jaw and grab the counter to keep myself from charging at him on the other side of the room. Through our entire relationship, he told me underground supper clubs were stupid and wouldn't let me host one, and now here he is, the first to arrive at The Dupont Circle Supper Club, with a date in tow. What a hypocrite. I could scream.

The doorbell rings again. Rachel must grasp my proximity to a full-blown nuclear meltdown because she wraps her arms around Adam and Millie. "Why don't we move into the living room?" she says. "Hannah, can you answer the door?"

I let in the next wave of guests and the next after that, and once everyone is chatting and drinking in the living room, I meet Rachel in the kitchen and grab her by the elbow.

"Why didn't you tell me Millie and Adam were on the guest list?"

"Because they *weren't* on the guest list. Here, look." She hands me a copy of the guest list. "Millie used pseudonyms for both of them. She e-mailed from a fake Gmail account."

I glance down the list. "*John Adams and Betsy Ross?* Those names didn't arouse any suspicions?"

Rachel sighs. "I didn't think anything of it at the time. Sorry."

"Great. So now I have to feed my ex-boyfriend and The Hemorrhoid, who—correct me if I'm wrong—appear to be dating."

Rachel peers into the living room. "It does look that way."

"Great. Awesome. Fantastic. As if I didn't already have enough to worry about tonight."

"Relax."

Rachel wraps her arm around my shoulder and leads me to the stove top, trying to calm me down as we launch into the prep work for the first course. She tells me time and again everything will be fine—we'll pull this off, we'll clean up with time to spare, I should forget about Adam and Millie. But it doesn't matter what she says. This dinner is already a disaster, and it hasn't even started.

With every passing second, the evening gets progressively worse. As I thread the hot dogs onto skewers and dip them in the cornmeal better, Rachel continues her pleas for me to *slow down, relax, take a deep breath.* But nothing she says or does relaxes me, and if anything my anxiety and rage feed on each other until I feel like a woman possessed. I thrust the corn dogs into the pot of sizzling oil and yank them out in an aggressive jolt that sends hot oil spattering across the kitchen. I drop the entire bowl of curried mustard all over the floor and send a knife hurling across the room when I lose my grip. I overcook three of the corn dogs and nearly burn the turkey legs, but no matter how hard I try, I cannot focus.

Rachel storms back into the kitchen with a stack of dirty plates after the first course, at which point I am about to burn the potatoes. "Hannah, come on!" she snaps. "Get your head in the game."

But I can't get my head in the game. My head is fighting multiple fronts and losing all of them. I'm worried about Blake coming home early, I'm worried about dinner taking too long, I'm worried about Adam and Millie mocking my cooking and making me feel like a failure. I cannot handle all this pressure.

Rachel and I plate up the confit turkey legs, each tender piece of meat covered in a silky, garlicky gravy that I manage to drizzle all over the meat and all over the floor. I pile a side of deep-fried Brussels sprouts on each plate and then fan out a helping of "poker-chip potatoes," which—I regret to report—are indeed slightly burnt.

Carrying the plates with Rachel into the dining room, I lock eyes with Adam, who follows my every move as I proceed into the dining room. I can't place his expression. Is it desire? Regret? Pity? Whatever it is, it's pissing me off, and yet I cannot look away. My eyes remain glued to his face.

This wouldn't be such a problem if I weren't carrying four plates up and down my arms and if Millie weren't sitting next to Adam, watching my every move as well. But as soon as I notice Millie's interest, I lose my footing and trip over the leg of one of the dining room chairs and go flying across the room, sending the four plates soaring through the air like Frisbees.

The plates crash to the ground, sending gravy and Brussels sprouts flying across the room, streaking Blake's pale cream walls and leather couch. The room goes silent.

"Sorry!" I shout from the floor, where I am splayed out like a squashed bug. "I'm okay. Everything is fine."

"I hope one of those wasn't *my* plate," Millie mumbles under her breath.

I pull myself up from the floor and brush off my apron. "I'll clean this up. Rachel will take care of you in the meantime."

By some miracle, the plates—a mix of Blake's, NIRD's and Rachel's—haven't shattered, but there is food scattered all over the floor—blobs of gravy and flakes of fried Brussels sprouts and squashed disks of potatoes. I scoop up the remains as best I can and pile them on separate plates and carry the plates back into the kitchen.

"Rach, please tell me we have some extra Brussels sprouts and potatoes."

She glances into the pans on the stove. "You do. But as for the turkey legs . . ."

"We'll brush them off and add more gravy," I say, lowering my voice. "It'll be fine."

"The ones from the floor?" Rachel whispers.

I nod. "The ones from the floor."

I bought thirty-six turkey legs for this dinner: no more, no less. I cannot afford to throw any of them out.

We brush the dust and lint off the four turkey legs and replate them with new sides and a new dose of gravy. From this point on, I leave the serving up to Rachel because, quite clearly, I am incapable of functioning like a normal human being.

Once everyone has been served, I join Rachel in the area between the dining and living rooms and begin explaining the theme of the dinner in more detail to both rooms. I tell them the first official U.S. state fair took place in Detroit in 1849 and that state fairs were originally intended as livestock exhibitions, eventually transforming into the fairs we know today, with rides and games and deep-fried everything. As soon as I start talking, my confidence slowly returns, creeping back with each smiling face I see. *You can do this*, I tell myself. *You have nothing to be nervous about.*

Then, halfway through my spiel, Millie lets out a groan from the middle of the dining room table.

"I didn't realize each course was going to involve a *lesson*," she says, rolling her eyes.

I abruptly cut off my speech and narrow my eyes. "Well then maybe you shouldn't have come."

She holds up her hands defensively and raises her eyebrows. "Whoa, sorry. Don't get the chef mad."

"You know what?" I tap my foot frenetically against the floor as I glare at her. "No, never mind. Just . . . shut up. Okay? Shut up. Shut. Up. Shut up, shut up, shut up."

The other guests stare at me in horror as I sputter a stream of "shut ups," which, apparently, is the only witty and piercing comment I can think of at the moment.

"Nice," Millie says. "Classy, as always."

Adam puts his hand over Millie's. "Millie, stop. Not now."

"Don't defend her," Millie says. "Why do you always defend her?"

I cackle loudly. "That's a joke. He basically spent our entire relationship defending *you*."

Millie's pursed lips relax slightly, and the room is filled with the sound of people shifting nervously in their seats as they watch this soap opera play out in front of them. If I knew how to make this conversation go away I would. Unfortunately I do not.

Rachel, however, does. Before I can make a further ass of myself in front of our thirty-six guests, Rachel yanks me by the arm into the kitchen and throws me behind the stove. "Enough," she says. "What is *wrong* with you tonight?"

"Nothing is wrong," I say, sticking the thermometer in the oil for the funnel cakes. "Leave me alone. I'm fine."

But I'm not fine, and we both know it. Adam and Millie have shaken my confidence, and any ability I had to ignore them and concentrate has entirely vanished. It's not as if I wish I were the one sitting beside Adam. But when I see him sitting next to Millie, it confirms everything I always feared—that he always harbored feelings for her, that I was never quite good enough, that I will perpetually be two steps behind both of them. Why does Millie win at everything? She got all the accolades at work, she gets Adam, she gets to sit there and laugh while I drop turkey legs on the floor and burn the potatoes. While I flounder and squirm under my parents' watchful eye, the two of them sail through life, succeeding at pretty much everything they do. It isn't fair.

I glance at the thermometer as Rachel tosses the dirty dishes into the dishwasher. The oil is cold. "Shit!" I say. "I forgot to preheat the oil for the funnel cakes."

Rachel turns on the heat under the pot. "Don't worry. I'll handle it. You get the sno-cones ready and whisk together the batter for the funnel cakes." She heads back into the dining room to finish clearing the plates, and I grab the pear-ginger ice from the freezer and begin scooping it into a series of small shot glasses.

I don't wish I were in Millie's position. I don't. But when I see the two of them together, giggling at each other's jokes and sharing food off each other's plates, I realize what I miss, what I have been missing these past four months, is the intimacy of a relationship.

I never thought I'd say that. As an only child who lacked a boyfriend for most of her life, I thrived on independence and solitude. I never needed anyone else, and I was happy to keep it that way. It wasn't until I met Adam that I learned what it meant to lean on someone else, to function as part of a unit. No sooner had I become accustomed to the joys of codependence than Adam ripped it away from me. Now I miss the companionship and the closeness, the regular kisses and "Just-Add-Water" social life. I want to pluck out all the good parts of our relationship and assemble them into something new and better and wonderful. I don't want to be alone anymore.

As I scoop the last of the pear-ginger ice into the shot glasses, a deep, smoky odor wafts past my nose. I sniff the air, which suddenly smells bitter and charred. Weird. Is something . . . burning? I whip my head around, and that's when I see the unthinkable.

Two-foot flames erupt around the pot of boiling oil, which has overflowed onto the stove. The blaze rages ever higher, catching onto the dish towel next to the stove and setting the roll of paper towels on fire.

"RACHEL!"

Rachel scurries in from the dining room, her eyes wide as she catches sight of the fire, which now stretches across the six-burner range. The kitchen fills with smoke and, right on cue, triggers the fire alarm, which blares throughout the house with an earsplitting wail.

"OH MY GOD!" Rachel shouts, covering her ears.

The dining and living rooms break out in chaos. People throw back their chairs and scurry into the kitchen and hallway, covering their ears as they shout at each other.

"Everyone stay calm!" I yell.

No one listens. Half the guests grab for their coats and make a beeline for the door as the fire continues to rage in the kitchen. Out of the corner of my eye, I see Adam grab Millie by the elbow and mouth, "Let's get the hell out of here." They run out the front door and leave. Assholes.

Rachel fills an empty pot with water and throws it on the fire, which only intensifies the flames, sending them roaring into the hood over Blake's stove.

"WHAT ARE YOU DOING?" I shout. "DON'T USE WATER ON A GREASE FIRE!"

Rachel's eyes fill with tears. "SORRY!"

Seconds later, the phone rings.

"Don't answer that!" I shout. "It's probably the alarm company. We're not even supposed to be here."

Rachel growls. "Thanks—I hadn't realized."

The phone rings and rings and rings, and one of the guests rushes into the kitchen. "Where is the fire extinguisher?"

I open a canister of baking soda and begin tossing it on the flames. "I don't know."

He flashes a panicked look. "What do you mean you don't know?"

"I don't live here."

His eyes widen, and he backs out of the room as he whips out his cell phone to call 911. "Jesus Christ."

Rachel dashes into Blake's hallway and opens his coat closet. "Found it!"

She comes back, pulls the pin, and begins spraying everything— me, the fire, Blake's drapes and floor and ceiling. How the hell am I going to explain this to Blake? By telling him his kitchen just spontaneously caught fire, and we tried to put it out? Oh god, this is horrible. Horrible!

"What are you doing?" I shout at Rachel. "Don't spray me!"

"I'm putting out the fire!"

"Move faster!"

"I'M TRYING!"

The guests pile out the door while Rachel showers the kitchen with fire retardant foam, and all I can hear is the blaring fire alarm, which blasts at an unholy decibel level. Even as the flames die down, the alarm continues shrieking its alert to the entire neighborhood.

"AAAAH, SHUT UUUUUP!" Rachel screams as she sprays the fire extinguisher across the kitchen.

Suddenly, mixed in with the cry of the fire alarm, I hear the fire trucks howling down the street in the direction of the house.

Rachel and I lock eyes. *Shit.*

The howl of the fire trucks intensifies as they barrel in our direction, and then the sirens stop. The front door bursts open, and three men in thick boots and black-and-yellow firefighter uniforms storm down the hallway into the kitchen.

"Everyone out!" shouts the firefighter in charge, yelling above the din of the smoke detector as his colleague disables it. "Everyone out now!"

The alarm shuts off, and the house goes silent, and any lingering guests scurry out the front door. The firefighter in charge grabs me by the shoulder. "This your place, ma'am?"

I fidget with the box of baking soda, my ears still ringing. "Um . . . actually . . . it's complicated."

"Yes or no, ma'am?"

I clear my throat. "No."

"Then I'm going to have to ask you to step outside." He turns to Rachel. "You the owner?"

She shakes her head. "No."

The firefighter lets out an irritated sigh. "Could someone tell me who the damn owner of this house is?"

"I am."

Rachel and I whip our heads around and see Blake standing in the kitchen doorway, dressed in a tuxedo and holding his cell phone in his right hand, his eyes darting anxiously around the kitchen. And that's when I know for certain that the hell of this evening isn't even close to being over. No, in a classic twist of Hannah Sugarman luck, the hell has only begun.

forty-one

blake's forehead twists into knots. "Can someone please tell me what's going on?"

The firefighter nods in the direction of the stove top. "It appears there's been a grease fire in the kitchen, sir."

"But . . . that's impossible. I've been at a gala all night." He waves his cell phone. "The only reason I'm here is because I got a call from my security company about a fire alert. Luckily I was only a three-minute cab ride away."

The firefighter shifts his eyes from Blake to me to Rachel. "I'm going to have to ask the three of you to step outside while we inspect the property. Sir? Ma'am?" He gestures toward the doorway.

The three of us walk down the front hallway and out the front door, my hair and apron covered in soot and chunks of food. A crowd has congregated outside the house, some of them neighbors, some of them guests of The Dupont Circle Supper Club.

When we reach the bottom of the wrought iron stairway, Blake turns to me, his brow still rumpled into thick creases. "Who are all these people? Why were you in my kitchen?" He glances down at my apron, and the blood rushes to his face. "Were you . . . throwing a party in my house?"

I grab the iron banister to keep from passing out. I might throw up. "No," I say. "Not exactly."

"*Not exactly?*" His face has turned the color of a red grape. "What the fuck does that mean?"

I have never heard Blake use the word *fuck*. I have also never seen him this angry. A thick vein pulses across his forehead, and he clenches his jaw and flares his nostrils and, oh my god, I think he might kill me.

"I . . . I . . . it's not what it looks like."

"Oh, really? So you *weren't* throwing a party in my house?"

I suppose the phrase *it's not what it looks like* is only effective when whatever "it looks like" is far worse than whatever "it (actually) is." In my case, however, the opposite is true, and so I have no response that will not result in my immediate eviction.

As I stare at Blake, my chin quivering and my eyes filling with tears, a stranger strolls past the crowd and asks what the hell is going on.

"Dude, The Dupont Circle Supper Club went down in flames tonight," someone bellows. "Literally."

Blake shifts his eyes from the crowd to his house and back to me again. His gray eyes fill with incredulity, then realization. The ice cream in his freezer, the missing port and scotch, my familiarity with his kitchen—all of the pieces come together at last. He shakes his head, his face painted with the pain of treachery and betrayal.

"You're fucking kidding me," he says, his voice gradually rising. "You're fucking *kidding* me!"

"I . . . we didn't . . . I mean . . ."

"How long has this been going on?"

I bite my lip and wipe the tears away from my eyes. I cannot bring myself to speak. Neither can Rachel, who has stood silently beside us, watching the horror unfold before her eyes.

"Answer me," Blake says. "How long has this been going on?"

Before I can answer, a young woman with cropped strawberry blond hair taps Blake on the shoulder. I recognize her as one of the guests from the dinner tonight. "Excuse me," she says. "Are you Blake Fischer?"

He frowns. "Yeah."

"The Blake Fischer who ran for Dupont Circle ANC?"

"Yeah, why?"

"I'm a blogger for DCist. Is it true you were running The Dupont Circle Supper Club out of your house?"

Blake glares at the blogger and then at me. "I don't know. Was I?"

My lip quivers. "No," I say. "I was."

The blogger stares at Blake. "But that is your house, right? You live here?"

Blake sighs. "Could you leave us alone, please?"

Her eyes dart back and forth between us. "Sure. Whatever."

She grabs her iPhone from her purse and begins tapping into it as she walks away, and Blake buries his head in his hands. "What a nightmare."

The firefighter approaches the top of the stairway and waves Blake inside, telling him they've extinguished the fire in its entirety. I motion for Rachel to stay outside and proceed to follow Blake up the stairs, even though I'm pretty sure he wants to vaporize me at the moment. I almost wish he would.

Blake runs his hands over the top of his head as he takes in the damage to the kitchen. "Jesus," he says.

A thick miasma of smoke hangs in the air, and the smell of scorched matter permeates the room. The formerly white cupboards are all a grimy gray, bespattered with streaks of black ash and soot. The ceiling, too, is dark and dingy, and the knobs to the stove top have all melted into the counter.

"The damage actually isn't that bad," the firefighter says. "Your stove top being in the middle of the room and all, none of the walls caught fire. The blaze was mainly confined to the breakfast bar area."

Blake snorts. "Oh. Hooray. Fantastic."

The firefighter shrugs. "Hey, buddy. I've seen worse. You lucked out. Nothing your homeowner's insurance shouldn't cover." He turns to me. "But you, ma'am, need to be more careful in the kitchen. Deep frying is no joke."

"Oh, don't worry, sir," Blake says. "She won't be cooking here ever again."

Blake escorts the firefighters outside, leaving me alone in the kitchen to stew in my own anxious juices. What can I say or do to possibly make this okay? I need Blake to understand how deeply sorry I am—how awful I feel for lying to him, how terrible I feel for setting his kitchen on fire, and, above all, how much his companionship has meant to me over the past few months and how much I don't want to lose that.

Blake returns a few minutes later, his black bow tie undone and hanging around his neck and his tuxedo jacket folded over his arm. His sleeves are rolled up around his elbows.

"Blake, I'm so sorry. You have no idea how sorry I am."

"Don't I?"

"I—I didn't mean for it to turn out this way," I say, wiping the splotches of soot off my face.

He sneers. "What, you didn't mean to set my kitchen on fire?"

"No—I didn't mean to use your house at all. I just . . . everything spun out of control."

"How, exactly?"

I clear my throat. "Well . . . my friend Rachel and I planned to hold a supper club out of my apartment, just to see if I could do it, but then the apartment flooded, and since you gave me a spare key to your house . . ."

"Hang on," Blake says, interrupting me. "Let me get this straight. You and your friend decided to run an unlicensed restaurant out of my basement—*my* basement, which I own and happen to let you rent. And when you ran into a problem, you decided it was okay to move the whole thing upstairs into a part of the house you don't pay for, using a bunch of furniture and kitchenware that isn't yours."

My throat tightens. Recited out loud, the scenario sounds even more absurd than it did in my own head. I stare at Blake, biting my lip to keep it from quivering. I can't believe I let this happen. All along, I knew I was doing something wrong—something profoundly dishonest—and yet I kept doing it anyway. What was I thinking?

"I . . ." My voice cracks and shakes. I am on the verge of losing it. I take two breaths and try again. "I . . ."

"You what?" Blake says.

"I'm sorry."

Blake goes silent and stares at the ground. Then he looks back up at me and fixes his gray eyes on mine. "You lied to me, Hannah. To my face, for months."

"I know, and I am so, so sorry. I feel awful."

"Why, because you got caught?"

"No," I say, my voice shaking. "Because I didn't mean to hurt you."

"Maybe you should have thought of that before you decided to turn my house into a speakeasy. Didn't you realize what this could do to my career? Did none of those conversations we had mean anything to you?" He shakes his head and looks up at the ceiling. "All those weekends I was away, I'd get excited about coming home because I'd think, 'Maybe I'll run into Hannah. Maybe I'll have an excuse to talk to her again.' And the whole time, you were running a borderline illegal operation out of my house."

"Blake, I didn't mean to—"

"I stuck out my neck for you, Hannah. I got my friend's aunt to look at your application for L'Academie. I wrote you an unsolicited letter of recommendation. I took you to fucking Bistro du Coin so that you didn't have to spend last weekend alone. And what did you do for me? You sabotaged my political aspirations and lied to my face." He tosses his jacket over his shoulder. "I can't believe I let myself care about you. What a fucking joke."

Blake turns his back to me and starts to walk out of the kitchen. "Blake—wait!"

He turns around and locks his eyes on me. The whites of his eyes are pink and glassy. "What?"

"I'm . . . I'm so sorry. What can I do to make it up to you?" Blake stares at me and says nothing. "I care about you, too, Blake. Please, what can I do? Tell me what I can do."

Blake lets out an exasperated sigh and heads back down the hallway. "I don't give a crap what you do," he shouts back at me. "Just leave my keys on the counter and get the hell out of my house."

i t's official: I've ruined everything.

I now have no job, no boyfriend, no supper club, no income stream, and an ex-friend landlord who hates me. And, on top of all that, my parents keep leaving me increasingly agitated voice mails, messages to which I cannot reply due to all of the factors listed above. As one might expect, I am completely freaking out. What am I going to do? This is a problem no amount of carrot cake or brisket can solve.

And now Blake is gone. *Gone.*

The morning after the fire, I banged on his door, holding a container of honeycomb ice cream in one hand and my check-book in the other, but he didn't answer and hasn't answered in the seven days since. Not that I should be surprised. The story of Blake Fischer and The Dupont Circle Supper Club has made the rounds, first appearing on the DCist blog and eventually making its way into the Metro section of the *Washington Post.* I try to comfort myself by pointing out that the story appeared on page three, below the fold, but I know Blake won't take any comfort from that at all, not in the digital era. According to the article, he is stepping down as neighborhood commissioner.

The article also said he has left town while on "temporary leave" from his job on the Hill, which explains why he hasn't answered my repeated knocks on his door or any of my phone calls. If he loses his job because of what I've done, I may never get over it.

Strangely, the articles make precious little mention of me, even though I am the buxom hostess in question, which makes the situation doubly unfair. Blake doesn't deserve this humiliation. This fiasco is entirely my fault. But if there is a way to make amends for what I've done and set things right, I don't know what it is.

My only choice, I decide, is to return to the message I began composing the day the *Post* article came out, and so the Saturday after the fire I flip open my laptop, and I write:

Your article about Blake Fischer and The Dupont Circle Supper Club ["Dupont Commissioner Goes Down in Flames," Nov. 16] portrays Mr. Fischer as a willing participant in the supper club's underground activities. This is not the case. As the sole proprietor of The Dupont Circle Supper Club, I ran the operation in Mr. Fischer's house without his knowledge, on weekends when he was visiting the home district for his employer, Congressman Jay Holmes (D-FL). Every aspect of the supper club, from its conception to its implementation, was my doing, and mine alone. Mr. Fischer knew nothing about it until I set his kitchen on fire last weekend.

Though I realize this will have little impact on the public's perception, I feel it necessary to mention that Blake Fischer is one of the most upstanding, inspiring people I've ever met. He cares passionately about making his neighborhood and community a better place and lives his life with guts and integrity. He is also very kind. It would be a disservice to the Dupont Circle neighborhood and the city at large to punish him for my own misguided actions. He deserves better.

Sincerely,

Hannah Sugarman

I skim the letter two times, and then, satisfied with my mea culpa, I click SEND and forward the message to the *Washington Post*.

Tuesday morning, the *Post* prints my letter. I sign onto my e-mail, hoping for a response or acknowledgment from Blake, but to my dismay, he hasn't written. Neither has anyone else.

What surprises is how much I want Blake to write—how much I want to know how he is doing and where he is living and whether he thinks he could ever forgive me for what I've done. But I haven't seen or heard from him in more than a week, and I'm beginning to think I may never hear from him again, except in some sort of legal eviction notice.

I do, however, hear from Rachel, who calls Tuesday morning as soon as she sees the *Post*. "I saw your letter," she says. "Why didn't you mention me?"

"I didn't see the point in ruining both of our lives. Blake was my landlord, not yours. This one is on me."

"But that's a lot to lay on yourself."

"Maybe, but you actually have something to lose—you're applying to Johns Hopkins, you have a boyfriend, you have a job. I, on the other hand . . ."

Rachel sighs into the phone. "Well, thanks. I just hope you'll be okay."

"I'll be fine," I say.

"Any interest in meeting up for a cup of coffee before I take off for Thanksgiving?"

I glance down at my T-shirt and raggedy Adidas pants and wonder if, with a little makeup and styling, I can manage some sort of quasi-athletic, postcollegiate student look. I decide I do not have the energy to try.

"Nah. Thanks, though. Are you leaving today?"

"Yep," she says. "What about you? Are you going to your parents'?"

I let out a protracted sigh. "Not sure. They're still trying to get out of my aunt's thing in upstate New York. They're supposed to let me know tonight whether I should buy a ticket for Philly or Buffalo."

"Thanksgiving is, like, two days away. Aren't you nervous there won't be any tickets left?"

"Right now, that's the least of my worries." I wander into the kitchen and pour some Puffins into a bowl and drizzle them with a little milk. I don't want to talk or think about my parents right now. "How are things at the office, by the way?"

"Less fun without you. But not all that different. Mark is still crazy. His new research assistant is totally confused and overwhelmed. Millie is still the same pain in the ass. The usual."

I freeze with my spoon in my mouth at the mention of Millie's name. "Has Millie mentioned the party at all?"

"Ugh, don't get me started," Rachel says. "Ever since that article appeared in the *Post*, she has been *freaking out*. So has Adam, apparently."

In a sad commentary on my current mental state, hearing this news makes me unexpectedly happy. I picture Adam's and Millie's faces when the fire alarm went off and they spotted the flames erupting from the stove—how panicked they looked, the way the two of them slinked out of the house without trying to help, content to let me and the kitchen burn to a crisp. Millie sees everything as a competition, but if Adam is as spineless as his actions that evening imply, dating Adam is one competition I'm happy to let her win.

"What else is new? How is Jackson?"

"Dreamy as ever," she says. I can feel her blushing through the phone. "We both sent in our Hopkins applications, so fingers crossed." She pauses. "Any word from Blake?"

I shovel a spoonful of cereal into my mouth. "Nope. Nada."

"Not even an eviction notice?"

"No. Thank god." My phone beeps, and I pull it away from my ear: MOM CELL. I groan. "My parents are calling on the other line. I've been avoiding their calls all week. I should take this."

"Do they know about the supper club?"

I let out a hoot. "Are you kidding? They'd both go into cardiac arrest. After shitting themselves. I haven't even told them I left NIRD. Like I'd tell them I nearly burned down my landlord's house while I was running an underground supper club."

"O-okay," she says, in a tone that suggests my behavior is totally insane—which, I will concede, it most definitely is. "Well, you better get that call. Talk to you soon."

I hang up with Rachel and answer my mom's call, deeply dreading this conversation. "Hi, Mom. What's up?"

"Hannah? Where *are* you?"

I clear my throat. I should tell them the truth. I will tell them the truth. Just not now. I'll tell them . . . at Thanksgiving. Which, admittedly, is only two days from now. But I feel strongly that those two days will make all the difference. Why? I couldn't say. Probably because I'm a big, fat coward.

"I'm . . . at work," I say. "Where are you?" There is silence at the other end of the phone. "Mom?"

"You're at work? Where?"

I swallow hard. "IRD. Why?"

"Well that's funny. Because right now your father and I are at IRD, sitting in Mark's office. And from what he tells us, you don't work here anymore."

And just when I thought my life couldn't be any more of a mess, Murphy's Law rears its ugly head and shows me, yet again, there are an infinite number of ways for the universe to fuck my life, and it appears nature is hell-bent on exploring each and every one of them.

CHAPTER

forty-three

In some cruel twist of fate, my parents decided it would be a fun surprise to visit me in Washington and bring Thanksgiving to me, since they so desperately wanted to get out of Aunt Elena's ridiculous dinner. I cannot imagine why they thought this would be a good idea, but I'm guessing it has something to do with their complete lack of understanding when it comes to me and what I might consider a "fun surprise." Admittedly, if I'd sucked it up and discussed my unemployment with them weeks ago, I wouldn't be in this position. Hindsight, twenty-twenty, blah blah blah.

My parents ask me to meet them at the Tabard Inn in Dupont Circle, a request I cannot decline because, well, they're my parents and they drove all the way to DC and I am a big, fat, lying liar. I throw on a gray wool sweater and a pair of black pants and hustle down Eighteenth Street toward N Street. I scurry up the front steps to the Tabard Inn, a small, independent hotel sandwiched between a series of row houses on a narrow, tree-lined street. A tall man in a suit holds open the glass-pane door to the inn, and I inch my way through the lobby. The hotel's restaurant is tucked in the back of the hotel, and that is where my parents plan on meeting me.

I scan the restaurant for my parents, but they haven't arrived, so I park myself next to the broad stone fireplace in the lobby. The fireplace roars with orange and yellow flames, and I secretly wish they would leap from their stone confines and consume me, so that my parents will not find me here. I clench my fists, jamming my fingernails into the squishy pocket of flesh along the bottom of my palms, squeezing tighter and tighter with the hope that I won't feel anything because this is all a dream. My parents aren't actually in Washington. This is not really happening.

But my palms sting and itch, and with each breath I fill my lungs with the smells of burning wood and baking bread. And when none of the patrons around me morphs into a goblin of the night, I know for certain this is all very real indeed.

My breath shortens, and I suddenly feel as if the walls of this room are closing in on me and there is no air in the entire building. What am I supposed to tell my parents? That I quit my job? That I told the head of HR to shove my statement up her ass? That I've spent the past few months hosting an underground supper club out of my landlord's kitchen and almost burned down his house two weekends ago? Yes, I'm sure all of that will go over well. Forging my own path in the face of their disapproval has never been my strong suit, and instead of feeling strong and sure of myself, I now feel weaker than ever.

My parents walk into the lobby and spot me standing by the fireplace, their faces painted with confusion and worry. As my mom draws close, she reaches out and folds her arms around me, pressing my face into her chunky wool cardigan as her fluffy bob tickles my forehead.

"Oh, Hannah," she says. And then, "What the *hell* is going on?"

And so it begins.

"Maybe we should sit down before we talk about this," I say.

"Yes," my dad says, raising his salt-and-pepper eyebrows. "That sounds like a good idea."

We settle into our table, and right away a few former colleagues recognize my parents and stop by our table to say hello. The Professors Sugarman offer artificially light and cheery responses, as if nothing—nothing at all!—could possibly be wrong.

The last thing they want is for other people to witness their daughter's complete meltdown.

Once we're on our own, my parents speak in monosyllables as they decide what to order, feigning deep interest in the contents of the Tabard Inn menu, as if they are reading through a classified State Department document or the president's personal diary. My mom pulls at one of her wavy auburn locks, nervously tucking and untucking it from behind her ear as she presses her lips together, an act that accentuates the small wrinkles around her mouth, which run from her lips like small tributaries.

"The trout looks nice," my dad says.

"Mmm," my mom replies, nodding. The trout, the chicken. We are all pretending to be engrossed in something other than what's actually on our mind: the very unpleasant conversation that lies ahead.

I look out onto the cobblestone courtyard through the window behind our table. No one eats in the courtyard this time of year, but in the summer Adam and I would sit out there for brunch and stuff ourselves with homemade doughnuts and French toast. On a cool day like today, we would burrow into the restaurant's cozy interior, with its roaring fireplace and black-and-white checkered floor. Today I'd like to burrow my way right into the wall until I disappear.

The waitress takes our order, and as soon as she leaves, my dad picks up where we left off.

"Okay, *what* is going on?"

I grab a piece of focaccia from the breadbasket and stuff it in my mouth. "Where should I begin?"

He scrunches his shoulders by his ears. "Oh, I don't know, maybe the part where you quit your job three weeks ago and decided not to tell us?"

"Okay. I didn't want to work there anymore. So I quit. End of story."

My dad raises an eyebrow. "Hannah . . ."

"What?"

"You've ignored our calls and e-mails for the past three weeks. Obviously there's more to it than that."

I reach for another piece of bread. "You think?"

"Listen, you were getting antsy. Your mother and I knew that. But we thought you were planning to stick it out until you went to grad school."

"I'm not going to grad school, so sticking it out wasn't really an option."

"I thought you signed up for the GREs?"

"I did. I canceled."

My mom clucks her tongue. "Hannah, we've discussed this dozens of times. If you expect people to take you seriously, eventually you have to go back to school and get an advanced degree."

"No, that's what I have to do for *you* to take me seriously."

My father sighs and shakes his head. "That's not true."

"Uh, yes it is. You and mom would rather I make myself miserable pursuing a career like yours than do something I actually enjoy."

"That's not *true*," he repeats. "Listen, what you have to understand is that no job is fun all the time. Look at your mother and I—we have to do all sorts of things we don't want to do. Grading exams, reading shoddy research papers. But we take the bad with the good. That's the real world."

"Frankly," my mom says, "I don't understand why your generation thinks work should be a never-ending party—constant fun, fun, fun."

I huff. "Uh, maybe because your generation raised us to be this way."

My mom widens her eyes. "Excuse me?"

"My childhood was scheduled by the minute—tennis lessons, SAT practice, theater rehearsals, bassoon lessons. I was programmed to *expect* fun."

My mom smirks. "Since when is SAT practice fun?"

"It isn't. But the point is, every minute I was on to something new. If I got bored with something, that was fine because an hour later I was onto something else. I never had to deal with perpetual boredom. I never had to worry about making my own way in the world."

My dad rolls his eyes and shakes his head. "And this is your excuse for quitting a perfectly good job? Because your mother and I were too generous when you were a child?"

"No—that's not what I'm saying."

Gah, talk about derailing the conversation. This is not where I was headed.

"I appreciate all the opportunities you gave me," I say. "I know how lucky I am. Really I do. But it's taken me a while to figure out I was in the wrong line of work, and now that I have, I see my job at IRD was a bad fit. That's all I'm saying."

"But how can something be a bad fit when you were obviously so good at it?" my dad asks. "Some of the papers you coauthored with Mark knocked our socks off. That doesn't happen when a job is a bad fit."

"Competence doesn't necessarily equate with happiness," I say, grabbing a triangular cracker from the breadbasket. "I was good at singing, too, but you don't see me running off to be a pop star."

My dad snorts. "Of course not, because that would be ridiculous."

"To *you*!" I say, pointing at him accusingly with the tip of my cracker. "It's not ridiculous to anyone who is passionate about music or singing. The reason I didn't pursue becoming a singer— or a writer or a painter—isn't because I thought those careers were silly. It's because I figured out pretty early that those careers would never fulfill me."

"It doesn't sound as if anything will 'fulfill' you," my mom says under her breath as she grabs for her water glass.

"Hey—that's not fair."

"Well, honestly Hannah, every time we talk about this, you seem to have an unrealistic notion of the sort of satisfaction you're supposed to derive from a job. It's called *work* for a reason. It isn't supposed to feel like a vacation every day."

"I don't expect work to feel like a vacation. But I also don't expect it to feel like a prison sentence."

"Okay," my dad says, sighing loudly. "Then what are you planning to do, now that you've quit?"

I take a deep breath and steady my voice. "I'm applying to culinary school."

"Oh, here we go again with the cooking thing," my mom says, rolling her eyes. "You're going to be a glorified *waitress* again?" She says it like I've decided to become a stripper or a call girl.

"No. Not a waitress. A caterer. A cook."

"And have any culinary programs accepted you yet?" my dad asks.

"Not really."

He clears his throat. "Not *really?*"

"Not yet," I say. I still haven't heard from L'Academie. I have no idea where I stand.

My mom grabs aggressively for her glass. "So what you're telling us is that you quit a perfectly good job for a pipe dream. Is that what you're saying?"

"No, I wouldn't put it that way . . ."

She shakes her head. "This is ridiculous, Hannah. Let us talk to Mark. I'm sure we can get your job back at IRD. Or at least let us make some calls to some of our colleagues in town to see what other opportunities are out there."

"*No!*" I shout. The people seated around us turn and stare. "No," I repeat, lowering my voice. "I don't want my job back. Haven't you listened to anything I've said?"

"We have," she says, "and I realize this all sounds very exciting to you. But you're only twenty-six. Your father and I have years of experience on you, and though it's difficult for you to appreciate this, we aren't suggesting you go to grad school or work at a think tank because we want to make you miserable. We're suggesting these options because we know how many doors they could open up for you. We've been around the block. We've seen lots of friends pursue wacky dreams, only to end up failing. Remember Uncle Sol's music store? And Jim Gillibrand's solar start-up? Both of them failed. It happens all the time. Your cooking adventure could blow up in your face."

"And if it does, I'll come up with an alternate plan. I'll work at Starbucks if I have to. But I refuse to go back to IRD or any place like it."

My mom throws her hands in the air. "I give up. You're not making any sense at all. Alan, would you talk to her?"

In the wake of my mother's fit, the waitress returns to deliver our entrées. The three of us shift in our seats as the waitress places the plates in front of us, my parents affecting a cheery disposition for her benefit, as if the waitress has any interest in our conversation or its tone. All she wants is a nice tip.

"Alan," my mom hisses as soon as the waitress leaves. "*Talk* to her."

My dad swallows a bite of his trout and takes a deep breath. "Hannah, the way you're talking—it's foolish to sabotage your entire career over one bad experience."

"Unbelievable," I say, stabbing my mushroom tart with my fork. "It's like we're talking in circles. It isn't foolish to sabotage a career I never wanted in the first place and definitely don't want now. You guys always talk about my 'career goals,' but the problem is, those have always been *your* career goals you've projected onto me. And I went along for the ride for a while, but if I'm being honest, they were never the goals I wanted for myself."

"That's because you never knew *what* you wanted," my mom says. "We were trying to give you structure. To give you focus."

"Of course I didn't know exactly what I wanted. How is someone who is sixteen, seventeen, twenty-one, supposed to know for certain what she wants to do with the rest of her life?"

My dad sighs. "You don't know. You pick something, and you work hard at it."

"Well I did pick something, and I worked hard at it, and I wasn't happy. I kept trying to explain that to you—to tell you how miserable I was—but every time I did, you either ignored me or convinced me I was being a spoiled brat."

"That's not fair," my mom says.

"It's not? Every time I tell you how much I love cooking and baking and all of those things, you give me a ten-minute lecture on how those are hobbies and how you didn't work hard all these years—how you didn't break down all these 'barriers'—so that I could end up back in a kitchen. Come on, Mom, how many times have you given me that speech?"

"But, what I meant . . ."

"What you meant was cooking isn't an acceptable career for your daughter."

My mother looks down at her plate and sighs. She hasn't touched her meal. "A lot of that is in your head, Hannah."

"Really? Because I don't think it is."

"I know I haven't always been supportive of your interest in food," she says, "but all this disapproval you're talking about—a lot of that is what you *heard*, not what I said."

"Oh, please! Let's hit the rewind button and go back three minutes ago when you nearly crapped yourself at the suggestion I might go to culinary school. And what about your offer to get my job back for me? That's not exactly an endorsement of my choices, Mom."

She grabs her water glass and takes a long sip before laying the glass back on the table. "I was only trying to help," she says. "I want the best for you. That's all I've ever wanted."

I close my eyes and let out a long sigh. "Listen. What I'm trying to say—what I've been trying to say for a long time—is I understand all the sacrifices you made for me. The bassoon lessons, the SAT tutors, the fencing practice—I know all of those things cost money. I'm sure that's why you never bought a bigger house and why you kept that rusty Volvo for all those years. You wanted to give me every opportunity, and I'm grateful for that. But that doesn't mean I'm going to want the same things in life you want for me. I've tried for a long time to be the next Professor Sugarman, and it isn't me. It never has been."

My parents catch each other's gaze at this last comment and, as if I have removed a critical block from a wobbly Jenga tower, their resolve begins to crumble.

My dad scratches his scruffy beard. "Well, if you were so miserable and felt passionate about pursuing another career, why didn't you just do it?"

"Because . . ."

But I can't finish the sentence. Why *hadn't* I just done it? Because then I couldn't use my parents as an excuse anymore. I couldn't sit around and blame them for my misery and talk about what I'd rather be doing; I'd actually have to go out and *do* it, which would mean opening myself up to uncertainty and insecurity and failure. And if I failed at the one thing I'd always wanted to do, well, how would I explain that to them? To myself?

"Because," I say, "I didn't want to disappoint you."

My dad sighs and shakes his head. "Oh, Hannah. We've never been disappointed in you."

"Really? Because it feels that way sometimes."

My mom rubs her temples. "Maybe I *am* a little disappointed. But not in you. In your interests, I guess. You have to appreciate how hard I worked to get where I am. I didn't have any of the opportunities you had—and not because my parents didn't provide them for me. I was a woman living in a different time. I had to fight my way in. And for me to watch everything being handed to you and then have you turn it all down—when you have such potential—well, I suppose I'm having a lot of trouble with that."

I look at my mom, whose hazel eyes glisten as she plays with the stem of her water glass. "I have so much respect for you and your career, Mom. You're amazing—I've always thought you were amazing. And sometimes I wish I could be just like you. But I'm not just like you. I'm me. And I want to be a cook."

My parents look at each other across the table, their faces pale and riddled with wrinkles and laugh lines, and a part of me wants to jump back in and qualify everything I said so that I don't lose my parents as my psychological safety net, the one easy excuse for why I'm stuck in the wrong career. But I don't. Because even if their pressure pushed me down the wrong road, on some level I know my own fear and self-doubt kept me chugging along that path.

"Well," my mother says, after a prolonged silence, "I have to be honest. I do not like this. I do not like the idea of you throwing away all these years of hard work for some fantasy."

"Judy," my father says.

"Let me finish, Alan. But even though I think you are probably making a huge mistake, I'm not going to stand in your way. Because if I do, lord knows you'll hold it against me forever. You're right. You're an adult now, and you can make these decisions for yourself. But that also means you shouldn't expect your father and me to bail you out when this whole plan implodes. You're on your own."

"That's fine," I say.

But in that moment, my mother's words tighten around me like a noose. *I'm on my own.* No bailout money, no backup job waiting in the wings, no magic wand to fix my problems. Life outside the bubble isn't going to be easy—which, I suppose, is something I always knew and is why I've waited years to have this conversation. It's a lot easier to complain about feeling trapped than to do something about it.

"I thought this lunch might end with you disowning me or something," I say.

"That's ridiculous, Hannah," my mom says. "You're our daughter. We love you. We will *always* love you." She reaches out and clasps her hand around mine. "Even when you make foolish decisions."

"Judy," my dad says again, this time more forcefully.

She shrugs. "I'm just saying."

It is the most I can expect from my mother. Giving me her

blessing does not change the fact that she hates this decision and probably always will. But I suspect a part of her recognizes there is nothing she can do about it, that I am an adult and no longer subject to her directives, and so this new career path is as much a change for my professional life as it is for the nature of our relationship. She isn't so much giving in as she is letting go.

We finish eating and pay the bill, and my parents walk with me toward my apartment. As we walk down N Street toward Eighteenth, my mom reaches down and grabs my hand. I look up at her, and she smiles. It's a forced smile, tense around the eyes, but for now it's enough. She's trying.

"So tell me more about culinary school," she says. "When did you apply? How did this come about?"

"It's kind of a long story . . ."

"We're professors on sabbatical," she says, squeezing my hand. "We've got plenty of time."

I study my parents, whose expressions I would hitherto have called anxious or critical, and maybe they do feel that way, just a little. But for what feels like the first time in years, I also see interest—genuine interest—in their eyes, as they try to figure out what sort of bizarre trail I'm blazing, far away from their well-trodden path. And if they're ready to listen to how all of this began, I'm ready to tell them.

I grab my dad's arm with my free hand and pull both my parents into a coffee shop on Connecticut Avenue. "Let me start at the beginning," I say. "See, I have this landlord . . ."

forty-four

i miss Blake. There, I said it.

I've tried not to miss him. I've tried not to think about him. But I can't help it. An eerie silence has filled the house in his absence, haunting this basement apartment for what has now been two full weeks. No matter how hard I try to think about something or someone else, as soon as one of the pipes starts clanging in the wall I assume Blake is home, but then I realize he isn't, and there I am thinking about him again.

When he first left town, I was, on some level, relieved. At least I'd be able to stay in this apartment a little longer while I searched for a new place—a search that has, to this point, been entirely fruitless. And hearing him thumping around upstairs or seeing his face would only remind me what a terrible person I was. Who needs to be reminded of that? I lied to him. I took advantage of his generosity. I ruined his political prospects. I made so many mistakes—all of them foolish, none of them excusable—and having Blake around would only throw those mistakes back in my face.

But the longer Blake has stayed away, the more I've yearned for his companionship—a development I most certainly did not anticipate but is nonetheless true. I miss his corny jokes and his cherubic smile and his optimistic realism. I miss his little adventures and his pep talks and his knack for knowing just the right thing to say—as opposed to Adam and Jacob, who knew exactly what to say to get into my pants. Deep down, neither of them really gave a crap. But Blake is different. He actually seems to care about who I am and what I want and how I can get the most out of life. And that's why I want him to come home and why I hate not knowing when or if he will.

Part of me wonders if he might not come back at all—if he might take off for Tampa or San Diego or the Florida Keys, someplace where he could buy a boat and fish and eat too much fried shrimp. That's what I'd do, if I were him. I guess he'll have to come back at some point because all his furniture is still here. Plus, I crawled onto his deck and peered through his back window and saw his KitchenAid mixer sitting, unscathed, along his soot-covered counter. No one would abandon a perfectly good KitchenAid. That would be cruel.

Infinitely crueler, though, is the prospect of abandoning *me*, especially when that abandonment stirs up all sorts of feelings I don't know how to deal with. Blake is . . . well, he's Blake. He wears sweater vests and Ninja Turtles pajama pants and frequently refers to me as Sugarman. I convinced myself he was my dorky landlord, useful for a gourmet kitchen and maybe a laugh now and then. But now I see I had everything backward, and I've screwed everything up, like I always do.

The only thing I've managed not to screw up, surprisingly, is my relationship with my parents. Our lunch at the Tabard Inn felt like being pounded by relentless, crushing waves, but once lunch was over, the tide receded, and our rough patch was left a little smoother by that sudden swell of emotion. There are still fissures beneath the surface, but we managed, nevertheless, to spend a quiet and enjoyable Thanksgiving in Washington. My parents booked a table at the Blue Duck Tavern for Thanksgiving dinner, and, as we feasted on Red Bourbon turkey, creamed spinach, and croissant bread pudding with pears and sausage, we shared stories about Blake and Halloween and their time in London. We shared a bottle of Pinot Noir and talked and talked and talked, as if we hadn't talked in years, and that's when we realized we hadn't. It felt good to talk like that, like three adults, instead of two adults and their aimless kid. I glazed over my involvement in an underground supper club, and I said nothing about the fire I started in Blake's house, mostly because I'm not clinically insane. There is only so much I can throw at my parents at once without causing them to burst into flames.

The Sunday after Thanksgiving, my parents drove back to Philadelphia, leaving me to return to my disorganized, unemployed clusterfuck of a life. Now two weeks have passed since the supper club inferno, and I still haven't heard from Blake. I've called, I've e-mailed, I've written a letter that appeared in the *Washington Post*, but nothing has worked. I also haven't heard from L'Academie de Cuisine—a worrying sign.

Determined not to let everything in my life fall apart, I spend the rest of my Sunday scouring the Internet for other culinary programs with January start dates, from Le Cordon Bleu to the French Culinary Institute. At this point, I don't even care if the program is in DC. I'll move anywhere—Boston, New York, San Francisco—if it means I can give this cooking thing a shot.

After a night of researching culinary programs, I lie in bed Monday morning and try Blake's phone for the millionth time, but like each of the 999,999 other calls, this one goes straight to voice mail. I snap the phone shut and roll over on my air mattress.

This sucks.

My phone buzzes in my hand, and I bolt upright. Blake? Oh, please, please, please.

But of course it isn't Blake. It's my mom.

"Hey, sweetie," she says. "How are you?"

"I'm okay. What's up?"

"Well, I've been thinking. About culinary school . . ." Oh, here we go. "Your father and I didn't mention this to you last week because . . . well, we weren't entirely sure how we felt about the whole thing."

"Okay . . ." Great. I thought we'd resolved this.

"But, see, the thing is, years ago your father and I set aside a little money to help pay for your grad school. And now that it appears you aren't *going* to grad school . . . we've been struggling with what to do with the money. On the one hand, we'd be happy to add it to our retirement fund. But after much discussion, we decided that wasn't fair, since the money was meant for you. So we've decided to give it to you now, and you can do with it whatever you like—whether it's culinary school, or some other professional endeavor."

"Wow—Mom. I don't know what to say." I feel a lump forming in my throat. "That's . . . I . . . Thank you. Thank you so much."

"You're welcome. Use it well." She presses her phone to her chest and tells someone she'll be there in a minute. "I have to go. Oh! But in the meantime, I also have a lead for you."

"A lead?"

"Do you remember David Levy?"

I cross my legs and lean back against my pillows. "He was a few years above me in high school, right? Lived on our street?"

"Exactly. Well, I ran into his mother, Barbara, yesterday at Acme, and it turns out David lives in Washington and is doing very well for himself—runs some sort of consulting firm, apparently."

"Mom, is this a setup? Because I'm not interested."

She makes a loud *tsk* sound. "No, this is not a setup. Would you let me finish?"

"Sorry."

"Anyway, David is looking to throw a holiday party at his office in a few weeks, but the caterer just backed out, and he's looking for someone to fill in at the last minute, and apparently everyone else is booked. I gave Barbara your number to pass along, so don't be surprised if you hear from David in the next day or two."

"That was sweet of you, Mom. Thanks. But . . . I don't think I'll be able to do it if the party is at his office. I don't have a catering license."

"You need a catering license? Couldn't you just sort of . . . do it on the sly?"

"I'm . . . trying not to do too much on the sly these days. But thanks for the reference. Could be useful in the future."

"Ah, well. It was a thought."

I can't help but grin. "I thought you weren't interested in this 'foolish career path' I'm pursuing."

My mom sighs into the phone. "Listen—I'm still your mother, okay? I'm allowed to toot my daughter's horn if I want to."

"By all means, toot away."

"Well, if I won't, who will?"

I press myself deeper into my pillows and smile. "Thanks, Mom. For everything."

She presses the phone to her chest again and tells someone to *take a message, for god's sake, can't you see I'm on the phone*, and then brings the phone back to her ear. "My pleasure," she says. "Now get out there and give 'em hell."

The rest of my day gets eaten up by culinary school applications— researching them, applying to a few, calling and hanging up on L'Academe de Cuisine multiple times—and by the time I finish, it's almost eight o'clock, at which point I'm too tired to braise the pork chop I'd planned to eat for dinner. I yank open one of my kitchen drawers and pull out a take-out menu for City Lights of China. Pork dumplings, here I come.

As usual, the delivery guy knocks on my door at the most inconvenient moment possible: when I am half-undressed and in the middle of taking off what little makeup I put on today. He is at least fifteen minutes early.

"Coming!" I yell as I wipe my face and throw on the first pair of pants I can find, a baggy pair made of heather gray cotton with a big grease stain on the right thigh.

I grab my wallet and unlatch the front door, but when I open it I see the caller in question isn't the Chinese delivery guy. It's Blake.

He stands in my entryway, wearing a navy button-down, jeans, and a pair of brown loafers. His hair sticks out in all directions, and he looks pale and drawn, as if he hasn't slept in days. He clutches his car keys in his right hand.

"Hey," he says.

I cannot bring myself to speak. It's as if a tornado is ripping through my brain, spinning all my emotions through my head and jumbling them all up. Part of me wants Blake to grab me and hold me and tell me he missed me and forgives me for everything, but another part wants me to grab *him* and apologize profusely for everything I've done. And still another part wonders why I chose to wash off all my makeup and put on pants that make me look as if I peed myself. This is a new low.

Blake scratches his jaw and looks past me into my apartment. "Could I come in for a minute?"

I follow Blake's gaze and note the stacks of clothes and papers scattered across my floor. "Um . . . I don't know," I say. At the moment, both my own appearance and that of my apartment scream *homeless person*. "My place is . . . sort of a mess."

Blake offers a faint smile. "It couldn't look worse than mine."

Right. Of course. Because I set your kitchen on fire. Duh.

I show Blake into my apartment, and we weave our way around the piles of junk on my floor. Blake shifts his weight from side to side as he stands in the middle of the room.

"Could I get you some water?"

"Nah, I'm okay," he says, clutching his keys in his hand. "Thanks, though."

"So listen," we say in unison.

Blake extends his hand. "You first," he says.

"No, go ahead."

Blake fidgets with his keys as he stands beside my beanbag chair. "I saw your letter. In the *Post*."

"Oh?"

"I appreciate you setting the record straight." He pauses as he flicks the key ring around his finger. "That was an admirable thing to do."

My heart flutters. "I wanted people to know the truth. I still feel awful about what I did."

He shrugs. "Well, you should."

"I do."

"Good." For a moment, I think I see Blake reveal the barest hint of a smile, but it passes so quickly I can't determine whether it's an actual smile or a figment of my imagination.

"I'll pay to repair the damage," I say. "At least as much as I can afford."

Blake waves me off dismissively. "My insurance is covering it. The damage isn't as bad as it looks. Although if you want to chip in for a new set of pots and pans, I won't argue."

"Pots and pans. Sure. Consider it done."

He gives his key ring another flick. "Cool."

"So . . . have you been staying in Tampa?"

He nods. "Yeah. With my uncle."

"Ah."

"My leave of absence is up this week, though, so I'm back on the Hill tomorrow."

"Oh. That's nice."

"Yeah."

The air between us is thick and charged, and yet our conversation continues in monosyllables and tightly knit sentences. There's so much I want to say—that I missed him, that I'm so happy he's back, that what I want, more than anything, is for him to give me another chance. But every time I try to say those things, what comes out instead are banalities like, "Ah" or "That's nice."

"You might want to start looking for a new place," Blake says.

"I—oh."

Blake offers a noncommittal shrug. "Come on—I can't exactly let you live here after what you did."

I pull on the edge of my sweatshirt. "Well, I mean, you could . . ."

He smirks. "Yes, I suppose I could. But I don't think it's the wisest decision, do you?"

"Actually, yes. Yes I do."

Blake holds back a smile. "We can talk about it later this week. I . . . this is a tough one for me." He clutches his keys in his hand and raises his eyebrows. "I'll see you later."

He turns and heads for the door, and as I watch him walk away I feel Blake slipping through my fingers like hot sand. Why can't I tell him I don't want him to leave? That I don't want to be alone anymore, that I missed him so much?

"Wait!" I call after him. "Don't go."

Blake turns, his expression indifferent. "Is there something else we need to discuss?"

"No. Yes. I don't know—maybe." I scrunch up my shoulders and gesture toward the beanbag chair. "Do you want to sit down for a minute?"

He glances at his watch. "I . . . there are . . . I have things to do."

"Oh." My shoulders slump. "Okay."

Blake bores into me with his gray-blue eyes, holding my gaze as I feel a lump develop in my throat. "I guess I'll see you around," he says.

I open my mouth to respond, but instead I start crying— blubbering like a total basket case, with a quivering lower lip and a sniffly nose and tears streaming down my face. I'm not quite sure why I am crying like this, a fact that only increases the volume and pitch of my wails. Admittedly, the catharsis feels fantastic, but I don't love that I'm howling like a lunatic in front of Blake.

Blake slowly approaches me, his eyebrows knitted together. "Uh . . . what's wrong?"

I try to answer, but every time I speak, I start choking on my sloppy, unrestrained sobs. I can only imagine what I look like right now—probably like a slobbery, swollen psychopath.

"Are you . . . okay?"

"I—I . . ." I still can't get the words out. *I really like you, Blake. And I don't want you to go.*

Blake comes closer and tentatively brushes my hair off my face as he looks into my eyes. His expression is one of utter mystification, as if dealing with a hysterical young woman is far outside his comfort zone—alien and awkward and infinitely strange.

"I wish I could help you, but . . . I don't know what's wrong. What's going on?"

I wipe the tears from my eyes and breathe in quickly through my nose to keep a river of snot from running down my face. I pull the bulky sleeves of my sweatshirt over my hands and look into Blake's eyes.

"Don't leave," I say.

"Sorry?"

"I have some things I want to tell you."

"What things?"

I feel my lip start to quiver. "I . . . I missed you, Blake."

Blake fumbles with his keys and nearly drops them on the floor. "Sorry, what?"

I shrug. "When you left, I missed you. I missed everything about you."

Blake stares at me, his eyes wide and still. I feel as if he is seconds away from telling me he missed me, too, that he forgives me for everything. But instead, he says, "Is that so?"

I nod as I wipe my eyes with the back of my sleeve. "And I know you'll probably never forgive me for what I did. But I . . . I . . ."

I sniffle again, the sobs threatening to return. Why can't I tell him? Why can't I tell him I feel more like myself when I'm with him than I do with anyone else? Because I'm afraid. Not that he won't reciprocate, but that he might, and then someday he will change his mind. Or maybe he won't change his mind, but he'll turn into Adam, and I'll be right back where I started.

Blake rests his hand on my shoulder. "You what?"

I dab my eyes. "I think you're wonderful."

Blake blushes. "Well . . . thanks." He clears his throat and awkwardly removes his hand from my shoulder. "You're not so bad either. Some of the time."

I stifle a smile. "You make me better, Blake."

"Better at . . . ?"

I shrug. "Just . . . better."

Blake presses his hands together and stares up at the ceiling. He lets out a protracted sigh. "Then why did you lie to me?"

"I don't know. I shouldn't have. But all that started before . . . before . . ."

"Before what?"

I fix my eyes on his. "Before I realized how much I liked you."

Blake goes silent and rubs his chin with his thumb. He matches my stare, trying to maintain his stern expression, but the softness in his eyes blows his cover. "It was cowardly, you know. The supper club."

"Cowardly? What do you mean cowardly?"

"Cooking in secret like that. You were too afraid to stand up to your parents and do what you wanted out in the open, so you did it in secret to keep them happy. You were trying to have your cake and eat it too—no pun intended." He flashes a genuine smile for the first time this evening. "Sorry—old habits."

I smile back. "I like your old habits."

"You might be the only one . . ."

I step closer to Blake and grab his hand. "I'm applying to culinary school. I never would have done that without you. I was being pathetic. You made me see that."

"I never said pathetic."

"You didn't have to."

Blake smiles and glances down at his hand, which I'm holding in mine. "I don't know if I'd listen to a former Dupont Circle neighborhood commissioner, if I were you."

"Former? Can't you step back in?"

He shakes his head. "I don't think so. Not after everything that happened."

"But it wasn't your fault. It was my fault. You had nothing to do with it."

"Yeah, but it happened under my nose. It makes me look pretty dense."

I interlace our fingers and rub my thumb against his. "That's not true. I was pretty stealthy."

The edges of his lips curl upward, and he pulls me a little closer. "I guess you were."

I tilt my head upward and stare into Blake's eyes. "Blake, I need you to know—"

But he brings his finger to my lips and leans in closer, until I can feel his breath on my cheeks. I close my eyes, and just as I feel his lips graze mine, the doorbell rings. The Chinese delivery guy. Classic.

I lean my forehead into Blake's chest and sigh. Blake pinches my chin with his fingers and looks me in the eyes. "I've wanted to kiss you since I met you four months ago," he says. "Whoever that is can wait two minutes."

He pulls my face into his and kisses me softly on the lips. His lips are smooth and warm, and I cannot describe the sensation of kissing him other than to say it feels like coming home. I grab his shirt and pull him in closer, ignoring the banging on the door because the only thing I'm hungry for is Blake, and he's right here, holding me in his arms, and I don't want him to let go. Not yet. Maybe not ever.

In the light from my laptop, I watch Blake's half-naked body rise and fall atop my air mattress, the sound of his snoring falling somewhere between a rumbling motor and a purring kitten. Somehow my knowledge of this intimate detail—that he snores, *how* he snores—is like finding another edge piece in a complicated puzzle. I still have a big hole to fill, but at least I have the makings of a frame: how Blake sleeps and snores and kisses, what makes him smile and makes him sad, where he goes to be alone and when.

And what I know, more than anything, is that I want to find all the pieces to this puzzle—to complete this picture someday and make it whole—and I hope, oh I hope I am one of those pieces.

I roll onto my side, away from Blake, and as I do I hear him rustle beneath the sheets. He draws close and wraps his arm around me, pressing my body into his bare chest as he kisses my shoulder.

"I think I might be falling in love with you," he mumbles, his voice thick with sleep.

I can't tell whether he is awake or not, but I reply anyway, whispering into the stillness of the room. "Me, too."

When he squeezes me, I know he heard, but soon he starts snoring again, and I realize there's a good chance he won't remember this moment in the morning. Were I sleeping next to someone else, I might worry; I might jostle him awake to validate this emotional exchange. But with Blake, I know I don't have to. Tonight we came close to saying those precious words—the *I* and the *love* and the *you*—but I know for certain it won't be the last.

On the first Sunday in January, I find myself standing in my kitchen at 1774 ½ Church Street, swirling together a mixture of butter, cream, and sugar on my tiny stove top. Tonight I am cooking dinner for Blake in my apartment, my last home-cooked meal as a nonculinary student. Tomorrow I begin my program at L'Academie de Cuisine.

My acceptance came late in the game, only a week or so before Christmas. According to Blake, the letter had been mailed to his address instead and got lost among the piles of bills and insurance notices. The program requires a long commute all the way to Gaithersburg, Maryland—a thirty-five-minute drive, or a heck of a long Metro and bus ride. Eventually I'll rely on public transportation, but for my first week, Blake is letting me borrow his car. That he is allowing me to borrow anything of his after the supper club debacle is a testament to how much he must like me.

As I stir the pan of cream, the unmistakable whiff of roasting nuts floats past my nostrils. I panic: I burnt the pecans. *Crap.*

I rip open my oven door, grabbing at the sheet pan with a gloved hand. I lay the pan on the counter, shaking it back and forth to inspect every russet-colored nut. The pecans are fine, perfectly toasted, although a minute longer would have put them over the edge. Crisis averted.

I dump the pecans onto a sheet of parchment paper to cool and return to the stove, where the rest of my carrot cake filling bubbles away, its creamy whiteness giving way to a light golden brown. I could have chosen any dessert for tonight's dinner—cheesecake, ice cream, Sacher torte, chocolate mousse—but choosing the carrot cake was a no-brainer. I've never made it for Blake before, and I wanted something special to celebrate his reinstatement to the Dupont Circle ANC. Besides, everyone loves my carrot cake. Everyone.

Blake found out last week that the Dupont Circle Advisory Neighborhood Commission had read my letter and requested to meet with him to reconsider his resignation. They took a vote, and aside from one crotchety commissioner, they all voted to reinstate him as the commissioner for Ward 2B07. Truthfully, I think they were just happy they didn't have to find a replacement, since Blake's opponent moved to Maryland after the election. But either way, Blake is back and in the clear, with no stigma attached to his name—other than dating me, of course.

The good news is that the health department has decided not to fine me for holding an unlicensed restaurant out of Blake's town house. Someone from the Food Safety and Hygiene Inspection Services Division sent me a curt letter in the mail, my first and final warning to terminate the operations of The Dupont Circle Supper Club immediately, and so—for now, at least—The Dupont Circle Supper Club is no more. Not that I needed an official warning. The memory of Blake's kitchen ablaze will provide all the restraint I need for quite some time.

I scoop the cake filling into a bowl to cool, toss my apron onto the counter, and gather together my bags for the Dupont Circle farmers' market. I haven't been in weeks, ever since the fire, but today I plan to pick up the ingredients for our dinner. If past experience is any indication, I will buy enough food to feed the entire House of Representatives.

When I arrive at the corner of Twentieth and Q, the Dupont market is already in full swing, although not as swinging as it was a few months ago. The winter market caters to the die-hard fans, those who won't be kept away by freezing temperatures or a little snow, and so the usual deluge has slowed to a thin but steady stream of regulars.

I take my customary practice lap, scouting out the best-looking celery root and potatoes and pricing out the Brussels sprouts and kale. The winter sky hovers above me like liquid mercury, silvery and bright, casting shadows around the dozens of colorful tents.

"Hannah, Hannah, bo bana!"

Shauna calls to me from beneath her green-and-white tent, smiling widely as she rubs together her gloved hands. I skip up to her tent and lean across the ice tray to give her a hug. "Long time no see," I say.

"Where have you been? It's been, what, almost a month?"

"Life got . . . complicated. But I'm back! And I need two petit filets."

"Take your pick," she says, pointing to the corner of the ice tray. "We have a few packages."

I scan the tray for two suitable filets, which I plan to sear and serve tonight with a red wine reduction, celery root puree, and roasted Brussels sprouts. I grab two filets, along with some chicken breasts and a packet of bacon, and hand them to Shauna. "That should do me for now."

Shauna grabs her calculator and tallies up my goods. "A lot less than you used to buy," she says. "Scaling back?"

I chuckle. "Something like that."

"Yeah, well, keep an eye on those flames tonight, huh?" She winks. "Kidding, kidding. But remember, whenever you decide to—*ahem*—throw some sort of underground party again, I'm here for all of your butchering needs."

"Finest pork in America, right?"

Shauna raises an eyebrow. "Damn straight."

We load the meat into one of my bags, and I stop by a few more stands to load up on celery root, potatoes, kabocha squash, butternut squash, and Brussels sprouts. By the time I finish, my load rivals the weight of a small rhinoceros.

Standing in the gated area of the market, I shuffle toward the opening facing Massachusetts Avenue, never fully lifting my feet off the ground. Every few steps I drop the bags on the pavement, shake out my arms and begin again. I'm fairly certain I've already pinched a nerve in my neck, and at any moment, my left shoulder might dislocate.

"Need any help?"

I whirl around and find Blake standing in front of a table of mushrooms, wearing a thick jacket and a pair of gloves. The winter cold has stained his cheeks and nose the color of bing cherries.

I rest my bags on the ground and wipe my brow with the back of my hand. "What are you doing here?"

He laughs as he comes close. "I know you, Sugarman. When you said you were heading to the farmers' market this morning, I knew there was no way you'd buy anything less than your body weight in food."

I survey the bags around me, all overflowing with squash and tubers. "Am I that transparent?"

"Not transparent. Consistent." He eyes my bags. "Wow, you really went to town, huh? That one squash is as big as you are."

"Almost—but not quite."

"And not nearly as cute." He grabs me by the waist and pulls me in for a kiss, his thick hands resting on my hips. "Here, let me help you."

Blake grabs three of the bags, the heaviest ones, and I throw the last over my shoulder. We walk toward Massachusetts Avenue, flanked on either side by tents and open crates. Ahead of us, a dozen or so people push past each other on their way through the wide gate.

"So where to, Sugarman? What's next?"

Around us, the market bustles with activity—the guitar player on the corner and the people walking their dogs and the couples sharing croissants as they laugh at each other's jokes. The city pulsates with energy on every corner, the same energy that has swirled through its veins for weeks and months and years, and yet somehow it all seems more alive because of the person standing next to me.

"Home," I say. "Take me home."

The next morning, at the ripe hour of 6:15 A.M., Blake and I stumble out of my apartment and walk toward his parking space at the corner of Eighteenth and Church. We spent the night together, as we have for the past two weeks, his arm wrapped around me throughout my fitful sleep. Normally after a meal of that size and caliber, I would have slept like a baby, but ahead of my first day of culinary school, I barely slept at all.

He wraps his arm around me as we approach the corner and rubs my shoulder. "You ready?"

"I think so."

He gives my shoulder a squeeze. "You'll be great. I know it."

I give my hair a twist, tying it into a knot on my head. I've followed L'Academie's instructions to the letter: hair up, no jewelry, wearing casual clothes and a pair of kitchen clogs. My chef's jackets will be waiting for me when I arrive, as will my black-and-white checkered pants, scarves, hats, and copies of our textbooks for the year: a 1,224-page reference called *On Cooking*, and *Le Répertoire de la Cuisine*, a guide to the cuisine of French cooking legend Auguste Escoffier, written by his student Louis Saulnier and containing some six thousand dishes. I still can't believe this is actually happening.

When we get to Blake's car, he wraps his arms around me and pulls me tight. I lace my arms through his and press my head against his chest, listening to the *thump-thump* of his heart, strong and steady like a metronome. I close my eyes and squeeze Blake tighter, wanting this feeling, this closeness, to last forever. But I have a thirty-five-minute drive ahead of me, and so I pull away and kiss him softly on the lips.

"Time to go," I say.

Blake gives me another squeeze and then hands me the keys

to his car. I hop inside, toss my purse onto the passenger's seat, and stick the key into the ignition as I lower the window in front of Blake's smiling face.

"I'll talk to you tonight," he says. He leans in and gives me one last kiss. "Good luck."

I stare into Blake's eyes, which shine like polished silver in the early-morning light. "Thanks. I couldn't have done this without you."

He grins. "Sure you could have. You just needed a little push."

I smile and, turning away from Blake, peer through the front windshield. Today it begins. A new chapter. A fresh start. A long-awaited commencement. My future is uncertain—full of potential pitfalls and failures, full of possible heartbreak and loss—but it is, nevertheless, mine. My future, and no one else's. I can't say I have any idea what awaits me at L'Academie de Cuisine, but there's no way to find out but to dive right into the mud pit of the unknown and wiggle around until I'm good and dirty. Today is when it all starts, and I can't afford to waste another second.

I blow Blake a kiss, raise the window, and put the car into gear. Then I step down on the gas pedal, and I drive.

Recipes

Old-Fashioned Braised Brisket

ADAPTED FROM KELLY ALEXANDER

Serves 8

As Hannah Sugarman knows, the number one rule of brisket making is to make the brisket a day in advance. It's always better the second day. If you don't own a Dutch oven or a pot big enough to hold the brisket, you can sear the meat in a big frying pan and then transfer the meat and vegetables to a roasting dish or casserole and cover with aluminum foil.

1 tablespoon kosher salt

1 tablespoon ground black pepper

1 tablespoon paprika

2 teaspoons oregano

1 5- to 6-pound brisket, trimmed of some of its fat

3 tablespoons vegetable oil

3½ cups low-sodium chicken stock, store-bought or homemade

1 14½-ounce can diced tomatoes

2 bay leaves

3 medium yellow onions, peeled and thinly sliced

3 cloves garlic, peeled and chopped

Preheat oven to 350°F. Mix together the salt, pepper, paprika, and oregano in a small bowl. Rub the spice mixture all over the brisket.

Over medium-high heat, heat the oil in a heavy, ovenproof pot with a tight-fitting lid, just large enough to hold the brisket snugly. Add the brisket to the pot and brown on both sides, about 10 minutes per side. Transfer the brisket to a platter and pour off the fat from the pot. Return the pot to the stove top and add the stock, tomatoes, and bay leaves. Bring to a simmer, scraping up any browned bits stuck to the bottom of the pot. Return brisket and any accumulated juices to the pot and scatter the onions and garlic over the meat in an even layer. Cover the pot, transfer to the oven, and braise for 1 hour. Uncover the pot and continue to cook the brisket for another hour.

Push some of the onions and garlic into the braising liquid surrounding the brisket. Put the cover back on the pot and return to the oven, continuing to braise the brisket until it is very tender when pierced with the tip of a sharp-pointed knife, up to 2 hours more (for a total of 4 hours). You can check after an hour to monitor its progress; your knife should slide into the center of the brisket easily when the brisket is done.

Remove brisket from the pot and place in a 9-by-13-inch baking dish. When braising liquid is cool enough to handle, remove the bay leaves and puree in a blender or food processor, or with an immersion blender. Pour the pureed liquid over the brisket, cover the dish with aluminum foil, and refrigerate overnight.

A few hours before serving, remove the brisket from the refrigerator. Take the brisket out of the baking dish, wiping off any sauce, and place on a cutting board. Slice the brisket across the grain, then transfer slices back into the baking dish. Let stand at room temperature for 1 to 2 hours, covered.

Preheat oven to 350° F. Cover the baking dish with aluminum foil and place in the oven for 30 to 45 minutes, until the liquid is bubbling and the meat is warmed throughout.

Pretzel Bread

....

FROM SHERRY YARD

Makes 8 pretzels

DOUGH:

1¼ teaspoons active dry yeast

½ cup warm water

¼ cup buttermilk

2 tablespoons light brown sugar

¾ teaspoon sugar

1½ teaspoons vegetable oil, plus more as needed (I use olive oil)

2 cups bread flour

1½ teaspoons salt

SIMMERING LIQUID:

2 quarts water

¼ cup amber beer

¼ cup baking soda

¼ cup packed light brown sugar

TO FINISH:

vegetable oil

2 tablespoons coarse sea salt

Make the dough: In a 16-ounce measuring cup, dissolve the yeast in the water and let it sit for 5 minutes, or until cloudy. Add the buttermilk, brown sugar, sugar, and vegetable oil and mix well.

Place the flour and salt in a bowl. Add the liquid mixture and knead until smooth.

Brush a large bowl with vegetable oil. Scrape out the dough

and place in the bowl. Cover with plastic wrap and let it sit at room temperature for 1 hour.

Line 2 half-sheet pans with parchment paper and brush with oil. Lightly oil your work surface and your hands. Remove the dough from the bowl and press into a 6-inch square. Cut into 1½-by-3-inch rectangles. One at a time, shape each piece into a pretzel. (Cover the pieces you aren't working on with plastic.) Roll each piece out into a 24-inch-long rope. Shape into a U, then crisscross the ends halfway up, twist them together like a twist tie, and pull the legs down over the bottom of the U. Place the shaped pretzels onto the lined baking sheets. Cover them with lightly oiled plastic wrap and allow to rise for 30 minutes, or until not quite doubled.

While the pretzels are rising, place the oven racks in the upper and lower thirds of the oven and preheat to 450°F. Cut the parchment the pretzels are on into squares to facilitate lifting and transferring the pretzels into the water bath.

In a 10-inch-wide stainless steel pot, combine the water, beer, baking soda, and brown sugar and bring to a simmer. Two at a time, lift the parchment squares and carefully reverse each pretzel off the parchment into the simmering water. Cook for 10 seconds and flip, using a skimmer or slotted spoon. Cook for another 10 seconds, and with the skimmer, lift each pretzel above the pan to drain. Then transfer each back to the baking sheets, rounded sides up. Brush with vegetable oil. Dust with coarse salt.

Bake, switching the sheets from top to bottom and rotating from front to back halfway through, for 15 minutes, or until the pretzels are chestnut brown. Be sure and check the bottoms— mine got a little toasty! Remove from the oven and serve warm.

Smoked Gouda Grilled Cheese with Caramelized Asian Pears

Serves 1

This recipe makes enough for one grilled cheese sandwich or 4 grilled cheese "squares," but you can easily scale the recipe up to make as many as you'd like. These would also be tasty on honey-wheat bread.

CARAMELIZED PEARS:

1 tablespoon butter
1 teaspoon sugar
4 ¼-inch-thick slices Asian pear

ASSEMBLY:

1 tablespoon butter, softened
2 slices brioche or challah, each ½-inch thick
½ tablespoon spicy honey mustard, preferably Honeycup
½ cup grated smoked Gouda cheese

Make the pears: Melt the butter in a small frying pan. When the bubbling subsides, sprinkle sugar over the butter and stir. Add the pears and cook for 2 to 3 minutes per side, until lightly golden but not mushy. Remove the pears from the pan and set aside.

Assemble the sandwich: If you want to be fancy, trim the crusts off the bread. Spread butter on one side of both pieces of bread, making sure you spread all the way to the edges of the bread. Spread the other side with a thin layer of honey mustard. Don't use too much mustard—that stuff is powerful! With the mustard side facing up, spread half the grated cheese on top of one slice of bread. Layer the caramelized pears on top, then sprinkle on the rest of the cheese. Put the other piece on top, with the buttered side facing up.

Heat a griddle or skillet over medium-high heat. When hot, place the sandwich in the pan and cook for about 1 minute on each side, until the bread is golden brown and the cheese has melted. Serve whole or cut into 4 squares for hors d'oeuvres.

Braised Green Beans with Fire-Roasted Tomatoes

ADAPTED FROM ED BRUSKE, AKA THE SLOW COOK

Serves 6 to 8

These beans taste even better if you make them a day ahead. Reheat them gently on the stove before serving.

2 tablespoons olive oil
1 medium yellow onion, thinly sliced
1 pound green beans, trimmed
1 14½-ounce can diced, fire-roasted tomatoes, with their juice
2 thick slices bacon, diced
1 teaspoon fennel seeds, ground in a mortar and pestle
½ teaspoon salt, plus more to taste
Freshly ground black pepper

Heat the olive oil in a heavy pot or Dutch oven with a tight-fitting lid over medium heat. Add the onion and cook, stirring occasionally, until tender, about 5 minutes. Add the beans, fire-roasted tomatoes and juice, bacon, ground fennel, ½ teaspoon salt, and pepper to taste, and bring to a simmer.

Cover, reduce heat to very low, and simmer gently until tender, about 3 hours, stirring and tasting the beans occasionally. Season with additional salt and pepper to taste.

Curried Deviled Eggs

Makes 12 deviled eggs

Feel free to add as much curry to these eggs as you like, depending on how strong you want the flavor to be—anywhere from 1/2 teaspoon to 1 1/2 teaspoons or more. For the best flavor, make sure your curry powder is fresh. You can easily double, or even triple, this recipe.

6 large eggs
1/4 cup mayonnaise
1 teaspoon Dijon mustard
1/2 teaspoon curry powder, or more to taste
1/2 teaspoon lemon juice
1/2 teaspoon minced chives, plus more for garnish
Pinch cayenne pepper
Kosher salt and pepper to taste
Paprika for garnish

Place eggs in a medium saucepan and cover with cold water, making sure the eggs are covered by at least an inch of water. Over medium-high heat, bring the water to a boil. Once the water reaches a boil, remove the pan from the heat, cover, and let it sit for exactly 14 minutes.

After 14 minutes, drain the eggs and place them in an ice bath to stop them from cooking. Let the eggs sit in the ice bath for about 10 minutes, then peel the eggs and discard the shells. From end to end, cut each egg in half. Scoop out the yolks and place them in a medium bowl and lay the whites cut side up on a platter.

Mash the yolks with the back of a fork, or, for a finer texture, press through a fine sieve. Add mayonnaise, mustard, curry powder, lemon juice, chives, and cayenne and stir until well combined and smooth. Season with salt and pepper to taste (you will need at least 1/8 teaspoon of salt).

Scoop filling into a Ziploc bag or a disposable pastry bag and snip off a corner of the bag with scissors. Pipe the filling into the egg whites. Garnish each egg with a sprinkling of paprika and more chives. Serve right away or chill and serve cold.

Devils on Horseback
(or, Bacon-Wrapped Dates Stuffed with Honey-Laced Mascarpone)

Makes 12 stuffed dates

2 tablespoons mascarpone cheese
¾ teaspoon honey
¼ teaspoon fresh lemon juice
12 Medjool dates
6 slices applewood smoked bacon

Preheat oven to 400°F. In a small bowl, mix together the mascarpone, honey, and lemon juice. Using a small knife, cut a slit down one side of each date to remove the pit. Stuff each date with ½ teaspoon of the mascarpone mixture, filling the cavity. Close up the date.

Cut each bacon slice in half, so that you end up with 12 slices about 4 to 5 inches long. If the bacon is very, very fatty, trim away some of the excess fat. Wrap each date with a slice of bacon, securing the bacon in place with a toothpick. Place dates on a rimmed baking sheet and bake for 5 to 6 minutes. Turn dates over and continue baking for another 5 to 6 minutes, until the bacon is crisp. Drain on paper towels and let cool for about 5 minutes. Serve.

Turkey Leg Confit

ADAPTED FROM *FOOD & WINE*

Serves 6

To make a proper confit, you should use duck fat, which you can buy online from D'Artagnan. However, if you're anything like Hannah Sugarman, you might not have easy access to multiple pounds of duck fat, not to mention available funds. So this recipe uses half olive oil and half vegetable oil, both of which are easier to come by. If you'd like to use duck fat, substitute melted duck fat for the olive oil. You can easily double this recipe.

6 garlic cloves, peeled
2 tablespoons kosher salt
2 heaping teaspoons fresh chopped thyme
Finely grated zest of half a large lemon
½ tablespoon juniper berries
½ teaspoon black peppercorns, plus freshly ground pepper
6 turkey legs (12 ounces each)
3 cups olive oil
3 cups vegetable oil
2 cups low-sodium turkey stock or broth
   (or substitute low-sodium chicken stock)
2 tablespoons all-purpose flour
¾ teaspoon balsamic vinegar
Pepper

Place 4 of the garlic cloves in a food processor with the salt, thyme, and lemon zest. Pulse until finely chopped. Add the juniper berries, peppercorns, and pepper and pulse just until slightly cracked.

Preheat the oven to 325°F. Arrange the turkey legs in a single layer in a medium, flameproof roasting pan, just large enough to hold the turkey legs snugly. Rub the legs all over with the salt mixture. Let stand for 30 minutes. Smash the remaining 2 garlic cloves lightly with the back of a knife. Pour olive and vegetable oils over the turkey legs and add the smashed garlic cloves to the pan. If the legs aren't completely covered by oil, add a little more to the pan.

Roast the turkey legs for about 2 hours, turning them every 30 minutes, until the meat is very tender and pulls away from the drumsticks. Transfer the legs to a large pot and carefully strain the fat over them, stopping when you reach the sediment and any caramelized pan juices. Reserve the garlic cloves. Let the turkey legs cool to room temperature, then refrigerate in the pot overnight or for up to 5 days.

While the turkey legs are cooling, return the garlic to the roasting pan and set the pan over one or two burners, depending on the size of your pan. Add a cup of the stock and bring to a simmer over moderately high heat, scraping up the browned bits on the bottom and sides of the pan and mashing the garlic into the juices. Strain the pan juices into a large measuring cup, let cool, then refrigerate for up to 5 days.

On the day you plan to serve the turkey legs, preheat the oven to 350°F and remove the turkey legs and reserved pan juices from the refrigerator. To remove the legs from the pot, gently rewarm the turkey legs over moderate heat, just until the fat melts. Remove the legs from the fat and transfer them to a roasting pan; reserve 1 tablespoon of the fat. Roast the turkey legs for 25 minutes, turning once or twice, or until golden and crisp in spots. Transfer the turkey legs to a platter, cover loosely with aluminum foil, and keep warm.

Pour off any fat from the roasting pan and set the pan over one or two burners, depending on the size of your roasting pan. Add the remaining cup of stock and the reserved pan juices and bring to a boil, scraping up any browned bits stuck to the bottom and sides of the pan. Pour the pan juices into a medium saucepan and bring back to a boil.

In a small bowl, blend the flour with the reserved tablespoon of fat. Whisk the flour paste into the pan juices and simmer over moderate heat, stirring, until the gravy thickens and no floury taste remains, about 10 minutes. Stir in the balsamic vinegar and season lightly with pepper. Serve the turkey legs with the garlic gravy.

acknowledgments

This book is dedicated to my mom and dad, who have always encouraged me to follow my dreams and be my best self. Thank you for always believing in me. I couldn't ask for better parents, and I love you so much.

A million thanks to Alanna Ramirez for being my book's first champion, and to Scott Miller and everyone at Trident for your hard work and dedication.

I am forever grateful to superstar editor Jill Schwartzman, who is truly one of the best in the business. Thank you for seeing something in my manuscript and for helping me take the story to the next level. Your input was invaluable, and I am lucky to have you in my corner.

To Sam O'Brien, who took over so effortlessly and helped bring this book to publication: thank you for your sharp insights, your enthusiasm, your hard work, and your sense of humor. You made every step of this process fun and exciting, even when we were just doing copyedits. You rock.

Many thanks to everyone at Hyperion, especially Elisabeth Dyssegaard, Ellen Archer, Maha Khalil, Kristin Kiser, Diane Aronson, Karen Minster, Shelly Perron, Jennifer Daddio, Christine Ragasa, Bryan Christian, and Georgia Morrissey. I hit the jackpot when I landed at your publishing house.

Lucy Stille—thank you for your constructive suggestions and infectious enthusiasm. You had me at "adorable and delicious."

A big hug and a kiss to Sophie McKenzie, for being my first reader and cheering me on throughout the process. You are a talented author in your own right, and I'm lucky to have you for a sister-in-law.

Thanks to Kim Perel, for giving early advice, and to Liz Roller Dilworth, Eve Gutman, and Bethany Lesser for lending their professional expertise to answer my (potentially annoying) fact-checking questions.

Mandi Schweitzer—many thanks for your input in the later stages of production. Your advice was beyond helpful. And to Amber Wheeler, Sally Pressman, Marin Levy, Lauren Alexander, and Sallie James—thanks for supporting me along the way and for being such wonderful friends.

And finally, a big thank-you to Roger, for everything. I couldn't have done this without you, and I wouldn't have wanted to. You gave me pep talks when I needed them, listened when I needed to vent, and read this book more times than anyone probably should. Thank you for encouraging me to take a risk and for supporting me every step of the way. You are the best decision I ever made.

reading group guide

Introduction

Dana Bate's first novel, *The Girls' Guide to Love and Supper Clubs*, introduces us to Hannah Sugarman, a savvy, intelligent, and frazzled young woman living in Washington, DC. What's the trouble? Everyone wants her to be someone she's not. Her boyfriend and his wealthy, judgmental parents want her to be more polite and accomplished; her parents want her to pursue advanced studies in economics; her boss wants her to commit even more time to his political think tank. What does Hannah want? To cook great food. In an attempt to balance all these things, she starts a secret, underground (and somewhat illegal) supper club in her landlord's fancy town house while he's away. And it's a hit. The success, however, inevitably conflicts with not only her other responsibilities, but her sense of who she is and wants to be. Fortunately, Hannah's passion for preparing knock-out food is always there—to distract, to soothe, and to empower.

Discussion Questions

1. What are Hannah's various problems and challenges as the novel begins?

2. Early in the novel Hannah tells Adam's parents they're living together and is accidentally overheard insulting Millie's cooking at Millie's party (11, 39). Adam later chides her that she's "physically incapable of keeping [her] mouth shut" (46). Hannah's mother, the professor, later tells her, "You are a strong woman . . . Some man isn't going to muzzle you" (62). Is Hannah a "strong woman"? Or is she a strong personality? How do you feel about these various instances of Hannah "speaking her mind"?

3. What are the various effects—positive or not—of the different hierarchical systems at work in the novel: Adam's family's social class, Hannah's parents' academic standing, Washington DC's political environment, to name a few?

4. In what ways does the food and restaurant industry create similar hierarchical or exclusionary systems? How does Hannah deal with this hierarchy differently than the others?

5. One issue throughout the novel is the tension between the kitchen as a confining or even oppressive place for women and one that allows for creativity, freedom, and even power. Which seems more the case for each of the characters—Hannah, her mother, Rachel, or Sandy Prescott? Why?

6. Thinking about Hannah bringing a carrot cake to the Prescotts, drowning her sorrows in ice cream, or starting a supper club, what are some of the different uses of or intentions for food throughout the novel?

7. In what ways is preparing and eating food an emotional experience?

8. At the second meal of the Dupont Circle Supper Club, "everyone at the table is talking about the foods they grew up with as kids and crave whenever they visit home" (145). What role does

memory or nostalgia play in our enjoyment of food? What are some of your own personal comfort foods?

9. Of all the dishes Hannah prepares, which would you most like to try? What's the best food you've ever actually eaten, and who prepared it?

10. What motivates Hannah to deceive her landlord? Greed? Excitement? Desperation? Fear? Or something else?

11. What might be valuable about a supper club experience that restaurant dining doesn't provide?

12. Should supper clubs be illegal? Regulated? Why or why not?

13. When finally confronting her parents about her unhappiness, Hannah's father asks her, "Well, if you were so miserable and felt passionate about pursuing another career, why didn't you just do it?" (352). Her answer is that she didn't want to disappoint them. To what extent should this be a concern of Hannah's?

14. About her strong abilities concerning her job, Hannah says, "Competence doesn't necessarily equate with happiness" (348). What are your thoughts on this statement?

a conversation with dana bate

Q: *How did you come to decide, given your background in science and journalism, to write a novel? What were the particular challenges of moving from nonfiction to fiction?*

A: Are you suggesting it's weird that I majored in molecular biophysics and biochemistry, only to become a broadcast journalist who eventually quit her job to write romantic comedies? Because I'm not seeing that at all.

In all seriousness, from the time I was a little kid, I always loved both writing and science. In high school, I was a member of the literary society (where I wrote a LOT of bad poetry), but at the same time I was also a big chemistry nerd. When I was sixteen, I studied creative writing at Oxford for the summer, and then when I started school in the fall, I dove into advanced placement chemistry. When I got to college, I realized pretty early that I had to choose one or the other. So I chose science. It was challenging, and I learned things I knew I'd never learn if I just read about it on my own time.

But I missed writing and telling stories, so I started writing for the *Yale Scientific Magazine*. Then, during my senior year, I started working on a news radio program, and I fell in love. I was able to tell stories again! After I graduated, I went for my master's in journalism at Northwestern University, and then I became a full-fledged journalist. But even in journalism, I missed the creativity and flexibility of fiction. So when my husband had a chance to do some work in London at the end of 2009, I quit my job, moved to London with him, and started the first draft of what eventually became *The Girls' Guide to Love and Supper Clubs*.

Journalism provided a wonderful foundation for writing novels, both in terms of discipline and the craft of writing itself. I say *foundation* because I had to build quite a lot on top of what I'd already learned. In journalism, you work on concrete deadlines, but at least in the early days of writing a first novel, any deadlines are ones you set yourself. I had to treat those deadlines as seriously as if they'd been set by my editor. I also had to adjust to a world where I'm in charge, where the characters do and say whatever I *make* them do or say. In journalism, you're always writing about what actually happened, and you're (rightfully) penalized for taking any liberties with the truth. But in fiction, the writer creates the truth—a total change of pace from nonfiction and one I really enjoyed.

Q: *Could you discuss any relationship or similarities that might exist between scientific lab work and that of the kitchen?*

A: As far as I'm concerned, baking is just a big chemistry experiment where you can eat the results. At its heart, baking *is* chemistry. You have your materials (ingredients), methods (weights/volumes, instructions, baking temperature, baking time), data and results (does everything look the way it's supposed to, and how many cookies/bars/muffins/cakes did I immediately stuff in my face?), and analysis and conclusion (would I make this again, and does this recipe belong in my recipe Hall of Fame?). In baking, as in a titration or ligation reaction, weights, volumes, times, and temperatures matter. If you take liberties with any of those things, you could end up with some burnt cookies or a cake that overflows onto the bottom of your oven.

But that's baking. Cooking is a little different. There is still the same respect for ingredients and cooking times, but there is also room for more creativity. Feel like throwing a handful of fresh herbs into the pot? Go for it! Want to throw those leftover vegetables into a risotto? Why not? Skilled bakers (and chemists) can fiddle with recipes as well, but I think it's easier for a cook. In that way, I'd say writing is more like cooking than baking: you need to respect the process, but you can also blow the process up and do it your own way and come up with something really great.

The one major advantage both baking and cooking have over scientific lab work is that you not only can eat the results, you can share those results with others, too!

Q: *What's interesting and valuable about deconstructing traditional—and sometimes unhealthy—foods in order to create gourmet versions, as Hannah does in the novel?*

A: For a lot of people, including myself, two of food's greatest virtues, aside from providing us with the energy to live, are its ability both to surprise and comfort. I'm sure many people have a short list of comfort foods they go to when they need a pick-me-up (chocolate, mac 'n' cheese, scrambled eggs, and mashed potatoes often appear on these lists. . . . They certainly appear on mine). At the same time, those same people probably remember the first time they tried a new dish that is now a favorite—their first quiche lorraine, their first curry, their first crème brûlée. For anyone who loves food, there is something very exciting about trying a dish that catches you by surprise.

When you deconstruct a dish, as Hannah does, you take familiar or comforting flavors and present them in a new way. So you get the best of both worlds: surprise and comfort in one dish.

To be honest, I'm not sure Hannah's versions are any healthier than the originals (in the case of the pork sandwich, her version is probably *less* healthy), but that's another issue altogether. . . .

Q: *Is there a legal version of the supper club, perhaps a nonprofit model?*

A: Interesting question. I'm sure there is some way to structure a supper club so that it doesn't need approval by the health department. One way most supper clubs have avoided legal trouble is by suggesting a "donation" or "contribution" rather than an outright fee. That way they can claim they didn't demand payment; they merely received a collection of generous donations. That's what lands most supper clubs in a so-called gray area, and in most cases, health departments leave them alone. Some sort of nonprofit model would probably protect supper clubs even further—although my guess is that, for most cooks, running a supper club would remain a side hobby.

Q: *Your acknowledgment of and thanks to your parents suggest a much more supportive relationship than Hannah experiences. What made you want to add that conflict?*

A: I am lucky to have two parents who have always supported my choices—even when I was skipping from science to journalism to fiction. That isn't to say my choices didn't baffle them at one time or another. But I think they always trusted me and knew I would throw myself into whatever discipline I took up and would make the most of it.

But not everyone I know has had that experience. In high school, I was surrounded by other students whose parents seemed to have all of these rules—about what classes they must take, what colleges they must apply to, what activities they must participate in and add to their résumés. A lot of "must"s. All of this came from a loving place (who doesn't want the best for their kids?), but it always seemed very controlling to me.

Then, after college, several friends and acquaintances in their mid-twenties were having quarter-life crises. They were all highly educated and had followed enviable paths—Ivy League colleges, prestigious law and med schools, competitive jobs. Theoretically the world was their oyster, and yet these friends seemed unhappy and, in many cases, paralyzed. It occurred to me that, with some of them, they were following someone else's dreams and not their own—their parents' dreams, or some path they felt "society" expected of them. They'd spent so many years scoring As and getting into the best schools and landing the most competitive jobs that they'd lost sight of their own passions; they were just going through the motions, until they reached their mid-to-late-twenties and started asking, "Is this really what I want to be doing?" So, to riff on that idea, I decided to create a character who hadn't lost sight of her passions but was too afraid and insecure to act on them, and I wanted to explore her relationship with her parents to see how that influenced her choices.

Q: *What are you working on now? More food-themed writing? Fiction? Nonfiction?*

A: I'm currently revising my second novel, which also contains food themes, but in a more subtle way than *The Girls' Guide to Love and Supper Clubs*. At this point, I'm keeping the plot under wraps, but I can say the book is a separate, stand-alone novel, with entirely new characters and situations. But for those who enjoyed my first book, the second will have some of the same ingredients: humor, relationships, family, and, of course, food.